T0265889

A DEATH IN
DIAMONDS

ALSO AVAILABLE BY S. J. BENNETT

HER MAJESTY
THE QUEEN INVESTIGATES MYSTERIES

Murder Most Royal

All the Queen's Men

The Windsor Knot

A DEATH IN DIAMONDS

HER MAJESTY
THE QUEEN INVESTIGATES

S. J. Bennett

CROOKED
LANE

NEW YORK

Copyright © 2025 by S. J. Bennett

Published in the United States by Crooked Lane Books, an imprint of The Quick Brown Fox & Company LLC.

Crooked Lane Books and its logo are trademarks of The Quick Brown Fox & Company LLC.

Library of Congress Catalog-in-Publication data available upon request.

ISBN (hardcover): 979-8-89242-090-7
ISBN (ebook): 979-8-89242-091-4

Cover design by Nick Stearn, illustrations by Iker Ayesteran

Printed in the United States.

www.crookedlanebooks.com

Crooked Lane Books
34 West 27th St., 10th Floor
New York, NY 10001

First Edition: January 2025

print line

For my grandmothers, Joan and Jessie

'We need the kind of courage that can withstand the subtle corruption of the cynics so that we can show the world that we are not afraid of the future. It has always been easy to hate and destroy. To build and to cherish is much more difficult . . .

I cannot lead you into battle, I do not give you laws or administer justice but I can do something else, I can give you my heart and my devotion to these old islands and to all the peoples of our brotherhood of nations.'

The Queen's Christmas Message, 1957

PART 1

VIVE LA REINE

PARIS, APRIL 1957

CHAPTER 1

The Queen knew instantly that she had made a fatal mistake, figuratively speaking.

'*Mais bien sur, madame. Ça arrive.*'

During the candlelit dinner at the Louvre to celebrate her second night in France on this, her first state visit, she had merely mentioned, perhaps a shade too wistfully, that she had never seen the *Mona Lisa*. The Salle des Caryatides was packed with *le tout-Paris*. Every minister, grand hostess and eminent dignitary was here, it seemed, sitting elbow to elbow, dressed in their finery, watching her closely. However, beyond the odd statue and ceiling, she had yet to see any art.

Now, after a brief consultation among the luminaries of the museum, two porters were carrying the Leonardo into the room, resplendent in its ornate gilt frame. They leaned it against a chair for her to look at, and it was the most extraordinary moment: those two famous eyes, staring impenetrably back at her from under their heavy lids. One knew the image so well as an illustration that it was astonishing to come face to face with the real thing. The Queen felt for an instant how so many people must feel, perhaps, coming face to face with *her*.

The portrait carried a huge weight of expectation, but was remarkably human in scale, close to, in the flickering light. Behind the eyes, the Queen saw a young woman, beautifully composed and a little bit self-conscious in the act being scrutinised. *I know how you feel*, she thought. The artistry was wonderful, of course, but it was hard to concentrate while everyone was leaning forward to see her reaction.

'*C'est merveilleux, n'est-ce pas?*' she said, fully aware that this might well be the understatement of her visit.

Shortly afterwards, when they were joined by yet more of the great and good in yet another lavish salon, the spotlight on the Queen herself was even more intense. Hundreds of people jostled together, eager to greet her, and sharp elbows dug into nipped-in waists as they jockeyed for a better view. At one point the crowd surged forward in a wave and the Queen felt the press of the throng. She was quite hemmed in and there was no room to breathe. For a moment she was almost frightened. It was gratifying to be so popular, but right now, she would be grateful to get out of the evening with her clothes and person intact.

Thinking of what her grandmother, Queen Mary, would say, she steadied herself and put on a brave face. But as she looked out over the sea of eager faces, two stood out. One was not looking in her direction exactly, but at someone in the crowd behind her. His face was briefly twisted into an unguarded scowl and there was a look of savage hatred in his eyes. The Queen had seen that look only a few times before, as a teenager at Windsor, when officers or their families had described some of the worst atrocities of the war. She knew who he was, understood his history, and guessed who he might be staring at.

The other face was scanning the room with undisguised disdain, the mouth crimped in frustration. At last, the eyes found hers, and instantly the face went blank. But the Queen had seen enough. This was someone she knew very well.

She had work to do when she got home, because it was clear that someone from inside her closest circle had been trying to sabotage this visit. Her response would be delicate and difficult, and she wasn't sure who she could trust.

★ ★ ★

In the car on the way back to the British Embassy, she said to Philip, 'Did you notice, they served us oysters tonight?'

'Yes, very good ones.' He gave her a knowing grin, before frowning slightly. 'I didn't think you liked them, though. Did you eat 'em?'

'No, I didn't. Actually, I'm quite fond of oysters.' She returned his grin. 'But I simply can't eat them abroad.'

'I think we can trust the Frogs, on this occasion. They'll hardly try to poison you. And they do oysters better than anyone. Always did.'

'I don't doubt that. It's not the French, it's the oysters themselves. One never knows. And an upset tummy would be a disaster.'

'I suppose it would. Pity. They were top-hole.'

The Queen adjusted her fur around her shoulders and glanced out at the twinkling lights on the Place de la Concorde. They would be back at the embassy soon. She loved this grand square by the river, with a backdrop provided by the classical Crillon Hotel, a central ancient obelisk, topped with gold, and a general air of panache. But it did not escape her memory that a king and his family had literally lost their heads here.

Should she tell Philip what she was really thinking?

The limousine traced the edges of the square and drove down the Rue Royale. The last time she and her husband were here in '48, she had been secretly pregnant with Charles. Oh, to be twenty-two, newly married and hopelessly in love, in Paris for the first time, while everyone went wild all around them, still carrying the joy of Liberation. What a trip that had been.

She didn't think, before they arrived two days ago, that they could possibly repeat that experience – not now she was the grand old age of thirty, with two children at home and all the cares of state, and the endless unfounded marital rumours one had to endure. But tonight, the Parisians thronged the streets as enthusiastically as ever. She was touched beyond measure. Philip was right: she doubted very much indeed that they had tried to poison her, or undermine her with a dodgy *huître*.

And yet . . .

The Queen asked for little when she went abroad. She had a strong constitution and decent stamina, was happy to work to a punishing schedule and ate almost anything that was put in front of her. However, shellfish were a rare but firm exception. One simply couldn't fulfil one's duties if one was doubled over with stomach cramps; her Private Office always made that clear. Nevertheless, last night she had been served six oysters *à la sauce mignonette avec fraises et champagne*, as if nothing had been said.

It would be easy to put it down to a simple muddle. Inevitably, little things were always going wrong and usually it was terribly funny. But there had also been the question of the missing speech.

Twenty-four hours ago, her reply to the toast from the President of

France was set to be the *pièce de résistance* of her first day in France. It was a reminder that she spoke fluent French and a hymn of praise to the Entente Cordiale that bound two nations whose joint sacrifices had won a war against terrible odds. The text wasn't long, but it had been weeks in the making and she had practised it endlessly.

Then, an hour before she was due leave for the Élysée Palace to deliver it, her private secretary had approached her, pale as death, and announced that both it and all copies and carbons had gone missing. He and the ambassador were desperately scrabbling to put something new together, but she knew it wouldn't be the same. There was a high risk that speaking unfamiliar phrases in her second language would lose most of the speech's power.

By a stroke of luck, she had remembered that one of the later drafts of the original had come back from the typing pool at Buckingham Palace with a couple of excellent suggestions, in perfect, idiomatic French. It had occurred to the Queen that the secretary in question might have kept a carbon of her own, and she must have done, because fifty minutes later she was dictating it down the telephone to the private secretary himself. Disaster was averted.

That temporary loss of the original, on its own, one might have put down to misfortune. But all copies and carbons? Really?

And now, on top of those near disasters, the unguarded look of disgust directed at the pressing crowd around her at the Louvre shed a new light on everything. Someone most definitely did not want this visit to succeed. Someone in her own circle. Someone she had always trusted implicitly until tonight.

The Queen recognised that on this evidence of missing carbons and unexpected shellfish and sour expressions, it would be easy to say she had a young mother's overactive imagination, or that she was tired and emotional after two busy days abroad and developing an unhealthy complex of some sort. None of which she dared be accused of, when this visit was so important.

Anyway, at this moment what could she or Philip do? As the car turned left into the Rue du Faubourg Saint-Honoré, she kept her thoughts to herself.

CHAPTER 2

'Well done, Your Majesty,' her private secretary told her the next morning, a trifle patronisingly. 'I think we can chalk last night down as another success.'

'Thank you, Hugh. It was a bit of a crush. There were moments I wondered if they were going to swallow me whole.'

Sir Hugh Masson smiled as if her observation were merely a joke. He hadn't been on the receiving end of that tidal wave of attention.

This morning, her three pinstriped senior courtiers were lined up neatly in front of her at the ambassador's residence, ready to discuss the new day. Sir Hugh was accompanied by Major Miles Urquhart, the deputy private secretary (or DPS, as he was known); and Jeremy Radnor-Milne, her press secretary. Solid, traditional and dependable, they were chief among 'men in moustaches', as Philip called them – a collective term for the old guard the Queen had inherited from her father.

Sir Hugh Masson's solid grey whiskers were counterbalanced by a large pair of black-rimmed spectacles that emphasised his bookish tendencies. 'The prime minister wanted me to let you know how pleased he is with how everything's going, ma'am. Your evening gowns are a particular hit. The choice of flowers of the French fields for the decoration was much admired.'

'Mr Hartnell did try very hard with the embroidery.'

'It's good to see British design compete with the French,' Miles Urquhart, the DPS, added cheerfully. 'And outclass them, you might say.' He sported a russet 'tache that bristled with delight and national pride. Urquhart was always absolutely certain that the British monarchy was the best institution in the world and the answer to almost any problem, even fashion-related. The Queen found it quite challenging to live up to such high expectations.

'Oh, I hesitate to say we outclass Dior and Balmain,' she demurred, 'but I'm glad we can hold our own.'

'One begins to understand why they wanted you as head of state.'

She shook her head. 'That was very odd, wasn't it?'

It was still astonishing to her, and not helpful in managing Urquhart's expectations, but – unknown to all but the British prime minister and his closest circle – the French prime minister had indeed raised the idea of a Franco-British union on a visit last year, with her as its figurehead. It had taken them all aback.

'After all they went through to get rid of the last lot,' she added. 'Mr Eden was right to say no. Anyway, I get the impression it was all the scheme of Monsieur Mollet alone. Nobody's mentioned it since.'

Jeremy Radnor-Milne laughed a little too loud. 'Haha! You're well out of it, ma'am. France hasn't covered itself in glory recently. They seem rather desperate, if one may say so.'

The press secretary wore a thin black line of facial fuzz modelled on the actor David Niven's, in an attempt to suggest the actor's military derring-do and suave urbanity. Like Urquhart, he was conspicuously patriotic and he was probably referring to France's ill-fated attempt last year to maintain control of Egypt's Suez Canal by sending in the troops. However, the United Kingdom had done the same, and come out of last year's Suez affair equally disastrously.

Gone were the days of gunship diplomacy, when the old imperial powers could sail in and sort out problems abroad with a little show of muscle. One needed the Americans on board now and, as Mr Eisenhower had made it very plain from Washington that he was not going to get involved, the French and British were forced to make an ignominious retreat. At home, Mr Eden had lost his premiership because of it.

'The talk here is all about making friends with the Hun,' Urquhart said, with a shake of his head. 'This new treaty of Rome. The "Economic Community", whatever they call it. You wouldn't think France and Germany had been at each other's throats for the best part of a century.'

'I suppose that's what they're trying to avoid,' the Queen pointed out. 'But I'm not so sure everyone's behind the treaty.' She addressed herself to her private secretary. 'I wanted to tell you, Hugh, the Comte de Longchamp is not in favour at all. You know his war record – what the Nazis put him through. And my papers tell me he has the ear of his president.'

'How do you know, ma'am? Who told you?'

'I saw it on his face last night,' the Queen said. This had been the first of the two odd expressions she noticed at the Louvre. 'A look of pure hatred, directed at the German ambassador standing behind me. I know it was the German ambassador because he has the most frightful breath. Somebody really ought to tell him at some point. Not ideal for a diplomat.'

'I'll pass the news on,' Sir Hugh promised.

'Not the bit about the breath.'

'Oh, that, too, ma'am. The Foreign Office will be delighted. Thank you.'

They moved on to her itinerary for the day, which was set out in five-minute increments from now until midnight, describing exactly where she would be and whom she would expect to meet, from the workers at a Renault factory to the Mayor of Paris. She noticed that there were two comfort breaks, of five minutes each, and planned to limit her liquid intake accordingly.

At the end, she mentioned the oysters.

Two sets of bushy eyebrows furrowed in horror and the lips of Jeremy Radnor-Milne pursed in confusion under his thin black moustache.

'Shellfish,' Sir Hugh explained in hushed tones, before turning back to the Queen.

'Did you eat any, ma'am?'

'No. I was terribly rude. I had some of the sauce mignonette.'

Radnor-Milne's jaw had dropped. He gaped like a fish. 'I . . . I . . . I don't see why on earth they would have—'

'Some chef must have got carried away with the menu,' Urquhart snapped, puffed up with indignation on her behalf. 'I'll have a word.'

'Please don't bother,' the Queen said. 'It's too late now.'

She had been watching them closely. The men in moustaches all seemed equally aghast, just as they had done two days ago when her speech went missing. These were men whose service her father had prized, and she relied on them completely in order to carry out her job. One of them, she now knew, was lying to her. What about the other two?

Chapter 3

Bobo Macdonald – Margaret, or Miss Macdonald to everyone except the immediate royal family – had a few whiskers of her own, but she was very much *not* one of the men in moustaches. She was the Queen's dresser and more: her original nursery nursemaid, her confidante, the only person except her sister to have shared a childhood bedroom with the young princess, and the only one trusted nowadays to prepare and preserve her clothes. There was nowhere Bobo didn't travel with her mistress. She had even accompanied the royal couple on honeymoon.

That evening, she was on duty while the Queen got ready for her last night in France.

'What do you think?'

The Queen was peering at herself anxiously in the cheval mirror in her dressing room at the ambassadorial residence. Her third evening gown of the visit was a new step: the first time she had ever worn a body-skimming column dress, instead of one with her signature full skirts, like her mother's.

The silk glittered in the lamplight, heavy with handsewn crystals. It was a beautiful creation, but was it too much? Or not enough? Its designer, Hardy Amies, had also created the peacock-blue gown she had worn last night. When he showed her the sketch for it, she had wondered about the strong colour. He suggested it worked because 'you are a *femme de trente ans*, ma'am'. It was the unkindest thing he had ever said to her, and she had told him so.

Perhaps to make up for it, Mr Amies had put her in this shimmering silver column, which was just the sort of thing Marilyn Monroe might pick. Could this *femme de trente ans* get away with it?

'You look magnificent. Your best frock yet. Och, you know you do, Lilibet. Look at you!'

At least Bobo was convinced about this one. The Queen turned to check her silhouette from different angles. She missed the comforting swish of net skirts. Last November, when she had met Miss Monroe at a film premiere, the actress had been in a golden figure-hugging dress that might as well have been a bathing suit. The Queen herself had chosen a black velvet crinoline, narrow at the waist and roomy everywhere else, and was grateful for the confidence it gave her. Poor Marilyn in her golden frock had chewed all her lipstick off by the time they shook hands.

She had been the sweetest thing to talk to, though. Marilyn was staying near Windsor at the time, and they talked about how nice it would be to meet up there too, not that either of them had the time. The Queen had the impression of a bold but fragile creature, like a young racehorse or a wild deer. She had wanted to lend her a fur and wrap her up.

Anyway, that was then. Now, *she* was the one in the slinky dress. She needed a second opinion. 'Bobo, can you call the duke for me?'

To everyone but the Queen, Prince Philip was 'the Duke of Edinburgh', or 'sir'. He didn't have a Bobo of his own to call him by a nickname and be treated as a trusted friend. Certainly not since he had recently lost his own much-missed private secretary in a divorce scandal. At least he had her.

Bobo spoke to the page outside the door, who passed on the message to Philip in his dressing room. The reply came back that he would be a couple of minutes, which gave the Queen time to touch up her lipstick and put on the jewellery that Bobo had laid out for her. While she fiddled with the earrings at her dressing table, Bobo sought to calm her mistress's rare attack of nerves.

'Did you see the newspaper headlines? The French are calling themselves monarchists! It's just you and the Chelsea murders on the front pages at home.'

'The Chelsea murders?' the Queen asked, turning round with the left earring in her hand. 'What murders?'

'Oh, it's dreadful. Two bodies, found in one of those little mews houses off the Old Brompton Road. It was all over *The Times* and the *Daily Express*.'

'How do you know?'

'The ambassador gets them by air from London. The housekeeper showed me.'

'Did they say who they were?'

'Not yet, dear. Just that it was a man and a woman, and she was no better than she should be. The awful thing is, it seems almost certain the Dean of Bath did it, or one of his guests.' Bobo shook her head. 'He rents the house where it happened for his visits to London. He looks such a mild-mannered man in the photograph, although they say he had a good war – so not *that* mild-mannered.'

'Was it definitely murder?' The Queen knew the dean in question a little. An upstanding member of the Church of England and a charming occasional dinner guest at Windsor.

'Oh yes, dear. It was all very violent. And a little bit suggestive.' Bobo pursed her lips and her eyes gleamed. 'The girl was wearing nothing but satin lingerie and diamonds. Lying on the bed like Snow White, the papers said, but they probably make that sort of thing up, don't they? And I don't think I've ever seen Snow White depicted in her smalls.'

'Who was depicted in her smalls?' Philip asked, striding into the room and looking somewhat distracted as he inserted a cufflink into a recalcitrant cuff.

'The dead woman in Chelsea, sir,' Bobo explained.

'Oh?' He didn't look up. The cufflinks were gold, held together by a delicate chain, and fiddly to use. 'And how did she die?'

'According to the papers, they were both strangled and the gentleman was stabbed in the eye. Isn't it wicked what some people can do? It beggars belief.'

'Oh, I can believe anything of some people,' Philip said. He glanced up from his shirtsleeve. 'You wanted to ask me something, Lilibet?'

The Queen had put on her earrings by now. She placed her tiara in position and stood up again, saying nothing, because she wasn't quite sure how to ask for what she wanted.

He looked her up and down.

'New dress?'

'Yes.'

'Haven't seen you in that style before.'

'No.'

'It's different. Very . . . sparkly.'

'Oh.'

There was a short silence.

'Isn't she a picture?' Bobo said, with an edge of Scottish censoriousness in her voice.

Philip took his cue at last.

'You look ravishing, my darling.' He grinned rakishly and strode towards her. 'If Ava Gardner was a couple of inches shorter . . .'

He took his wife's hands in his and kissed her palms, one after the other, and she was reminded how irresistible he was himself, and how hopelessly devoted she was. Not just because of his Viking-blond looks, but for his ability to make her weep with laughter one minute and to be quite serious the next, as he was now, aware of how important this visit was, how much was asked of her, and how much she needed him.

'Good, well, that's settled, then,' Bobo said. 'Your tiara's a bit wonky, dear. Don't forget the necklace. I'll go and fetch your fur.'

★ ★ ★

Outside the room, at the top of the stairs, a small group was gathered. It consisted of the ambassador, two military equerries who assisted the royal couple in their public duties, Sir Hugh and Philip's new private secretary, all ready to accompany them down. They were speaking in low voices but the words 'Cresswell Place' were audible.

'What's that?' Philip asked. 'What're you talking about?'

'The murders in Chelsea,' the ambassador explained. 'Have you heard?'

'Oh that. Strangling and stabbing,' Philip said, fiddling with his second cuff. 'Those the ones?'

'Yes, exactly. Hardly the modus operandi one would imagine of the members of the Artemis Club.'

'What?' Philip's head jerked up.

'Well, apparently the dean was dining at the club that night and he brought a small group back to play cards. Nobody else went in or out, apart from the victims, so . . .' The ambassador trailed off and coughed. 'I'm aware you're a member of the Artemis, sir.'

Philip's face tightened. 'I am.'

The ambassador laughed nervously. 'I don't mean to imply . . . Rather, the people who came back with the dean that night were all above board. Decent men, spotless reputations. You knighted one of 'em last year, ma'am.' He nodded to the Queen. Nobody had said anything about her dress yet, but they were men, so they wouldn't. 'They apparently accompanied the dean home for a quick game of canasta.'

Sir Hugh intervened with a slight cough. 'So they claim. The awkward thing is, according to the press reports, the dean told the charlady not to clean upstairs the next day, as she usually did. He then returned to Somerset, and she only discovered the bodies when she went upstairs a week later.'

'Gosh, so when did they die?' the Queen asked.

'I suppose it would be a week ago last Sunday,' Sir Hugh said, rapidly calculating. 'The thirty-first. That would be the night of the card game. They must have been lying there all—'

'Damn!' All eyes turned to Philip. 'I've bust a cufflink. You!' He held out the offending article to the young equerry standing nearest to him. 'Find my valet and get replacements. Quick, or we'll be late.'

He caught the Queen's eye and she could see how irritated he was. They looked like the Britannia cufflinks he'd had personally designed to commemorate his recent trip to the Southern Hemisphere.

'I suppose they'll say in the papers that I was involved somehow,' he grunted.

His new private secretary coughed. 'They already are. I'm sorry, sir, I haven't had the chance to update you. I've just read the piece. They noted that you dined at the club that night too.'

Philip glowered at him. 'And did they equally note that I was tucked up safe in bed by eleven?'

'They didn't.'

'They wouldn't.' He gave a theatrical shrug and glanced at his wife. 'I only have my security detail and Her Majesty to plead my case.'

At this, five pairs of eyes turned quizzically to the Queen. After the minutest of pauses, she smiled back at them with a raised eyebrow and a little shrug of her own. They allowed themselves a chuckle.

'The papers didn't suggest you were part of the dean's party, sir,' the private secretary assured him. 'Merely that you were in his set.'

'I'm damned well not. Who is this blasted dean anyway?'

'Bath,' the Queen told him.

'Oh. Yes, we do know him, vaguely. Decent sort. Worked at St George's Chapel. Hardly a friend.'

'Cufflinks, sir.'

The pink-faced equerry was back, spurs clinking on the boots of his uniform, hand outstretched with the replacement links in his palm.

'Let's go,' Philip said. 'I can fix these in the car. Bring the papers, too. I can read 'em on my lap, nobody'll know. Time to be zoo animals again.'

* * *

The final event of the day was to be a river cruise down the Seine, and the Queen had been hugely looking forward to it. What could be more romantic, in April, than a trip under the bridges of Paris, accompanied by her husband, with the Eiffel Tower behind them, and in the distance the illuminated towers of Notre Dame?

What she had failed to imagine, and perhaps she should have done because it was there in black and white on her itinerary, was that the President of France would be sitting on her other side. They were on his launch after all. Both he and Philip were positioned at arm's distance from her, too far to chat comfortably to the president, and certainly too far for Philip to tell her what he really thought of all the tableaux that had been set up for them to admire along the banks.

It was difficult to see very much, because there was a spotlight trained on her face from a few feet away. She could just about make out that the river was lined with thicker crowds than ever, all craning their necks to see and packed so tightly one worried they might push forward and fall in. If it were possible to spend a *less* romantic evening in Paris, it would take some doing.

Nevertheless, her new dress sparkled obediently under the lights and her cheeks grew numb from smiling. Philip, grinning at a floodlit tableau of Napoleonic soldiers near Les Invalides, seemed to be enjoying himself. He always did, on the water.

As they glided along, the Queen thought about what Bobo had said about the Artemis Club, and the night the murders must have taken place. She pictured the poor girl, strangled to death in a room with a man who was essentially a stranger, wearing nothing but silk and diamonds. A true pause for thought, when one happened to be wearing silk and a large array of diamonds oneself.

What an awful way to die. She must have felt so terribly alone.

The Queen realised she wasn't concentrating and glanced out to see several ranks of floodlit choristers singing ethereally in front of Notre Dame Cathedral. Soon, the launch was floating past the Île Saint-Louis, and the sky lit up with a sudden explosion of fireworks.

Her initial surprise gave way to gradual delight. She imagined an anonymous young couple in the crowd, his arms around hers, his chest warm and solid against her back, craning their necks towards the fireworks together, unseen.

Yes, that would be lovely.

She turned her head to the president and called out something pleasant and diplomatic, in French. The spotlight still trained on her face, they headed back the way they had come.

CHAPTER 4

'Just a simple lunch,' the Queen Mother said. 'For the three of us. You must be exhausted after your trip. You need to get your strength back, Lilibet.'

The Queen was delighted to be back at Windsor Castle, after a packed five-day schedule in France. She had spent a joyful evening with the children and another hour playing with them this morning. They were keen to know about their gifts, which were inevitably too delicate to play with, but they soon forgot about them anyway in a ridiculous game of chase with their father, who was just as happy to be in their company as they were to have him back.

After all that excitement, it was comforting to be among the familiar art and antiques of her mother's residence at Royal Lodge in the castle grounds. She declined a spot of champagne in the sunny morning room because she had several meetings coming up, but her mother and sister both accepted a glass from the butler's tray.

'What's Philip up to this afternoon, do you know?' the older Queen Elizabeth asked.

'Flying. He wanted to take advantage of the good weather. Down to Southampton, I think.' The Queen smiled gamely, as if every minute that Philip was in the sky didn't worry her just a little bit. It wasn't the flying so much as the landings. A wartime Spitfire pilot had once said every landing was just a controlled crash, really. There had been one or two close shaves in the past. Philip thought them terribly funny. She didn't.

'Lucky him,' the Queen Mother said with a grin, knowing exactly how her daughter was feeling and choosing not to get involved. 'You were both so marvellous in Paris. Weren't they thrilled to have you back?'

'Mmm,' the Queen agreed with a shy grin. 'A little bit too much, sometimes.' She told them about the crush at the Louvre.

'God, a *museum*,' Margaret groaned. 'They might have at least taken you to Montmartre, or a show. I hear the new one at the Crazy Horse is eye-popping.'

'They'd hardly have taken me there!' the Queen protested. 'And we did see Édith Piaf last time.'

'Édith Piaf!' Margaret made a face like a squeezed lemon. 'Yves Montand, *he's* the one these days. Did you see Mr Dior, by the way?'

'We did,' the Queen agreed. 'Very briefly. He wasn't looking terribly well, poor man. He was *very* complimentary about you, Mummy. He told me that whenever he wants to think of something really beautiful, he remembers the clothes Mr Hartnell made for you in 'thirty-eight.'

The Queen Mother glowed with pleasure. 'My white wardrobe? For the Paris trip? What a darling man. One was in mourning for your grannie, of course, but *French* mourning is so very interesting. *Le deuil blanc.* Like Mary Queen of Scots.'

'But with parasols,' Margaret added. She turned back to her sister. 'I do think you might have worn *one* Dior gown. You're in danger of looking old-fashioned.'

Their mother's smile became a little more fixed. It wasn't always easy to have a younger daughter at home, still rather pointedly recovering from the most famous broken relationship of the decade. Especially when the older one was happily married. And the sovereign of countries whose land mass circled the globe.

'Lunch is served, ma'am,' the butler announced, to her great relief.

They went through to the dining room, where the table was set and the footmen were ready to serve. The older Elizabeth knew her elder daughter's tastes were simple, so she had asked for just a consommé, a little salmon en croute, some green vegetables and potatoes from the gardens at Sandringham and a light lemon posset, served with a rather good Pouilly-Fuissé from her personal cellar. Conversation over pudding turned to Clement Moreton, the poor Dean of Bath, whose unimpeachable life as a cleric was currently being dissected by all the newspapers.

'I feel so *sorry* for the man,' she said. 'He's a delight. A *very* good card player, but not in that way, you know. Just a charming, sensible companion. And his sermons are always so *short*. Cissy's beside herself. They all are.'

Cissy, the dean's cousin and childhood friend, was one of the Queen Mother's ladies-in-waiting. She was good with dogs and very popular. The Queen made brief noises of sympathy, and asked if he was friends with Philip, which her mother thought she should be more likely to know herself.

'They might have made friends in the war,' the Queen Mother acknowledged, 'but Philip was at sea and Clement was with the Royal Artillery, so I doubt it. Clement served with great distinction, you know. It's quite impossible that he was involved in this business, and not just because Cissy says so. I have literally seen the man upend a glass on a piece of paper to transport a spider safely outside. Admittedly, he did see some *horrors* in Germany, but war is war, isn't it, and quite a separate thing? And then there's the question of the tart in the tiara. What did they say she was called?'

'Gina Fonteyn,' Margaret said promptly. 'Like Margot.'

'Who?'

'The ballerina, Mummy.'

'Margot Fonteyn? My God, are they related?'

'No! Margot's called Peggy Hookham really, and goodness knows what the tart's real name was. The papers said she was Italian.'

'Anyway, what about her?' the Queen asked her mother.

'Actually, I was thinking of the tiara,' the elder Elizabeth said. 'Clement told Cissy that the police showed him a picture of the diamonds, in case he knew where they came from. Of course, he had no idea, but he said the tiara was made up of roses and daisies in pink and white diamonds, with pale green peridots for the leaves. It's quite an unusual combination and it reminded me so much of the Zellendorf tiara, from 'twenty-four. Cartier, very delicate, made for Lavender Hawksmoor-Zellendorf. It was supposed to resemble an English country garden. So pretty. I wondered about trying to buy it for you, Margaret, when it came up for auction last year, but of course it was much too expensive.' She sighed. 'One has to manage one's spending money so carefully.'

Margaret looked disappointed. 'Margaret *Rose*,' she said pointedly, stressing her middle name.

'Well, exactly.'

'Who got it, Mummy?'

'I don't know, that's the thing. Not that I didn't ask, but everyone was very tight-lipped. Some foreign johnny I imagine. They have all the money nowadays. An American, probably, or the Aga Khan, or the Shah. Anyway, it disappeared. Such a pity as it's a lovely piece.'

She stopped, sensing that while her younger daughter still looked wistful and slightly cross about the diamonds, the older one was staring at her with a hint of criticism. She raised her hands defensively.

'You see, one didn't know the girl, but one does know tiaras. What I meant to say was, if it *is* the Zellendorf, how on earth did she get hold of it?'

★ ★ ★

After lunch, the Queen suggested a walk outside, but instead Margaret inserted a cigarette into a long-handled holder and had one of the footmen light it for her.

'Hmm.' She stared up ruminatively through the smoke. 'Cresswell Place. Anything goes on in that street. I think it's exactly the sort of place you'd find a body and stolen diamonds.'

The Queen turned to her. 'Oh?'

'Absolutely. I've been there a couple of times. There's an artist who hosts these fabulous little parties. Tiny mews house, like a doll's house, really. You can hardly squeeze everyone in. They play the saxophone and dance on the stairs, it's terribly funny. You never know if you're going to be talking to a stockbroker or a demi-mondaine, or a spy. Or me.' She arched an eyebrow. 'I can see why the dean liked it there.'

Her mother was shocked.

'I very much doubt that's why he chose the street. Cissy says Clement is humiliated beyond belief. And so unsettled. To think that sort of thing was going on under his roof! And what if he'd been in when the killer came?'

'I don't think you could confuse the dean of a major English cathedral for a jewel thief and his paramour,' Margaret said through another puff of smoke. She eyed her mother. 'You know, I still don't have a tiara of my own.'

The Queen said nothing at this, but was privately exasperated. The point was certainly *not* the tiara. Perhaps Margaret harked back to it because she really didn't have one of her own, whereas the Queen couldn't remember exactly how many she had access to. Such thoughts made her judge her sister less harshly than she might otherwise. On a good day, Margaret was the soul of generosity.

'. . . yourself.'

'Hmm?' Margaret had been saying something she had missed.

'I *said*, you'll be going that way soon anyway, so you can see the place for yourself.'

'Will I?'

'Mummy said you're visiting Deborah Fairdale in the Boltons. Creswell Place is right next door.'

'Oh! Yes we are. For drinks on Friday.'

'Well, look out. You'll be practically on the murderer's doorstep.'

Margaret said it with something approaching relish. The Queen was very much looking forward to seeing her friend, but that aspect of the visit came as a bit of a shock. And also, she realised, an opportunity.

CHAPTER 5

The thing Fred Darbishire really wanted to know – and it was a big thing – was why he'd got this gig at all. It should by rights have gone to Chief Inspector George Venables, who regularly nabbed the best cases in Chelsea and Kensington. Venables was on the cusp of being made detective superintendent at a record juvenile age and everyone circulated around him like little planets. A double murder on his doorstep? A society vicar in the frame? The mention of the Duke of Edinburgh, and the cover of every newspaper in the land, alongside the Queen and the Duke in Paris? Venables would normally go for it like a shot.

But apparently the Criminal Investigation Department's darling was 'indisposed'. Or he had holiday booked. The rumours varied and Darbishire believed none of them. Nothing short of his own deathbed would keep George Venables away from something he really wanted. So here was Darbishire, a mere detective inspector, along with his trusty, useless sergeant, Woolgar, in charge of the whole shebang, and expected to be grateful instead of suspicious, which he was.

He stood at the entrance to Cresswell Place, a cobbled street of mismatched two-storey mews houses just off the Old Brompton Road. Darbishire happened to know, because his uncle Bill was interested in etymology, that 'mew' referred to the moulting feathers of birds of prey, and the first mews – on the site of the present National Gallery in Trafalgar Square – was built to house the king's hunting hawks while they moulted. Uncle Bill wasn't so interested in the monarchy, so Darbishire didn't know which king, but one long ago enough to have gone hawking.

That mews burned down and was replaced by stables for the royal horses, which kept the name. Afterwards, mews streets like this were built to house the horses, carriages and, later, the cars and servants of the grandest London houses. Since the war, hardly anyone could afford servants like before, so these places had become chichi little pieds-à-terre for the posh set. From hawks to horses, and from housemaids to Hooray Henrys. Uncle Bill would sniff at them: *once a home for horseshit, always a home for horseshit.* But now, it seemed they were good enough for the Dean of Bath and his ilk. And for men with their high-class escorts dripping in diamonds.

The house rented by the Dean of Bath at number 44 was a two-up-one-down affair in faded pastel pink, which had originally been built to serve one of the grand Chelsea villas of the Boltons. Like most of its neighbours, it retained the inbuilt garage it came with. According to the dean, the garage space was rented separately for parking a vintage motor, and the owner of the vehicle confirmed this. There was no longer an internal door between the garage and the rest of the house, and no indication the garage had been used that night, so that person was out of the frame for now.

'I don't see why we have to go back inside. We've got the pictures,' Detective Sergeant Woolgar muttered.

Len Woolgar was six foot four, built like a brick shithouse, and unbelievably lazy for a man in mint condition. Put him in a rowing boat on the river and he was a demon – practically Olympic standard, so they said at the Yard, which was why he'd joined the force. The Metropolitan Police boat crew was top class. But put him on an actual police job, requiring thought and dedication to duty, and he was a liability. He was usually hungry. He would be now, but he'd had two egg sandwiches for tea before they left. A third created an unsightly bulge in the pocket of his coat.

'It's not the same if you can't stand in the room and look around it,' Darbishire told him. 'We might miss something.' By which he meant *he* might miss something. Woolgar would miss everything, guaranteed.

The constable guarding the front door of number 44 gave them a respectful nod. 'Afternoon, sir. Sergeant.'

'Any trouble?'

'Only a few pressmen. Nothing I can't handle. There's one at the far end taking a picture of you now.'

'So there is.'

Darbishire took the house key from his pocket and let himself inside. Woolgar followed.

'Watch yourself on the—'

'Arse!'

The sergeant had beaned himself on the low door lintel again. You'd think, being six foot four, you'd learn to duck eventually.

The door opened straight on to a long, narrow living room with a kitchenette at the back, the right-hand half of the downstairs space being taken up by the garage. At the far end, a little window above a Belfast sink overlooked a small yard with an ivy-covered wall. Woolgar's presence seemed to fill the modest seating area at the front, where the canasta game had taken place. It was furnished with two rickety card tables and bits of old mahogany furniture that still showed evidence of a dusting with fingerprint powder.

The only new piece was a chrome drinks trolley, well stocked, which Darbishire suspected was the tenant's own addition. You wouldn't necessarily expect a senior member of the Church of England to be a demon with a cocktail shaker but, having met the man, Darbishire suspected he probably was.

Clement Moreton and his three fellow members of the Artemis Club had made liberal use of the trolley on the night of the thirty-first. The dean had treated them to a cocktail of his own construction featuring lemon juice and vodka. He claimed that was the cause of his headache the following morning and the reason he told the charlady not to linger any longer than strictly necessary, and not to clean upstairs.

'*She's noisy. She rattles round the place like a Sherman tank. I don't make a mess. I'd only been there overnight and I was going home that day anyway, so I assumed another week wouldn't make much difference before she changed the sheets . . .*'

The guests that night had comprised a university professor who had been friends with Clement Moreton since his Oxford days, a widely respected circuit judge and a canon at Westminster Abbey. All were known to each other, but did not socialise as a unit. According to their matching testimonies, each man had been out of sight of the others for a matter of a few minutes, no more.

To Darbishire's right, an open staircase was set against the wall that divided the living area from the garage. Between hands of canasta, Moreton and the other three men went upstairs once each to use the facilities. There was no lavatory downstairs – no room for one.

Darbishire thought back to the pathologist's comment from an hour and a half ago.

'Not my place to do your job for you, but if one of those highfalutin clubmen card players did it, I'll eat my hat.'

Darbishire's own visit to the Artemis Club yesterday had proved a disappointment. It sounded a grander institution than it was, physically at least – which was little more than a doorway off a street near Piccadilly, leading up to a few rooms for drinking and gaming and a private dining room. He wondered if Bertie Wooster's Drones Club was a bit like this. Except that one had a swimming pool, so possibly not.

Anyway, pool or no pool, membership of the Artemis included half the aristocracy and most of the Cabinet. Darbishire knew a thing or two about what went on in those exalted circles and wouldn't put anything past them. The problem was not where the dean and his guests came from, but the layout of the mews house when they got here. There was simply no way to murder two people upstairs in the way it was done and come down those open stairs without your physical appearance afterwards being observed by all concerned. So, either they were all in it together or the guests, at least, were innocent. They claimed not to know anything about the couple upstairs, but then they would, wouldn't they?

He climbed the stairs with a heavy tread. He knew what lay ahead.

'The one thing I don't get, sir,' Woolgar said on the way up – and Darbishire was intrigued by what was coming next, because there were at least a dozen things he himself didn't get – 'is, you know, the couple . . . Why they didn't, you know . . . do it.'

'Mmm.'

Woolgar's tread on the stairs was heavier than his. The whole house seemed to rattle.

'I mean, she's all dressed up. She's a tart, isn't she? They've got the house to themselves. According to that witness statement, she comes in at ten forty-five, lets the bloke in around eleven. Assuming that witness is reliable, they've got a good forty, forty-five minutes to themselves before the clubmen get back . . . But they don't . . . you know.'

The pathologist had just now confirmed his initial finding that there was no evidence of sexual activity between the couple, as Darbishire had reported to his sergeant.

'Which suggests they were surprised by someone else before they had the chance to,' he muttered.

'Except nobody else came in the front way until the dean and his mates got back,' Woolgar pointed out, 'and there's no sign of forced entry from the back. *Forty-five minutes*, guv. Longer, if they waited while the others played cards downstairs, and then the dean came up on his own and killed them afterwards for whatever reason. What did they *do*?'

'Perhaps they played cards themselves. Or talked philosophy.'

'D'you really—? Oh. Right. Sorry, sir.' Woolgar still never quite knew when to take his guvnor at face value. 'So, what . . . ?'

'I don't know, Sergeant.'

By now Darbishire had reached the landing. To his left lay the bedroom used by Clement Moreton. It was spartan and uninteresting, except for the green glass vase that had been taken away for processing by the laboratory. Behind it was a bathroom: small, modern, yellow-tiled and garish, accessed from the landing. Forensics had spent a lot of time in it, because apparently so did the killer or killers, who were unfortunately very good at cleaning up after themselves.

To the right lay the door to the larger second bedroom that ran from front to back, above the garage. This was where the bodies had been discovered. Moreton swore blind, or as much as a churchman ever did, that he never entered this room. His story was that the rental agency told him it was used for storage by the landlord and kept locked. He claimed he tried the door once and the handle rattled uselessly, as he expected it to. He didn't need the space so didn't worry. It was why the rent was cheap. The charlady confirmed this story, though she said that when she finally came upstairs a week after the murders, the door had sat ajar, which is what made her curious.

And yet, the room wasn't filthy with dust and grime when the police first entered. If the char didn't normally go in to keep it clean, who did? Another question.

The bedroom door sat open today and Darbishire walked inside.

The room was dominated by a big brass bedstead topped with a fat mattress, stripped of all bedding. It sat against the back wall, facing a bay window that overlooked the cobbled street. This was where the blonde was found, lying on her back, arms crossed over her chest, with a posy of flowers tucked inside them. The male victim was curled on the floor at the foot of the bed in a pool of blood, trousers round his knees, with a slim blade sticking out of his right eye. No wonder the char's screams were heard halfway down the street.

Woolgar hovered in the doorway and cracked his knuckles.

'What did Deedar say, sir?'

The pathologist visited by Darbishire was called Johnson, but was universally known as Deedar. It related to all the Sheffield steel involved in his profession, apparently. Sheffielders were known as 'Dee-Dars', because of the way they said 'thee' and 'thou' for 'you'. As a native of Aberdeen, Johnson didn't do this, so it had taken Darbishire a long time to work out the etymology of the nickname. By now, most officers assumed it was something to do with police sirens. But the inspector didn't trust easy answers. He tended to ask questions until he got the hard ones.

Darbishire also knew that Woolgar hadn't missed today's appointment at the mortuary with him because of a misunderstanding about timings, but because the smell of formaldehyde made him sick. If there was a future great detective inside that burly frame, it had a very long way to come out.

'It's largely as we thought,' he said. 'Did you make any progress with the other girl, by the way? The original one?'

Woolgar shook his head. 'She's vamoosed, no surprises. Beryl, her name is.'

'I don't need the name, I need the individual.'

Beryl was the lucky girl who was supposed to be meeting up with the male victim on the evening of Sunday the thirty-first – a blonde, like he'd requested from the Raffles escort agency. For some reason, this girl – Gina – had stood in for Beryl at the last minute.

Darbishire didn't believe in luck. Another question.

A modern ladies' vanity unit upholstered in smoky blue velvet sat under the window, topped with a triple mirror and an empty Venetian glass ashtray. It didn't align at all with the battered antiques downstairs: this room was kept for special assignations and decorated as such. There was also a large art deco wardrobe in the far corner, ideal in size for a couple of men of murderous bent to wait, unseen, for their victims – except that it was found to be full of catering-size boxes of tins of spam and a broken chair, awaiting repair. There wouldn't have been enough space to house a five-year-old.

In his forties, with the slicked-back hair of a Mediterranean or South American, the male victim had been identified by the papers in his pockets as Dino Perez from Argentina. The Raffles escort agency had been the first to confirm the couple's identities, although they had initially misidentified the girl. They said Perez had told them he was staying at the Dorchester, but the hotel had no record of him.

Darbishire walked over to the far side of the bed. He wanted to picture the scene as Deedar and his team thought it went, see if it worked.

'According to the forensics, Perez would have been standing between the bed and the door when the killers came in, with his back to them. The state of his trousers suggests his concentration was elsewhere. He was stabbed in the side with a slim blade, about six inches long, almost certainly the knife that was jabbed into his eye post-mortem. Given the way the knife twisted as it went in, it was likely he turned and caught them off guard.'

It would have been a painful wound, but not fatal straightaway. Hardly the most efficient way to kill a man.

Woolgar watched silently from the doorway, where the assailants must have entered, knives out. He was trying to picture it too.

'Somehow Perez got free,' Darbishire went on, moving towards the bay window. 'There was a struggle. He got as far as the foot of the bed, where they managed to cosh him on the back of the head. Right-handed, Deedar thinks. Why they didn't do that first, I don't know. Still no sign of the cosh. Perez fell . . .' he checked against the blood-stain on the carpet '. . . here. And that's where he was garrotted. Using cheese wire, or something like it, Deedar says. The stocking we found round the neck was superfluous. The wire'd already gone halfway through his windpipe.'

Woolgar nodded. 'Belt and braces, you might say.'

You might, though Darbishire wouldn't. It was an odd thing to do, though. Were they squeamish, these thugs? Did they want to cover up the wound with the stocking? Or in their fury, did they both want a go? That made sense, given the stag-handled flick knife someone ghoulishly parked in his eye afterwards. It was a slim, evil-looking affair, of the type the Italians called a stiletto. He'd seen many like it before.

'Definitely two of them, then?' Woolgar asked, taking out his notebook.

'If not, why didn't the girl intervene?'

'Perhaps she did.'

'If she did, why didn't she scream the bloody house down while she was doing it? Nobody on the street heard a peep. They all heard the char clear enough a week later.'

Woolgar scratched his chin.

'So there were two at least – one to go for him, one to keep her quiet?'

Darbishire had assumed this from the start, and Deedar agreed. 'Hence the bruising on her arms and legs. She didn't scream, but she fought against it. She knew what was coming.'

'She could have been the one killed first.'

'Not impossible,' Darbishire conceded. 'But the bruising suggests otherwise. They used the missing stocking on her, by the way. The seam's still visible on her neck.'

Woolgar winced. He wasn't good when it was a woman. He definitely wasn't cut out for long mornings in a mortuary.

'She was washed before she was put in position,' Darbishire added. 'Curious, no? Not all over, but enough to get rid of whatever blood was on her, which would've been mostly his. Wet towel dumped beside the bed. No decent prints anywhere. Then she was laid out in that ritualistic way, with the purple flowers—'

'Lilacs, guvnor.'

'Lilacs, if you say so . . . taken from the vase in the other room. Shoes put on her bare feet, tiara arranged nicely in her hair, even if the updo was missing a few pins by then. They didn't rush. No sense that they were under pressure or worried about witnesses.'

Which is why the Artemis crowd were in the clear. None of them would have had time for all the artful arrangement, and to clean themselves up too. Or the opportunity to hide the girl's missing dress and the stocking used to strangle her.

'What if . . .'

'What if what?'

There was a light in Woolgar's eye. 'How about if it was some sort of satanic ritual and *he* was the collateral damage . . . ?'

'Nice idea. Except, Gina Fonteyn wasn't supposed to be there, remember?'

'What if it didn't matter *who* she was? What if—?'

'That's enough of the "what ifs", Woolgar. If you set out to do that sort of thing to a girl, you don't ensure you've got a jumpy gangster in the middle of it all, do you?'

'No, sir,' Woolgar conceded, reluctantly.

It wasn't a cult. It was a gangland revenge killing of some sort, surely? That's what they thought at the station, too. The East End visiting the West End, with a cosh and a garrotte.

'Interesting that they didn't take the diamonds,' Darbishire added. This, too, had been bothering him.

'Perhaps they thought they were paste?'

'Even so, good repro gems are worth a bob or two.'

Woolgar shrugged. 'Dunno, sir.'

On that, they agreed. The inspector preferred not to think of the young woman's face in the mortuary just now. Human faces do not fare well after a strangling and a week lying undiscovered on a bed. Her peroxide hair, soft and curled and lacquered into a sophisticated style, looked horribly out of place against the skin. Her eyebrows and eyelashes were dark, he'd noticed. As was – and it was necessary to look – the rest of her. The limbs were slim and athletic. It could easily have been the body of the twenty-three-year-old she'd told the agency she was, though Deedar thought she'd knocked a few years off her real age.

'Wrong time, wrong place,' Darbishire concluded. 'Unlike Beryl, who so conveniently wasn't here.'

'Yes, guvnor.'

'And why were they in this room at all? When any minute a senior member of the clergy might come and find them at it?'

'Dunno, sir.'

Darbishire pointed at Woolgar's notebook. 'We need another word with that charlady. I suspect that's how the girl got the key to let herself in.'

'At least we know how they got out,' Woolgar suggested.

When the police had first arrived, they found the back door

unlocked and unbolted, but otherwise untouched. Moreton swore he always kept it bolted from the inside, hadn't touched it for months, and the char swore she hadn't touched it either, so if they were telling the truth, the killers couldn't have got in that way. Moreton said he couldn't remember seeing if the bolt was in place before heading home to his cathedral on the Monday morning, so it was probable that they had escaped via the little yard.

'Getting out was easy. It's still the entry we need to worry about.'

Woolgar's shoulders slumped. 'So we're back to the dean.'

'We're back to the dean.'

Who, in Darbishire's considered opinion as a policeman with twenty years' experience, couldn't have done this. Not physically, on his own, and not psychologically in any way, shape or form. Having met the man, the inspector could easily imagine the Very Reverend Clement Moreton killing someone in self-defence, but not like this. Not with that girl watching, and then kill her as well, and go to his dentist for his Monday morning appointment in Harley Street and back to his cathedral as if his worst care in the world was toothache, as every witness swore he'd done.

Besides, there were those forty-five minutes to account for between Perez's arrival at number 44 to join Miss Fonteyn, and Moreton's return from the Artemis Club with his friends at a quarter to midnight. Darbishire really didn't think the tart and her client had spent them playing cards, or talking philosophy. They were together here at eleven, and almost certainly dead by eleven thirty. Killed by persons unknown. Who teleported, like something out of H. G. Wells.

Woolgar pocketed his notebook and they headed back outside, into the pink light of a spring evening. Darbishire rolled his shoulders, glad to be in the fresh air. He wondered about the main witness that night: the young woman in the mews house opposite, up all night with her baby, who saw the comings and goings of Perez and Fonteyn, the dean and his guests. Her statement fitted in with the reports of taxi drivers and the suspects themselves, so she wasn't making it up. But she didn't see the men who must have done it. She had been interviewed by one of the sergeants and was very helpful at the time. Obviously, given her importance, Darbishire needed a personal word and soon, but like Beryl, the missing tart, she seemed to have gone to ground.

Once again, he wandered down to the end of the street, to get a sense of the yards behind the houses and their relationship to the gardens of the grand villas beyond. They were separated from each other by a motley collection of sturdy walls and flimsy wooden fence panels. The killers may have escaped across a series of yards until they were further down the street, but it seemed more likely they went straight over the ivy-covered wall of number 44 into the garden behind. Some of the ivy roots had been pulled away and a couple of crushed shrubs the other side of the wall were vaguely suggestive of a heavy landing, although the damage could equally have been made by a large animal. It hadn't rained, and there were no telling footprints in the earth. There never were.

'Off home, sir?' Woolgar asked.

Darbishire nodded. He lived only a couple of streets away, in a nice new block of flats purpose-built for the police on one of the few local bomb sites, a couple of years ago. This area had been miraculously spared by the Blitz – as if the golden denizens of the nearby stucco villas had been protected by the Luftwaffe themselves. There had been some tragedies, of course, and some empty sites, even now, like missing teeth. But mostly it was a place of Edwardian mansion flats and cheap hotels, of large Victorian houses, churches and schools, all muddling along comfortably together between the medley of shops along the King's Road to one side, and bedsits of the Old Brompton Road to the other.

Darbishire liked it round here. He liked to keep it tidy. He didn't like it when someone strangled and garrotted two people to death and left their bodies for a traumatised charlady to find. He intended to deliver whoever did it to the hangman's noose as soon as he could.

After saying goodbye to his sergeant, he picked up an evening paper at a corner shop. There was a round-up of Her Majesty's trip to Paris, with a picture of her on a boat on the River Seine, looking very regal in a shiny silver dress and a big white fur, and a tiara like the one she wore to get married in. She must have been having the time of her life.

CHAPTER 6

By the following Monday, the royal couple were back at Buckingham Palace and life was humming along at its brisk, London pace. One floor below the Queen's private apartment in the North Wing, the press secretary put his head around the private secretary's office door.

'I'm looking for the Eisenhower file. Need it for a briefing this afternoon. HM's got the call with the president at four. Have you seen it?'

Sir Hugh Masson looked up from the papers he was reading. 'No, Jeremy. It'll be in Miles's office. Did you hear about the first time the Queen encountered him? Or didn't, rather.'

'Eisenhower? No.'

Sir Hugh smiled and sat back in his chair.

'I heard this first-hand from the King. It was 'forty-two, and General Eisenhower was visiting Windsor Castle. Eisenhower was supposed to have a little tour before the official introductions, but the King and the family were sitting out on the terrace when he saw the general's party heading their way. The King knew it would cause a terrible fuss if the general was made to encounter them *au naturel*, like that, without warning, so he got them all – the Queen and the young princesses too – to get down on their knees and hide under the tablecloth until the party was out of sight. They were hooting with laughter. Didn't say a word afterwards. Very funny.'

Jeremy Radnor-Milne smiled politely. 'How sweet. But as I say, I need the file itself.'

Sir Hugh shrugged. 'It's probably on Fiona's desk somewhere.'

'It isn't, I've looked.'

'Have you checked the cabinets?'

The press secretary's slim moustache wiggled in irritation. He had indeed checked everywhere obvious in the filing room, where the absent Fiona worked occasionally.

'The thought did occur to me. I've got that typist girl helping me look. The trouble is, Fiona seems to keep things in the most extraordinary places. We found the Danish paperwork on one of the radiators in Miles's office. All the Cheshire research was in a basket marked 'Dog Biscuits'. God knows how *she* finds anything. No wonder the speech went missing.'

Sir Hugh rolled his eyes. 'Don't remind me. Why doesn't she leave it to the secretaries?'

The press secretary grimaced in agreement. Though he, Masson and Urquhart all shared the title 'Secretary' in one form or another, none of them did secretarial work of any sort, nor would they know how to. That was for the typists. The Honourable Fiona Matherton-Smith was a rare bird indeed: a woman untrained in secretarial arts, who was one of the higher breed designated with a capital 'S', like them. Her official title was Assistant Private Secretary and she assisted them all, but she was especially useful – although 'useful' was a loose term, in Fiona's case – when it came to helping the deputy private secretary set up royal visits or manage Her Majesty's correspondence. She was very easy on the eye, but paperwork was not her strong point.

The sound of pounding leather soles on the carpet in the corridor was followed by the appearance of the DPS himself, Miles Urquhart, looking anxious. 'Any idea where Her Majesty is? I can't find her.'

Sir Hugh leaned back in his chair and grinned. 'You've lost the Queen?'

Urquhart glowered. 'Don't joke, Hugh. Has she taken the dogs for a walk? Her diary's empty. I assumed she'd be doing paperwork but she's not upstairs.'

Sir Hugh checked his own copy of the royal schedule, running his finger down the appointments for the day. 'She's having a dress fitting, apparently. Mr Hartnell. It should be in your copy too.'

'Well, it isn't,' Urquhart complained. 'Dammit! I need to talk to her. Just had Washington on the phone. They've brought the call forward. The president can only do it in half an hour.'

Sir Hugh was startled. 'What?'

Radnor-Milne threw up his hands in horror. 'That bloody file!'

'I've found it, sir.'

There was a woman standing in the doorway. One of the junior secretaries, in a serge suit and sensible shoes, clutching a familiar-looking manila file. Radnor-Milne groaned at her. 'Too late now.'

'I can't go to HM if she's in a state of undress!' Urquhart wailed. 'That's what Fiona was for.'

'We could get a lady-in-waiting,' Radnor-Milne suggested.

'It'll take too long.'

'Where is Fiona, anyway?' the private secretary asked. 'Why isn't she back yet?'

'Still under the weather,' Urquhart complained. 'Her mother's taking her away, she said, for her nerves.'

'Her *nerves*?'

The DPS's florid cheeks went pinker with disgust. 'That's what she said. What is it with women? Why can't you trust them? *Her* nerves? What about *my* nerves? Christ!' Urquhart shot an anguished look at the typist in the doorway. 'Hey, you. McGinty. Jane, is it? You'll do, at a pinch. Can you take a message to Her Majesty?'

The woman clutching the folder stared back at him.

'Don't look like a startled deer, girl! You've met the Queen before.'

'I haven't, sir.'

'Oh. Well, you're doing it now.' Urquhart checked his watch. 'Tell her the American president will call in twenty-five minutes, at twelve instead of four, and we know that's not what we agreed but there's not much to be done about it. She can make it to her desk if she runs, or of course we can have a telephone brought to her, but I imagine she'll want privacy.'

'*Runs*?' the secretary asked faintly.

'What?'

'Did you say "if she runs"?'

'Yes. Have you seen Her Majesty run?'

'No, sir.'

'Well, she does. She likes the exercise. You should see her when one of her dogs goes off after a rabbit or the children get too close to the lake.'

'Yes, sir.'

'What are you waiting for? You know where the fitting room is?

South Wing, next to the old chapel door. Off you go. You'll need a decent turn of speed yourself or HM will require a Derby winner if she wants to get to her office on time.'

★ ★ ★

Joan McGraw (her names included neither Jane nor McGinty, but she was very low in the pecking order and put up with it) paused for a moment outside the private secretary's office in the North Wing. She couldn't quite believe what she was about to do. But she had no time to lose and precious little time to think. She flew down the red-carpeted corridors in her sturdy lace-ups, past gilt-edged doors to state rooms and priceless marble statues, sweeping staircases and several frowning footmen, until she eventually reached the dowdy limewash and linoleum of the administrative offices in the South Wing.

She was grateful to have been her school's cross-country champion, but she was still out of breath. The royal fitting room was to her right, with a page in uniform standing outside the door. She took a moment to calm herself.

The page knocked on her behalf and a very familiar voice said, 'Come in.'

Joan did so, to find three middle-aged women and a very dapper gentleman in a pinstriped suit standing around the monarch, who was pinned into a white calico dress which Joan recognised as a 'toile' – a pattern for the real thing – while one of the women fussed at the fabric round her bosom.

The Queen gave Joan a casually curious glance.

'Yes? Is it something important? We're rather busy.'

Joan curtseyed, averting her eyes from the pushing and pulling of royal flesh inside the fabric. She explained about the call.

The Queen glanced at her watch. 'There's enough time to take it at my desk. You can come with me. I'll finish this later. Mr Hartnell, I'm so sorry. I hope you understand. We really mustn't keep the president waiting.'

The designer was obsequious in his forgiveness. Her Majesty disappeared behind a screen with one of the women and emerged five minutes later wearing a sensible skirt and twin-set, and a grin.

'We have twelve minutes. Odds on we can make it in ten. Sugar, off we go.'

For a moment, Joan assumed that Sugar was a nickname for the woman who had accompanied the Queen behind the screen, but it turned out to be a corgi, who had been lounging in front of a fireplace. The dog cheerfully shadowed her mistress at a brisk trot as they set off back across the palace. Joan jogged along too.

'Why isn't Fiona here?' the Queen asked as they sped along. 'Hugh would normally have sent her to find me. Is she still away?'

'Yes, ma'am.'

'For how much longer?'

'It's not certain ma'am, but—'

'Yes?'

'I sense it will be quite some time.'

'What makes you think that?'

'I'm afraid I can't say.'

It wasn't 'nerves'. On a brief visit to the Private Office two weeks ago, Joan had observed Fiona being sick in the lavatories. Fiona told Joan in passing that she had been doing this every morning for the previous month, and wondered if she had caught some sort of tropical disease. Joan had been the one to break the news to her. She still remembered the look of dumb shock in Fiona's eyes.

Joan could have told the men in the Private Office as much, but she wouldn't have betrayed a confidence and anyway, they didn't ask her. The Queen turned her head to give Joan a look of surprise. It wasn't normal for staff not to be able to tell her things. But she didn't press the point.

'Have you taken over from her?'

'Oh, no, ma'am. I'm just a typist. I happened to be around when Fiona, um, had to leave. I was able to help out in a small way.'

'Not such a small way if you're still there. My DPS is a notorious taskmaster. Well done.'

By now they were approaching the ornate Ministers' Staircase, heading for the undistinguished lift nearby that went to the Queen's private apartments. Joan basked in this unexpected praise.

In the lift itself, they took the opportunity to catch their breath and size each other up a little. Her Majesty was a disconcerting mix of perfectly normal and hypnotically familiar. Joan found it hard not to stare. There was an odd modesty about her for someone whose image was so famous. Her face was almost bare, except for a little lipstick and powder, her bushy eyebrows resolutely unplucked, her pale skin smooth and unrouged. What she lacked in vanity she made up for in self-possession. Joan was the taller of the two by several inches, but the Queen was still clearly and comfortably the boss.

The Queen sensed a certain confidence in Joan, too. Though she was 'just a typist', she was obviously enjoying her little adventure. She had an attractive, open face with freckled skin and Titian hair (Philip would have called it ginger) neatly rolled in a slightly old-fashioned style. The Queen noticed she didn't wear a wedding ring and wondered what the story behind that might be. After the war, there were so many. Anyway, here she was.

As they shared a smile, each saw a woman with a job to do, a practical sort, up for a challenge. There was an intelligent spark in Joan's hazel eyes that the Queen liked very much. In the tight proximity of the creaky lift, with the clock running down, she recognised a kindred spirit.

As the lift reached its destination, Joan finally plucked up the courage to ask something that had been on her mind.

'Ma'am, while you were in Paris, how did the speech go? I mean, I hope you got it in time.'

The Queen stopped and looked at her closely.

'It was *you*.'

Joan blinked. 'Yes, ma'am.'

'You found a carbon? Was it in a bin or something?'

Joan was surprised. 'No, ma'am. They'd all disappeared. But I could remember it.'

'What? The whole thing? By heart?'

'Yes.' Joan was bemused.

The Queen tipped her head to one side and looked at her harder still. 'It went very well, thank you. Do you have one of those, what do they call it, photographic memories?'

'I don't think so, ma'am. I just . . . if I see something, I can generally remember it.' Joan felt acutely embarrassed. She didn't understand why other people had trouble recalling the images they had recently seen. What was so difficult about it? Like her father, she'd been able to do it all her life. He didn't understand the problem, either.

'I think that *is* a photographic memory,' the Queen said. 'Ah, here we are. Outside my study with . . . what?' She looked at her watch and smiled. 'Three minutes to spare!' She paused on the threshold and turned back. 'What's your name, by the way?'

'McGraw, ma'am. Joan McGraw.'

'That's Irish, isn't it?'

'Yes. My grandfather was Irish.'

'Mmm. And you speak French fluently?'

'I do. My mother was French. I also speak German.'

The Queen nodded thoughtfully. 'How old are you, if I might ask?'

'I'm thirty-seven, ma'am.'

She nodded again. 'I see. Did you have an interesting war?'

They held each other's gaze for just long enough for Joan to signal that she knew what the Queen meant. 'Interesting' wars for clever young linguists at the time tended to involve spying or, in Joan's case, decoding work at Bletchley Park, before moving on to other, equally interesting things.

'Yes, ma'am.'

The Queen gave her the briefest nod. 'Yes, well, thank you for your message. And now I must see what Mr Eisenhower wants from me.'

★　★　★

That evening, the Queen had a question for Sir Hugh as he discussed her schedule for the following day.

'I gather Fiona won't be coming back for a little while. Is that right?'

'Ah. Do you? I—'

'She wasn't an ideal APS anyway, Hugh. She was always confusing Austria and Australia.'

Sir Hugh was alarmed. He was very fond of Fiona. She was the great-niece of a duke, one of his own distant cousins, and an excellent horsewoman with a weakness for cocker spaniels and couture fashion she couldn't afford. She could be a little scatty, in an endearing way, but he would argue she made up for it with her cheerful nature, the boxes of pastries she brought in each morning, made by her family's exceptional London chef, and her uncanny ability to know when he, Miles or Jeremy needed soothing or cheering after a fraught encounter.

'She was deb of the year, ma'am, if you recall. I think it's simply a matter of training. With time, she—'

'Anyway, we need someone new. I like the girl I met yesterday. I think she shows promise.'

'The redhead? McGinty? She's just a typist, ma'am. She—'

'So she told me. I think there's more to her than that. She helped you out in Paris, didn't she?'

'Dictating over the telephone? Yes, she did, but—'

'She got us out of a hole. I'm very grateful. Don't search for a replacement for Fiona just yet. Let's see how this one gets on. And her name's McGraw.'

'Ma'am?'

'Not McGinty. You're thinking of the nursery rhyme. Thank you *so* much, Hugh.'

This was a dismissal, and he knew it. He was astonished.

'Ma'am.' Sir Hugh bowed and left.

Afterwards, the Queen smiled to herself. His grey whiskers had quivered with indignation at the very idea of a lowly secretary taking on such a valuable role in the Private Office. As she had known they would.

It was inevitable that the men in moustaches would provide acute resistance to a girl with an Irish name, a *typist*, no less, taking her place alongside them. But the Queen needed an ally, someone outside the close-knit institutional world she had inherited from her father. She sensed this morning, looking into those clever, frank hazel eyes, that she had found one.

Hence her forcefulness with Sir Hugh just now, which was rare. Her private secretary wasn't going to make Joan's life easy, but he would at least give her a chance, because he had no choice. The rest would be up to her.

CHAPTER 7

Inspector Darbishire made his way to the interview room at a police station in Southend. After a nationwide search lasting two weeks, Beryl White had finally been tracked down by a sergeant working for the Vice Unit. DS Victor Willis had discovered the missing escort at the home of her brother and his family. She refused to return to London, so Darbishire and Woolgar travelled to Essex while Willis stayed with her to ensure she didn't do a flit.

'Nice work, Sergeant,' Darbishire acknowledged, as the man waited at the door to greet them.

Willis gave a friendly smile. He had a record of helping out with reluctant witnesses. His slick good looks and a kindly manner seemed to have a special effect on women of ill repute.

'Would you like me to sit in with you, sir?' he asked, eyeing Woolgar, who lurked further down the corridor.

'That won't be necessary,' Darbishire assured him, although he briefly wondered what it would be like to employ Willis's sharp wits and good looks, instead of Woolgar's bulk and lively imagination. 'Anything I should know? What frame of mind is she in?'

'I told her she could have the duty solicitor if she wanted, sir, but she declined.'

Darbishire nodded. Silly girl – but he wasn't complaining. It was easier for him if there was no lawyer to interfere with his line of questioning. Given the approach he planned to take today, it helped a lot. 'Still being difficult, is she?'

'Oh no, sir. She just wants it over with. I told her as long as she cooperates and tells us everything she knows, she'll be all right. She should be a good girl. I gave her a decent talking-to.'

Darbishire wasn't entirely happy with this. It should have been a job for the duty solicitor she didn't want – but he assumed Willis had done his best. He called Woolgar over and they went in, leaving Willis to make his way home.

Beryl White was precisely what you would expect a high-class escort to be, that is, young and beautiful, with skin like silk and a nose like something off a Greek sculpture, perfectly coiffed platinum-blonde hair and a buttoned-up dress fitted a size too tight, to show off her assets. The Raffles agency advertised its services as offering 'pleasing feminine company for uplifting conversation with the discerning gentleman'. It was quite plain that it wasn't chiefly conversation that got uplifted in her company. But perhaps she was good at that, too.

As Darbishire sat down opposite her, he noticed the frequent glances she gave DS Woolgar from under those long eyelashes of hers. Once again, he managed to fill the room with his looming presence, though he had positioned himself behind his boss, near the door. She seemed intimidated, but if she was afraid of what Darbishire thought she was afraid of, it might help for her to know that the police could also be a force to be reckoned with.

'So, Miss White—'

'Call me Beryl. Everyone does. Except . . . my gentlemen.'

'What do they call you?'

Beryl slid her eyes to meet Darbishire's. 'Whatever they like.'

He held her gaze. He was aware that he was about to do the same, in a way.

'With all due respect, I prefer Miss White.'

'"With all due respect,"' she echoed, raising one sculpted eyebrow. 'May I?' She fished a packet of cigarettes out of her handbag and lit one, eyeing Woolgar once again through the smoke.

Darbishire got down to business.

'You've been away from London for some time, Miss White. Would you like to explain why?'

'I needed some sea air.'

'And why was that?'

She shrugged and glanced around the little room. 'Can't a girl need a bit of a break sometimes?' Then, catching his stern expression, she stared down at the table between them. 'I lost a good friend,' she added, subdued.

'You made yourself very hard to find. You must have known we were looking for you.'

She shook her head adamantly. 'I had no idea. My brother's family don't get the papers. It was just a little break, that's all. I've got nothing to hide.'

We'll see, Darbishire thought.

'Tell me what happened the day of the thirty-first. You were due to see Dino Perez, as arranged by the agency. He'd asked for you specifically, the day before.'

'Not specifically, no,' she corrected him. 'And it was two days before, not one. He was out of town, but he said he'd like company when he got back. His last companion was . . . otherwise engaged. I suppose I was closest to what he wanted.'

'Which was?'

'A princess.'

She looked at him archly and let the words hang in the air. The way she carried herself, her bone structure, the way her blonde hair caught the light . . . He could see why the agency picked her.

'Any princess in particular?'

'No.' She hesitated. 'A blonde.'

'What happened next?'

Beryl started off composed. 'I put the date in my diary. But the next day I woke up with the most god-awful headache. A real blinder. I could hardly see.' Her eyes briefly widened, as if she was reliving it. 'Once it comes it stays for a day or two and I'm out of it, and afterwards I'm good for nothing. So I told Gina, God bless her, and she said she'd step in for me. And she did, the next day.' She paused, lips trembling. 'I'll blame myself forever.'

She glanced away with a shuddering breath. Her act was touching, but slightly over-rehearsed, in Darbishire's opinion.

'Why ask Gina yourself?' he asked. 'Why not get the agency to sort something out?'

Beryl shrugged. 'Once you say yes to a job, it's up to you to get it done. Besides, I knew Gina would do it. She owes me. *Owed* me.' Her long eyelashes brushed her pretty cheeks with tears.

He came in gently for the kill. Having spoken to the agency, he knew about the request. 'There's something I don't understand, Miss White. Why ask Gina to stand in for you, if Mr Perez wanted a blonde?'

A slight frown formed between Beryl's eyebrows, and for an instant she looked a bit rattled.

'What d'you mean?' she asked.

'Gina was normally a brunette, wasn't she? She is in all her photographs. She had very recently dyed her hair – to become a blonde, like you, yes?'

Beryl took a moment to restore her composure. 'She was dark, yes, but she didn't want to be. She'd seen the sort of clients I got. She'd been interested in changing her look anyway.' With a steady gaze, she added, 'Gentlemen prefer blondes, you know.'

Darbishire didn't, personally. His wife's hair was jet black before the grey started to appear. But then, he didn't think of himself as a gentleman, either. He moved on.

'So, she peroxided her hair?'

'Yes.'

'Did you help her?'

'No.'

'And did you provide any of her clothes?'

'No. We're different sizes.'

'And the tiara?'

'What about it?'

'Real diamonds. Was it yours?'

Beryl stopped and stared at him as if he was from Mars. 'Yeah,' she drawled. 'It was my second party tiara. I kept it with my bleeding crown jewels.'

'You'd never seen it before?'

'No. I hadn't. Still haven't – except that drawing in the papers.'

'You didn't need one . . . professionally?'

'I had a little paste thing.' She glanced at the stub of her cigarette, now finished, took another one from the packet and lit it. 'Nothing special. Got it from a shop in Brighton, in the Lanes. I offered it to Gina but she didn't need it. Found something better, didn't she?'

'Evidently she did. Any idea how?'

Beryl took a drag and shook her head.

'Are you sure you didn't provide it?'

'No!' She seemed genuinely surprised by the question. 'How could I? Why would I?'

'Nobody gave it to you, or asked you to—?'

'What are you getting at?' she asked, brow furrowing. 'D'you mean another of my gentlemen? No.'

This was not what Darbishire meant. If a gang had planned this murder and stolen a tiara to order, or if they'd had one lying around after a robbery and decided to use it for fun, it was plausible – just – that they had given it to Beryl to pass on to the unfortunate Gina. This was one of his theories. But he believed her surprise at the suggestion. She simply wasn't a good enough actress to fake it.

'What did you know about Perez?' he asked, changing tack.

'Nothing.' Her gaze was shifty again.

'He was a client of the agency,' Darbishire pointed out.

'He wanted company a few times, yes. But I'd never met him.'

'You said his last "companion" was otherwise engaged. Was that deliberate? Did you ask to take over?'

'No! She didn't want him! She—' Beryl caught herself and stopped suddenly.

'She what, Miss White?'

'Nothing,' the girl said. Her attempt at breeziness was undermined by the stiff set of her shoulders.

'Don't lie to me,' Darbishire barked. 'Don't even think about it. Why didn't she want him?'

Beryl stiffened further. 'Look, it was nothing. She just said that he wasn't the most . . . gentlemanly. It's not exactly news. They're not all saints. There was something in his eyes, she said . . . But that's all I knew, I swear.'

The agency hadn't mentioned this. They weren't entirely forth-coming with information, Darbishire had noticed. Given that it was illegal for them to profit from prostitution, they had to be careful what they said.

'What about Gina?'

'What about her?'

'Did she know about him, too?'

The escort shifted uncomfortably and crossed one elegant leg over the other. 'I might have told her. She was just grateful for the job. Look, can I go? I don't know anything. I wasn't even there!'

'That's the *point*, Miss White,' Darbishire insisted, stepping up a gear. 'You weren't.'

'W-what d'you mean?'

Sensing he was on the right track, he pushed on.

'There's something you're not telling us. And if you don't come clean, this won't end well for you.'

She flicked another frightened glance towards Woolgar. Darbishire looked round to see if his sergeant was glowering at her in a threatening way, but he seemed as impassive as ever.

'That house,' Darbishire said harshly. 'Why did they go to Cresswell Place in particular?'

'I don't know!'

'Why not a hotel?'

'I told you, I don't *know*! I assumed Mr Perez asked to go there.'

'You *do* know, Miss White. We've talked to the char who cleaned at number forty-four. She's admitted that room was used for occasional assignations by the agency. Gina Fonteyn somehow had the keys, but Perez was expecting *you*. Admit it – you gave the keys to her. You'd been there before and—'

'Not for months!' she insisted. 'I didn't touch those keys, I swear!'

'Let me put a theory to you,' Darbishire suggested.

'OK, but—'

'I think you arranged where Gina Fonteyn was going to meet up with Dino Perez. Somewhere nice and quiet, without witnesses like a hotel clerk. I think you made sure you were out of it, but you let somebody else know too. There are some dangerous characters involved, Miss White. Men who know how to hurt a pretty face. Maybe there was money in it for you, or maybe you were just scared out of your wits, but you did something you're ashamed of. And you fled London as fast as you could to get away from it—'

'I swear! I never—'

'But you can't escape, Miss White. Not from these people. Not without our help. You need to be honest with us or we can't protect you.'

She trembled and looked desperately towards Woolgar. What *was* it about him? Darbishire briefly wondered if he had another sandwich stuffed in his pocket and she thought it was a gun. Should he throw the man out? He would, if she did it again. Darbishire turned and glared at him, then straightened and lowered his voice to reassure her a little. Perhaps he'd overdone the threat.

'We *can* protect you, Beryl, but you have to help us. Can you? For Gina's sake? Because I don't think you meant any of this to happen.'

Beryl stared him full in the face, wide-eyed and noticeably pale.

'Meant it to happen? *Meant it?* What are you getting at? Of course I didn't mean it. I just . . . Gina *wanted* to go with him. I didn't know where they went, I swear. D'you think I'm in *danger*? I just went away because I was feeling rotten, like I told you. My head.' She pressed the heels of her hands to her temples, as if to demonstrate. 'What dangerous characters? I don't even know any. I mean, I know *some*, but none as would do this. Would they? I don't understand. I—'

'There, there. Calm down. As I say, we can protect you.'

She glared at him again. 'You can't,' she spat, to his astonishment. 'What do you mean by that?'

Her whole demeanour changed. She had been openly panicking, but now she sat back in her chair and her lip curled. 'Since when did the likes of you ever protect the likes of me?'

For the first time, Darbishire sensed he was seeing the true Beryl White. And she had a very low opinion of him, of the Metropolitan Police, and of everything that had happened here so far, despite his best assurances.

For the next half-hour, he grilled her as hard as he could about who might have set up the meeting with Perez, what she knew and what they did to buy her silence. But the silly girl was scared witless, and for a full thirty minutes he got nothing further out of her at all.

CHAPTER 8

The Honourable Fiona Matherton-Smith had a beloved spaniel called Monty, and Joan knew this because Monty's empty dog basket still took pride of place beside the radiator in the deputy private secretary's office, which she now also shared. In the week since she had been offered the job of assistant private secretary by Sir Hugh (with obvious shock and reluctance on his part, and absolute astonishment on hers), Joan twice tried to move the dog basket, to make way for much-needed filing cabinets, but Miles Urquhart wouldn't hear of it.

'The place isn't the same without Monty,' he opined. Joan tried not to take it personally, but a treasured spaniel was one of the many things Fiona possessed and she did not. Others, in no particular order, included a title, a famous family chef, an outsize bottle of L'Air du Temps (a gift from an admirer, found in a desk drawer next to the paper clips) and a personal acquaintance with at least half the men who had been at Eton in the last twenty years.

It wasn't easy to make up for these deficiencies. However, for what it was worth, Joan had an innate ability not only to find important documents in Fiona's idiosyncratic horizontal filing system, but to put them back in places where other people – notably the private, deputy and press secretaries – could find them too. There was also her memory for names: both of the senior men around the globe who needed to speak to the Private Office, and for their secretaries and assistants, who purred like kittens to be remembered and suddenly made all transactions easier.

On her first day, Joan installed an impressive typewriter on her desk, and though the DPS insisted the noise of the keys would drive him mad, her ability to anticipate and type up the notes and memoranda he needed saved him precious minutes in a busy day. She couldn't bring in Parisian-style pastries, but she wasn't a fool and she arrived instead with bags of fresh bagels and cinnamon babkas from the East End, which were always gone by ten o'clock.

Every half-hour, Urquhart would give her a new task, or a head would pop round the door and the private or press secretary would add something for her to do. It was mostly menial work and the thanks were always perfunctory, but Joan didn't care.

She was at the centre of the world and loving every minute.

Within twenty-four hours of her arrival, someone from the White House had called to sort out the Queen's sleeping arrangements for her stay in Washington in October. Urquhart, who found such details beneath his dignity, had left her to it.

Joan had since met the prime minister, the lord chancellor, the Archbishop of York and the chairman of the BBC. She saw Her Majesty almost daily, to deliver or pick up the red boxes of official paperwork for the Queen to review. And because Joan mastered the files so quickly, she became the expert on the schedules for the upcoming royal visits. Other members of staff were coming to rely on her. They would always address their questions to the DPS, but they increasingly turned to Joan for the answers.

There was something she needed to discuss with the Queen, but their brief conversations had been taken up with immediate plans for the Easter weekend and Her Majesty's birthday. Meanwhile, the only problem lay with the secretaries (lower case), who were once so friendly. When Joan used to pop across from the typing pool, they would include her in their tea breaks and their gossip. But since her elevation to a capital S, they looked on her with suspicion. The nicer she was to them, the more distant they became.

Still, the job itself was a dream, she knew she was doing it well, and for now that was enough.

★ ★ ★

'The new girl's a disaster, ma'am. I'm sorry, but there we are.'

Miles Urquhart stood stiffly before the Queen in her study. It had taken him a few days to get this little meeting in Her Majesty's diary, but at last the time had come. His russet moustache quivered with righteous indignation: to be expected to work alongside a little know-it-all Irish minx! What had Her Majesty been thinking? It was demeaning, demoralising and it had to stop.

'Oh? What's she done?'

Urquhart briefly closed his eyes. What *hadn't* Joan done?

'She doesn't know her place, ma'am.'

'And what is that?'

'To be my assistant,' he said gruffly, sensing more resistance from Her Majesty than he had anticipated. 'To learn fast and do as she's told.'

'I see.'

'And she has been sadly disappointing on both counts. I didn't want to bring this to your attention, ma'am. Normally I'd deal with it myself, but I know you suggested the girl personally and I thought you ought to know before any action was taken.'

'Bring what to my attention, Miles?'

Where to begin?

'She's frequently late. She's cocky. She doesn't know her limits. She almost made a complete hash of a sensitive issue in Washington, classic example, and I've only just rescued it. And—'

'I thought Hugh said she was flying through the filing and doing rather well.'

'That was at the start, ma'am. Before we found out her true nature. I'm not surprised she can't cope, of course. Girls of her class aren't cut out for this sort of work.'

The Queen pushed back her chair and sat with her hands in her lap. She looked composed, but had she sported a moustache, it might have bristled tellingly too.

'Oh. You mentioned an issue in Washington . . . ?'

He refrained from rolling his eyes, but a tic went off in his cheek at the memory of it. 'This was on Saturday, ma'am. I only found out on Sunday but as it was your birthday, I didn't want to bother you. And as I say, I've dealt with it.'

'I'm sure you have, Miles. Dealt with what?'

'A ridiculous breach of protocol. Joan tends to chat to every Tom, Dick and Harry who calls up, regardless of status. She made friends with some secretary at the White House and took it upon herself to overrule your sleeping arrangements for October. I might not have noticed, but she pointed it out to me herself, as if she was proud of it.'

'And what did she do, exactly?'

Urquhart's tic beat faster. 'The protocol is quite clear. All leaders visiting the White House stay at Blair House on Pennsylvania Avenue, as they've done since Churchill's unfortunate visit to the executive residence in 1942. I gather he was known to wander about the White House at night with a little more freedom than the president found acceptable. Given that history, it makes it all the more embarrassing that Joan and this American secretary took it upon themselves to change your schedule and move you and the duke back to the executive residence for your stay.'

'Did she?'

The Queen's eyes widened. Again, her upper lip didn't amplify her emotion, and Urquhart assumed horror, like his own.

'Don't worry, ma'am. I've spoken to my man in Washington. He's busy putting it right before the president gets to hear about it. We would hate him to think we have no respect for tradition, for privacy . . .'

'I see,' the Queen said. 'Have you spoken to Joan about this? Did she explain?'

'She said she discussed it with Jeremy, but he denies it. I'm afraid she can't *absolutely* be relied upon to tell the truth. Another class trait, possibly. To be charitable, one might assume that perhaps she feels overwhelmed.'

The Queen cut across him. 'If you *had* spoken to her, Miles, she might have told you that I wrote a note following my discussion with the president last week. Mrs Eisenhower very kindly invited the duke and me to stay with them in the White House. I was touched by the gesture. It was a sign of our personal friendship.'

'Ma'am, I—'

'Of course, I accepted. You didn't see my note? I do hope you can talk to your man in Washington before the president *does* get to hear about the new arrangement. I'd hate us to look ungrateful.'

Urquhart stood rigid with dismay. 'Yes, ma'am.'

'And silly, and uncoordinated.'

There was a pause.

'Yes, ma'am.'

Urquhart was stung. It was rare for Her Majesty to issue a rebuke, but when she did, she chose her words well. *Silly and uncoordinated.* If Sir Hugh were to hear of it . . . It was all the fault of that stupid girl, of course, for not making herself clearer and then discussing the thing with Jeremy, and not himself, if indeed she'd talked to anyone. She had been nothing but trouble, apart from the filing – which any office girl could do. It was what he was trying to *say.* He returned to his point.

'She didn't show me the note. But, that's not all, ma'am. I really can't have her working for me.'

'I hate to mention it, Miles, but she doesn't actually work for you, she works for me.'

'Well, technically, ma'am.' He caught the look in HM's eye and corrected himself. 'I mean of course she does, but . . .'

'You mentioned lateness?'

At least Her Majesty was listening, and keen to get to the bottom of the thing.

'Twice, at least,' he explained. 'Swanning in at past nine a.m.'

Fiona, bless her, was rarely in by ten, but always looked divine when she arrived with her darling Monty. Joan, if anything, looked more frazzled and unkempt when she was late than when she crept in on time.

The Queen nodded. 'Oh dear. And "cocky", I think you said? In what way?'

Had he said 'cocky'? Well, she was.

'McGraw's attitude to punctuality speaks for itself, ma'am. She's a typist: she should be able to keep office hours if anyone can. She's been here five minutes and she's getting ideas.'

'Ah.'

'It's not a surprise, as I said.' At last, Urquhart could play his ace. He looked suitably sombre; it didn't do to crow when delivering the coup de grâce. 'Jeremy's been doing some research. Due diligence, you might call it, and we've discovered she has a history of this sort of thing.'

'Oh?'

'McGraw's war record. Gross insubordination. Far worse than we might have imagined. I'm not surprised she doesn't talk about it. I'm afraid, given what we know, we can't possibly keep her in the Private Office after this.'

'May I see it?'

Urquhart dutifully held out the manila folder he'd armed himself with before leaving his office.

'Of course, ma'am. It's all there in black and white. I'm sure when you read it, you'll see what I mean.'

CHAPTER 9

Joan found herself summoned to the Queen's presence at half past six, as she was preparing to tidy up her desk. It would be the first time in five days that she'd finished before 9 p.m., but she didn't mind this little delay – in fact, she was excited. There was a lot she wanted to discuss with Her Majesty if she got the chance. She arrived at the door of the royal study on the second floor in a buoyant mood.

The look on the Queen's face put paid to that.

'Good evening.'

Joan curtseyed warily. 'Good evening, Your Majesty.'

'We don't have long. I'm due downstairs shortly. I've been reading about your war record.'

Joan's good spirits evaporated.

The Queen sat at a heavy, Chippendale pedestal desk set at right angles to the room's bow window, with the darkening sky behind her left shoulder. There were comfortable chairs elsewhere in the room, but the cluttered desk was a place of work. Tonight, a bulb in an Anglepoise lamp illuminated the incriminating document sitting on the royal blotter.

'The DPS unearthed it for me. I'm afraid we have a bit of a problem.'

A bit of a problem.

The room was quiet, except for the sound of Joan's new life crashing down around her. She stood straight and still, using everything she had to stop her eyes from even glistening.

'You were demoted, I understand.'

'Yes, ma'am.'

'Oh dear.' The Queen looked up. 'I actually remember the incident, though I didn't know your part in it. My father told me about it.'

'He did?'

'Yes. Everyone was concerned about Brigadier Yelland losing his command of Longmeadow in the run-up to D-Day. You worked for Yelland, I understand?'

Joan nodded. The headquarters at Longmeadow marked the end of her 'interesting' war.

Before arriving there, she had already been moved from Bletchley to Trent Park in Middlesex. At the latter, her role had been to interview senior German prisoners of war. She had been chosen because she was young and female, which instantly wrong-footed them and proved a good way of tripping them up. To that she added her linguistic ability, a certain hard-headedness and natural investigative skill, so that the work had come easily.

She wasn't pleased when an admiral at Naval Intelligence tasked her to assist Brigadier Yelland at his secret HQ in the spring of 1944, but the new job came with a promotion and the assurance that the high-ups in Whitehall were keeping an eye on her career.

Longmeadow Hall in Dorset turned out to be the headquarters of some of the most important intelligence gathering on German forces in France, prior to D-Day. It was staffed by the best and brightest officers from across the Allied forces, working in great secrecy and under extreme pressure. But Yelland struggled with organisation and morale was at rock bottom under his command. Joan was drafted in as his assistant in the hope that a woman's touch would smooth over any problems, without ruffling the sensitive feathers of the brigadier himself.

As soon as she understood the nature of the D-Day plan, Joan realised how much faith they had put in her. She was honoured to be involved, but Yelland was beyond help and didn't want it. He was in the grip of a severe drinking problem and incapable of listening. He would make mistakes, blame others, alienate important people and retire to his room with a bottle of gin. She endured this regime for six weeks with a growing sense of dread, knowing how much depended on the work they were doing. In the end, she jeopardised everything, made a secret trip to London, and took the biggest risk of her life.

And paid the price, or so she thought.

She had lost her job at the base, and any hope of a career. When the war ended, nobody in the Admiralty wanted to employ her. She was lucky to get secretarial work where she could find it. The typing pool at Buckingham Palace had been her first full-time job in years.

It would all be in the report sitting in front of the Queen tonight.

'General Eisenhower was aware something was wrong at Long-meadow,' the Queen told her, folding the manila cover shut. 'As I'm sure you know, several staff members had already complained through the proper channels. But you didn't do that.'

'No, ma'am.'

'In fact, you took it upon yourself to go straight to Admiral Butt in Naval Intelligence, who reported what was going on directly to the prime minister. As a result of your trip, Yelland was sacked within forty-eight hours.'

Joan was thrown back to the week of her court martial. Her crime of 'gross insubordination' had been thrown in her face by a very super-cilious major, extravagantly whiskered, who had ground her reputa-tion into the dust. She had overstepped the mark, broken the rules by taking matters into her own hands, and shared secrets of national importance. She should have used official channels. She wasn't to be trusted. She was lucky to escape without a dishonourable discharge.

The Queen carried on. 'As the report states several times, in the armed forces it's essential to go through the chain of command. You had a duty to report your concerns to your immediate superior.'

Joan bowed her head. 'Yes, ma'am.'

'But you didn't.'

'I tried, ma'am, but—'

'Who *was* your immediate superior?'

Joan sighed. 'Brigadier Yelland, ma'am.'

The supercilious major at the court martial had found no irony in this at all.

'Mmm. Who else was there, holding a senior position at Longmeadow?'

Joan tried to hide the memory of her frustration. 'No one, ma'am.'

There was a grim look in her eyes as the Queen glanced back at the file. She seemed to be mulling over what to say.

Joan made a snap decision because she realised she may not have much time.

'Ma'am?'

The Queen looked up. 'Yes?'

'Before I . . . before you . . . I just need you to know that I've come across something disturbing in the Private Office. I know you may think this is just sour grapes, given what you've just said, but I assure you it isn't.'

'Go on.'

'It was something in the Denmark file a couple of days ago. About your state visit next month. It's odd, but there was a request for the Duke of Edinburgh to be escorted on his individual excursions – he's making two of them, as you know – by a particular young lady from the Danish Embassy. I thought it was unusual, because of course she's based here in London, not Copenhagen, so I double-checked with the duke's private secretary and he said he knows nothing about it. The request certainly didn't come from him. He doesn't know Miss Kern and he's pretty sure the duke doesn't either. The thing is . . .' Joan paused, and noticed the Queen's blue-eyed gaze gathering a touch of frost.

'Continue,' Her Majesty said tightly.

'The thing is, ma'am, she's very striking, this woman, Ingrid Kern. She has shining blonde hair, you know the sort, and I understand she stands out on the diplomatic circuit. Her presence would be noticed. People would ask questions, and as things stand, they'd be hard to answer.'

Joan knew what she was implying. Prince Philip was known to have an eye for pretty women, especially blondes. Equally, they had an eye for him. When his engagement was announced in 1946, there had been a song about the loss to the debutante world of the dashing 'Philip Mountbatten RN'. Recently there had been talk while he was touring the Pacific at Christmas. His private secretary's wife had asked for a divorce while they were away, and rumours were still flying around about what both men had got up to on *Britannia*. Today, if he was seen with a blonde who shouldn't be there, conclusions would be drawn as fast as newspapers could be printed.

In the silence that followed, the frost turned to ice.

'Did you find out who asked for her?' the Queen asked in glacial, clipped tones.

'No, ma'am. I didn't dare go too far because . . . because . . .' Joan knew she sounded ridiculous, and especially in light of the reason for her presence here in the first place. But in for a penny, in for a pound.

She went on defiantly, 'Because I don't know who to trust, ma'am. Everyone in the Private Office seems incredibly dedicated, but . . . The way the text of your speech went missing in Paris – that just can't happen. There are too many backups, it's just not possible. For example, I'd kept a carbon of my own draft of it, as a memento, if you must know. It was in the drawer of the desk I was using, but that copy disappeared too. The head of the typing pool was going frantic. The whole thing was just so . . . *strange*. And when I asked casually about Ingrid Kern this morning, everyone claimed never to have heard of her. But someone put that note in the file, ma'am. It was typed and unsigned. Before I go, do you want me to rescind it? Anyway, I thought you should know.'

'I see. Please do.'

'And there's the issue of Blair House in Washington. That was odd too.'

'I know about Blair House,' the Queen said quietly, dismissing it. Her thoughts were elsewhere. 'A misunderstanding.'

'Oh. I'm sorry, ma'am.'

Joan ground to a halt. She'd said everything she needed to say, and it was probably too much, as usual. Her father had always told her she needed to learn diplomacy, and she meant to, but what always tripped her up was a fierce regard for what felt right at the time, or what she thought that was, anyway, and she just couldn't shake it. She looked briefly around the lamplit room, with the dogs snoozing on the floor and the family in photograph frames, and felt in her bones how much she'd have enjoyed working for this woman, and how sad she was to give it up.

'Don't be,' the Queen said.

'I beg your pardon?'

'Don't be sorry.' The Queen seemed to gather herself. 'Not for the Blair House business. And thank you for warning me about Miss Kern in Denmark. In fact, I'd been meaning to ask you to do some work for me.' She sat back and smiled faintly. 'I wasn't sure if you were ready, but it seems you've been doing it anyway. That makes things much easier.'

'But I thought . . . ?'

'Ah, yes. The chain of command. Your act of gross insubordination.'

Joan said nothing.

'For the good of the country.'

Oh. That wasn't how the bewhiskered major at her court martial had put it. It sounded quite different when the Queen described it.

The Queen pushed the report away from her. She smiled. 'That's what my father thought. General Eisenhower too.'

'Did they? But—'

'The chain of command . . . It does rather require every link to be reliable, doesn't it?'

Yes, it did. Yelland was an incompetent bully in a position of extreme sensitivity, and he was the only person Joan was allowed to turn to with her complaint. She had never regretted causing his departure. So, Her Majesty appreciated irony after all.

However, Joan hadn't forgotten how the conversation started. 'You said there was a problem, though, ma'am. With my record.'

'Oh, there is.' The Queen gestured at the file. 'You were demoted from third officer back to ordinary Wren, and as far as I'm concerned you should have been promoted. However, I can hardly undo the decision-making processes of the navy. Rather, I can, but I won't. I rely on my admirals, and they rely on me.'

'Oh,' Joan said, feeling suddenly like a cork rising from the bottom of the ocean.

'But we'll think of something. "Gross insubordination". At least you can't go over my head. Where would you go?'

The monarch kept a straight face, but Joan permitted herself a grin. 'I'm not sure there is anywhere, ma'am.'

'Well, quite.'

The Queen glanced at her watch and reached for the telephone on her desk. She told the palace operator to tell the duke that she would be with him in five minutes before leaving for the Boltons. Then she turned back to Joan.

'I mentioned getting you to do some work for me.'

Joan's pulse quickened. 'Yes, of course. What is it?'

The Queen briefly outlined her concerns from Paris. She completely agreed about the inexplicable strangeness of the missing speech. On top of that, she described the unwelcome presence of the oysters and the unguarded expression of annoyance at her warm welcome at the Louvre, worn by one of her own courtiers.

'And now this girl, Ingrid. It confirms my fear that my foreign visits are under threat. It might seem as if I'm overreacting, but I think I know when something's off.'

'I see.'

'I need you to find out what this pattern means. It's a lot to ask. For obvious reasons, you'd be acting alone. There's no one else I can . . . D'you think you can manage it?'

'Yes, ma'am.' Joan had visions of Elizabeth I entrusting Lord Walsingham with similar missions. It sounded lonely and dangerous . . . and right up her street. 'Yes, of course I can. Do you have any idea who it might be? Someone to keep an eye on?'

'I do. But I have no idea why he would behave in such a way. I won't tell you who it is for now. I find if I say something, people tend to take it as gospel. I want to see if you come to the same conclusion by yourself. And anyway, he might not be acting alone.'

'I understand, ma'am.'

'Now, I'm afraid I must go. I'm already late.'

Throughout the discussion, Joan had the impression that something else was preying on the Queen's mind – more worrying, even than the fact that one of her closest advisers might be undermining her and was, in fact, a traitor. What could be worse than that? Joan also sensed that there was no one the Queen could talk to about it – no one at all. Which begged a few questions.

She had a lot to think about.

CHAPTER 10

The Victorian villas of the Boltons were a cut above most Chelsea houses. They sat in opposing crescent shapes either side of an oasis of green, where St Mary The Boltons church catered to a select little congregation. Deborah Fairdale's home, which she shared with her husband and daughter, was the largest and loveliest of them all, as befitted a Hollywood star who had become as much loved on the West End stage as she was in America.

Born to a music teacher and his wife in South Carolina, Deborah never expected to be sharing jokes with the king of England and Sir Laurence Olivier, but after starring alongside Cary Grant, she had come to England to perform in a Noël Coward play, fallen for a Brit and stayed. In her West End dressing room back in 1937, Paul Locke had led her to believe he was a car mechanic, which was sort of true, but really, he was a racing driver. Now, at the grand old age of fifty-two, and minus a leg after the Battle of Monte Cassino, he ran his own racing team. He didn't mind being 'Mr Fairdale' half the time, when really she should be 'Mrs Locke'. It was one of the many things Deborah loved about him.

Together, they were the couple that every London socialite wanted to know. Miss Fairdale was a proud Southern girl and tried to maintain her home state's reputation for hospitality. When it came to the Queen and the Duke of Edinburgh, she always liked to have someone special for them each to meet. They couldn't always socialise with who they chose, and the duke in particular had an endless appetite for interesting people in the arts and sciences, so Deborah liked to mix it up a bit.

She had been excited all week, thinking of this particular soirée, but it wasn't going the way she'd planned at all. Paul had found her a rocket designer whom Prince Philip would adore, but her special guest for the Queen was horribly late, and in the meantime all anybody wanted to talk about was murder. Deborah had tried several times to shift the conversation on to more enlightening topics, but by the second martini she realised Her Majesty was as interested as anyone else.

For her part, the Queen was having a fascinating time. She had grown up with some of the best gossips in the country – her mother's household – so she was used to the interest that many people took in other people's business. Tonight, she had her own reasons for being among them, so she didn't judge. In fact, she was grateful.

'So, tell me,' the wife of a press baron asked, 'can you really see the place where it happened from your house?'

'Not quite,' Deborah admitted. Standing beside the grand piano in her double-aspect living room, she gestured beyond the balcony windows. 'The mews house backs on to a garden about five houses down. If you lean out of our top floor bathroom you could probably see the roof.'

'Oh my God! How thrilling! Did you hear anything?'

'Not a peep,' Paul said smoothly, circulating with the cocktail shaker. 'Although to talk to my wife, you'd think it happened in our basement.'

Deborah struck a theatrically affronted pose.

'Paul! Don't be rude. We did have the police round, to ask if we'd seen any sign of fugitives, but of course we hadn't. I'm ashamed to say I was disappointed.'

'How do you know there *wasn't* anyone hiding in the garden?' an old Hollywood pal of Deborah's asked.

She cocked an eyebrow. 'Are you suggesting my garden is an overgrown jungle, by any chance, Carole? True, it's so full of trees and bushes we wouldn't have seen a thing, but the chickens would have clucked the place down. They get furious if their sleep's disturbed. And Gregory would have gone absolutely *berserk*.'

Gregory Peck was the name of Deborah's cockerel, who was infamous in the Boltons for his dawn alarm. He was only kept alive by the fact that the neighbours were grateful for her little flock's fresh eggs. Gregory was touchy and territorial, and he'd have crowed the place down if anyone had leaped over their garden wall. But that night he'd been perfectly quiet until dawn.

'Did anyone else see anything?' the rocket designer wondered.

'The police have been tramping round all the gardens, looking for clues,' Deborah said. 'As you can imagine, Gregory didn't approve. If someone *had* got in, they could've run down the little side passage, I suppose. I asked Mike, our chauffeur, whose house is on the street . . .'

'Your chauffer *lives there*?' the press baron's wife asked. 'Practically next door?'

'Five doors down.' Deborah and Paul were among the few residents of the Boltons who could still afford to keep the original mews house on.

'He must know something?' Carole said, with her lovely Californian twang. 'Did he see the people going in? Or coming out? Were they in cahoots? Don't you love that word? Cahoots. It's the only thing that makes sense.'

'Mike didn't see a thing. Not that night. But . . .' Deborah lowered her voice and they all leaned in. 'He's heard stories about other couples. Going into that very house. On other nights.'

'The dean's house?'

'Uh-huh. They were always very *proper*,' she added, using the British term. 'Well dressed in their dickie bows and furs. They'd be dropped off by cab and disappear straight inside.'

'No!'

'Oh yes. He has it on good authority. The thing about Mike is, he'll talk to anyone. He's a fount of knowledge. Never talk in the car, that's what I've learned. Chauffeurs say nothing, but they hear *everything*.'

'So the dean's house was a . . . knocking shop?' Carole's companion, a big game hunter, asked, with a sidelong glance at the Queen. She felt dreadful for poor Clement Moreton, but didn't want to interrupt the conversation.

'I dread to think what it was,' Deborah said. 'Perhaps he was running a very upmarket bedsit. Who knows?'

'Did your man hear anything that night?'

'Well . . . he thinks he heard a gunshot,' Deborah admitted, with a look of innocent mischief that had been one of her calling cards in Hollywood.

There was a communal intake of breath and then the questions came thick and fast.

'A what?'

'Gunshot?'

'Are you serious?'

'That never got mentioned,' the press baron's wife remarked, looking peeved that her husband's many papers had missed it.

'Well, I *know*,' Deborah agreed. 'So maybe it was a car backfiring, but Mike swears he heard something. At around two or three in the morning, All I know is, it didn't set Gregory off, so it wasn't in our backyard.'

The conversation moved on to other topics and the big game hunter decided to tell the Queen in great detail about the drama of his recent visit to Tanganyika. She waited for half an hour, wondering if the subject of what had happened in the mews would come around again. Keen for more information, she eventually did the only thing she could think of, and spilled the remains of her martini on her dress.

'Oh, how clumsy. Deborah, you wouldn't mind helping me sponge this off, would you?'

Miss Fairdale, nominated for two Oscars, was always a good sport. They perched side by side on the edge of the bathtub, doing the best they could with a damp flannel on the satin skirt. The Queen took the opportunity to ask after Deborah's daughter, Bridget. 'She must be quite grown up now.'

'Oh, she's certainly that, ma'am. She's seventeen and she hates me.'

'I'm sure she doesn't!'

'She tells me she does, in no uncertain terms. I'm bourgeois and conventional. I'm too concerned with my appearance. I don't care about the future.'

'Gosh, that sounds rather exhausting.'

'Oh, she loves me to bits. You've got all this to come, ma'am. How are your babies?'

'They're very well,' the Queen said. 'Anne's determined to do everything Charles can do, and better. But it's hard if you're six and your brother will insist on being eight and a half.'

'I doubt she lets that get in her way.'

'No, she certainly doesn't. And if she thinks I'm bourgeois and conventional, she certainly hasn't told me so. By the way, I wanted to ask you something . . . Paul's a member of the Artemis Club, isn't he?'

Deborah nodded. 'Yes, ma'am.'

'Did he hear any rumours about the thirty-first?'

'About the dean and his guests, you mean?' Deborah asked, dabbing gently at the skirt with a fresh flannel. She sounded relaxed and light, but the Queen knew what a very good actress she was.

'About anything, really,' she replied, trying to maintain the same light tone and wondering if she was pulling it off as effectively. 'The club or . . . what happened afterwards.'

Clearly, she wasn't Hollywood standard. Deborah gave her one sharp, penetrating look.

'There are always rumours,' she said carefully. 'I wouldn't pay them any attention, ma'am.'

The Queen had hoped she wouldn't need to. Deborah's answer confirmed her fear that she very much did.

Meanwhile, the actress tilted her head back and dabbed at the skirts one more time. 'There. I think we're done! I don't think we've made the stain any worse, anyway.' She went to put the flannels in a laundry bin and added, 'You know what men get up to when they've had a few too many. High jinks and stupidity. I make a point of not asking Paul for any details. I'm sure I'd be so disappointed if he told me.'

The Queen felt reprimanded. Deborah was one of her most candid friends and if she wouldn't talk, no one would. Perhaps that was a good thing, all things considered, but the Queen dearly wished her friend had made an exception for *her*.

'Thank you *so* much for all that dabbing,' she said, standing up and brushing her skirts down. 'Does the stain show?'

They decided it did, but that everyone outside would pretend not to notice, and made their way back to the party.

When they got there, Philip was turning down an offer to race in Paul's Lagonda at Goodwood.

'My God! The men in moustaches would never let me! They'd be dragging me out by the lapels.'

'You must have some fun sometimes,' the big game hunter insisted.

'I never do. Not allowed. My life is simply too boring for you to imagine.' Philip glanced across at the Queen. 'Isn't it, darling?'

She smiled at him blandly. 'I wouldn't say *too* boring. I'd like to think we do the odd interesting thing.'

'We don't! We never do!'

She would have loved to prove him wrong, but it was time to go. She still had paperwork to catch up with back at her desk, and a very busy day tomorrow. Their hosts accompanied the royal couple to the hall.

'I suppose the next time we'll be seeing you is at the palace, next week,' Paul said, taking the Queen's fur from the butler and giving it to Philip, who placed it round his wife's shoulders.

'The palace?' Philip queried. 'God, poor you. Why?'

'Because it's Bridget's presentation – had you forgotten? It's her coming out year.'

'Oh, I had. She's a deb, is she? We'll look out for her, won't we, Lilibet? Poor kid.'

'Poor kid?' Paul asked.

'Lining up like a lamb to the slaughter. It can't go on,' Philip said. 'I always feel so absurd, nodding to them all. And they look like frightened rabbits and afterwards their mothers are the cat that got the cream.' He didn't mention that his sister-in-law had unkindly remarked that the presentations had to stop because 'every tart in London' was getting in.

'Well, I'll be the cat that got the cream,' Deborah said. 'And Bridget may well be a frightened rabbit, but you'll smile at her, won't you?'

Philip looked sheepish. 'I promise I'll make an exception for Bridget.'

'And I know you've already said you probably can't make it, but we'd love to see you at her party next month,' Paul added. 'Debutantes are passé, I get it. But we're pulling out all the stops anyway. Bill Astor's given us the use of Cliveden. It's a masked ball, and the theme's Shakespeare. You can go incognito if you like.'

The Queen was wondering what to reply, when the doorbell rang and Deborah's hand flew to her heart.

'Oh! At last!'

Her other special guest had finally arrived. A distinguished-looking black man in a smartly tailored dinner suit was divested of his overcoat by the butler. The Queen took in his gently waving hair, his lugubrious eyes, his familiar smile . . . She was amazed, and thrilled, and only sorry they were leaving. Deborah had done it again.

'Ma'am, I'd like to introduce Mr Duke Ellington,' Deborah said. 'He was held up at the 400 Club, but we forgive him.'

The musical maestro bowed. 'I'm sorry I'm late, Your Majesty. A little matter of paid employment. I got here as fast as the audience would permit.'

The Queen beamed at him. 'How wonderful to meet you, Mr Ellington.'

'Likewise, ma'am.'

'Is this your first visit to London?' Philip asked him.

'No, sir. That was back in 'thirty-three.' Ellington turned to the Queen. 'Long before you were born, ma'am.'

He held her eye. Having, in fact, been born in 1926, the Queen admired his gallantry. 'Oh, really?' she said, throwing him a cool look, letting it stand.

The maestro's eyes twinkled. 'Yes, indeed. I remember I played four-hand piano with your uncle, the Duke of Kent.'

'Was he any good?'

'Not bad, for a prince. He sat in on drums with the band as well. There was no getting away from him. Anyway, it's nice to be back. Do you like jazz?'

'I've loved it all my life,' she assured him.

'I promised Miss Fairdale here that I'd play a little something. Have you got time for a song or two?'

The Queen thought about her busy week ahead. She should really go home and get some sleep, but right now, at this minute, she was in heaven. She took off her fur and handed it back.

CHAPTER 11

As April drew to a close, the Queen and Prince Philip got ready to embark on a packed programme of visits round the country. Joan was not invited to join the men in moustaches on these trips. Miles Urquhart had managed to convince Sir Hugh that there wasn't room for her on the royal train.

One morning as she waited to pick up the red boxes, Joan heard the confident tread of Dilys Entwistle's court shoes as they clacked down the linoleum of the North Wing corridor. The private secretary's personal secretary stopped at the DPS's open door and coughed. Joan looked up from her desk.

'Sir Hugh would like a quick word before he goes,' Dilys said.

Joan frowned. 'With me?'

'Yes, Miss McGraw.'

Joan saw the way Dilys pinched her lips when she said 'Miss McGraw'. She had suggested that Dilys should continue to call her Joan, as she had in Joan's typing pool days, but the other woman primly insisted on 'Miss McGraw' now. Joan felt judged and found wanting. But it didn't do to let it show.

'I'm coming. Do you have any idea what it's about?'

'None at all. Sir Hugh doesn't let me into his confidence.' With a sour look, Dilys waited to accompany her down the corridor.

An uneasy truce had emerged between Joan and the men in moustaches in the days since the Queen had made her feelings known about the 'gross insubordination' report. Joan's place in the Private Office was safe for now, but Urquhart, whose office she shared, had effectively sent her to Coventry. His detailed instructions for what Joan was to do while he was away were delivered via *his* personal secretary, Sarah, even though she worked down the corridor and Urquhart's desk, by contrast, was literally opposite Joan's.

It hadn't escaped her notice that Urquhart was also the person in charge of the royal couple's upcoming Danish schedule, where Ingrid Kern had made her strange appearance. Technically, it was easier for him than anyone else to sabotage the Queen abroad. But in reality, any of the three men had access to the files and diaries in question, and were senior enough to instruct staff to do their bidding and keep quiet about it.

Of all of them, Urquhart was the least likely to get away with it, Joan thought. Now that she was experiencing his more childish and stubborn side, she saw a man who simply couldn't hide his feelings. Dealing with him was a walk in the park compared with Brigadier Yelland.

So far, she hadn't seen much of Jeremy Radnor-Milne, the press secretary. He was either locked away in his office or out wining and dining his contacts, but Joan noticed he had a large framed photograph of the Queen on the wall behind his desk. The real person working one floor up wasn't enough for him, it seemed.

Sir Hugh Masson also hadn't crossed paths with Joan much, but she knew that he was a canny operator, respected for getting difficult things done without losing good relationships. Sir Winston Churchill himself was an admirer and a friend.

The private secretary's own war service wasn't easy to investigate, meaning he had probably worked in military intelligence, and he was understated and academic in his manner. Some people mistook his politeness for weakness. They did so at their peril. He would make a formidable adversary, she thought – if that's what he turned out to be.

Sir Hugh's office sat across the corridor from Joan's and exactly two floors under the Queen's, overlooking the treetops of Green Park beyond the palace wall. The room was tall and airy, with Georgian windows, a marble mantelpiece and several pieces of antique furniture. It spoke of quiet power and a strong sense of history. Unlike Her Majesty, he kept his desk free of memorabilia, and immaculately tidy. He indicated a wing-back chair beside the fireplace. Joan took it.

'We appear to have a problem,' he said, sitting down opposite her. He removed his spectacles and gave them a polish. 'With your accommodation.'

'I see.' Joan paused. She had been preparing for much worse. 'No, actually, I don't see. What problem?'

'As you know, your lack of punctuality has caused Miles great concern. I've looked into it, and I understand that you travel across London each morning from Bow – a matter of six or seven miles. Is that right?'

'Yes.'

'Which would be all right, I suppose, if the buses were reliable, but I gather there have been various traffic incidents recently. It's quite unsustainable. Her Majesty has made it clear that she wants you to be on hand, and I don't want you getting here tired and flustered. And we really can't have the Queen's temporary APS eating jellied eels on Brick Lane, or whatever else they do.'

Joan's hackles were rising fast. She did her very best to keep calm.

'I wouldn't say I was ever flustered—' she protested, but he cut her off again.

'The women in the Private Office do not live in Bow. It's in the East End of London. Too far, in every sense. It risks making you look unprofessional.'

'I—'

'So I've arranged alternative accommodation. Something more suitable, closer to home. A decent address in Pimlico. It's walking distance from the palace – a good twenty minutes, but think of it as exercise.'

Oh. This was a complete surprise.

'That's very kind of you, but . . .'

'But what? I'm not really offering, Joan. I'm informing.' He pursed his lips and regarded her across steepled fingertips.

'I see, but I'm afraid . . . I don't see how I can afford it,' Joan admitted.

Didn't he think she'd live closer if she could? As it was, a bedroom in her aunt's flat, shared with her three young cousins, was the best she could do.

'Westminster rents are problematic,' Sir Hugh agreed. 'I understand that. And good places are hard to find – unless one knows the right people. You're smiling. I read that to mean that you don't know the right people, and I do, and you're probably right. As it turns out, we know someone who can help. The rent is perhaps still a little out of your league, even on higher wages . . .'

'My wages are higher?'

'Didn't anybody tell you? Yes, quite considerably. Even so, that part of Pimlico might be a stretch, but don't worry about it for now. The important thing is that you're here when we need you, and that you get safely home.' He shook his head. 'One doesn't like to think of what can happen the other side of Fleet Street.'

'It's pretty friendly,' Joan assured him. 'You'd be surprised.'

His nose twitched, as if he'd thought of something. 'I notice you don't really have the accent, by the way,' he said. 'How did you avoid it?'

'What do you mean?'

'Cockney. Growing up in the East End . . .'

'I didn't,' Joan said. 'I went to school in Cambridge. My father works there.'

'Oh! Does he? At the university? What college?'

'St Anselm's.'

Sir Hugh brightened suddenly. 'Ah! I had no idea. What's his field?'

'His field?'

'Academically. One of my godsons is up at St Anselm's now, reading Classics. I wonder if he might know him.'

Joan gave him a wry smile. 'I'm sure he does. My father's the head porter.'

Sir Hugh looked momentarily derailed. 'Ah. Oh. Mmm. I see. Important job.' The warmth of genuine interest faded, to be replaced by something more distant, if not unkind. 'I remember I was scared witless of the head porter at Trinity. Six foot four in his bowler hat.'

'My father's six foot five.'

Sir Hugh frowned. 'Wait a minute. My godson mentioned something . . . He wasn't at the Somme, was he? Decorated for valour?'

Joan nodded. Vincent McGraw was a bit of a legend among the undergraduates, having single-handedly rescued four officers of the Coldstream Guards who were trapped under fire in their collapsing trench. He was nearly seven feet tall in his head porter's bowler, powerful as a boxer, firm but fair, the nighttime nemesis of drunken student revellers. At home, he was soft as a pussycat, a prizewinning solver of *The Times* crossword, and a soppily fond single parent to his only child.

'You must be very proud of him,' Sir Hugh suggested.

Joan shrugged. 'I am.'

After that, Sir Hugh's expression was neutral. He didn't give away whether he was pleased to be working with the daughter of a hero from the First World War or alarmed at having to make conversation with the offspring of a college servant. He steepled his fingers again.

'The thing is, it's going to be all hands to the pumps until we find your replacement. Fiona's replacement, I should say. We have a particularly intense few months ahead. Lots of diplomatic visits abroad. Denmark is . . . Denmark. Always good to be friends with the Scandinavians. And they're related, of course.'

'I'm sorry, who are?'

'Her Majesty and their royal family. So is the duke. That always helps. But then we have the trip to Canada and America coming up, and that must *absolutely* not go wrong. Canada is a jewel in the Commonwealth crown. Her Majesty already knows the country and is fond of it. And the United States . . . I need hardly say . . . after Suez . . .'

'I understand,' Joan said.

Sir Hugh looked sceptical. 'Washington's reaction to the intervention in Egypt was alarmingly hostile. They threatened our economic stability.'

'I know,' Joan said. 'It must have come as a shock to Mr Eden, after the close relationship during the war.'

'It did, rather. He had overplayed his hand.'

'And I suppose they're still angry about Burgess and Maclean.'

Guy Burgess and Donald Maclean were British diplomats who had suddenly fled to Moscow in 1951, provoking a national scandal. Both had worked in Washington on sensitive issues while reporting to the Foreign Office and – as it turned out – the KGB. Too late, it had been discovered that they had been pouring secrets into Russian ears for years.

Sir Hugh gave Joan an appraising glance through his spectacles. She sensed that transatlantic political tensions hadn't been Fiona's strong point.

'Anyway, there are bridges to rebuild,' he acknowledged. 'And Her Majesty is Mr Macmillan's secret weapon. To be deployed with deadly accuracy and devastating effect. She must dazzle.'

'Do they want to be dazzled?'

'In my experience, everybody does. A few inverted snobs think they don't, but they end up being the most dazzled of all. We have the advantage that she is an attractive young woman. And a dutiful one.

The Queen may lack the education of her courtiers, but her instincts are good.'

Yes, they are, Joan thought. *Possibly better than yours.* She said nothing.

'She seems to like you, so I imagine you'll spend plenty of time in her company when we get back. If any issues arise, I want you to bring them to me directly. May I have your assurance on that?'

'Absolutely,' Joan lied.

'Excellent. Good luck. And let me know if there are any problems with Dolphin Square meanwhile. Her Majesty wouldn't have raised the issue if she didn't want it solved, so I'll assume you'll say yes? You can move in at the weekend.'

'Dolphin Square?' Joan asked.

Sir Hugh frowned. 'Didn't I say? Your new address. Large block of flats near the river. It's several blocks, in fact. A few MPs use it as their London pad. My aunt used to live there for a while. It's perfectly respectable, and above all, *safe*. Ah, Dilys. Yes?'

His secretary had arrived to announce that his next visitor was waiting to see him.

Back at her desk, Joan wondered if Sir Hugh thought he had just bought her complicity with the offer of a posh address. He certainly wanted to know what she – and Her Majesty – were up to. But Joan didn't really blame him for that. If she had been in charge of the Private Office, she'd have wanted to know too.

If the private secretary was working against the Crown, he was covering his tracks extremely well. It was hard to imagine sounding more dedicated to supporting it. But equally, that meant he understood what the stakes were. If he *did* want to undermine the Queen, he'd know exactly how to do it.

Could he be in the pay of a foreign state? Joan wondered. Had the Soviets managed to recruit him in the thirties, like Burgess and Maclean? Surrounded by Georgian architecture and antiques, it was hard to imagine anyone more British. But, if they wanted a spy, wasn't that precisely the sort of person they would pick?

CHAPTER 12

Back in London after his brief trip to Essex, Inspector Darbishire was happy to be on home turf again. It was accidental that Cresswell Place happened to be so close to where he lived with his wife and daughters. However, it had turned out to be quite useful in this case because he was still trying to speak to a couple of key witnesses, and they were turning out to be stubbornly difficult to get hold of, except by telephone in one case, which had thrown up more problems than it solved.

They were never in during working hours, so he had taken to popping round to their houses in the mews first thing in the morning, or after tea, to see if he could go over their statements. Still no joy. Now it was nearly ten o'clock at night and every self-respecting Londoner – those that didn't go gadding about in gentlemen's clubs, or serve the ones who did – was on his way to bed. Would Mrs Gregson from number 23 be at home? Darbishire was increasingly curious to find out.

He was still working on the theory that the murdered couple were lured to their deaths because of something in Mr Perez's murky business dealings. Darbishire and his men had interviewed all Miss White and Miss Fonteyn's recent clients, who were a motley selection of financiers and playboys, expatriates and industrialists. In Miss Fonteyn's case, there was even a lovesick poet who couldn't afford her, like something out of the opera. Most were acutely embarrassed to be questioned, but none looked the type to garrotte a man, or had any discernible reason to do so. Perez, on the other hand . . . Perez was travelling on forged documents and Darbishire was still waiting for information about where they came from. There lay his answers, he felt sure.

The *why* of the murders would surface any minute; the *how* they already knew. But the exact *when* continued to elude him – and how it was done without anyone else in the street noticing. The answer surely lay with Mrs Gregson, the key witness, who lived almost directly opposite the dean's house. She must have made a mistake about who went in and out, missing the murderers entirely, but she swore blind at the time that she was completely accurate.

Mrs Gregson was a young mother who had been nursing a restive baby at her living room window that night, and was probably sleep-deprived. She spoke to a couple of detective sergeants from his team the day after the bodies were discovered. She had a remarkable memory for timings, and claimed it was because she was desperate to get the tot to nod off, and kept looking at the clock.

Darbishire knew she'd got the arrival and departure of the Artemis Club crowd right because the times were corroborated by the cab driver who'd brought them to Cresswell Place and two others who'd picked the guests up later. There would be no shame in admitting she got something else wrong – but something odd was happening. He needed to sort it out.

Unlike its pastel neighbours, Mrs Gregson's house at number 23 formed part of a short row of houses in the Arts and Crafts style. The top half was hung with terracotta tiles that gave it airs and graces beyond its station, in Darbishire's opinion, as if it thought it was a cottage in Tunbridge Wells. He knocked at the door. A young man answered, whom Darbishire had met before. He was thin, pasty-faced and nervous. Or, not nervous so much as wary. There was a difference.

'Ah, Mr Gregson?' The young man nodded. 'I'm sorry to disturb you at this late hour. Is your wife back?'

'Back?' The man blinked.

'Only, you said last Monday she'd gone to her mother's. Because of the stress. Quite understandable. But I found the telephone number for the address you gave me in Shropshire – her parents live a long way away, don't they? – and when I rang, they said she'd gone out for a walk with her little girl. She was very helpful when she rang back. She confirmed everything she'd told us before. But I'm confused. I think we must have got crossed wires somewhere.'

'Oh?'

The young man was wearing a hand-knitted sweater with rather a large hole in it, Darbishire noticed. The sort of hole a wife would normally mend. But Mrs Gregson had a baby to take care of, so perhaps that explained it. His whole face was trying to form a shape of bland politeness, but the wariness seeped from every pore.

'It's just that my Mrs Gregson . . . your Mrs Gregson indeed . . . has a little boy, not a little girl, doesn't she? That was what she said in her original statement. Not the sort of thing a mother gets wrong!' Darbishire's face formed a jovial grin around his shrewd eyes.

'Ah.' Mr Gregson looked momentarily confused himself, but his frown soon cleared. 'They must have meant she was out with her sister's little girl. They're staying there too, with my parents-in-law. Linda, my wife, helps out when she can. Perhaps she took them both out.'

Darbishire nodded. 'Mmm. That makes sense. Thank you.'

'Not at all,' Mr Gregson said with a smile of . . . was it relief?

'May I come in, by the way?' Darbishire asked. 'I don't want to keep everyone on the street awake.'

'No,' he responded sharply. 'It's just . . . I'm doing something for work. I'm a photographer. It's all very delicate. Can't disturb it. Sorry.'

Photographer. Hmm. Darbishire didn't know that much about photography but perhaps it explained the pervasive, unpleasant smell emanating from somewhere in the background.

'Oh dear,' he said easily. 'I'll have to stay out here then. I wonder what the neighbours will say. Ha!'

Mr Gregson was intransigent. 'I'm sorry I can't help you any further.'

Darbishire shook his head. 'But I'm sure you can. When Mrs Gregson called me back, I had a few questions about the baby that night, the night of the murders. I asked if perhaps she had colic – like I say, I was getting my wires crossed – and your wife said she'd been sick with it for weeks, but she was getting better. *She*, you see. A little girl. Not a little boy, as my sergeant noted down the first time he spoke to you both. Named Francis. Is that correct?'

'Sorry, what? Oh, yes – Francis. That might explain it. The different spellings.'

'Mmm. But not the different pronouns.' Darbishire's face still smiled and his eyes were shrewder than ever.

'I see what you mean. I don't know what my wife was thinking.'

'Nor do I, Mr Gregson. And my men and I have been talking to people up and down the street, as you know, and a few times we've mentioned the young woman with the colicky baby, and do you know what? Nobody's seen that baby. Not a soul.'

'We keep ourselves to ourselves. My wife hasn't been well.'

'Or heard it. A colicky baby that cries through the night?'

'He doesn't cry if we soothe him.'

'So he's a he now?'

'He was always a he! My wife is confused! She misunderstood you. She hasn't been sleeping.'

'I did wonder about that,' Darbishire said. Then his voice hardened. 'About that baby. There's no birth record of a Francis Gregson, or indeed Frances Gregson – I looked for both – in the last two years. Your wife is either in grave danger, or she never existed either. Which is it, Mr Gregson?'

'Listen,' Mr Gregson said, his face transformed, his body hunched with a new sense of urgency. 'Everything she said was true, I swear it. Everything about what happened opposite. I was awake most of the night with her, and I saw it too. We don't know who did it, and we've nothing to gain by lying. We just wanted to do our duty. Yes, she's frightened. Frightened for her life. Do you blame her?'

Darbishire was unmoved. 'Given how little she saw that's of any real use to us, I rather do. If anything, she's been wasting police time so far. Tell her I'd like to see her at the station in the morning. You too, sir. If you're not there, there will be consequences. Goodnight, Mr Gregson. Sleep tight.'

He crossed the street to the western side, to his second elusive witness.

Number 42, a couple of doors down from 44 (the houses in the mews were numbered sequentially), was the London residence of a William Pinder, civil servant. Mr Pinder, who definitely existed, as confirmed by the War Office, had spoken to the police a couple of times, to assert that he was alone at home that night, having taken a sleeping draught, and he saw nothing, heard nothing, knew nothing. Darbishire had a couple of supplementary questions to ask, but Mr Pinder, too, had recently been out when his officers had called by.

The inspector knocked without much hope but, to his surprise, the door was answered within a minute.

'Yes?' a female voice demanded through a tiny crack. Her cut-glass accent was apparent in one word. It reminded him: Mrs Gregson's accent on the telephone had been posher than her husband's just now. Should he read something into that? Or was he just being a snob?

'Police, ma'am,' Darbishire explained. 'Would you mind . . . ?'

The woman opened the door by about a foot, to reveal that she was in her dressing gown and slippers, with her hair in curlers under a little pink net and a blanket over her shoulders.

'Can I help you?'

'Are you Mrs Pinder, by any chance?'

'Marion Pinder, yes.'

'I'm Detective Inspector Darbishire, CID. So sorry to disturb you. Is your husband in?'

She frowned. 'No. He's, er . . . no. He's in the country.'

'Not Shropshire, by any chance?'

She stared at him. 'Surrey. He's staying with his parents. What?'

She'd spotted the massively sceptical look on Darbishire's face. But coincidences did happen. He gave her the benefit of the doubt.

'Why isn't he staying with you, if you don't mind me asking? I mean, from what he's already told us you share a home in Reigate with the children. He just stays here during the week for work, yes?'

Mrs Pinder scowled and pulled the blanket tighter around her. She, too, had no intention of inviting him in. Darbishire was a friendly man by nature and this aspect of the job didn't always appeal to him: alienating bystanders in the interests of investigation. However, he was good at it.

'Bill normally stays here,' she agreed. 'Sunday night to Thursday. But he's not well. I'm just sorting out some things here.'

'Is he infectious?'

'No! Nothing like that. We just . . .' Her face hardened. 'We needed some time apart, if you must know. Or we did. Now I'm wondering . . .' As her voice trailed off she looked lost and sad. Darbishire sensed she needed a solid shoulder to cry on, but it wouldn't be his.

'Can you ask him to get in touch with me? One of your neighbours claims to have heard a gunshot the night of the murders—'

'Gunshot?' She almost leaped out of her skin.

'Yes, and unless it came from number forty-four, where we have no evidence of it, it must have come from this property, if it came from anywhere at all. The house in between is empty, you see.'

'I know. But there wouldn't have been a gunshot. We don't even have a gun. My husband was fast asleep, as I said. He's been finding it difficult to rest recently so he took a significant amount of sleeping powder. I know because he was very groggy when he spoke to me the next morning. He'd have slept through anything. Who said so, anyway? Was it those bastards from across the road?' She flicked her eyes to the space beyond Darbishire's shoulder. 'Don't believe a word they tell you.'

He was so surprised by the crystal-toned profanity coming from under those curlers that it took him a moment to recover.

'What about them? Do you mean the Gregsons at twenty-three?'

'The Gregsons? No. You mean the Hallidays. But they moved out last month because of the flood. I was in town for the ballet and I saw them put all their things in a van.'

'The flood?'

'Yes. One of the pipes sprang a leak. Mrs Halliday said it was going to take weeks to dry the place out. She has trouble with her lungs, so they found somewhere cheaper in Earl's Court.'

'Very interesting.' It had not escaped Darbishire's notice how garrulous Mrs Pinder had suddenly become. 'But if you didn't know the Gregsons, who were you referring to?'

She pursed her lips and clammed up again.

'Which "bastards" did you mean, Mrs Pinder?'

'You'll have to ask my husband. Now, if you'll excuse me, I need to go to bed.'

She shut the door in his face. Darbishire turned around to examine number 22, directly opposite. This was where she had been looking when she swore. It was part of the Arts and Crafts row and slightly taller than the others. An extra floor had been added above the pantiles, with a couple of windows at roof level, overlooking the street.

Darbishire mentally consulted his notes. The current tenants were academics of some sort, who had been pleasant but largely unhelpful as witnesses. According to their statements at the time, they saw nothing of the goings-on at number 44, but one of them claimed to have heard a motorbike roaring away in the distance after the so-called gunshot, which enhanced the theory of a backfire.

Darbishire knocked on their door, but nobody answered.

He had arrived at Cresswell Place with one set of questions and found himself going away with a completely different set. What was wrong with William Pinder, if anything? Who, or what, were the Gregsons, and why were they prepared to live in a dangerously damp house while they pretended to look after a non-existent baby? Had he been worrying about the wrong witnesses anyway? Who, underneath it all, were the 'bastards' at number 22?

What had Gina Fonteyn and Dino Perez got themselves into?

CHAPTER 13

The following day, as soon as it could be arranged, Darbishire was back at Cresswell Place armed with warrants, several burly constables and a ram to break down doors if necessary.

It *was* necessary, because neither door at numbers 22 and 23 was answered. Both houses turned out to be deserted. Inside, number 23 smelled powerfully of drains and mould. It had officially sat empty since the Hallidays left a month ago, exactly as Mrs Pinder suggested. Number 22, by contrast, was unnaturally neat and tidy. Its paperwork was superficially in order, but the department at King's College where the academics who rented it supposedly worked had never heard of them, and they had somehow managed to live in the place for several weeks without leaving a single fingerprint.

There was one minor consolation: Mrs Pinder was reluctantly persuaded to let them into her home at number 42. The team did a thorough search, but found no evidence of a gun having been discharged. Nor was there any sign that any of the slightly shabby walls had recently been redecorated. Darbishire took the opportunity to venture out into the yard at the back, whereupon a dog in the yard of number 41 instantly set up a cannonade of furious barking. The same dog, as the saying went, who had curiously done nothing in the nighttime. Darbishire made a mental note.

Sergeant Woolgar was highly impressed with this turn of events, which only showed how much he knew. Young Chief Inspector Venables, on the other hand – now happily reinstalled behind his desk – gave Darbishire a chuckle and an ironic salute.

'I hear the mews was a busted flush. Commiserations, George. Drink later?'

After work, the two men left the station at Lucan Place, and headed for a pub near Cadogan Square that Venables claimed to favour. It was a strange little interlude. The star of Kensington and Chelsea was perfectly friendly, but after five minutes on the subject of his recent absence, Darbishire still couldn't really tell whether to commiserate with him on needing to take a walking trip for health reasons, or congratulate him on a nice little holiday.

He had assumed Venables wanted to tease him about his 'busted flush' this morning, but instead, the chief inspector chatted about Fulham's recent track record in the Second Division and his concerns about the effect of rock and roll on the youth of today, especially young women.

'I've been looking at footage of Elvis Presley. The bobbysoxers lose their minds, you know. They've even been known to . . .' he lowered his voice '. . . lose control of their bladders. God help us all when he comes to Britain.'

Darbishire's girls were four and seven, so he wasn't unduly worried. He found the new music foot-tapping enough, but he preferred the big band sound for dancing. Still, he was making a mental note to look out for footage of one of those concerts when Venables put down his empty pint glass, stood up and said he needed to be somewhere. It was hardly worth coming this far for that odd, disjointed chat. They said goodbye outside the pub and Darbishire headed west, for home, thinking of his sweet little girls.

Perhaps it was because he wasn't paying proper attention that the sudden hand on his shoulder came as such a shock. He turned round, tensed for a fight. None came, but the hand remained firm and exerted a lot of pressure considering the diminutive size of the man applying it.

Darbishire's new companion looked determinedly ordinary. A pale face under a brown trilby, a standard mackintosh, soft-soled brown shoes. He swung Darbishire around, heading south.

'Let's keep moving, old man. Easier that way.'

Darbishire did as he was told. He felt something dig in his back, through his coat. He didn't know if it was a knife, or a rolled-up newspaper, or a gun. They walked down past the square at a fair clip. The road was busy enough with cars, vans and pedestrians. If his new companion tried to steer him into a side street, out of public view, Darbishire would make a move, but for now, he wanted to hear what the man had to say. He remained tense, ready for action.

The other man's casual tone belied the strength of the grip on his shoulder.

'I come bearing a message. With your best interests at heart. It won't take long.'

'Who sent you? I talk to organ grinders, not their monkeys.'

'I'm terribly sorry, old chap. Monkey it is. Believe me, if you knew who the organ grinder was, you'd be flattered.'

'What message?' Darbishire asked.

'The Chelsea murders. You're doing an excellent job, very thorough. Admirable. We're right behind you – we want the villains caught as much as anyone. Happy to assist in any way. But you're going up a blind alley, I'm afraid, old chap. A dangerous blind alley. We'd appreciate it if you left well alone.'

Who on earth had the chutzpah to threaten a detective inspector in broad daylight, in the centre of London? They were still surrounded by people, although, in the nature of Londoners, none of them took a shred of notice.

'I'm a policeman,' Darbishire muttered. 'I don't leave well alone. It's my job not to.'

'All very admirable, as I said. But it won't help you here. The witnesses have told you all they can and they haven't lied. Monkey or not, I can assure you of that.'

Darbishire was not assured. 'I assume you mean Gregson. Who on earth squats in a mould-covered, stinking flat, purely so they can mislead a police investigation? What's going on? What don't I know about?'

'Nothing that need concern you. Nothing of any illegality whatsoever.'

'Oh? I suppose the neighbours wiped a building down of its fingerprints because they were feeling tidy. This isn't my way home, by the way.'

'I know.'

The little man pushed him left at the corner of Cadogan Gardens. His tone was still light.

'You're probably imagining criminal gangs and drugs and all sorts of unpleasantness. Were they were planning a bank robbery, like *The Lady-killers*? Excellent picture, very funny. Have they kidnapped the scion of a royal family? Or did they keep a mouldering body in the basement? I can assure you none of these things are true.'

Darbishire had been imagining exactly these things, or variations on them. He was more sure than ever that he was dealing with a gang. Who else would send someone with a prim little voice who called you 'old chap' and looked like a cut-price Humphrey Bogart? The incongruity of it all was what made it seem most likely. But the specific denials were a surprise. Were they to distract from another possibility that he'd missed? Or a tissue of lies?

'Excuse me if I don't take the word of a total stranger who accosts me in the street.'

The man relaxed his grip. 'I understand your hesitation. But I wanted you to hear it from us personally. No hard feelings. Carry on the good work. Just . . . focus on what was said, not who said it. Be a good boy. It's to everyone's advantage.' He raised his free hand for a moment, as if waving to a distant friend. 'Ah, this is me. It's been good to have this little chat. Don't forget what I said.'

A black cab pulled up smoothly in the road beside them and he climbed into it almost without breaking step. The taxi pulled out into the traffic of Sloane Street and Darbishire watched as it disappeared in the direction of Hyde Park. He had no idea who the man was, or who he was working for, but he had to admire the slickness of their operation.

And Venables was in on it. That's why he took Darbishire to that particular pub. It was so obvious that the chief inspector didn't feel the need to pretend to hide it. Which meant that either this went all the way to the top, or Venables was in with some extremely shady characters. Either way, pursuing those elusive witnesses wasn't going to lead anywhere.

His initial suspicions about this job had proved spot on. Turning for home, Darbishire smiled grimly to himself.

CHAPTER 14

Philip was right when he talked about the need to end the outdated flummery of court presentations for young, marriageable debutantes. They might have worked well in the days of Queen Charlotte, but in 1957 the Georgian tradition had become decidedly quaint. And it took up so much time. The Queen had already decided that next year would be the last of them, though it had yet to be announced. However, after her wonderful evening with Duke Ellington, she decided to make an exception for Bridget Fairdale's coming out ball.

The Queen was very fond of Deborah, and the word 'incognito' had clinched it for her. She loved dressing up, always had, and she adored people-watching when she got the chance. It would be so much easier if not everyone was watching her. In addition, the theme was Shakespeare, which made it easy to rustle up an appropriate costume. And the venue was Cliveden, which would make a magnificent backdrop for whatever Deborah chose to do.

Philip had no difficulty deciding on his costume. For a Danish prince – even one who had given up his title – the chance of going dressed as Hamlet was too good to miss. He copied the black velvet doublet worn on-screen by Laurence Oliver, which showed off his pale blond hair. The children were delighted with it when the royal couple went up to the nursery to say goodnight. On the other hand, the Queen was pleased to see that Anne had to stare at her for a minute before recognising her at all.

Cliveden lay higher up the reaches of the River Thames, a half-hour's drive from Windsor. Originally a home of dukes, it had been bought and restored by William Waldorf Astor, the second richest man in America, who had chosen to settle here after a family dispute. He was responsible for building the original Waldorf Hotel, which was now part of the Waldorf Astoria, used by a succession of presidents and princes. She would be staying in it herself when she went to New York.

At Cliveden, William's daughter-in-law, Nancy Astor, had updated the decor along with her fellow Virginian, Nancy Lancaster. Cliveden's interior put Windsor Castle's decoration to shame in many ways. While the Queen had antiques and tapestries that had been in her family for centuries, some of them were getting a bit tatty, unlike the Astors' fixtures and fittings, many of which had once belonged to Louis XV, all now restored to their full glory. The benefit of American money was obvious. And the Queen did not have the luxury of carpeted bathrooms, which Nancy Astor seemed to think of as quite normal. Even going to the lavatory at Cliveden was a treat.

Tonight, the grounds were ablaze with electric light and lanterns. Deborah Fairdale had asked Cecil Beaton to provide the theatricals, and the drive from the fountain to the main house was thronged with fairy creatures in woodland costumes inspired by *A Midsummer Night's Dream*. There was even a donkey on the front steps, bedecked with flowers.

Deborah and Paul met the royal couple in the entrance hall. The Queen had always loved this room because of the romantic couples carved above the banister posts on the stairs. These too were wreathed in roses. The actress looked magnificent in a waist-length red wig as Titania. Her husband was a Grecian Oberon.

After the usual formalities of greeting, Paul grinned at the Queen. 'I hardly recognised you in those breeches, ma'am. And the hat with the feather! Let me guess . . .' He frowned and hesitated.

'She's Viola,' his actress wife cut in, 'disguised as Cesario, aren't you, ma'am? I love the breeches, they're quite the thing on you. Have you worn them before?'

'I was Aladdin at Windsor once,' the Queen admitted with a grin. Philip, who was visiting while on embarkation leave during the war, had been quite taken with her performance.

'Ah, a fellow thespian,' Deborah proclaimed. 'And a cross-dresser. Isn't it the best? Oh, here she is.'

Their daughter Bridget appeared from the direction of the garden, looking desperately young and lovely, with several male admirers in tow. She had chosen to be Ophelia, draped in ropes of herbs and wild-flowers, which the Queen thought rather unfortunate, given what happened to the poor girl in the end.

She dropped into a rather perfunctory curtsey, but gave the Queen a genuine smile of welcome.

'I didn't think you'd come, Your Majesty. I thought you'd have much better things to do.'

'On an evening like this, I can't think of anything nicer.'

'Oh I can.' Bridget rolled her eyes.

'Really?' This seemed surprisingly ungrateful.

'I mean, here we are guzzling champagne and there are people in the Pacific getting ready to end the world.'

Bridget gave the Queen a look of heartfelt fury and a couple of her admirers nodded in approval. They had longer hair than usual, the Queen noticed, and one had a juvenile attempt at a beard. University students, she thought. She recognised the type. Their bows to her were minuscule.

Deborah was making earnest gestures at her daughter to shut up or change the subject, but Philip was interested.

'D'you mean the hydrogen bomb?' he asked. The words seemed odd coming out of the mouth of an Elizabethan prince in doublet and hose.

'Yes! Of course! I can't believe we're doing it.'

A bearded admirer – another Hamlet – stepped forward. 'It's Armageddon, isn't it, sir? We should be out there, stopping it.'

'If we don't do it, somebody else will,' Philip pointed out. 'That genie's out of the bottle, I'm afraid.'

Deborah looked despairing: this was supposed to be a party. But Philip was enjoying himself. The university students gathered round him, all talking at once, and they wandered off together, with Bridget in tow, arguing the merits and otherwise of mutually assured destruction. Deborah followed them like an anxious mother hen, glancing back to the Queen with a look of horror.

'I'm sorry, ma'am,' Paul said, grabbing a couple of champagne coupes from a passing waiter. 'Bridget's having one of those moments. She's mad on a boy who's a physicist at Oxford. Convinced the world's about to end. Forget Cecil Beaton – she'd rather be on a rowing boat in the middle of the ocean, chanting for peace.'

'But we've *got* peace,' the Queen said.

Paul shrugged. 'You and I know that, ma'am. They take it all for granted, these young people. They want us to go around shaking hands with Soviets and turning swords into ploughshares. They don't know what's going on behind the Iron Curtain . . .' He stopped and slapped his forehead. 'I'm sorry. Enough! Let me start again.' He reset his face to its normal, suave, gently amused setting and asked, 'Have you heard about Bill Astor's new swimming pool?'

Bill Astor was the redoubtable Nancy's son and a fellow horse owner.

'Didn't he have it put in with the money he won when Ambiguity won the Oaks in 'fifty-three?' the Queen asked, grateful for the change in subject. Although she was rather jealous of that little win. She wouldn't mind winning the Oaks herself.

Paul grinned. 'Of course you'd know! Nancy wouldn't let him have one at first, but Bill can afford it now. It's in the walled garden. Would you like to see it?'

The Queen was pleased at the chance to go outside, and she was always curious about swimming pools. They were such an extravagance but also very practical for one's health. Paul accompanied her as they wandered past the converted stables, where Bill lived, to a lovely walled space where a body of water a bit smaller than a tennis court glinted temptingly in the moonlight. Four women in bathing suits and rubber caps performed tricks together in perfect time. What Shakespeare would have made of synchronised swimmers, the Queen didn't know. But they looked very graceful as they rose and twirled and disappeared under the water, save only for one pointed foot.

After that, a group of Guards officers appeared through a door in the wall and announced that horses and carts were taking guests down to the river. The Queen never missed an opportunity to meet a horse, and found herself cheerfully accompanied down the winding drive to the riverside.

She loved this spot. Windsor Castle had many things, including a medieval chapel and a thousand years of history, but it didn't have a riverside mooring where one could keep a boat. Here, on a gentle stretch of the Thames, several couples were taking to the water. It was a gentle evening in early May, and England was at its best. The Guards officers vied with each other to take her out on the river, but she politely declined. The boats were pretty to look at, but not entirely safe, she decided. Not with the flickering lights and the general level of inebriation. As the officers drifted away, she was happy to stand by the boathouse and watch.

It was easy to spot the debutantes who hoped the evening – or the summer – would end in a proposal. They arranged themselves as attractively as they could in the launches and rowing boats, looking doe-eyed at their partners. Others sat stiffly, looking out into the dark. At one point, she thought she saw Jeremy Radnor-Milne emerging from the Astors' famous electric canoe, but it turned out to be the real David Niven. He was wearing some sort of fairy headdress and was quickly surrounded by female admirers, much as Bridget had been surrounded by men. The Queen decided to join them – she was a fan, too – but as the film star headed for a buggy waiting to take revellers back up the hill, she felt heavy footsteps beside her.

'Your Majesty!'

She turned round to see the portly Duke of Maidstone, dressed as Prospero, clutching a hip flask. Bunny Maidstone had been a very good-looking man in his youth, but the contents of many hip flasks over the years had made him go to seed. He didn't seem to have noticed, and behaved like a matinee idol. Unlike the real film star, up ahead, who was climbing into the cart without her. It filled up with squealing women and set off.

'Bunny!' she said politely. The duke had been called this since his schooldays, for reasons lost in the mists of time. 'How are you?'

'All the better for seeing you, ma'am. You're looking delectable, may I say? Trousers! How funny. D'you mind if I tag along?'

The Queen did, but couldn't say so. She wished Philip was with her. He'd have told the duke exactly what to do in no uncertain terms, but she simply wasn't made that way.

'I didn't know you knew Deborah,' she said, to make conversation while they waited for more carts to come.

'I don't, really,' he admitted. 'But my elder boy races with Paul's outfit. He's got a bit of a thing for Bridget. She's fallen in with this Trotsky crowd, though. One hopes she'll grow out of it.'

'Mmm.'

The Queen looked desperately up the drive, but there was no sign of more horses.

'Did you see the Astors have got a swimming pool?' Bunny scoffed. 'Terribly infra dig.'

The Queen thought it infra dig to dismiss the prize possessions of one's host, but she had often noticed that some dukes thought themselves above that sort of nicety.

'I ask you!' he went on. 'Astors. They may be viscounts these days, but they'll always be hoteliers at heart.'

'We have a pool ourselves,' she reminded him. 'My father had it put in when we were little.'

'Ah yes!' Bunny took another swig from his hip flask. 'That makes sense. You wouldn't want the whole of London crowding in to ogle at two girls' adolescent bodies . . .'

'I thought this one looked rather charming,' she said quickly, eager to move off the topic of adolescent bodies – hers or anyone else's. A buggy arrived at last, with room for two, and Bunny sat snugly beside her. So snugly in fact that she said she'd rather get out after a couple of minutes and walk back across the lawns. She remembered Fiona Matherton-Smith's mother telling her once about 'NSITs – men who were 'not safe in taxis'. Bunny wouldn't try anything, but she knew how it felt.

The lawns were full of people, at least. Fairies cavorted around them and the sound of laughter came from behind a thick laurel bush. Several Romeos and Juliets passed in the opposite direction. There were a couple of Queen Elizabeths in farthingales and ruffs, which the Queen thought was cheating slightly. As Bunny insisted on walking her back to the house, which still seemed a long way away, she noticed that for once her costume was doing her no favours. No one recognised her and came to the rescue. She realised that she relied on this happening more often than she cared to admit.

Her attention was caught by a very beautiful woman on the arm of a man in a toga. She was wearing sandals, turquoise jewellery and a tight, gold lamé dress that reminded the Queen of the one worn by Marilyn Monroe.

'Cleopatra,' Bunny said, following her gaze. 'Clever. Oh my! Look who it is!'

'Who?' the Queen asked.

'That's Lucy Seymour, with her husband. Bit of an ice queen. No wonder Stephen . . . But anyway, I'm surprised to see them here tonight. Very brave. Ha!'

He bowed lavishly to them as they passed, and they both looked slightly horrified and walked on quickly. They, too, didn't recognise the Queen, although she thought the man in the toga looked familiar.

'Why brave?' she asked Bunny.

'Oh, didn't you know?' The duke gave her a conspiratorial look. 'I shouldn't be telling you this, ma'am, but everyone's talking about it. It was Lord Seymour who owned the tiara found on the Chelsea tart.'

'The one that went to auction? Was he the buyer? My mother was telling me about it.'

'Yes, ma'am. My nephew works at Bonhams. They were in a quandary about whether to say anything to the police. A client, you know. But someone would have said something eventually, so they told Scotland Yard, and now it's halfway round London. Of course, everyone thinks Stephen did it, but I can categorically assure you he didn't.'

'How do you know?' she asked.

'My brother was with him at Eton. He's a thoroughly good egg. A sound junior minister. God knows how he got caught up in this mess.'

The Queen knew Lord Seymour vaguely through his work for the Government. She found the man unobjectionable, but she thought the duke was being a little naive.

'Bunny, it's not unheard of for politicians to be involved with escort agencies. Or old Etonians.'

He laughed.

'Oh, no, ma'am. No indeed. But they try and stay out of murder.'

'I'd like to think they do.'

His lips twitched as he watched Cleopatra and her Mark Antony walk out of sight. 'The diamonds must have been stolen,' he mused. 'Curious how the tart got hold of them. The girl was obviously dedicated to her art . . .' He frowned impishly. 'I wonder who she was doing.'

'I'd have thought that was obvious.'

'No, *who* she was doing,' Bunny repeated. He took a swig from his hip flask and gave her an unsettling look. 'The tarts at Raffles have a speciality. Well known for it in clubland. Hasn't anyone told you?'

The Queen felt vaguely alarmed. 'Why would they?'

'Because it involved you, ma'am.'

They were getting nearer to the golden light and laughter from the house. One of her friends recognised her at last and waved, but the Queen ignored the chance to escape. She needed to listen.

She stared at Bunny. 'Me?'

'Mmm. They impersonate famous women. Liz Taylor, Vivien Leigh. Marilyn Monroe. They're very good, I'm told. Not that I'd know personally.' The leer that accompanied this statement made clear he would very much know.

'Poor Marilyn,' the Queen said faintly. She thought back to her encounter with the real Miss Monroe. So, prostitutes – to call a spade a spade – impersonated the actress professionally? How extraordinary. How uncomfortable for her. 'I don't see how that affects me, though.'

'Ah. Well, it's not just film stars. All sorts of famous women. The Duchess of Argyll, for example.' The duke coughed. 'I've heard your sister's quite popular.'

The Queen couldn't believe she was hearing this. She stopped dead. There was a sort of ringing in her ears. She couldn't answer for a moment.

'M-Margaret? Really?' She had thought Bunny was the one being naive, but it was plain he thought *she* was.

The duke made a poor attempt at looking ashamed of himself.

'Isn't it awful? Don't worry, ma'am, you aren't as much of a draw. I think the gentlemen are a little bit too intimidated.' He swept into an ironic bow. 'Anyway, your hair . . .' He gestured vaguely at her hat. 'The tart in the tiara was a blonde, so nothing to worry about. My money's on Lana Turner, or that new little French firecracker, what's she called? Brigitte Bardot. Or Grace Kelly. She's quite the—'

'Darling! Are you all right? I've been looking for you for ages.'

Philip's voice came from close behind her, and the Queen turned to him in shock and relief. The single look he shot at Bunny made the duke scuttle off into the night.

'Was he being a bore? Look at you! Pale as death.'

Instinctively, she pressed herself against the comfort of his velvet doublet, and he put his arms around her.

'Dammit, Lilibet, was he pestering you? I'll kill him if he was.'

Her heart gradually stopped racing and she gathered herself. When she was sure she could sound at least relatively light-hearted, she asked, 'Did you know about the tart in Chelsea? Bunny was telling me the most extraordinary things.' She outlined her recent conversation as calmly as she could.

'Oh that,' Philip said with a smile, as if it wasn't important. He straightened the feather in her hat, which had been squashed in their embrace. 'Yes, I did. Didn't think you'd be interested.'

'You'd be surprised what interests me.'

'Not bloody Maidstone, I hope.'

'Very much not.'

'Oh, listen.' He raised his head. 'They're playing Cole Porter on the terrace. Shall we dance?'

As they headed towards the lights of the terrace, she took his hand in hers and determined not to let him out of her sight for the rest of the night.

CHAPTER 15

The following morning, the Queen asked to see her private secretary after breakfast. In a few hours, Margaret and her mother would be popping across to Windsor Castle from Royal Lodge for lunch. They would both be keen for all the gossip from Cliveden last night. But first she had something to do.

She had spent an hour or two sitting bolt upright in bed last night, contemplating whether to tell her sister about what she'd found out about the Raffles agency. Margaret would be fascinated and quite possibly flattered. But even so . . . The Queen was annoyed at herself for letting Bunny see her personal shock. There had been a gleam in his glassy eye as he told her the story last night, as if he were enjoying her reaction.

No, she had decided not to tell Margaret. The whole thing was too disturbing.

However, the information had its uses.

When she was ready, her page knocked on the door to announce Sir Hugh's arrival.

'What can I help you with, Your Majesty?' he asked.

'I'm afraid I had rather a shock last night. I found out that I might be connected in some way with the murders in Chelsea.'

'You, ma'am?'

'The escort agency in question has . . . specialities.' The Queen maintained a steady look as his eyebrows shot up. 'You perhaps know about them. Lots of people seem to. Apparently, those specialities concern me. So I'd like to see the police reports.'

'But, ma'am . . . !'

'Is there a problem?'

'You aren't involved at all, I assure you! The girl in question was a blonde, for a start.'

'She had dyed her hair. I read it in the papers.'

'Yes. But before that she specialised in Vivien Leigh and Elizabeth Taylor . . .'

Goodness. Sir Hugh really *did* know a lot about it. 'Was that in the papers?' she asked.

'No, but one learns these things.'

'I see. Well, last night I learned some of them too.'

Sir Hugh's whiskers twitched with indignation. 'Ma'am, I'm sorry. Who on earth had the impudence to—?'

'It doesn't matter. But it will be reassuring to see how the police are getting on. You don't see any obstacles, do you? To getting the report, I mean?'

He hesitated for several seconds before reluctantly shaking his head. He really didn't want her to see this report for some reason, which made her want to see it all the more.

'N-no obstacles, ma'am. But I imagine the Criminal Investigation Department will be very surprised to be asked.'

'Perhaps.'

She held her nerve and didn't waver. Whatever the reasons for his own reluctance, he was right about the CID. It was true that she didn't usually involve herself directly with murder cases. Her official reason for doing so this time was tenuous and unsavoury, as she privately admitted to herself, but it would do. She wasn't sure exactly what she was looking for, but she'd know when she'd found it.

'Thank you very much, Hugh.'

He took this as the dismissal it was.

As the door closed behind him, the Queen felt a little sorry for her private secretary. He must be wondering what on earth she was thinking. But Philip had broken a cufflink at the mention of the goings-on in Cresswell Place, and things hadn't been quite right ever since.

This wasn't the first little mystery she had encountered. She had been solving them since childhood, but not always without pain, heartache and disappointment, so she had learned not to trust her inner thoughts even with the people she most loved. Their ideas of what was in her best interests and her own weren't always aligned. Her interest this time was deeply personal and she would have to keep it to herself.

She didn't think her husband was involved in anything nefarious – not exactly. She didn't know anyone else in the world more dedicated and sincere in everything that really mattered. But Philip loved risk and silliness too. Was that it? Not all his friends were entirely reputable. Every time she thought about it, she felt a bit dizzy. And then she remembered that all you can do is keep going, trust in God and try your best to do the right thing, however small that might be.

She hoped the police report would be reassuring. At least, one way or the other, she would know.

PART 2

DAPHNE TO THE RESCUE

CHAPTER 16

'Good Lord, Joan McGraw. Who'd you have to sleep with to get this?'

'Auntie Eva! Stop it!'

Joan faced her grinning aunt across the art deco sitting room of the chichi flat in Dolphin Square. *Her* flat. It was clean and smart, with a bedroom all to herself and a downstairs lobby where she and her aunt had just passed two women in mink jackets, who had given them a friendly 'hello'. Instead of the bus, Joan now had a brisk, pleasant walk through Westminster. She could no longer bring in babkas as peace offerings to the men in moustaches, but replaced them with sticky buns from a Pimlico bakery, which were almost as popular.

'I thought the building was a hospital when we drew up outside,' Auntie Eva said. 'So grand.'

'It was one, during the war,' Joan agreed. 'And the HQ of the Free French.'

'La-di-da! Look at you!'

Eva was amused by Joan's turn of fortune but, of the two of them, she was the one who looked the most at home here. Eva was a dressmaker who worked for fashionable ladies who couldn't afford the top designers. Using the latest patterns, her suits and dresses were easily as stylish as the ones Joan saw in magazines. On her clients, it was difficult to tell them from the couture originals. *It's all about fit and fabric*, she would say. Right now, in a slim-fitting H-line tweed dress and jacket, copied from Dior, she looked as well turned out as Deborah Fairdale – and not unlike her, if you gave her an expensive hairdresser and overlooked the nose.

Joan ran her hand along the edge of a plush blue sofa. The living room had a small, round dining table at the far end, next to an archway that led to a kitchen with a gas-ring stove and its own electric refrigerator.

'Did you say it was the private secretary who put you here?' Eva asked.

'Yes. It's owned by a Major Ross. An absentee landlord. Sir Hugh Masson has organised everything.'

'A man of sense,' her aunt pronounced with a nod. 'You can't look good for the Queen if you've traipsed halfway across London.'

'It's not about looking good!' Joan protested.

'What is it about then?' Eva raised a perfectly plucked eyebrow.

'It's about the work. We connect. It's about getting things right.'

'Well, if you say so . . . Talking of which, if you ever get the chance to look at the boning in her evening gowns, can you let me know how Mr Hartnell does it? Because I'm sure he has a new technique.'

'It's not about her evening gowns either!' Joan insisted with a laugh. 'I don't get to look inside them.'

'More's the pity.' Her aunt sighed. She walked over and gave Joan a hug. 'We're going to miss you, you know. The flat won't be the same without you.'

'No. Alice can have a proper bed instead of a mattress on the floor.'

'She never minded. She adores you.' Eva placed a gloved hand affectionately against Joan's cheek.

'I love her too,' Joan said, squeezing her aunt's slim body tightly. 'And you.'

Auntie Eva had the same figure as her mother, who had died when Joan was a teenager. These hugs always brought a wave of nostalgia that threatened to overwhelm her. Alice, the youngest of the three cousins whose room Joan shared, had her mother's vivid red hair and the same dusting of freckles across her nose. She would miss all the girls, but even so, Joan deeply savoured her new-found independence. It felt like her last chance.

After nearly four decades on this earth, Joan's life fitted into four suitcases, two of which belonged to Auntie Eva. As she unpacked their contents onto her bed so her aunt could take the empty luggage home with her, she found an unexpected package tucked into one of them. It was a brown paper parcel, neatly tied with ribbon.

'Oh, that's for you,' Eva said airily. 'I ran it up last night with some scraps I had left over. Open it later.'

After some more close-hug goodbyes, Joan went back to the package in her bedroom. She unwrapped the paper and held up the folded garment inside. It was a jade silk kimono, lined with more silk in a cherry blossom pattern. Auntie Eva had certainly not made it out of 'scraps': the fabric alone must have cost her a fortune. It was fit for a princess – or the sort of lady who mixed with neighbours in mink coats and reclined on plush blue sofas. Joan slipped it on over her dress and wondered what might happen to jinx this moment. Because it felt too good to last.

CHAPTER 17

I t was now the second week in May, more than a month since the
bodies in Chelsea had been found. Sir Hugh arrived at the Queen's
study to go over her diary.

'I've allowed an extra fifteen minutes in your schedule this morning, ma'am. The police report you requested arrived on my desk last
night. I've had time to go through it. If you'd like me to . . .'

'Thank you, Hugh.'

There were one or two things in particular that the Queen wanted
to know, but it would be better if she didn't ask directly.

'First of all, ma'am, I can confirm that it was a blonde princess that
the male victim asked for. He probably meant Princess Grace of
Monaco, which would explain the tiara. I hope that puts your mind at
ease . . .' he looked uncomfortable '. . . with regard to your family, et
cetera.'

'Not entirely,' the Queen said. 'But do go on.'

'Inspector Darbishire has also made excellent progress in establishing how the murders were done.'

'Not Chief Inspector Venables?' the Queen interrupted. 'I was
rather expecting him to be in charge.' She was familiar with Venables
from several high-profile investigations, which always made the front
page of the papers.

'Not this time, ma'am. He was, er, otherwise occupied. But Darbishire is very thorough. And discreet.'

Sir Hugh's eyes met hers with a look of brief intensity. She wondered if it was merely an effect of the light on his spectacles.

'Does he need to be discreet?' she asked.

'Always,' he said, without further explanation. The Queen was about to press the point, but her private secretary moved on smoothly.

'You'll be pleased to know the Dean of Bath has been all but ruled out, although he's still on the suspect list.'

'Oh good. Does he have an alibi?'

'Far from it, ma'am. But, without going into detail, it was a crime requiring two people to, um, subdue the victims. There's no evidence he had an accomplice, or indeed a motive. It has since been established that the house was used entirely without his knowledge for illicit assignations.'

'Ah. I knew about that.'

'Did you, ma'am?' Sir Hugh was too polite to express surprise verbally, but his bushy eyebrows shot up, leaving his spectacles behind.

'Deborah Fairdale told me.'

'Oh, I see.' Sir Hugh retrieved a page of notes from the file tucked under his arm. He quickly consulted them. 'However, there remain some unanswered questions. If the murders happened when the police think they did, then the dean either just missed the killers, or slept through the whole thing. Why didn't he notice that the flowers he had bought for his bedside the day before were missing? Or that the back door was unbolted? Or – most importantly – that the door to the second bedroom, opposite his own, had been left partially open, as the charlady found it the following week? He would have to be very unobservant indeed.'

'Did he give a reason?' the Queen asked. The Clement Moreton she remembered was a sharp, quick-witted man, as you had to be if you were going to beat her mother at canasta, which he had done more than once.

'He put it down to toothache, ma'am. He was in London in the first place so he could see his dentist in Harley Street on the Monday morning. He drank a little too much the night before, he says, to dull the pain. A hangover didn't help.'

'I see.' This seemed plausible. The Queen knew how painful toothache could be. Earaches too . . .

'Anyway, Inspector Darbishire strongly suspects a link with a London gang. He's already found out that Perez was consorting with some dubious characters. He was from Argentina, ma'am. The inspector's in touch with Buenos Aires.'

'You say he knows how the murders were done?'

'Yes. As I say, it's best if I don't go into details, but Perez was attacked first, almost certainly, and Fonteyn killed as a witness. Perez was taken by surprise in the, um, bedroom and left where he fell. The knife was applied afterwards, in some sort of vengeful act. Or possibly as a message. All very sordid.'

'Was there anything about a gunshot?' she asked.

'A gunshot?' The eyebrows shot up again. 'Miss Fairdale, ma'am?'

'Actually, yes.'

Sir Hugh glanced through his notes. 'Um . . . here we are. Two witnesses in the mews reported something of that sort, at about three in the morning. But one of them heard a motorbike roaring off at about the same time, so it was almost certainly a backfire. There's no sign of any bullet, casings or damage that might have been caused by one.' He glanced up from the file. 'There are some witness statements that don't quite make sense. That's often the case early in an investigation, I believe . . .'

'But they've had six weeks, Hugh!'

'Five, from when the bodies were discovered. These things take time.'

The Queen tried not to sound personally invested in any way. 'And there was nothing else in the street that night? To explain the gunshot, I mean?' She didn't mean that exactly, but it would do.

Sir Hugh gave her that odd look again. 'I can't imagine what that might be, ma'am,' he said evenly. He held out the file. 'You can read it for yourself if you like.'

'Perhaps later. Leave it with me. Thank you.'

'There *was* an anonymous phone call, later on that Monday morning. It came from a public call box on the King's Road. A muffled voice, telling the operator that there had been a terrible accident in the mews. But the operator didn't catch the full address, and the police went round and found nothing. They've only recently realised it might be important. In the meantime, the focus has turned to Lord Seymour, the Minister for Technology. You heard about the tiara?'

'I did, last night. He bought it at auction. Have they spoken to him yet?'

'Not in person. He's been taken up with Government business, you know. He's given a statement explaining that the diamonds were stolen from the safe at his home.'

'*Has* he?' the Queen said, raising an eyebrow.

'Quite, ma'am. Inspector Darbishire is hoping to interview him imminently. Fortunately, he has the prime minister and half the Cabinet as his alibi. He was with them at a dinner in the House until after ten thirty on the night of the thirty-first. He went straight home, where the servants and Lady Seymour can vouch for him. As alibis go, it's a pretty good one.'

'That's a relief,' the Queen said. 'I'd like to think my ministers are . . . not cold-blooded killers, at least.'

'No, ma'am. Seymour's well regarded. Mr Macmillan himself has said he's destined for high office. This discovery of the tiara has caused an obvious strain. The police have yet to confirm that there *was* a robbery. And if a gang had stolen the diamonds, it's very hard to understand why they'd let them be used out in public, so to speak. But I suppose the tar—woman in question was wearing them to a private encounter, so perhaps that explains it. If Seymour *was* involved, then why he'd use his own diamonds to dress her is even more beyond comprehension. But Darbishire's pursuing every avenue.'

'And are there any others? Avenues, I mean?'

'The initial theory about a gangland execution is the main one for now. It's quite possible that a fellow escort was involved. She was supposed to be with Perez that night, but she somehow managed to swap with Miss Fonteyn. Darbishire isn't convinced by her excuses. It's all very lurid and unfortunate, but nothing remotely related to the family.'

'Whose?'

'Yours. I hope that reassures you, ma'am.'

The Queen wasn't reassured, but didn't say so.

'Thank you very much for updating me, Hugh.'

'My pleasure, ma'am. If I hear anything else of interest from the CID, I'll let you know.'

The Queen smiled, but her tone was firm. 'A weekly report would more than suffice,' she said, sensing that otherwise she would probably get nothing. 'And I can read it personally, to save you the time.'

'I assure you, ma'am, it's no—'

'I'm quite happy to read it myself.'

Nonplussed, Sir Hugh nodded obediently. 'Absolutely, ma'am. I'll see it's done.'

CHAPTER 18

Darbishire took his secret warning seriously. He fundamentally refused to give in to whichever dark forces had approached him, but he was a pragmatic man. They knew who he worked with. No doubt they knew where he lived. They would know he had a wife and two precious little daughters, whom he'd lay down his life for. He wasn't going to make any dangerous moves until he understood exactly what he was up against.

Meanwhile they didn't want him to stop the investigation, which he had no intention of doing anyway. He had plenty to do that didn't involve lifting up stones and seeing if the inconsistent Gregsons crawled out from under them. For now, he was busy. In fact, he was about to interview a Government minister concerning the matter of some inconveniently located diamonds.

He had put on his best suit today – of the two that he possessed – and his favourite tie. It was navy blue and slightly narrower than was traditional. He liked to think it gave him a certain air. Woolgar, needless to say, had traces of egg on his lapel which he tried to brush off with one hand when they were pointed out to him.

'You need to get yourself in hand, Woolgar,' Darbishire said, not unkindly. He sent his sergeant off to the lavatories to do a better job of it. Lord Seymour was a VIP. For the sake of the Met, they need to look their best.

The minister lived with his wife and servants in a large house on Smith Street, a gentle stroll from Westminster Abbey and the political cut and thrust of Whitehall. When Darbishire and Woolgar knocked at the polished front door, it was answered by a butler who took their hats and showed them upstairs to a book-lined room, lit by a large Georgian window, with the promise that the minister would be with them shortly.

'Not bad, sir,' Woolgar pronounced, giving the walnut bookcases and antique carriage clock an approving eye.

'All right if you can afford it,' Darbishire admitted.

Seymour had inherited a family business and a small property empire, which he had made bigger by investing in car parks after the war, buying up old bomb sites and exploiting them in ways no one else had thought of. All this while rising rapidly through the ranks of the Conservative Party. It was widely thought that Mr Macmillan had great plans for him.

He had avoided meeting the police for two weeks since the auction house leaked news of the tiara, citing travel abroad and urgent Government business. Darbishire expected someone lofty and dismissive, but the man who arrived two minutes later was smooth and smiling, warm in his handshake, keen to look you in the eye. He apologised profusely for the delay in seeing them and asked them to make themselves comfortable in a couple of club chairs. Ashtrays were placed beside them by the butler before he withdrew. Seymour offered them cigarettes. Darbishire refused, but he could see why this man had gone so far in politics.

'I'm sorry to disturb you while you're so busy, sir.'

'You're not disturbing me at all, Chief Inspector. Only too happy to help.'

Seymour crossed one immaculate, pinstriped leg over the other. His face bore faint traces of a suntan, his jowls a hint of good living– but he'd retained much of his youthful attractiveness. His eyes were friendly behind wire-framed spectacles and something about his high forehead suggested a keen intelligence. Or perhaps it was all those leatherbound volumes behind him. Anyway, Darbishire found himself thinking it wouldn't be hard to vote for the man.

If he hadn't strangled a tart to death and stabbed and garrotted her companion, obviously.

'As you know, I'm investigating the events of the night of the thirty-first of March. You've been good enough to give us an account of your whereabouts that night . . .'

'Of course, I'm only sorry that I need to explain at all. Awful business, awful.'

Darbishire ran through the minister's alibi for the early part of the evening, which had been corroborated by fellow ministers and staff at the House of Lords.

Seymour gave a light laugh. 'There's many people who will lie for you in life, Chief Inspector . . .'

'It's just Inspector,' Darbishire corrected him. He'd let it go the first time, but if it was an attempt at flattery or bribery, it was important the minister understood that Fred Darbishire didn't work that way.

'Really? Is it?' Seymour seemed stumped for a moment. 'I do apologise, Inspector. As I was saying, many people will lie for you, but not the barmen of the House of Lords. Nor the policeman at the gate. I have no memory of when I left, exactly, but if they say it was twenty past eleven, then you can be certain that's when it was.'

'Quite. However, you say you walked home. When you got here, fifteen minutes later or thereabouts, there were only John Richards, who I assume is the man who greeted us at the door, and your wife to vouch for you. And they, I might say . . .'

'. . . Are less reliably dispassionate,' Seymour finished for him. 'What can I tell you? Richards has been with us for twenty years. He would certainly lie without a second thought, if he believed it was in my best interests. My wife, on the other hand, is pure as the driven snow. She wouldn't lie if her life depended on it, to save me or to sink me, but you have only my word for that.' He smiled again. 'You're very welcome to meet her and judge for yourself. She's out this morning, but at your disposal in general terms.'

'Thank you. I will,' Darbishire said. For all the good it would do. He already knew what Lady Seymour would say, and whether or not it was true, she couldn't be compelled to give evidence against her husband in court, so it wasn't a rabbit he intended to spend much time chasing.

There was also the fact – though Darbishire didn't raise it now – that even if Seymour had caught a cab and raced to Chelsea, for which they had no evidence, he would only have had five or ten minutes before the dean and his guests had arrived at Cresswell Place. There was no way Seymour could have conducted the bloody murders and cleaned up in time, and no evidence of him and the dean knowing each other or colluding.

On the other hand, Seymour could easily have hired someone else to do the dirty deed while he was at the House. The perfect alibi. What Darbishire needed was a motive.

'Did you know Dino Perez?' Darbishire asked.

'As I told you in my statement, I did not,' Seymour said. 'I never met the man, or heard of him.'

'And Gina Fonteyn?'

This time, Seymour cocked his head. He coughed. 'I knew *of* her. I might as well give you full disclosure. Her popularity at Raffles was hardly a national secret.'

Bravo, Darbishire thought. Because he'd done his homework. He knew Seymour was a valued client of the agency. He appreciated all the good old conversation they offered the discerning gentleman. He would certainly have heard of Miss Fonteyn, and to deny it would be foolish. It appeared the Minister for Technology was not foolish.

'But you never met?'

'Never. She wasn't my, er, type.'

'Do you know any of the men she saw?'

Seymour raised his eyebrows and shifted in his chair.

'Really, Inspector. I have no idea. I'm not in the habit of questioning my friends about their nocturnal escapades.'

'But you say Miss Fonteyn's popularity was well known.'

He looked uncomfortable. 'It was talked about in the club, you know, in general terms. Unfortunate banter, when some men had had too much to drink.'

'Which club?'

'White's.'

'Not the Artemis?'

'I don't think so. I haven't been there in a while.'

'So, you have no idea how she came to be wearing the diamond tiara you bought last year.'

'None at all, as I said in my statement. The tiara was taken, and I can only assume that whoever took it gave it to her to use, for reasons I can't begin to imagine.'

'You must admit, that seems unlikely,' Darbishire persisted.

Seymour's gaze was frank. He smiled slightly. 'I do admit it, certainly. I realise what a position I'm in. But it's the truth.'

'Do you mind showing us the safe?'

'With pleasure.'

Seymour was about to get up, when Darbishire raised a hand.

'I'm sorry. One more question first.'

'Yes?'

'Have you ever visited Cresswell Place? You neglected to mention it in your statement.'

There was a flicker in Seymour's eyes, and Darbishire saw him hesitate and calculate. It was the first time he'd done this. He inclined his head.

'Yes. Once. I . . . went there with another escort from Raffles. I wanted somewhere low-key. They suggested number forty-four. That was several months ago.'

Good decision, Darbishire thought. I'd have found that out eventually. And if he was worried about any fingerprints or other evidence at the house, it was a nice way of explaining them.

But they hadn't found his fingerprints. The char was a pretty thorough cleaner. No wonder she sounded like a Sherman tank.

'Thank you. Oh, and one other thing. Sergeant Woolgar, the photograph?'

Woolgar pulled out a picture of the stag handle flick knife found in Perez's eye. It was a German made gravity knife, Deedar said, designed to be used one-handed. The minister winced.

'Do you recognise this knife?'

'Yes, absolutely I do.' Seymour looked up. 'It was stuck in the victim, wasn't it? The man, I mean. I saw it in the papers.'

'It was. Had you seen it before?'

He looked at the picture a bit more closely and pursed his lips. 'I can't be sure. I've seen a lot of knives like this in my time. As I'm sure you have, Inspector. Sorry. Shall we go?'

'After you, sir.'

They headed for the dining room, which was on the same floor as the library. Seymour lifted a Venetian oil painting of the Grand Canal off its hook, and indicated the safe set into the wall behind it. It was about eighteen inches by twelve, with two brass handles and a central keyhole set into the door. Darbishire had seen hundreds like it.

'It was put in five years ago,' Seymour explained. 'The best that money could buy at the time. I use it for keeping bond certificates and essential paperwork and so on. My wife uses it for her pearls and the other jewels she wears on a regular basis. The tiara had been at the bank, but I'd got it out two weeks before to give to her for her fortieth birthday.'

'When was that, may I ask?'

'Last week. Until the auction house contacted you about it, I had no idea it wasn't still on the top shelf, in its box, where I'd put it. As I said in my statement, I didn't see the description of the diamonds in the gutter press – we don't read that sort of thing. When Bonhams got in touch, I was certain they must be wrong: it couldn't be the Zellendorf. But when I opened the door to check, all my wife's jewellery was missing, along with the tiara and a couple of rather valuable watches I'd inherited from my father.' He looked helplessly at them both. 'When exactly we were burgled, we don't know, but we've had workmen in and out. My wife's been redesigning the drawing room and bedrooms. I've given the names of all the relevant businesses in my statement. The safe was as I'd left it, externally. I keep one key on my fob and the spare at the bank. Neither was used. Whoever got into it knew what he was doing. It was an expert job.'

Darbishire could think of half a dozen experts off the top of his head who could do it. He'd never store anything truly precious in a safe like this.

'How much was it all worth, do you think?' he asked.

Seymour frowned at him slightly, as if such questions were improper. People this rich didn't like to talk about it. 'Oh, upwards of twenty thousand pounds,' he said. 'It's in the hands of the insurers. They like to question the value of everything as soon as one puts in a claim. And naturally, they're awaiting the result of your investigation.'

'I'm sorry to hold them up.'

Seymour caught the barb in Darbishire's voice, but didn't rise to the bait.

'I'm sure you'll take as long as you need to,' he said evenly. 'You have my full support.' He breathed out a small sigh and looked towards a group of cherry trees swaying in the breeze beyond the dining room window. 'It does me no good either, to be caught up in all this. I realise how unconvincing it looks, that we didn't know.'

'Correct,' Darbishire agreed. He checked his notes. 'You said in your statement that the last time you looked in the safe was on the twenty-fifth, six days before the murders.'

'Yes. I needed some paperwork.'

'Your wife didn't need her other jewellery in the meantime?'

'No. She had her pearls out anyway. We only put them there when we go away. She rarely uses the other pieces.'

'If you don't mind me asking, sir – why the tiara at all?'

'Because of her fortieth birthday, as I told you. She was going to wear it to her party.'

'But why a tiara?'

'Isn't that for duchesses and the like?' Woolgar butted in. Darbishire had been searching for a polite way of putting it.

For the first time, Seymour gave in to annoyance. He drew himself up to his full height, which was still several inches shorter than Woolgar. 'Because we're going to America, if you must know. We'll be guests at a ball and dinner with the Queen, the UN Secretary-General and the Governor of New York. I'd like my wife to be appropriately dressed.'

'I'm sure she'll look very nice,' Darbishire said, momentarily forgetting that the diamonds were in a different safe now, in Scotland Yard.

Seymour had not forgotten. 'She won't be wearing the tiara. But yes, she'll look as lovely as she always does. She doesn't need diamonds. She never did.'

Darbishire caught Woolgar's eye, and though his sergeant had the sense to say nothing this time, he knew what he's thinking. Until now, the inspector had been far from convinced by the minister's stated devotion to the wife he regularly cheated on with prostitutes. But something in the way he talked about her suggested it wasn't impossible that this politician might, for once, be telling the truth.

Chapter 19

Joan woke with a start.

Was that the sound of a key in the lock? She sat up in bed, pulling the blankets around her. Moonlight streamed in through a crack in the curtains, casting an eerie glow over her new bedroom. It was full of unfamiliar shapes – but as her eyes adjusted she recognised these as her own clothes, draped over the furniture. Fully alert, she listened hard. Beyond the bedroom, a narrow hallway led down to the flat's front door. For a moment, there was silence. Then she heard a quiet footstep in the hallway.

She was not alone.

She armed herself with the heaviest thing she could think of, which was the hard-edged alabaster lamp base from beside her bed. As she reached out to unplug it from the wall, her thoughts were rapid, and mostly regrets.

She shouldn't have taken this flat, which was obviously too good to be true. The rent was minimal, and the place was smart, with fancy furnishings, a view of the river, and posh neighbours who wore mink coats and dined at the Ritz. The only catch was that it contained a second bedroom with a locked door that she'd been told she couldn't use.

Now, here, in the freezing middle of the night, Joan thought of the house in Cresswell Place. In the wake of the Chelsea murders, what single woman in London was mad enough to take a place with a locked spare room? Especially when, ironically, the key to her own bedroom door was missing. True, the flat had been recommended to her by Sir Hugh Masson himself. But hadn't the Queen told her, in no uncertain terms, that she couldn't trust him? Joan knew she'd been moving in dangerous waters, but she'd never begun to imagine that it could come to this.

The light in the hallway went on and heavy footsteps began to pad down the corridor towards her. The lamp base, unplugged, felt reassuringly chunky in her hand. Joan was only wearing her pyjamas, but there was no time to struggle into her dressing gown. To her vast relief, the footsteps turned off into the sitting room before they reached her. Was he a burglar, plain and simple?

But how would he have a front door key?

She realised how certain she had been that he was coming to kill her; she'd been ready to fight for her life. Now, she put her ear to the bedroom door and tried to hear what he was up to.

There was a grunt and a swear word. Whatever he'd come for, he wasn't pleased. Doors opened and closed. Then the footsteps got faster and closer. He was coming back down the corridor now. The bedroom door handle rattled. Joan stood back. The door opened and she raised the lamp base above her head.

'What in God's name?'

His voice was guttural and he stood stock-still, silhouetted against the light from the hallway. He didn't advance.

'Who on earth are you? Put that down, for God's sake.'

Joan lowered the lamp base slowly.

'Who are *you*?'

All she could see was the broad-shouldered shape of a man in a mackintosh.

'Who d'you think? I'm Ross. What are you doing in my spare room? Oh God – does McGraw have a bit on the side? Christ! Look, this isn't going to work. Put some clothes on. I'll meet you outside.'

He retreated to the sitting room, but Joan's racing heart took a while to slow down. It was a few minutes before she emerged from her room, wearing slacks and a Fair Isle knit, her hair brushed, looking militant but unarmed.

Major Ross, her 'absentee' landlord, was waiting for her in an armchair, with a finger of whisky in a tumbler in one hand and a cigarette in the other. He had taken off his mackintosh and was dressed in a thick woollen cardigan and corduroy trousers. He looked confused, amused and very unthreatening.

Ross motioned to the sofa and Joan perched on the edge of it. He gestured to a cigarette box on the coffee table between them. She didn't normally smoke, but she accepted both a cigarette and his offer of a light.

'So,' he began, leaning back. 'You're McGraw's . . . ?' He left her to finish the sentence.

He had an air of authority about him. Older than her: in his forties, probably. His hair fell into a cowlick that he brushed unconsciously from his face. His skin was freckled, like hers, and his eyes were tired. There was a certain cragginess to him.

'*I'm* McGraw,' she said simply.

He frowned. 'But . . . he was called John. I was distinctly told so. That's why I said he could stay.'

'I'm Joan.'

'Oh.'

They both realised what must have happened. Ross's face relaxed.

'That explains the damp stockings on the shower rail.'

Joan remembered that the bathroom was draped in her drying underwear. 'Oh no! I didn't realise—'

'I got rather a surprise.'

'Not half as big a shock as I did,' she said crossly. 'I was told I had the place to myself.'

'Well, ah. I'm not up often, but I do come over occasionally. They should have explained . . . But you shouldn't really be here. Anyway, I'm sorry. And for my language earlier. The shock, you know. Can I offer you tea?' The gentle sound of a kettle boiling on the stove was just rising to a keen whistle. He got up to deal with it. 'Or a wee dram?' There was an edge of a Scottish burr to his voice.

'I'll take the whisky. Actually, both.'

'Good idea.'

He dealt with their drinks and Joan settled herself in his comfortable little sofa.

'There's been a misunderstanding, obviously,' she said.

'Obviously.'

'The Queen's private secretary knew I needed somewhere to live. He arranged it incredibly fast. Something was bound to go wrong.'

Ross shrugged. 'A chap got in touch at the club. Said he knew someone – I could have sworn he said John – who needed helping out. I was happy to oblige. We used to have guests often, but we're not in town much these days. At least . . .' He paused. 'I am, but my wife isn't. Dashed awkward.'

It was more than awkward. Joan couldn't possibly stay in a flat with a married man. Dammit! She liked this place.

'What do you do in town, Mr Ross?' she asked, to take her mind off it.

He shrugged and lit another cigarette. 'Oh, you know, this and that. Very boring. Civil servant.'

'But you travel for work?'

'No. That is, I tend to stay at my club these days. It's more sociable. I was thinking of giving up the flat.'

Joan ignored the reference to the club. 'What sort of civil servant?'

'Hmm? You ask a lot of questions, don't you? Just the ordinary kind, you know. Briefcase and bowler hat. Very dull.'

'Yes, you said it was boring,' she observed. 'Where's your office?'

'Hmm? What is this, the inquisition? I might ask the same of you.'

'You know where I work,' Joan said. 'Buckingham Palace.' *You really are very evasive*, she thought. *This interests me.*

'Yes, but what do you do?' he persisted.

He was only trying to throw the spotlight back on her. She was already beginning to guess what he did. She knew other men who were evasive about their boring jobs and bowler hats.

'I work for the Queen,' she said. 'Temporarily.'

'Lucky you. How fascinating.'

When he smiled, his grizzled cheeks dimpled in a way that was undeniably attractive. His eyes were grey. Joan had always had rather a thing for men with grey eyes. Dammit again!

For an instant, the thought flashed into her mind That either Sir Hugh or Miles Urquhart had engineered this precise situation . . . But that was so far-fetched. And the chances of such a scheme working out were a thousand to one. She might be on a secret mission for the monarch, but that was no reason to become paranoid.

Those grey eyes were peering closely at her. 'I was just thinking . . . I'm sure I know you from somewhere.'

She smiled sardonically. 'Really?' It was the line so many pilots in the war had used.

He read her mind. 'No, really! I've been trying to place you. The Admiralty. No . . . I know! Dorset, 'forty-four. Longmeadow. Hmm.'

'I . . . Yes. Hmm.'

He'd been thinking aloud, but they both knew that the first rule of Longmeadow was that you didn't talk about it. Even now, its existence and the identities of the people who had worked there remained top secret.

Joan wasn't sure she remembered him, but men had come in and out all the time, and Brigadier Yelland had made her life very stressful. To have visited, Major Ross might well have been in Military Intelligence. And from the careworn look of him, he probably still was.

He smiled with just a corner of his lip.

'A long time ago. Another life.'

'Absolutely,' she said, though she sensed that for him, it wasn't.

They made small talk for a few minutes. He told her about the cottage in Hampshire where he was trying 'make something of the garden'. She told him about Bow, and how much she had enjoyed living there, but that it wasn't practical for work. Then she remembered what time it was and rushed off to the bathroom to denude it of stockings and handkerchiefs, which she had been drying against the bathroom tiles so they would be flat.

She looked at herself in the mirror and realised she was slightly flushed. Too much whisky, late at night. Her hair was a mess again and she put her fingers through it to arrange it, even though it was too late. Then she grinned at herself for being an idiot and went to bed.

CHAPTER 20

In the offices of Scotland Yard on the Victoria Embankment, Fred Darbishire looked up from his temporary desk. If he stood up a little and leaned to the left, he could see the River Thames through one of the office windows. On the opposite bank, where the Festival of Britain buildings used to be, they were building some sort of skyscraper between Waterloo Station and the Festival Hall.

He didn't know how tall it would be exactly, but there were dark mutterings among the officers at the Yard who cared about London's architecture. This was the city of Sir Christopher Wren and Nicholas Hawksmoor. Its skyline was defined by the dome of St Paul's and a familiar scattering of church spires. Now, where the bombs had fallen heavily, buildings were starting to go up that were higher than the tallest churches. Big, concrete things that looked as if they belonged in New York. They made him nervous. Woolgar was a fan, needless to say.

It's progress, sir, isn't it? Houses? Offices? We need them.

Darbishire needed open sky. He was not quite forty, but he was starting to feel old.

He sat back down and focused on a different kind of progress: his own.

The reason he was here, not at his desk at the Chelsea police station in Lucan Place, was that his reports now went all the way to Her Majesty the Queen, God help him, which meant they got vetted by every goddam senior pen-pusher in between. Every single thing about them had been altered, from the paper he used, to the secretary who typed them up, to the structure of his sentences. The only thing they *couldn't* change was what he had to say.

Did Her Majesty care about escort agencies and cleaning contracts? Darbishire doubted it. However, if she wanted to know the intricacies of arranging discreet meeting places in central London, she was welcome to fill her boots.

Under further questioning, the charlady at Cresswell Place had confirmed exactly what he suspected about the mews house, which was that it was one of several posh locations used for the assignations of some Raffles VIPs who didn't want to risk being spotted in a hotel. These locations used to be kept empty, she said, but the landlords started getting greedy and looked for tenants who might want the place on a Monday-to-Friday basis. One room would always be set aside and kept pristine for Saturdays and Sundays, without the renter's knowledge. The rent for the rest was cheap and high-quality cleaning services were thrown in. 'The churchman seemed just the right type,' she'd added, 'because he's always busy of a weekend, isn't he?'

Darbishire judged this a particularly stupid plan, because people don't always do what you expect them to do, do they? When asked, the receptionist at the letting agency said that tenants were supposed to call and check if they could stay over on a weekend, because it was written into their contracts that they couldn't, and technically they weren't paying for it. The receptionist swore blind that this wasn't a ruse to warn the Raffles agency in advance, but obviously it was.

The dean had in fact made such a call. But the office girl at Raffles said that it wasn't a problem, because they had nobody booked that night. Beryl White and Perez were not supposed to go there. Which raised, once again, the question of the keys.

Darbishire had another question, too. The Raffles agency and the letting agency needed to talk to each other to make this precarious arrangement work. It followed that the greedy landlords must be intimately connected with the owners or managers of the escort agency, but Darbishire hadn't had any luck yet establishing who they were, behind the convoluted front of Liechtenstein-based companies they'd set up. He was working on it.

CHAPTER 21

As the days of May sped by, the deputy private secretary huddled behind his desk in the North Wing corridor and buried himself in the preparations for Denmark.

The stress of the visit was getting to Miles Urquhart for some reason. Twice, he had broken his vow of silence to shout at Joan in front of all the typists. It was hard not to look hurt, but Joan just about managed it. She was used to the secretaries not offering her any solidarity, but she was surprised when the press secretary, of all people, invited her into his office and offered her a chair.

'I apologise for Miles. That was unpardonable. He can be a brute sometimes, but he doesn't mean it. He'll come round eventually, when he sees how indispensable you are.'

'Thank you, Jeremy.'

Radnor-Milne smiled, and his thin, chiselled face looked almost attractive. 'HM doesn't make mistakes about people. She's really quite brilliant that way, like her father.' He saw Joan frowning at this newfound friendliness. 'I'm sorry I've been ignoring you. Up to my eyes. But that doesn't mean I haven't noticed how hard you've worked on these trips. I'm sorry you don't get to come to Denmark with us.'

'It's alright. There's a lot to do.'

'Minding the fort and so on, like last month. Mmm.' He nodded. 'But I'd hate to think of you as Cinderella, busy filing all the time, with your nose covered in ash smuts from the fire . . .'

Joan grinned. 'I don't think Cinderella filed.'

'She would have, if Miles had been involved. Anyway, Fiona used to come out with us for cocktails and so on, and we had a grand time.

I suddenly realised that you haven't done anything with us socially yet, have you?'

'No,' Joan agreed. She had been pointedly left out of any plans.

'It's simply not good enough,' Jeremy said. 'My wife and I are going out with some people a couple of nights before we head off to Copenhagen. A little dinner at the Ritz. Will you come? I'm afraid I can't provide you with any eligible bachelors, but my brother will look after you. It's the least you deserve.'

'I'd love to. Oh, what should I wear?'

'Anything you like.' He smiled reassuringly. 'Don't worry, we're all very relaxed.'

★ ★ ★

Joan did worry. There was no such thing as 'anything you like' in London society. She spent a couple of days anxiously scouring magazines and talking it through with her aunt and some of her old friends from the Wrens. As she had suspected, a trip to the Ritz required a proper cocktail dress, which she didn't possess, and some form of glamorous wrap.

Auntie Eva was delighted to help, but she was a perfectionist. The dress was finally delivered to Dolphin Square two hours before Joan was due to wear it. She changed into it nervously, checking her profile for gaps or bulges. As far as she could tell, it fitted as well as her aunt promised it would.

'Bloody hell! Excuse my language.'

Hector Ross looked up in shock from his newspaper when she emerged from her bedroom.

'Do I look all right?'

'You know you do.' He seemed flustered. 'It's just . . .'

'What?'

'It's not very *you*.'

'What does that mean?' Joan asked, exasperated. If that's all he had to say, he might as well keep his thoughts to himself. 'There's more to me than serge suits, you know.'

'I can see that.'

She resented being criticised in her own flat – so to speak – when she was trying to build her own confidence. 'Why are you here anyway?' she asked. 'This is the third night this week.'

'Building work at the club,' he muttered. 'Not that it's any of your business. Where are you going?'

She explained about the Ritz, and the press secretary's invitation.

'Did he get that dress for you?'

'No! Of course not! My aunt made it.'

Joan did a little twirl. The finely pleated bodice of this black silk dress was engineered to fit her like a second skin. Below the waist, its skirts fell in clever layers, fluidly outlining her every move. She had new nylons, and shoes borrowed from one of the few girls in the typing pool who was still friends with her, and had left work early for a shampoo and set at the hairdresser's. Her normally wayward hair was now glued to her head in a complicated design, held in place by a multitude of hidden pins. She hardly recognised herself.

She was missing jewellery, but Auntie Eva assured her that her bare shoulders would 'work their own magic'. Joan hadn't been convinced by this, but looking at Hector's jaw, which still hadn't fully closed, she began to wonder. Even so, he was frowning, and his voice was gruff.

'Who will your escort be?'

She shook her head at him. 'No one, exactly. There's a party of us. Jeremy said his brother will look after me, not that I need it.'

'Tony?'

'Is that his name?'

Hector shut his jaw. Now he seemed to prickle. 'He's a very rich man. I'm sure he'll look after you very well.'

'I don't know what money has to do with it,' Joan shot back at him.

'He's married. You do know that?'

Joan didn't. She tossed her head as if she didn't care. She was feeling out of her depth and determined not to let it show.

'So you know him?' she asked.

'Of course. That's how I—'

The doorbell rang. Hector went to answer it while Joan ran to her room to get the black satin opera coat that Auntie Eva had made to go with the dress.

It was Tony Radnor-Milne, not Jeremy, who stood in the hallway. Joan instantly saw the likeness, but Tony was much taller, clearly the older of the two. He was clean-shaven, with the same long face and wavy hair as Jeremy, although his was flecked with grey. His fur-collared coat suggested a very expensive tailor and there was a swagger about him, as if he was usually the most powerful person in the room. Hector stood stiffly in his shadow. Tony caught sight of Joan and his face lit up.

'Miss McGraw, I presume. My goodness, my brother certainly didn't do you justice.' He glanced behind him. 'Major Ross, what fabulous company you keep.' Then he held out his hand to her. 'The others are waiting. Shall we go?'

Hector watched with arms folded as she swept past him. He reminded her at that moment of her father.

CHAPTER 22

The evening started well. Tony Radnor-Milne had ensured they had the best table in the Ritz's dining room, surrounded by gilt and mirrors and under crystal chandeliers – much as Joan imagined the Palace of Versailles. Other diners turned to look at their party, which consisted of the two brothers, Jeremy's sweet but rather mousy wife, Patricia, two foreign business friends of Tony's and their glamorous female companions.

The conversation round the table was easy and entertaining. Joan noticed that the men did most of the talking. One of the glamorous companions was French and spoke little English. The other didn't seem to have much to say – but didn't need to, because like the French-woman, she had the lips, cheeks, height and hair of a society queen or a top model. Joan said an inner prayer of thanks for Auntie Eva's dress. She couldn't hope to compete on the looks front, but at least her outfit was on a par with theirs.

There was something she needed to address with Tony early on, and she did so as politely as she could.

'I'm sorry your wife couldn't join us.'

'Oh, don't worry about Topsy. She's happily at home at the Abbey.' He lowered his voice. 'She doesn't enjoy company as colourful as this, shall we say.'

'Oh.' Joan had expected to feel sorry for poor, absent Topsy, but suddenly didn't.

Tony's business friends were from Hong Kong and Singapore. Both had been educated at British public schools, but their appearance attracted covert stares from among their fellow diners. Joan was sympathetic. When her father had first come to London, he had encountered signs in bed-andbreakfast windows saying, 'No Blacks, no Irish, no Dogs'. The thought of those signs kept a little fire of fury glowing inside her.

'Did you say the Abbey?' she asked Tony, to take her mind off it.

He planted his fork in a buttered spear of asparagus. 'Yes. Wroxham Abbey. Our country place. Goes back to the twelfth century but it's only been in the family since the sixteenth. You should come and see it. Do you ride? There are some excellent hacks in the park.'

'No, I don't ride,' Joan admitted.

'Shoot?'

'Yes. That I can do.'

'Excellent. We must have you down for the weekend. I'm sure Topsy would love to meet you.'

Courses came and went, along with a series of different wines. Joan could at least make sense of their French descriptions, but had never encountered them before. She noticed that the glamorous companions picked at their food, but seemed at home in the general surroundings. If anything, they looked bored. To her surprise, Tony didn't mind her own lack of familiarity with the complicated silverware. In fact, he was kind at explaining which of the vast array of knives and forks to use when. He asked who'd designed her 'delectable' dress, and gave her his full attention when she told him about Auntie Eva.

'Lucky you,' he said. 'We're going to have to take you out more often so we can see what else she can do.'

After the third course, his attention turned to the man sitting on Joan's left, and the chance of trade opening up with China. Joan had come across various Government background papers on the subject in the course of her work, and was at least as well informed on the latest developments as they were, but it was clear her opinion wasn't wanted. She caught mousy Patricia Radnor-Milne's eye, and shared a brief moment of solidarity. Both were used to being ignored when conversation moved to 'serious' things.

Joan didn't really mind. It gave her time to study the two beauties at the table. One wasn't speaking at all, but staring at her plate as if trying to memorise it for an exam. The other was laughing a little too loudly at her date's jokes and occasionally just about stifling a yawn. By the fifth course, Joan had worked out that she had only very recently met her partner, whose name she mispronounced. It took until the sixth course for her to realise what they were, and why they were there. *Oh my God*, she thought. *I'm dining with courtesans.*

She instinctively caught Patricia's eye again. The other woman's quiet resignation seemed to make sense. Joan wondered if this was something she was going to have to adjust to if she wanted to dine in high society. Did men do this on a regular basis? Did they do it so openly? Were such gorgeous women readily available? Joan had always assumed there was something grubby about a tart. Those she knew from Bow were poor and plump and 'obvious', as Auntie Eva would have put it. These two could easily hold their own at a royal reception, as long as they weren't asked to speak.

Tony turned to her and said, 'I'm so sorry, my dear, we were talking shop. Are you having a good time?'

'It's . . . educational,' she said.

'Oh Lord! I never want to be educational! Tell me a bit more about you.'

He was full of questions about her job, and what Her Majesty was like when alone with another woman. 'Does she kick her shoes off? I've always pictured her that way. Does she share tips on hair and lipstick?' Joan sensed the Queen probably did such things with her ladies-in-waiting, but certainly not with her. And she wouldn't have talked about it anyway. She was surprised he even asked.

Leaning back in his chair, Tony was approached by a couple of other diners, keen to press his hand with promises of meetings soon. His younger brother, by contrast, attracted only brief, distant nods, despite his key palace role. Joan realised that if the Radnor-Milnes were responsible for anything going on there, Tony, not Jeremy, would be the instigator of it. She would need to find an excuse to see him again, and soon.

Dessert came, and then coffee. Both the escorts looked bored out of their minds by now. Had life been like this for the dead woman in diamonds? Joan wondered. There was a ripple round the table and she realised that Jeremy was signalling to his wife, who nodded. He stood up and so did she.

'You must forgive us. Very busy day tomorrow, and a babysitter to get back to. Tony, don't give Joan the third degree. She's here to enjoy herself.'

Tony grinned.

'She's the soul of discretion. In such a pretty package. I tried and tried and she wouldn't tell me a thing.'

Without warning, Joan suddenly felt the warmth and weight of his hand on her thigh. At first, she thought it was a mistake. She moved her leg, but his hand moved with it. She felt herself go rigid, unable to speak. In theory, she knew what to do – stab him with the nearest fork – but this was the Ritz. Duchesses might be watching. Surely it would be overreacting to make a scene? For a minute, she couldn't move. Tony smiled at his brother's retreating back, as if nothing was going on at all.

When she couldn't bear it any more, Joan reached out and 'accidentally' knocked over Tony's glass of wine, so that several waiting staff hovered around them and both his hands were occupied in the clean-up operation. Soon, he was calling for the bill and making plans.

He addressed the table. 'The night is young. My little brother may have to scuttle off home, but we have the town to ourselves. Joan and I will be exploring the delights of the 400 Club. Will you join us?'

Joan sat rigidly beside him. He brushed his fingers lightly across the hairs of her arm. He smiled at her, and there was no threat in it, or even a question. It was as if the evening was always going to end this way.

The almost silent French girl stood up.

'Powder room,' she explained.

Feeling dizzy, Joan stood up to join her. They wended their way through the tables into the dimly lit lobby, where a pianist was playing to couples at small tables, and down the stairs to the ladies' cloakroom. When they emerged from their cubicles, the escort sat at one of the mirrors designed for makeup renewal and pulled out a lipstick from a little clutch bag.

'Ça va?' she asked Joan in the mirror. 'You look . . .' She shrugged, not finding the word.

'Pale,' Joan said in French, taking stock of her own face. 'Yes, I am.'

'You speak French!' the girl said delightedly in her own language. 'Are you all right?'

'Not really. I think I must go home. Tell Mr Radnor-Milne I felt unwell. Blame it on the oysters. No – don't do that. Say something disagreed with me.'

'Of course. If you like.' She frowned. 'He made a move?'

'He did,' Joan admitted.

'But you expected it, no?'

'No, I didn't,' Joan said.

And from the look the girl gave her, she realised she was the only person at the table who had been so innocent.

★ ★ ★

The concierge put Joan into one of the taxis queuing up outside the hotel. It took less than twenty minutes for her to get home to Pimlico in the night-time traffic. Joan knew somehow that Hector Ross would be waiting up for her and used the time to shed all the hot, bitter tears she could manage.

It mattered, because she prided herself on being clever and good at reading people. It mattered, because she thought that when she entered the new worlds of the Private Office and Dolphin Square, she had become a different person. One who was taken seriously. One who mattered herself.

She had braced herself for poor treatment by the Radnor-Milnes, but for three hours, she had honestly believed that Tony saw her as a senior member of the Private Office – a girl with the world at her feet, like Fiona Matherton-Smith, in a fairy-tale dress, with a shining future ahead of her. She mopped her wet cheeks with the back of her hand. What a fool. All he saw was a cheap little Irish tart who would sleep with him for her dinner and be grateful. No need to ask.

Posh girls like Fiona weren't exempt from bastards with a sense of entitlement, Joan knew that for a stone-cold fact. During an urgent, whispered conversation in a quiet palace corridor, the last APS had explained that one of her top-drawer boyfriends had assured her after a hunt ball that 'it didn't really count' if they 'got up close and personal' standing up. Fiona, who had never been told the facts of life, wasn't even sure what they had done under the voluminous skirts of her designer dress. Joan had encouraged her to talk to the family doctor. 'It'll be all right, won't it?' she'd asked, too shocked to even cry. Joan reassured her that it would, but privately thought it depended on what your definition of 'all right' was.

Joan had thought of herself as cynical and worldly-wise. Tony saw her as a joke. An available joke. All that talk of riding at the Abbey: of course he knew a girl like her wouldn't ride. When he asked about her family, he'd been privately amusing himself with how the other half lived. She saw herself now as Hector must have seen her: the bare shoulders, the sheer stockings, the sophisticated hair. Did he think that of her too?

'Cheer up, love!' She looked up to see the taxi driver watching her in the rear-view mirror. 'It might never 'appen.'

'It won't, trust me,' she muttered.

'Give us a smile, then. Oh, all right. 'Ave it your own way.'

They reached the river and she saw that they were only five minutes away from home.

As hot shame and fury coursed through her, she thought of something else. Had tonight's introduction been arranged deliberately? Not just to humiliate her, but to use her to get closer to the Queen? She remembered thinking that of the two brothers, if anyone was responsible for the plot it would be Tony. Sir Hugh seemed so upright, and Miles Urquhart so childish, that if she had to guess right now which of the three men in moustaches was trying to sabotage Her Majesty, she would say it was almost certainly Jeremy, in service of his brother. There was nothing she wouldn't put past either of them. Nothing at all.

The taxi pulled up outside Dolphin Square and she extracted a note from her evening bag to pay the driver. As she got out, the cold air hit her and she realised that shame and fury had been doing a lot of her thinking for her. She loathed Tony Radnor-Milne, loathed his brother for making the introduction, and his brother's insipid wife for assuming the worst of her. But that didn't mean to say they were traitors.

Only that they might be.

CHAPTER 23

Hector Ross was in his dressing gown, waiting for her at the open door to the sitting room.

'I'm making cocoa,' he said. 'Would you like some?'

She didn't answer, slamming the door behind her and heading for the sanctuary of her bedroom. The last thing she needed was a man fussing over her. But the bedroom walls were closing in on her and it didn't take long for her to realise she needed distraction.

She craved something sweet, and something strong. She would never be able to sleep like this. She emerged five minutes later, head held high, clad in thick pyjamas under her kimono. There was no hot water at this time of night. She would shower in the morning, as soon as she could.

Hector was still at the stove, stirring. How long did it take to make one cup of cocoa?

'Shall I add some for you?' he asked.

She nodded.

'Would you like a shot of brandy in it, perhaps? As a digestif?'

There was gentleness in his studied offhandedness. She gritted her teeth and had to wipe away her budding tears with the back of her wrist, when he wasn't looking.

When it was ready, Hector brought two mugs to the little round dining table and added brandy from a decanter. Joan cupped her mug with both hands.

After a minute, she lifted her head. 'How did you know?'

'I know Tony,' he said, simply. 'And I'd like to think I know you a little bit. I wasn't sure you'd get on.'

'He seemed to think we would.'

'Ah. Well, that's the point.'

She jutted out her chin. 'Why didn't you warn me?'

Hector looked aggrieved. 'I saw the looks you were giving me. You didn't exactly invite my opinion. So, what happened?'

'He invited me to a jazz club.' Hector raised an eyebrow. 'And he spent the meal telling me all about his ancestral home and his boys at Eton and his bloody shooting weekends.'

'Mmm, yes,' he said. 'He would. He was like that at Oxford. Although back then I seem to remember that it was other people's ancestral homes that he invited one to.'

'Does he do this to every woman he meets?'

'Only the ones he finds attractive.'

He tipped another generous slug of brandy into her near-empty mug, and she took a good glug.

'It's not Tony,' she said, dabbing at another infuriating tear. 'It's just . . . getting used to the new job, really. Not that I'm not good at it – I'm very good. But . . . it's hard to know where to fit in.' Now she'd started talking she couldn't stop. 'I'm not related to half of them, like Fiona. One of the men treats me like a speck of dust, another makes no secret of how much he'd love to be rid of me, even though I do half his typing, on top of my own work. I thought the third was all right . . . But, ha!' She rolled her eyes. 'Obviously not. I'm nice as hell to the secretaries, but they cold-shoulder me too. They were lovely before I got promoted and I'd swear I haven't changed.' She realised how much she was gabbling and was horrified. It was the brandy talking, and the shock. 'This is all hush-hush, do you understand?' she said, glaring at Hector across the table.

He shrugged and said nothing.

Joan looked down at her mug, which was inexplicably empty, reached for the decanter and poured herself some more. She waited for him to tell her off for blabbing secrets, or patronise her in some way for whining like a baby, which she had undoubtedly done, or drinking too much, which she was.

Instead, he asked, 'Do you mind if I smoke?'

She didn't. He offered her one of his cigarettes and she took it gratefully. It reminded her of Bletchley, standing outside the huts, looking up at the sky and praying for the citizens of Coventry and the

East End, the submariners in the Atlantic, the fighter pilots heading out to France. That's where she'd learned to smoke, not that she did it often as it made her wheeze. The taste of tobacco in her mouth brought back the camaraderie and terror, the intense pressure and a never-to-be-repeated lust for life that they had shared in the midst of it all. It was strangely uplifting.

'Well done for getting home safely,' Hector said quietly.

She was glad he'd changed the subject from her little rant. He seemed deeply relieved.

'Tony was never going to harm me,' she assured him.

But he *was*, and he had. Not only by what he did, but by what she didn't do. How hard was it to stab a man with a fork? Why couldn't she?

'He's a very successful man,' Hector said. 'If I could afford to put money in one of his companies I'd probably make a fortune. But that doesn't mean he isn't an outright bloody blackguard.'

Perhaps he hadn't judged her harshly as she'd left the flat this evening, after all, Joan thought. She had the impression that, sweetly, he would have liked to have ridden in on his charger and rescued her from Tony's evil clutches. Instead, he'd made her cocoa.

Then she thought of something else.

'You said you knew Tony at university. Was he the person who told you I was looking for somewhere to live?'

'Yes, that's right. I'd mentioned at the club that I was thinking of getting rid of the flat. A few days later he rang me up and told me about Sir Hugh's predicament, and you.'

'Mmm.'

But he *hadn't* told Hector about Joan McGraw – he'd mentioned John. And 'John' was somebody that Hector would be happy to share a flat with, occasionally. He might have said no to a 'Joan', but now that she was here . . . and given the kind of low-class girl she was . . . who knew what might ensue?

Joan was either very paranoid about Tony Radnor-Milne, or she was right.

CHAPTER 24

Darbishire put his empty glass down on the gingham-covered table.

'Another one?'

The inspector definitely didn't want a top-up of whatever gloopy green liqueur he was being offered. The first had been bad enough.

'Yeah, thanks,' he said. 'That'd be nice.'

'I thought you'd like it,' Jimmy Broad said with a grin. 'Got a bit of an edge. Unusual.'

Darbishire couldn't tell if the other man was teasing him or telling it straight. Either way, it didn't matter. One of Billy Hill's most trusted henchmen was talking to him face to face, and right now, he'd down a pint glass of that foul liquid if it helped.

Jimmy was solicitous. 'I 'ear you've been 'aving some trouble,' he said, filling his own tumbler with water from a rustic jug. 'With this little strangling case of yours. 'Ow can I 'elp?'

'It's kind of you to offer.'

'Anytime. You only 'ave to ask.'

Jimmy sat back and smiled from across the table. The besuited man sitting beside him in the dingy Notting Hill restaurant smiled too. So did the gorilla at the door, who made sure nobody else was getting in or out.

Darbishire did *not* only have to ask. The men of the Billy Hill gang didn't normally try to assist the police in any way – except by providing work for them to do. Everything about this situation was unusual, including the fact that the inspector was not tucked up in bed at this very late hour. His wife would be worrying about him. He was worried about himself.

'It's about Dino Perez,' he said, knowing Jimmy already knew this part. 'Or Nico Rodriguez, as I should call him. Known to the police in Argentina. Arms dealer. Fixer. International man of mystery, you might say.'

It had taken a while to find out Perez's real identity. He had no known friends and family either here or in Argentina, his forged papers were designed to be confusing, and the bloating and discolouration of his face when he was found hadn't helped at all. However, Buenos Aires eventually came up with a match, and now the information was flooding in. Rodriguez was of interest to police forces in four continents.

Jimmy nodded and said nothing.

'Quite the globe-trotter,' Darbishire went on. 'Contacts in the Middle East, North Africa. The man who could get you whatever you wanted. He liked to dabble in cocaine.'

At this, Jimmy raised a hand. 'I wouldn't know about that.'

Darbishire took this little denial on board. 'He had a taste for the high life, let's say. Gambling in Monaco and Morocco. Putting a packet on the horses over here. He was seen in the company of one or two of your associates, Jimmy, before he died. So, perhaps that's what you can help me with.' *God help me*, he added, privately. These encounters always looked so smooth in the movies, but he was sweating in his shoes.

'I'm not sure I can, entirely,' Jimmy answered. 'Not with what Rodriguez was up to in London, at any rate. What a man does with his leisure time is up to 'im, isn't it? It's a free country.'

Darbishire didn't bother to argue. 'Then why am I here?'

'It's what 'e *didn't* do,' Jimmy said.

'OK.'

'And what 'e *didn't* do, is rattle the boss. In fact, they were friends.'

'Your boss has been known to do a bit of damage to his friends,' Darbishire pointed out. Billy Hill was famous for it. Sudden, vicious violence. Plentiful blood and scarring. He enjoyed it, and it was the main reason he'd been the top dog in the London underworld for ten years and counting.

Jimmy assented. 'Ah, well, that's the thing. You know Mister 'Ill. 'Ow 'e likes to operate.'

'I do. He likes a knife. And one was found in Rodriguez's eye,' Darbishire added. Jimmy clearly knew it already and had something to tell.

'But what *kind* of knife?' Jimmy asked. 'That's the thing. The one in the eye was a flick knife, wasn't it? From America, or Italy?'

'Germany, in fact.'

'Doesn't matter. Mister 'Ill, as 'e will 'appily tell you, prefers the 'umble chiv. Nothing like a nice little razor blade to do the job. Slice down the face, always down, and you make your mark without doing something dangerous, like nicking an artery. You don't want to do that, because you might kill someone, see? Billy may be up for a fight – we know 'e is – but 'e doesn't like murder. Too many consequences. It isn't what you might call 'is "modus operandus".'

'So you're trying to tell me he didn't kill Rodriguez, or get anyone in the gang to do it?'

Jimmy leaned back, relaxed. 'That's the ticket. No reason to – like I said, they was friends. Plus, if 'e *did* 'ave a knife like that, 'e'd know what to do with it. See what I mean? Any one of us would. Not stick it in 'is side like some sort of 'andle.'

'How'd you know about that?' Darbishire asked.

Jimmy smiled. 'We've got friends at the Yard, same as you.'

'I see.'

Suddenly, Jimmy leaned forward until his face was right up in Darbishire's, and the smile was replaced with a snarl. 'I'm not sure you *do* see, Inspector. Mister 'Ill's played nice all these years, looking after 'is patch in London, keeping 'is 'ead down. And what's 'appened? The police are tapping 'is telephone! That's 'ardly cricket, is it, Fred? Can I call you Fred? 'E's fed up with it. Up to the back teeth. 'Is girlfriend's in jail, for a *minor* altercation. Those injuries'll 'eal without 'ardly a mark. 'E's thinking of moving out of town, and believe me, you won't want what's coming next, Fred. It'll make us look like choirboys.'

Darbishire took a sip of green gloop and swallowed. He tried to maintain a steady tone.

'Even so, I'd still like to know what Rodriguez was doing over here. And how he got involved with the Raffles agency.'

'What makes you think I'd know about that?'

Darbishire decided to show his hand a little. He and his team had been very busy recently. If Jimmy realised how much they knew, perhaps he'd be rattled enough to give some more. Billy Hill obviously wanted some sort of deal, or Darbishire wouldn't be here at all.

'Rodriguez was a gambler,' he pointed out. 'He liked to spend time in a club in Tangier called the Chamberlain, overlooking the Mediterranean. That club is partly owned by a company that has an interest in the Raffles escort agency. At least one of your associates is a regular customer of Raffles, and Rodriguez also liked to visit when he was in town. You can see the connections, Jimmy.' He raised his hands. 'What am I supposed to think?'

Jimmy took a sip of water, cleaned the top of his glass with a napkin, and sat back with a look of amusement.

'Looks like you've got it all worked out,' he said. 'A man likes to make a bet, and 'e's got an eye for the ladies, ipsus factus, 'e must be in with another man wot likes a bet and likes the ladies. I see your reasoning. Very clever, Fred. Well done.'

Darbishire tried to imagine how an actor like Dick Powell would look in this scenario: sardonic, inscrutable. He'd be hiding the fact that his adversary had never looked less rattled. That Jimmy had pointed out the holes in his best argument. That maybe there was no deal.

'We'll find out who owns those companies.'

'You go ahead, Fred. But just remember . . .' Jimmy leaned in again and patted Darbishire gently on the cheek '. . . the skin on their little boat races was pristine, from what I 'eard. No chiv. Wrong knife. No argument with Billy that you know of – or you'd 'ave told me. And I can assure you, there wasn't one. Never 'eard of the blonde. Billy's only got eyes for Gypsy, and she's black-'aired, as you know. Raven.' He sat straight and added, 'I like the sound of that nightclub, though. In Tangier, you said? I'll tell Billy. 'E's looking for somewhere new.' He yawned and nodded to the gorilla at the door. 'Nice chatting to you, Fred. It's always good to clear the air. You can see yourself out.'

With a final, defiant gulp of the green gloop in his shot glass, Darbishire did.

CHAPTER 25

Joan made sure it was her turn to collect the red boxes from Her Majesty in the morning. The Queen looked up from the last paper, before slipping it inside.

'Is there any news?'

'Not exactly, ma'am,' Joan admitted, knowing she meant her suspicions about the plot to undermine her. 'But I'd like to suggest a name.'

'Go ahead.'

Joan named Jeremy, the press secretary.

The Queen nodded gravely. 'What makes you say that?'

'To be perfectly honest, ma'am, no one in your Private Office likes me working here, but Jeremy pretends he does. Both Sir Hugh and Miles have given me good advice, whatever they think of me. Jeremy's brother propositioned me last night.'

The Queen's eyebrows shot up. 'Tony Radnor-Milne did?'

'You know him?'

'Not well. Poor Topsy. And I'm sorry. That can't have been pleasant.'

'No. But I'm afraid that's all I have. It isn't really proof of any kind. Is it Jeremy who you had in mind, too?' she asked.

The Queen fiddled with her pen. 'It is. I saw him surveying the room in Paris, where I was surrounded by excited Frenchmen and women, and he looked both disdainful and slightly furious. It's supposed to be a *good* thing if we're popular. He seemed to disagree.'

'He could have quite easily organised the disappearance of your speech,' Joan suggested. 'He has the senior ladies in the typing pool wrapped around his finger.'

'He might well have, but that's not how it was done, supposedly.'

'Oh?'

The Queen hadn't told Joan this part yet. 'Sir Hugh looked into it for himself when he got back from Paris. Apparently, the instruction had come directly from the Embassy there – and it had come from Sir Hugh himself.'

'Oh!'

'A junior girl swore that Sir Hugh had spoken to her personally on the telephone. If someone was doing an impression, it was a good one.'

Not Urquhart, Joan thought. His impressions were terrible. But Jeremy Radnor-Milne was good.

'And any of the three men could have slipped a message about my food preferences to the chefs at the Hôtel de Ville,' the Queen went on. 'Just as they could have typed that message about Ingrid Kern. Well, I'm not entirely sure Hugh or Miles has ever typed anything, but if it was part of a conspiracy, they could find someone who can.'

Joan agreed that none of these things was hard. 'The question is, why would they want to?'

'Quite. And until we know that, I don't want to interfere by starting a proper investigation. Whoever he is, he'd just stop for a while. I need him to carry on so we can find him. Ideally, before he does any real damage.'

Joan nodded. 'I'll do whatever I can.'

★ ★ ★

At lunchtime, she was surprised by the arrival of two dozen long-stemmed pink roses, with a note saying, 'I hope you're not allergic to these'.

Joan was relieved that Miles Urquhart was in conference with the other men in moustaches, so she had the office to herself. She removed the note and burned it in the fireplace with a lighter. She'd recognise the handwriting again if she saw it.

What to make of it?

She had assumed Tony Radnor-Milne would instantly see through last night's flimsy excuse, and had been worried about his reaction. She certainly hadn't expected roses. Was this some sort of double bluff? Or was he really so self-opinionated that he assumed she would only reject him if she was genuinely physically incapacitated?

She gave the bouquet to the secretaries.

'The smell makes me a little nauseous. I'm sure you'll enjoy them more than me.'

'But they're so heavenly! You must have made an impression, you lucky thing!' one of the younger women said, before the others stared her down for being spontaneous and friendly.

That wasn't the end of it.

'Ha! I hear you have a secret admirer,' Urquhart told her on his return to his desk. 'Tony Radnor-Milne, no less.'

'Not so secret, then,' Joan said. There was clearly no point denying it. 'How did you know?'

'Jeremy told me. Tony was quite taken with you, apparently.'

'I hadn't realised he was married,' she said, watching for his reaction. Was this part of the plot? Was Urquhart in on it after all? Why on earth was he being so friendly, suddenly?

'Oh, that! He means no harm. His wife, Lady Jessica, is quite intimidating. I'm not surprised he enjoys little distractions.'

Joan kept her seething to herself. 'He invited me down to the Abbey,' she explained. 'He wants me to go shooting.' Since they were discussing Tony, she might as well tell him everything. She didn't want there to be any secrets, or the suggestion of them. She felt compromised enough.

'Ah. He does that to all the pretty girls,' Urquhart said. 'Harmless fun, but I wouldn't go, if I were you. Lady Jessica – Topsy, we call her – doesn't like it. And it's her home, after all.'

'Yes, I suppose so,' Joan said, unsure why he needed to stress the point.

'I mean, her ancestral home,' Urquhart said. 'Tony married into money. And nobility. Topsy's the niece of the Marquess of Middlesex. Of course, Tony's a millionaire in his own right now, but the Abbey is hers, strictly speaking. It's been in her family for generations.'

'Oh. What about Tony's family?' Joan asked.

'Lawyers, I think. His grandfather worked at the Old Bailey. Why?'

'I didn't know, that's all.'

Urquhart grunted. 'He likes to give the impression he's the Lord

God Almighty, but he's terribly bourgeois. His father had to save for him to go to Eton.'

'I see.'

Joan resisted a sudden impulse to laugh. Urquhart's raging snobbery put him inadvertently on her side. So, the star of the Ritz was 'bourgeois', was he? His father had to save up for boarding school fees? The landed gentry performance was just an act? It probably didn't make him any less dangerous, but Tony had made her feel foolish last night, and now she knew *he* was.

'He's undoubtedly clever,' Urquhart acknowledged. 'He got a first in PPE, went into the City and made a fortune in rubber during the war, selling essentials to the military.'

'What, tyres?'

'Ah, um, yes, tyres . . . if you like.'

The penny dropped. 'Oh,' Joan said.

'There was a big demand for rubber in the army. It set him up for life. Now Tony has fingers in pies all over the place. He's very good at anticipating the next big thing. He's expanded into oil and plastics. Something to do with aviation – jet planes, I think. They need materials that can withstand high temperatures.'

'He told you about this? You know him well?' Joan asked.

'Not very well, but he was trying to get me to invest in one of his new ventures. However, I prefer the land. More reliable. Give me a decent farm and some tenancies any day.'

This was a side of the DPS that Joan hadn't anticipated. She had no idea that he was rich enough to mull over his investments. He never normally talked about money. Or indeed much with her at all, of course.

'And there's another thing,' he added. 'While we're on the subject.'

Subject of what? Joan wondered. 'Yes?'

'Major Ross. Jeremy said you're staying at his place.'

'Did he?' Jeremy was being very loose-lipped this morning.

'Yes. You know about Ross, I suppose. Damn sad story. Wife ran off with the family doctor.'

'No, I didn't know.'

Urquhart regarded her grimly. He was clearly trying to tell her something.

'Happened after the war. Ross was busy clearing up a lot of difficult situations in Europe. Away a lot, as he had been during the fighting, of course. His wife volunteered at the local cottage hospital. Fell for the sawbones. Wouldn't leave Ross, wouldn't exactly stay. Dashed awkward for all concerned.'

'I'm sure it is.'

'He was a bit of a hero. Perhaps you know. Various missions one doesn't talk about. More medals than he can easily account for. Dashed unfair. Awful for the man.'

'It sounds it.'

'As I say, she didn't exactly leave him in the end. Other people's marriages – none of our business.'

'I so agree.'

'Good. Yes, um. Good.'

Joan watched him go back to his papers, as if they had just had a robust conversation. She couldn't exactly tell whether he had been encouraging her to console the poor, sad war hero, or firmly warning her against going near him. She suspected the latter, which might explain Urquhart's decision to talk to her. It was good advice. Remaining unattached was by far the safest, most sensible thing to do.

She would have to abandon the flat at some point soon. It was such a shame. She would really miss the cocoa.

CHAPTER 26

On the 18th of May, the Queen and her entourage left for Hull, and from there to Denmark on the Royal Yacht *Britannia*, in a flurry of bags and boxes, and last-minute instructions for those left behind.

For a week, Joan had the run of the North Wing corridor to herself. The palace took on a different character when the royal couple were away. The pressure to provide perfect service to the family and hospitality for guests was replaced by a more methodical work rate, as each department used the time to take stock and prepare for more busy times ahead.

From her desk, she obsessively scanned all of the newspapers and the embassy updates for the slightest sign of anything going wrong. Ingrid Kern, she was relieved to see, had stayed in London. Joan knew how tiring the itinerary was, but in all the newsreels, the Queen looked cheerful and relaxed. The Duke of Edinburgh was busy, dutiful and happy enough to follow his wife around porcelain workshops and bottling factories.

Joan viewed these visits in an entirely different light now. Before, it had always looked easy enough to sit and wave, or stand and wave, or walk around and shake a few hands and nod at a piece of machinery. But knowing as she did that every ten-minute slot was accounted for, and each half-hour included a hundred people who could be inadvertently insulted if they weren't smiled at or asked the right question, and twenty pressmen who would be happy to capture the moment on celluloid if it happened, Joan saw each day as an endurance test.

The Queen insisted, even in private, that she loved it. 'People are so interesting, don't you think?' Joan still thought it was a strange gift, bordering on madness, to enjoy being in a goldfish bowl. No wonder the Queen enjoyed solitary dog walks when she got home.

★ ★ ★

This time, the royal yacht sailed back without incident and the men in moustaches crawled into the office a day later, somewhat grey after a choppy North Sea crossing. Not all of them enjoyed travel as much as Her Majesty.

After several cups of coffee and talk of minor triumphs, Miles Urquhart was forced to admit that Joan's assistance in setting up this visit 'hadn't been as bad as I feared'.

'Did everything go to plan?' she asked.

'More or less.' He digressed for several minutes about the set-up of the bottling factory, and the difficulty of declaring all the beer they were presented with at customs.

'There was nothing embarrassing? No slip-ups?'

'No, of course not!' he said. 'What do you take us for? We manage these visits with military precision. You'll see for yourself one day. Possibly.'

'I hope so.'

'Well, there was *one* embarrassment, I suppose,' he admitted. 'Poor Bobo Macdonald. She came down on the second day looking red as a tomato. Her cheeks and chin were itching like billy-o, poor creature. Coming up in hives. Her Majesty sweetly told her to go and rest, but of course Bobo was having none of it. "She needs me, and I'll be there. There's too much to do." She's made of Scottish granite, that woman. Sterling individual. She slapped on some calamine and carried on as usual with the frocks and furbelows. Reminds me of my own nanny. I think they manufacture them that way north of the border.'

'Was she ill?' Joan asked.

'I did wonder,' he said, 'but it went away after a day or two. It nearly caused an international incident because the housekeeper was convinced it was measles. She wanted us all quarantined. But Bobo seemed to think it was Her Majesty's makeup ointments. She'd been trying it out because it "smelled funny", if you can believe it. Obviously, she had some sort of sensitivity, or it might have been an allergy,

I suppose. Jeremy suggested wearing a yashmak for as long as it lasted. *Very* funny. Anyway, she's all right now.'

★ ★ ★

'It wasn't an allergy, was it?' Joan asked the Queen.

They were walking in the gardens of Windsor Castle together, while five corgis – all related – snuffled near the rose bushes.

'No, it wasn't,' the Queen said grimly. 'Bobo's face cream ran out, so I said she could use mine. She said it wasn't the smell that worried her, so much as the fact that it didn't *have* a smell. She knows Elizabeth Arden. It wasn't *quite* the right colour, either – too grey – but it was a new tube and the packaging had been intact. So she smoothed some on her face and within a matter of hours, her skin erupted.'

'Poor woman!'

'She was quite indomitable about it. I assured her I could manage perfectly well without her until she felt better, but she was positively offended by the idea. And the housekeeper at the residence was rather *mean* to her, but of course one couldn't say anything.'

'If the packaging looked untouched, it must have been a professional job . . .'

'I know,' the Queen said. She glanced across at the youngest corgis. 'Whisky! Sherry! Come back here this minute, you terrors. That's better. Go over there, with your mother. What was I saying? Oh, yes, the packaging. It's worrying, isn't it?'

'It's a step up in their behaviour,' Joan agreed. 'It suggests they have technical support. They're not entirely opportunistic.'

'It still feels so scattergun, though.' The Queen looked up at the castle, which loomed grey and solid in the background. She sighed. 'I mean, face cream! Honestly! And itching powder – that's what it must have been, some industrial version of it. It's such a schoolboy prank, isn't it? Like apple-pie beds and buckets on doors.'

'Did they take the tube to have it tested?' Joan asked.

The Queen gave her a sidelong look. 'They couldn't. By the time Bobo thought to look for it, half the residence knew about her skin reaction. Several servants had been in and out of our rooms, any one of whom might have spirited it away. I helped in the search personally, and there was nowhere we didn't check . . . But there was no sign of it.'

'Tony Radnor-Milne is interested in technology,' Joan said. 'He may well have contacts in the research world who could tamper with a new tube of cream and make it look untouched.'

'Sir Hugh's brother is a world-class chemist.'

'Oh.'

'Professor Masson has a whole Cambridge laboratory at his disposal. He's an expert in insulin manufacture. I can't believe he'd do anything so petty and juvenile. But if his brother asked him to, and said it was a joke . . .'

'At least it was only face cream, ma'am,' Joan said, in an effort to be encouraging. Her Majesty was looking very glum by now.

The Queen shook her head. 'Ah, but I'm not Bobo. I'm not sure I could have carried on with a raging itch and skin that looked like Vesuvius, in front of all those people . . . It wouldn't have been fair on them, as much as anything. It wasn't a pretty sight.'

'What would you have done, ma'am?'

The Queen didn't answer straightaway. She called the corgis to her and bent down to stroke the closest. When she stood up again, she stared thoughtfully at the sky.

'I don't know, Joan. I really don't know.'

CHAPTER 27

'Y̶ou're not aware of anyone who wishes harm on me, are you?' the Queen asked the prime minister at their meeting the following Wednesday.

It took place as usual in the pale blue sitting room in Buckingham Palace that she liked to use as an audience room. Hard to imagine here, among the porcelain and Canalettos, that she was worrying about something as mundane as the contents of a tube of Elizabeth Arden.

'Goodness me, no!' Harold Macmillan said, smiling at the outrageousness of the idea.

He was a confident politician who had settled quickly into the job. According to Sir Hugh, he had a note pinned to the door of the Cabinet Room in 10 Downing Street, saying *Quiet, calm deliberation / Disentangles every knot*. It was a quotation from *The Gondoliers*. Not only was it sensible advice, especially for the Cabinet, but anyone who could quote Gilbert and Sullivan as a mantra for running the country was a man she could do business with.

'Not the Russians?' she suggested.

'Oh no, ma'am. They may bluster, but I believe even they're quite fond of you, really. Why do you ask?'

'A few odd things have happened recently.'

She didn't elaborate, but he saw that she was serious. 'I don't think you need worry, ma'am. No friend wishes you ill, and if anything were to happen your popularity would only soar, and your enemies would suffer.'

'My enemies?'

'If you have any. Which, as I say, I doubt. For us as a country . . .

That's a different matter. These are choppy waters, ma'am, as you know. We need all the friends we can get – but you're good at getting them.'

'I wondered . . . Singapore and Ghana gaining their independence this year. Everyone had been quite charming to me in person, but behind the scenes . . . ?'

'Behind the scenes, they have a lot to say about the British Empire, ma'am, not all of it favourable. But they're complimentary about you personally. Were it not for your focus on friendship, things would have been much more difficult.'

'Are you sure?' she asked. That focus had been her father's legacy and she wanted it to be hers too. But was it working?

'Quite sure,' he said.

'What about the Americans? Not the president – I know he's an ally, and you worked with him in the war – but America is a big country.'

Macmillan gave her a warm, paternal smile and a look that suggested if he could have patted her on the hand, he would have.

'I'm not sure what troubles you, but I might remind you that my mother was from that great country. I speak as half American when I say that they are in awe of you too.'

'Surely not "in awe", Prime Minister?' He thought he was helping, but he wasn't.

He shrugged. 'You'll see. And you know how much faith I have in you, ma'am. I hope for great things from this trip. Since the flight of Burgess and Maclean . . .'

'I know all about Burgess and Maclean.'

'The ripples of their treachery still reverberate across the pond. I need hardly remind you, we're locked out of their atomic programme, we've lost the trust of the CIA . . .'

He *did* hardly need to remind her. She knew all of this. After the disaster of that flight to Moscow six years ago, and MI6's inability to do anything about it, the Americans were convinced that Burgess and Maclean weren't the only communist sympathisers at Cambridge to have been recruited by the KGB. It made her next state visit even more freighted with consequence. And she must do it without being able to trust the food she ate, the people she travelled with, or even the contents of her vanity case.

'. . . But I have great hope for the future,' he continued. 'I enjoyed my time working with General Eisenhower. He was tough on us during Suez, but he did warn us, and we didn't listen. Now we must. But we have a lot to offer the Americans. Our day is coming . . .'

'Is it?' she asked. 'I'm glad to hear you say that, Prime Minister. When I travel round the country, of course I'm opening new buildings and celebrating great history, but I hear so much anxiety. From farmers to factory workers . . . They don't understand our place in the world. They're worried about inflation. They don't know what's coming next.'

Was it an internal plot against her? she wondered suddenly. If so, why focus on her foreign visits? Did they want the country to be taken over?

Macmillan smiled at her again. 'I hear the same things in the party. They do like to worry there – it's something of a religion. But as I like to point out, part of the problem is that we're growing. We're making things and selling them like never before. We like to grumble, ma'am, but I remind them we're heading for a state of prosperity we've never seen before. Most people have never had it so good.'

For the first time, she smiled back.

'Really?'

He nodded, clearly pleased with his response and its effect on her. 'Take courage, ma'am. This is the new Elizabethan Age. Whatever warning signs you see, I wouldn't worry.'

The Queen normally liked to follow her prime minister's advice, but this time it would have been helpful if he *had* pointed out some nation or person in particular to worry about. Nevertheless, she found his words comforting, for the country at least. Ten years ago, the very dark days of the war had given way to the giddy optimism of peace. Perhaps that was around the corner again, though it was hard to imagine it.

CHAPTER 28

'It strikes me, sir,' DS Woolgar said, 'that somebody needs to go to Monaco in person. Get people talking. Find out exactly what Rodriguez was doing there. What he was buying or selling. Who he hung around with.'

Since the breakthrough from Buenos Aires, there had been talk of little else in the Chelsea police station beyond the activities of the nefarious Rodriguez around the edge of the Mediterranean and the Arabian Sea.

'And that would be you, Sergeant, would it?' Darbishire asked, as straight-faced as he could manage.

'I don't see why not, sir,' Woolgar told him, stoutly.

He was looking tanned and fit – fitter than usual – after a successful few days on the river. Woolgar had been absent with leave quite a bit in May, and the Metropolitan Police Athletic Club rowing eight had just come second in some sort of regatta challenge cup. They had stormed past the Australians and were pipped at the post – or 'beaten by a canvas', whatever that was – by the team from Harvard University. The young sergeant was very full of himself. And now he wanted to go to Monte Carlo on the investigation's budget.

'Speak French, do you?' Darbishire asked.

'I did it for my school certificate. Besides, they all speak English down there, don't they, sir? The thing is, I know the case inside out. I could ask all the right questions.'

'Do you picture yourself in a dinner jacket, by any chance?' Darbishire asked. 'With a gun in your pocket? And a large pile of chips and a wilting woman at the table? Are you by any chance James Bond?'

'Who, sir?'

'The spy. He gambles in French casinos. And why not go to Tangier, while you're about it? Rodriguez went there, too.'

'It has to be Monaco, sir. There was a man in the Harvard boat . . .'

'Oh Christ! Not the Harvard bloody boat again.'

'. . . And we were drinking together afterwards,' Woolgar persisted. 'They got very friendly after the third or fourth pint. He was talking about the Chelsea murders . . .'

Darbishire groaned. 'They're not talking about this in New York, are they?'

'Boston, sir. And yes, they are. It's in the papers because of the tart in the tiara. Diamonds always make the papers. So do—'

'I don't want to hear the theories of a Boston newspaper editor!'

Woolgar looked slightly hurt. 'He's not a newspaper editor. He's the number eight in the crew.'

'I don't care if he's the number fifty!' Darbishire realised he was sounding touchy about Woolgar's posh new friends, and about his own recent lack of progress, since the unexpected dead end with Billy Hill. 'I'm sorry. Go on.'

'His name's O'Donnell and his dad owns a boatbuilding company,' Woolgar explained. 'They travel a lot. Fancy places. And his dad was saying that last summer he ran into Lord Seymour at a spa in Switzerland. He goes there every year for a health cure, sir. He met his wife there . . .'

'And?'

'Lord Seymour was putting it about that he'd recently won a million francs on blackjack in a casino in Monte Carlo. So, O'Donnell – the father, but the son agrees – thinks that maybe he wanted to relive his big night when he got back to London. Seymour asks for a girl who looks like Grace Kelly, Princess Grace, as she now is. He gives her the tiara; there's no *way* it was stolen from that safe of his. *He* was the client, not Rodriguez – but he has some hold over the agency, so he gets them to tell us it was the *victim* who booked the girl, in the name of Perez, and they get Beryl White to lie about it too. I mean, it's obvious she wasn't telling the whole truth, sir.'

'I know that, Woolgar. But you're forgetting, Seymour didn't have time for any of this. He didn't leave the Houses of Parliament until after Rodriguez arrived in Cresswell Place.'

'Ah. That's what you're supposed to think, sir. But we only have one witness's word for it. Bear with me.'

Darbishire raised a sceptical eyebrow.

'Anyway,' Woolgar continued, 'Seymour meets with Gina Fonteyn, and somehow Rodriguez gets in and it all goes pear-shaped. He was fuzzy on the details, but O'Donnell – the son, not the father – pointed out that Rodriguez gambled in Monte Carlo, too. That's all over the papers now. He might have lost money to Seymour there, or won it off him, or maybe Seymour needed a favour, something dark and dirty, and they fell out, and that's why Rodriguez followed them in Chelsea. And Seymour turned on him. He was a commando in the war, sir, so—'

'Mmm, I see,' Darbishire cut in. 'And was he also a magician? Did he become invisible? Did he hypnotise the witnesses?'

'Not exactly, sir,' Woolgar said cheerfully, finding sarcasm no obstacle to his flow.

'Oh?'

'He shut them up, sir, didn't he? That's why you're not allowed to try and talk to them again.' He folded his arms and smiled. Point proven, he seemed to say. 'But if I could go to Monaco and do some digging . . .'

'Hang on, Sergeant.' Darbishire raised a hand. 'I'm not allowed to *what*?'

It turned out that his encounter with the mysterious man in the mackintosh was an open secret among the local CID. One of the keener officers on the case had gone to the deputy commissioner to try and get Darbishire thrown off for not pursuing the loose end with the Gregsons, and had been told 'in strictest confidence' 'not to go there'. Most of those who knew about it assumed the prime minister was behind the threat, or the Cabinet Office at least. They were taking bets. Some had gone for the Billy Hill gang, but increasingly thought it wasn't his style. Or 'modus operandus', as Jimmy would say.

Mr O'Donnell Junior of Harvard, Boston, USA, didn't know about the witness suppression, but Woolgar had tacked it on of his own accord. It explained some of the details that the oarsman had left out.

'So, your theory is,' Darbishire summarised, tetchily, 'that Seymour booked the girl, gave her the incriminating diamonds, got surprised by Rodriguez somehow, killed them both single-handed in self-defence, left the diamonds on her head, then escaped in full view of everyone and bribed or blackmailed whoever it took, to feed me lies about what happened, or not to talk to me at all?'

Woolgar paused to think. 'Um, that's about it, sir.'

'And no one has cracked?'

'Well, he's got away with it so far, hasn't he? If I could just go to . . .'

Darbishire shook his head. As a theory, it didn't make sense, but it didn't exactly *not* make sense either. You had to give the man top marks for trying.

'No, you can't,' he said.

CHAPTER 29

Early June meant the Derby, and a couple of days visiting the lovely course on the Epsom Downs. The Queen had high hopes for Aureole, her late father's horse, who had nearly won in '53, but agonisingly, he came second. She still hadn't won a classic race. However, she fancied her chances the following day in the Oaks, where she had two horses running, both in excellent form.

Philip didn't accompany her, because while he was an excellent rider himself, he wasn't interested in the endless display of other people's horses. She sensed he might have felt differently if he'd grown up with stables of his own. Instead, he was chairing a meeting at Windsor about his new award scheme. She didn't mind, because she had her mother and Margaret for company, and plenty of friends who were nearly as passionate about racing as she was – including Bill Astor from Cliveden, who had a horse running against hers.

Her mother, meanwhile, loved horses of all descriptions. The elder Elizabeth had a slight preference for jump racing over the flat, but was knowledgeable about it all. Margaret loved the opportunity to wear dresses that showed off her tiny waist, and hats that showed off her rich, dark hair. She had worried that wet weather wouldn't allow her to wear the outfit she'd chosen, but in the end the sun beamed fiercely, and she was content. To start with, anyway, but Margaret's moods rarely stayed steady for long.

'If the Duke of Maidstone paws me again, I swear I'll hit him with my handbag,' she announced, joining her sister in the royal box as they got ready for the first race.

'Paws you?' the Queen asked.

'Don't worry. I gave him a look to shrivel him to the size of a cherry stone. He's trying to set me up with his horrible son, who's having affairs with at least two women I know of. All he ever talks about is how much he's looking forward to the grouse season. What they see in him, I have no idea.'

'Probably ten thousand acres in Kent. Where's Mummy?'

'Oh, I left her downstairs, talking to the Dean of Bath. Clement Moreton – d'you remember? He's the one with the tart in the tiara.'

The Queen was horrified. 'The man's a suspect in a murder case!'

'I know! That's why she went over. According to his cousin Cecily, he's really not doing very well. Mummy was pleased to see him out and about. Looking very dapper, I must say, with a white rosebud in his buttonhole. He didn't seem *that* under the weather.'

'Well, I suppose that's good.'

'Unlike the Minister for Technology. You know, the one who *bought* the tiara. He looks absolutely dire.'

'Lord Seymour?'

'Is that his name?'

'Where was he?'

'Chatting to Mummy and the dean. And a very attractive woman in the strangest hat. His wife, I assume. I imagine the men were sympathising with each other. It must be awful to have the whole country assuming you committed a horrific murder. Even if one of them probably did. May I borrow your race card? I've lost mine.'

The Queen was dumbfounded. Her mother always thought that people worried too much about newspaper pictures, and that what mattered was to be kind to the people who deserved it, but the thought of her on the cover of the *Daily Mirror* in conversation with not one but *two* suspected murderers was too much. She called her racing manager over and sent him off to the rescue as quickly as possible. Then a thought occurred to her.

'Was my press secretary there, by any chance?'

'Jeremy?' Margaret asked. 'I've seen him around today. He has the tallest top hat you can imagine. It's as if he's wearing a chimney pot.'

'But was he with Mummy?'

'No. His brother Tony was, earlier. He rescued me from the duke.'

'Hmm.'

The Queen wondered whether her mother had been led into some

sort of trap. Was a press photographer waiting, ready to take a compro-
mising picture? It seemed the sort of thing the plotters might do,
although, as ever, why they would bother remained a mystery.

'Ah, Lilibet! What a lovely atmosphere out there.' Her mother
appeared at the door to the royal box, looking bright and cheerful.
'Everyone's so excited about the Oaks. I really think this could be your
day, darling. I know all the money's on Mulberry Harbour, but I
thought Carrozza was looking marvellous in the collecting ring.
Someone said you wanted me?'

'I just wondered where you were,' the Queen said, evenly.

'I was talking about the Highlands with Clement Moreton and
Stephen Seymour, and then your press secretary popped up and collared a man with a *very* large camera, and persuaded him not to take
any pictures. Very understanding, I thought. The last thing those two
men want is to be on the front pages again.'

'Oh.' The Queen felt wrong-footed. She forcefully suspected Jeremy and his brother of being behind the plot, and yet here her press
secretary was, doing the job he was paid for. It was hard to read anything into it but helpfulness. 'Why the Highlands?' she asked.

'Clement goes there every summer, to contemplate the world, you
know. I assumed he meant some sort of religious retreat, but actually,
he's a fly fisherman, like me. So, I invited him to Balmoral.'

'Mummy!'

'And Stephen Seymour is thinking of buying a castle on the west
coast, so I was recommending a few I know of whose owners would
be thrilled with the cash.'

'Why does he want to live in Scotland?'

Her mother looked surprised. 'I didn't ask. Why wouldn't he?'

The Queen smiled at this. As a daughter of the Earl of Strathmore,
growing up in Glamis Castle, home to Macbeth, her mother found
Scotland perfect in every way. She couldn't imagine anyone not wanting to cut themselves off in a draughty, windswept medieval building
overlooking nothing but moor and sea, and the foothills of rain-clad
mountains.

'Does Lord Seymour need to retreat from London?' she asked.

'Darling, I have no idea. He had a very romantic look in his eye,
though. He and his wife know the Arisaig estate quite well. I think he
was stationed there in the war. Lucy had a Scottish look about her today.

She was wearing the most beautiful silk tartan two-piece and a clever little thistle hat that was quite the thing. *Quite* the best-dressed woman at the Oaks. Her husband must spend an absolute fortune on her.'

Margaret looked annoyed. 'I was told *I* was the best-dressed woman at the Oaks.'

'Well, yes, they would say that, wouldn't they?' her mother said, adding just in time, 'And you look perfectly enchanting, darling.' Then she returned to her theme. 'Lucy really is very attractive. I can quite see why he bought it for her.'

'What?'

'The Zellendorf. It would have looked lovely in her hair. Lucy's perhaps a little old for something so summery. Personally, I'd have recommended a bandeau, but taste in tiaras is very personal, isn't it?'

'I wouldn't know,' Margaret muttered.

'It would have looked far better on you,' her mother said gamely. 'But it will be locked away now, won't it? Or else it will be notorious and sell for a fortune, which would be *dreadful*. I must say, they seemed a devoted couple, if rather sad, but that's understandable, in the circumstances. I wonder where he got his penchant for tarts and other men's wives.'

'Mummy!'

'Everyone knows, Lilibet. He's famously unfaithful. Men are so very complicated, aren't they?'

'I always thought they were rather simple,' the Queen said.

'Don't underestimate them, darling. What would the world be without them? Oh, look, they're lining up for the first race. Can somebody pass me my binoculars?'

CHAPTER 30

Carrozza won the Oaks, with a brilliant young jockey called Lester Piggott edging her over the finish line, and the rest of June rather paled by comparison, until Ascot brought more successes on the turf. July went by in a flurry of visits, from the Wirral in the north-west to Jersey in the Channel Islands, and all of them went off without a hitch.

There were times, especially when the Queen was reminded of her victories by the *Racing Post*, when she began to wonder whether she had imagined treachery and sabotage after all. Was the suspect face cream in Denmark just a faulty batch? Had she read too much into what happened in Paris? Until she remembered Ingrid Kern. That brief addition to Philip's Danish schedule had been no accident. Somebody wished her, and her marriage, harm.

The start of August was marked by Philip heading south to the Isle of Wight to join *Britannia* again and participate in the sailing festival at Cowes. He was joined by Charles for the first time, as a special treat before he went away to school. The Queen and Anne meanwhile would travel north by train, spend a few days at Balmoral and meet up with the princes later.

The royal diaries had been full since Philip's arrival in Portugal in February, and they were busy again from October. So the Queen was looking forward to high summer in Scotland, with islands to visit, grouse moors to walk on and rivers to fish in, and only the mizzle and midges to worry about.

But as she was preparing to leave for King's Cross to board the royal train for the overnight journey, Sir Hugh appeared at her study door with the same sort of expression he'd had when her speech went missing in Paris. Only, this time it was worse.

'There's been an article about you in a magazine,' he said.

This wasn't at all unusual. In fact, it seemed rare for magazines to publish without including an article about her these days. The Queen frowned at him. 'Which one?'

'The *National and English Review*.'

'Do we know it?'

'I read it occasionally, ma'am. It's generally quite sound. But I'm afraid this time the editor has had some sort of psychological episode. He's written things that are . . . Well, I won't bore you with them now, ma'am, but suffice it to say they are rude to the point of treachery, not just about you, but about the whole fabric of the court and . . .'

Pink with outrage, he struggled to finish the sentence. This was very unusual for her unflappable private secretary. The Queen was more curious than alarmed, though.

'Does it matter? Does anyone read what's in the *National and English Review*?'

'Not normally, ma'am. But the problem is that the *Daily Express* has got hold of it and Lord Beaverbrook has published an article roundly defending your interests. And so now of course everyone will read it. By the time you get to Scotland, I'm afraid there will be talk of little else.'

'Put a copy in my boxes. I'll read it on the way up. I'm sure we'll manage, Hugh. Who wrote it, by the way?'

'John Grigg – Lord Altrincham – the editor. He's a historian; an Oxford man, who should know better.'

'I'll read it with interest,' the Queen promised, still amused at Sir Hugh's pink-faced reaction.

★ ★ ★

She read it twice that evening, between Stevenage and Peterborough, and had to wait until morning, when she finally got to Balmoral, before she could commandeer a telephone to talk to Philip in Cowes. By that stage, he'd already been briefed by his private secretary. His rage reverberated down the line.

'The treacherous bastard! He should be hung, drawn and quartered! Who is this weasel?'

The Queen agreed up to a point. The article in question was much worse than she had imagined. It contained some very personal attacks that were quite upsetting. Her style of speaking was 'a pain in the neck'. The words 'priggish schoolgirl' lingered in her mind. Was she really like that? She'd always considered herself rather approachable and open-minded.

The author claimed to be on her side. She was a good person, he surmised, but surrounded herself with 'tweedy sorts' (no wonder Sir Hugh was apoplectic) and failed to connect with her people. The *Daily Express*, in coming to her defence with loyal outrage, had made a small problem infinitely worse. The trouble was, in August there was little real news to fill the front pages.

'It'll be all over the world by next week,' Philip shouted. 'It's already in the *New York Times*. How dare he? Six thousand people came to wave flags for you in the Forest of Dean. Six thousand! Did *they* think you were priggish?'

She really wished he wouldn't go on about that word. It smarted.

'They seemed happy enough,' she said.

'Bloody Altrincham had better watch out. Mind you, he's got a point about the men in moustaches. Tweedy sorts, was it? Ha! Spot on. You know my thoughts on Hugh and Miles. But . . . hire trade unionists and socialists to take over from them? What in damnation?'

'I'm not sure he thinks I should *really* hire them.'

'Then he makes you the butt of his joke!' Philip's outrage reasserted itself. 'And he has no right to attack you, by God. None.'

She felt sorry for whichever shipmates were accompanying him that morning. However, his temper was squally, and would probably blow itself out by lunchtime. The Queen on the other hand, more quiet and reserved, was still smarting when she went to bed. The line about her losing her 'bloom of youth' one day lingered in a particularly sour fashion.

She didn't only mind for herself. She didn't entirely agree with Philip about the men in moustaches. What was she supposed to do? Trade unionists and socialists were out of the question, but should she try to replace Sir Hugh and his ilk with thrusting young 'executives' who had no experience of monarchy or tradition, or any of the myriad unique aspects of her job?

However, at least one of the men in moustaches was not the man she thought he was, and she had to admit that she didn't feel safe. It wasn't only Altrincham's article she worried about, but whether it fitted into the larger pattern of disturbances. Was this what the saboteurs had been building up to? For now, all she could do was put a brave face on it and wait.

CHAPTER 31

Back in London, Darbishire sat late at the desk he had been assigned in Scotland Yard, reading over the typescript of his latest report and knowing that it would go to the palace, for reasons that had still never been fully explained.

Twice, this one had come back to him with question marks about his grammar. His assigned secretary had even been given a better typewriter, but he'd managed to get a smudge of newsprint on the second immaculately rendered page. No doubt it would come back again.

The problem for Darbishire wasn't his use of subordinate clauses, or grubby thumbprints from ten minutes spent catching up with the *Evening Standard*, but the fact that his report essentially said nothing. After all his high hopes, it was an elegantly worded temporary admission of defeat. His fears about this job, given that the mighty George Venables didn't want it, had been fully realised. And the one person in the world who seemed *not* to be trying to stop him was . . . Stephen Seymour.

Darbishire had received another visit. He was beginning to feel like a puppet with too many strings. The same bland gentleman in a mackintosh had accosted him outside Sloane Square tube station and they had 'gone for a walk together' down the road to Orange Square.

'It's come to our attention, forgive me for saying so, that you've been asking some rather aggressive questions about a member of the Government,' he'd begun.

Darbishire had pointed out that that was his job. It was then explained to him, in no uncertain terms, that Lord Seymour was *not* being protected, had *not* intimidated witnesses, but was already experiencing huge damage to his reputation and deserved not to suffer additional slurs.

The inspector couldn't believe they would take him for such an idiot. They *would* say that, wouldn't they?

The man in the mackintosh had said, 'You're probably thinking, we would say that, wouldn't we? I can see exactly why you would come to that conclusion. All I can say is, it's an interesting theory, but not the right one. I'm not suggesting Lord Seymour *didn't* commit the murders; it's your job to prove or disprove that point. Only that he didn't speak to the Gregsons. I mean, it was rather a far-fetched scenario, wasn't it? Haha. I'd hate you to get lost down that blind alley, Inspector. I'm sure you have better things to do.'

So now, assuming the man in the mackintosh wasn't lying, which of course he might be, Darbishire felt a fool for listening to Woolgar's half-baked fantasies. And if Seymour didn't do it (and if he did, how did he get away with it?), and Billy Hill didn't do it, who did? And who *was* protecting whoever it was? Darbishire was still inclined to think it was somebody in the Cabinet – or maybe MI5, for reasons he couldn't begin to fathom.

Darbishire wasn't happy, whoever it was. Two people had been horribly murdered, and he was being deliberately hobbled in bringing the murderers to justice. That did public confidence no good, so if it *was* someone in the Government or MI5, they'd better be thinking about that, too. And if a gang *did* have a stranglehold on the privates of the high-ups in the Met, then God help them all.

At least he'd had reasonable success tracing Nico Rodriguez's movements in the months before the murders. As well as his stints in Egypt, Oman and the watering holes of Morocco and Monaco, he had come in and out of London three times in that period, under the guise of delivering trade samples of some kind of industrial plastic. Darbishire suspected that almost certainly, he was smuggling small quantities of drugs or arms, or working out how to do it.

When in London, he stayed at the Marlborough, which wasn't a bad hotel, even if it wasn't quite the Dorchester. He won big on the horses and treated himself to cigars and champagne. He had visited the Raffles agency in person, at their little office just off Shepherd Market in Mayfair, to look through their books and find girls to his liking. Was he disappointed when he got Gina Fonteyn instead of Beryl White? If so, he overreacted a bit, didn't he? And that still didn't explain what happened to *him*.

Darbishire had interviewed Miss White once more since their last encounter – or rather, got DS Willis to do it, since he realised he personally had put the wind up her too much when he brought her in, and Woolgar seemed to scare the bejesus out of her with his mere presence. But Willis didn't come up trumps either. Gina Fonteyn's fellow tart either really did know nothing about the reasons for luring Rodriguez to Cresswell Place that night, or she was too terrified of the consequences of telling. Willis was known for getting results out of these women, so if he couldn't do it, no one could.

Darbishire's reports had neglected to include his clandestine conversation with Jimmy Broad of the Billy Hill gang. As with the man in the mackintosh, Darbishire was hardly going to take the word of a violent, hardened criminal like Jimmy effectively saying, 'my boss didn't do it'. But the trouble was that Jimmy's argument was, if not compelling, then at least plausible. The killers of Cresswell Place might have got away with it so far, but those murders were messy. They had the police crawling all over the place and, as Jimmy said, that wasn't Billy's style. He liked to keep them at arm's length if he could.

Darbishire had continued to investigate him anyway, and this *was* in this report. But in the updates he was forced to admit that there was no suggestion among the gang's known fences that they had been asked to offload the contents of Lord Seymour's safe, where the stolen diamond tiara was supposed to have been residing. No hint of a need for revenge against Rodriguez – a deal gone wrong, money missing, goods not delivered. And they still hadn't made any progress on those damned companies that owned the escort and letting agencies and the nightclub in Tangier where Rodriguez liked to gamble. Whoever owned them had excellent lawyers and accountants. Darbishire tipped his hat to them.

The typescript in his hands stressed that the investigation was still highly active. He had men out everywhere, carrying out interviews in their thousands. Privately, though, he was stuck.

And so, his report was full of travel itineraries and casino anecdotes and speculation about Lord Seymour's holiday haunts and the contents of Rodriguez's luggage. The text was correctly spelled, contained several subtle but telling instances of the subjunctive and was beautifully typed on the latest Corona. The next draft would be free of thumbprints by tomorrow afternoon. But it was also free of real progress.

In practical terms, Darbishire was no closer to discovering who placed the tiara on Gina Fonteyn's pretty head, or how two men, at least, came into the house unnoticed – or why they would want to – than he had been in April when he started. Her Majesty might admire his grammar, but she wasn't going to admire that.

CHAPTER 32

For several days, they didn't openly talk about Lord Altrincham's article.

The royal family were reunited on *Britannia* for a gentle cruise of the Western Isles. It was the one time of the year when they were truly alone (apart from two hundred very diplomatic sailors, who left them to it) and the Queen could just be Lilibet.

Philip was keen to pick up the outrage where he had left off, but she said, just once, 'Not now, if you don't mind. We're on holiday,' and he talked instead, with equal passion, about the new yacht race he had just launched in Cowes.

The scenery was mesmerically beautiful – purple islands on the horizon and silver sand beaches for family picnics. Charles and Anne competed to spot seals and basking sharks, but the Queen trumped them both when she caught a playful pod of dolphins in her binoculars. She was reminded of her mother's comments at the races: the west coast of Scotland was very close to heaven. She knew various Englishmen and Canadians who'd fallen in love with Arisaig and Mallaig. It wasn't so very difficult to imagine someone wanting to retire here after all.

★ ★ ★

Meanwhile, the members of the royal household muttered the name of the *National and English Review* in low, indignant voices. Everyone who'd travelled to Scotland consulted friends and developed their own thoughts, while back in London, Miles Urquhart visited the editors of all the major newspapers to assure them that the palace was both taking the article seriously, and not bothered by it at all.

The Queen waited until she got back to Balmoral, after a soul-restoring week at sea. The children were delighted to be reunited with their favourite cows and ponies. Philip went walking in the hills to view the work done on the estate since last year. She spent one day riding by the river and standing under the stars at midnight, tracing the constellations in the sky, the way her father had taught her. But she couldn't put it off any longer. She called a meeting in her study with Sir Hugh, Jeremy Radnor-Milne and Joan. It was time to decide what to do.

'What's the verdict, Hugh?' she asked.

'Mixed, ma'am,' he told her. 'There are columnists in Australia who think Altrincham should be sent to the Tower, and hacks in Canada who say he has a point. Down in London, as you may have seen in the papers, the editors are united against him. I pity the man if he dares show his face on the streets right now. They're enjoying this little opportunity to rally the nation. On the whole, the public is on your side. But not mine, I fear. I'm a "tweedy courtier" who makes you sound "prissy" against your better nature.'

'It's very easy to criticise the people who work hard in the background,' the Queen said, sympathetically.

'We're only here to serve you, ma'am,' her press secretary interjected. His upper lip wiggled with affronted loyalty. 'We're men of steel, we can take it.'

'Ah, but it's fair to say that my Scottish wardrobe is tweedier than yours,' the Queen pointed out. 'And I approve the speeches. Surely I'm responsible for what I say too?'

'Mmm. In a way, ma'am, but on the other hand . . . I think what one should properly consider . . .'

Radnor-Milne was caught between the disloyalty of agreeing that she should share the blame, and the rudeness of suggesting she was their puppet. He couldn't find a way around it.

'What do you think, Joan?' the Queen asked, while he fumbled for a reply.

'I don't always trust the papers,' Joan said, as the private and press secretaries turned in alarm at the sound of 'the typist' expressing an opinion. 'I think the public reaction's a bit more complicated than that.'

'Oh, and what might that be?' Sir Hugh asked, sceptically. 'The man on the Clapham Omnibus – your father, for example – what does *he* think?'

Joan was not impressed that the private secretary seemed to think of her father as a spokesman for the working classes. And anyway, his opinion wouldn't help.

'He's a little bit in love with you, ma'am,' she admitted. 'In his eyes, you can do no wrong. But my aunt . . .'

'Your aunt!' Radnor-Milne said, with a curl of his lip. 'I really don't think we all need to know what Joan's aunt in Bow thinks about Her Majesty.'

'No, I very much want to know,' the Queen said with a frown.

Joan wasn't sure Auntie Eva would want to be a spokeswoman for the working classes either, but she did have strong opinions, which she had been happy to share in a letter that Joan had received just yesterday.

'She agreed that the article was incredibly rude, but it made her wistful.'

Radnor-Milne was dismissive. 'Wistful, I tell you!'

'In what way?' the Queen asked.

'She said you're a working woman, and a mother,' Joan said. 'She works, and she's got three children herself. But she doesn't feel the same connection with you. Not like she did when . . .' Joan hesitated.

'When what?'

'When you were a young bride, ma'am.'

'One can't be a young bride forever,' the Queen muttered.

'Nobody could age more gracefully than . . .'

'Oh, do be quiet, Jeremy.'

Joan carried on. 'She said everyone was very low last winter, with fuel rationing and everything so expensive, and a new prime minister . . . but your speech was all about the Commonwealth. Which was all well and good, but . . .'

'It wasn't about home,' the Queen said thoughtfully.

'Not really. She wants peace between nations, obviously but . . .'

'I see,' the Queen said. *I was missing my husband, who was far away in the South Atlantic, and I ignored what was happening at home because . . .*

She wasn't sure exactly why she'd ignored what was happening at home. But she knew she had intended to inspire women such as Joan's aunt in Bow, and if that hadn't happened, she should do something about it.

From then, the conversation took an interesting turn. They all contemplated the possibility of presenting her as someone of flesh and blood, like her subjects, thinking and feeling with them – which she did – and not simply trying to pat them on the head with pleasant generalities and noble aspirations. The press secretary thought it was a dreadful idea: her noble aspirations were what made her so . . . ('Not now, Jeremy'). Sir Hugh sensed the new direction had possibilities, but had no practical solutions to suggest, beyond perhaps lending her name to a new cake.

'What about the "Elizabeth sponge", ma'am? A variation on the Victoria variety, but with a different jam, perhaps? We could hold a competition. It would highlight your interest in the domestic sphere. The curried chicken recipe at your coronation was a great success.'

The Queen bit her lip. Thinking back to the article, she had a vision of Margaret, aged eleven, standing hands on hips, yelling, 'You're such a *prig*, Lilibet.' At the time, she'd lifted her chin and walked off with great dignity. But she had been a bit of a prig, looking back. Perhaps her sister wasn't the only one to notice.

'I'm not sure a cake is the answer, Hugh.'

★ ★ ★

After their meeting, she asked Joan to stay behind.

'I assume I'm right. Your aunt wouldn't be appeased by cake?'

'I think she'd be pretty insulted, ma'am. She can make her own cakes.'

'Mmm.'

'Although lots of her friends would be delighted.'

The Queen turned to the bigger question. 'What did *you* think about this article? Could it be part of the campaign against me?'

'I've been wondering about it, of course,' Joan said. 'It seemed so obvious to start with. I assumed it was the start of something more overt. But, when I got my aunt's letter yesterday, I started to think . . .'

'That in fact he's being helpful?'

'Yes, ma'am. Or trying to be. The article itself was very polite. It wasn't a criticism of *you*, but more what my aunt said: that the monarchy needs to be less distant.'

Flattery shouldn't always be laid on with a trowel, the Queen thought to herself. Sometimes, hard truths were what one needed.

'So you don't think Altrincham's involved? I must say, neither do I.'

'More the opposite, actually,' Joan agreed.

'And what about Sir Hugh? You saw him just now.'

'He was trying, ma'am. Keen to do the right thing. He has been all week. I'm not convinced the answer's a new cake, but . . .'

'He seems to be acting in my best interests, as well as he can. And then there's Jeremy . . .'

Joan nodded. 'He wants you to do nothing, ma'am. And so does Miles Urquhart, by the way.'

'When it seems that "nothing" might be a dangerous course of action. But it's hard to tell excessive loyalty from a hidden wish to do harm.'

'I'll keep my eyes open,' Joan promised. 'If Sir Hugh *is* part of the plot it will be very hard to prove, but if it's either of the others I'm sure I'll get proof soon enough.'

'I admire your confidence,' the Queen said. 'The prime minister has made it painfully clear how important my visit to America is. If they follow the pattern, they'll do their damnedest to cause trouble in October. It only gives us a few weeks to stop them.' She sighed. 'And we still have to work out why.'

'We will, ma'am,' Joan assured her. 'Thank goodness for their incompetence.'

The Queen pursed her lips. 'But the face cream was too close for comfort. I can't always rely on Bobo to save me. I hope you find what you need.'

CHAPTER 33

Taking advantage of a quiet afternoon, the Queen joined Philip on a ride into the hills. It was lovely to be out among the purple heather and rain wasn't threatened for several hours.

'What's happening with Altrincham? Is he in the Tower yet?' he asked.

'Actually, we've been thinking quite a lot about everything he wrote,' she said. 'Joan's going to have a quiet word.'

'A warning?'

'No. A thank you.'

'A *thank you*? For all that rot about you?'

'It wasn't all rot,' she admitted. 'Apparently some members of the public agree.' She didn't mention Joan's aunt. Sir Hugh had taken soundings and discovered, to his disappointment, that she wasn't alone. 'It's lovely that so many people have leaped to my defence of course, but . . . one does have to learn. And change. A little.'

'Oh?'

Philip was thoughtful for quite a while. They rode on in companionable silence. Below them, the River Dee glistened in a patch of sunlight. An eagle soared lazily overhead. There was nowhere she would rather be. Nobody she would rather be beside than this man, who was eager to help and already thinking of solutions, she could feel it. His brain was never at rest. Part of Philip's rudeness – she knew he could be rude, even to her sometimes, though he fiercely berated anyone else who was – came from the fact that he was often two steps ahead of whoever he was talking to. He was a man who lived in the future, while she clung, a little too tightly sometimes, to the past.

'Look!'

She pointed at the sky. The eagle had been joined by another. They swirled in graceful, complicated patterns. The couple rested in their saddles and watched.

Eventually, the birds flew out of sight behind the hilltops.

'You're right, Lilibet,' Philip said firmly.

She had forgotten what they were talking about.

'Oh? Good.'

'An opportunity for change. This has come at the perfect time. Altrincham mentioned television. We should use it.'

Oh, gosh. Live television. Nothing more frightening. Her husband *would* pick on that. 'He said you were very good on it,' the Queen said tartly.

'Did he? Well . . . You were a fuzzy figure during the coronation. But you've got your Christmas message coming up.'

'Don't remind me.'

'You could practise when we're in Canada. You've got that thing in front of their cameras too.'

'I know! In French and English!' To several million people. She was terrified at the thought.

Philip carried on. 'There you are. It won't be in French at Christmas. It's the perfect opportunity. The technology's come on in leaps and bounds since 'fifty-three. It's much sharper now.'

'Is that a good thing?'

'Of course it is. You know how mad they go for you whenever they see you in the flesh. You could show off your new speaking prowess.'

'If I have any by then.'

'You will.'

'I'm hardly Robin Day,' she protested.

'It's not an interview – just a speech. But a *decent* speech – not one of those tweedy ones of Hugh's. Something modern, for the modern man. And his modern wife,' he added.

So, Philip did agree with Altrincham after all.

'But if Hugh can't help me write it, who can?'

'I can,' he offered, with a broad smile, before turning his horse to lead them both back towards Balmoral.

'Yes, of course you can,' she called after him quickly. 'But . . . um, I'd need a proper professional, don't you think?'

He turned round in the saddle. 'What about if we get Daphne in?'

'Daphne?'

'You know Daphne. We'd have to get her up from Menabilly. But I'm sure she'd love it here.'

Daphne? It was certainly a thought. The Queen hadn't considered working with a woman on something so important. But after all, why not?

Daphne was the wife of Philip's much-loved head of household, General Sir Frederick Arthur Montague Browning – 'Boy' to friends and family – who was a hero of the First World War. In the second, he had helped found the First Airborne Division and led his men through the horrors at Arnhem in 'forty-four. He was sociable, organised, military to his core . . . perhaps the last person one would expect to be married to a sensitive novelist like Daphne. Nevertheless, they made an entertaining couple, both in London, where Boy worked with Philip at the palace, and in Cornwall, where Daphne had her domain.

'We owe her the hospitality,' Philip said. 'We had such a day sailing with them on the Helford, do you remember? You almost fell in, but Daphne rescued you just in time.'

'I was perfectly safe. Just surprised when you tacked too hard.'

'I never tack too hard. Anyway, she's a bloody good writer. Not my sort of thing, but the general public seem to approve. She's probably deathly bored down in Cornwall. She'd appreciate the company, and do a damned good job.'

She probably would, the Queen agreed. Daphne was sharp, observant, quick-witted – another *doer*. She would certainly understand the problem, and be honest about what it would take to fix it.

'Yes, all right. Let's ask her.'

One had to be brave. If one didn't take on difficult challenges, and overcome them, how could one possibly ask one's people to do the same?

The Queen put to one side the rumours she had heard that Daphne was the woman Philip had gone to before proposing. His love was never in doubt, but nobody could deny the sacrifices it would take for a proud, successful young naval officer to marry a future sovereign and play second fiddle to her for the rest of his life. If he *had* spoken to Daphne at Menabilly, she had presumably advised him to go ahead with the marriage, because he had committed himself ardently and fully, as had Elizabeth herself. Doubts didn't matter, as long as you stuck to your decision. Marriage was a daily act of faith, she realised.

CHAPTER 34

Balmoral was built for entertaining, and quickly filled with family and friends. The fifteenth of August was Princess Anne's seventh birthday and one of those glorious, sunny days that the Scottish Highlands do better than anywhere on earth. They marked the day with a picnic in Balmoral's grounds organised by Philip, and games organised by the Queen Mother, who also participated with great gusto.

She was full of tales about her recent visit to Africa, representing her daughter in Rhodesia and Nyasaland. The Queen had been deeply worried about this trip, given what had happened on her own. She had implored her mother's officials to take the greatest care of her. And they had done. Nothing had gone wrong.

'Everyone was absolutely delightful,' her mother insisted gaily. People usually were, in her company. It was hard not to be, when she was obviously having fun herself.

Had a sabotage plan been tried, and failed? Was it luck that spared the older Elizabeth, or was it only the Queen and Philip who were at threat? The Queen didn't know.

She was distracted watching her children race around the grounds on a treasure hunt. They were giddy on attention and chocolate cake. Philip tried to calm them down a bit, but they didn't listen. He came to stand beside her, laughing.

'We'll pay for this tomorrow. They'll be impossible to get to bed, and then irritable in the morning. Charles especially. Anne's indestructible. Look at her!'

This reminded the Queen of something. It had been nagging at her for a long time, and the latest report from Inspector Darbishire had made it worse. She took advantage of her husband's good humour.

'That night in March,' she said. 'When you came home late . . .'

'What night?' He turned to her sharply.

'You know the one.'

'No idea what you're talking about.'

'I think you do. I'd find it very difficult to explain . . .'

His jaw was clenching. 'What's that got to with anything? Has anyone asked you?'

'Well, no, but—'

'A man's entitled to enter his own home whenever it suits him. And I wasn't late. It might have been a shade after midnight. If anyone asks you, send 'em to me. Hey! Charles! Wait for your sister, you little monster!'

He stalked off, leaving the Queen standing.

She bit the inside of her lip, hard, and smiled gamely for her mother when she turned to see if anything was wrong.

★ ★ ★

That night, lying awake in bed, the Queen felt very alone.

She worried for her family. The thing was . . . The Queen normally tried not to follow dark thoughts to their conclusion, because honestly how could one keep going if one did? But, the thing *was*, if somebody was trying to sabotage her and Philip, if they didn't want her as queen for whatever reason they might have, then where would it end?

If they somehow got rid of her, then what about Charles, what about Anne? What about Margaret, if her own little family was gone? It was awful to contemplate, but the Queen regularly had to review the secret official plans for just such contingencies. Royal families had been wiped out before. Her cousins in Russia had been obliterated forty years ago; other thrones had been lost this century in Germany, Bulgaria, Portugal, Romania, Italy; Philip's own family was sent into exile from Greece when he was a baby. She pictured him, a refugee on a boat, tucked up in a simple crate of oranges, reliant on the kindness of strangers. The dangers were real and recent.

She didn't just have herself to think of. She worried about Charles, who was a sensitive child, already becoming aware of the duties that awaited him and the sacrifices he'd be asked to make. Brave little Anne did seem indestructible, as Philip said, but even she had her vulnerabilities. Which brought one back to Inspector Darbishire's report.

The Queen propped herself against her pillows, contemplating her precious daughter. Back in the spring, Anne had suddenly come down with a terrible earache, an awful thing that she had probably picked up in the palace swimming pool. It had floored her with pain. Anne never cried usually, unless something happened to one of the animals, but that evening there had been floods of tears, and 'Make it stop, Mummy!' after bath time, which was heartrending.

The Queen had spent an extra half-hour with her, singing and reading from the *Golden Treasury of Verse*, before leaving her in the capable hands of Nanny. But afterwards, she had heard tears wafting downstairs from the direction of the nursery, and it had been impossible to sleep that night, too.

It was the last day of March, she remembered: the Sunday before she drove to Broadlands, where Philip would join her later, and from where they would ultimately leave together for Paris.

On that Sunday night, she had watched the clock tick down the hours, thinking of poor Anne's misery, until she had given up even trying to nod off again. She had picked up her Bible to read some verses from Psalms and the Song of Solomon, which she usually found soothing.

When she next looked up from the text, it was four thirty in the morning. Something had disturbed her: a noise in the passage outside her bedroom. She had listened keenly, wondering if Anne needed her, but in fact it was Philip, coming in. She had heard him muttering something to the footman at his bedroom door, down the corridor from hers. Then, finally, she had slept.

The next day she was extremely busy, and in the evening everyone had been distracted by a *Panorama* programme on the BBC about the spaghetti harvest in Italy. Apparently, the pasta grew on trees. Several people in the palace believed it implicitly – it was the BBC, after all – until it was announced to be an elaborate April's fool joke. Philip didn't interrupt the lively conversation afterwards to mention where he'd been the night before until almost dawn, and she didn't ask him: one didn't want to be a nag.

She had honestly forgotten about it, until the date of the thirty-first of March was mentioned in Paris, in the context of the Chelsea murders. After the brief, unexpected jerk of his hand with the delicate cufflink, Philip had smoothly used her as his alibi for the night. *I was in tucked up safe in bed by eleven. I only have my security detail and Her Majesty to plead my case.* His security detail were famously discreet. And who would question a queen?

But the footmen in the corridor knew better. And so must the guard at the palace gate that night, and the three or four other servants he would have encountered on his way in. One could rely on loyalty and discretion up to a point. It was dangerous to rely on it forever.

The mention of Cresswell Place had also clearly meant something to him. The Queen had half expected to see something in the police reports that might explain it, which was really why she'd asked for them. But there was nothing. What were they not telling her? The inspector had noted in the first report that the witnesses' evidence didn't entirely make sense, but he hadn't followed up on it in any subsequent update. Why?

Their little family felt assailed from outside and within. The Queen had shared this with no one, of course, because even her darling mother couldn't entirely be relied on to keep an absolute secret. She had hoped Darbishire would solve the case for her, but his latest report was thin, containing only minor updates about the male victim.

Rodriguez, as she now knew him, gambled at the Chamberlain in Tangier, which was interesting because it was a club favoured by the Duke of Maidstone, who had told her about the specialities of the girls at the Raffles agency. There was something about the names of the club and the agency that sparked a hint of a connection at the back of the Queen's brain. But she couldn't think of men more different than Sir Thomas Stamford Raffles, a wealthy collector who worked for the East India Company, or even A.J. Raffles, the fictional and rather wonderful gentleman thief, and Neville Chamberlain, the unfortunate former prime minister.

Meanwhile, the report didn't say anything about unusual visitors to Cresswell Place, or the gunshot – which the police seemed to have dismissed as a motorbike backfiring – or any of the aspects of the case she was most worried about.

She sat up late, in silence, thinking about it all, and the following morning, to Philip's surprise, it was she, not the children, who was irritable.

CHAPTER 35

Joan returned to England after three weeks north of the border. Sir Hugh – who took his only holiday at Christmas – would remain at Balmoral for the full summer break, apart from occasional weekends when he stayed with friends who owned nearby estates. The other members of the Private Office took it in turns to be by the Queen's side, alternating it with rare time with their families.

Relieved to have some freedom back again, Joan spent a happy few days with her father in Cambridge, racing him each morning to complete *The Times* crossword and punting to Grantchester with some of the graduate students, where they settled on the banks of the Cam with a bottle of squash and a box of buns from Fitzbillies on Trumpington Street.

She loved the timeless certainty of the old stone colleges. Often, first thing in the morning, before most people were about, it was possible to imagine she was living in the sixteenth century. In the evenings it wasn't much different, the college fellows insisted on inviting her into the candlelit Senior Common Room for sherry, so they could try unsuccessfully to extract details about her new job.

Arriving in Buckingham Palace's North Corridor on her first day back, she heard the sound of laughter coming from the secretaries' shared office. It was Dilys Entwistle's birthday and one of the others had brought in a cake. Joan noticed how they lowered the noise and looked guarded the moment she walked in.

'Would you mind getting the press secretary, Miss McGraw?' Dilys asked politely. 'He never turns down a slice of Victoria sponge.'

Jeremy Radnor-Milne had come down from Scotland with her,

when he had spent the long journey raging against Lord Altrincham and painting Her Majesty, like Mary Poppins, as practically perfect in every way. He thought any changes to her proposed speeches praising the Commonwealth were 'doomed to failure', but was grudgingly supportive of Sir Hugh's idea of an 'Elizabeth sponge' competition, as long as it was done in such a way that it wasn't disrespectful to her great-great-grandmother, Queen Victoria.

Joan knocked on his office door and opened it in one smooth movement – a manoeuvre she had perfected over the last few months, hoping to catch him in the act of doing something underhand. He hated her for it, but was too polite to say so. She was happy to take advantage of his good manners.

'Dilys is cutting her cake,' she explained. 'Why she's doing it at this time in the morning, I don't know, but she wants to know if you'd like a slice.'

Jeremy looked up from his desk with a rigid smile.

'Oh, is she? How nice. I remember signing a card last week. She's turning forty-five, I think . . . not that one should ever ask a woman her age. I suppose she'll be retiring soon. I'll meet you outside.'

He stood up without taking his eyes off Joan, made to close the file in front of him and changed his mind, leaving it open. She noticed how talkative he was being. He normally didn't have much to say about the secretaries.

The rapid speech and the eye contact, the fixed expression . . . They were all signs Joan had seen before, during her work with the captured German officers. When somebody didn't want you to know something, they often overcompensated. The more a prisoner smiled at her and held her eye, the more he fidgeted, the more she probed with her questions.

This time, Jeremy was clearly anxious for her not to look at his desk. He'd resisted looking at it himself, even when it would have been natural to.

At last – the door-opening ploy had finally worked. Joan just needed to know what she wasn't supposed to see.

'Oh my God! Was that a rat?' she shrieked, staring at the wall behind him and pointing at the skirting under the window with a trembling finger.

Jeremy swivelled to look 'Where?'

'Gone behind the bookcase. It was enormous!'

'I'm sure it's a mouse, Joan. You must be used to them by now. Surely they had them in Bow?'

'They did, but that was a monster!'

'I didn't see anything,' he muttered, turning back to his desk. 'And I haven't heard scrabbling recently. You have a vivid imagination. Now, shall we go and say happy birthday? Only a small slice, I think. I need to watch my waistline.'

He accompanied her out of his room, pushing her gently into the corridor by the small of her back, locking the door behind him as he usually did, and pocketing the key.

In the few seconds while his back was turned, Joan had made a mental inventory of everything on his desktop. Only one thing stood out: a recently opened letter, beside the antique Moghul dagger he liked to use as a paper knife. The wording of the letter was suggestive. The image on its letterhead looked vaguely royal, but she hadn't seen it before. Several people in the palace would probably be able to tell her what it was, but she didn't dare risk sharing her question with any of them. There was only one person she could think of to ask.

★ ★ ★

Hector Ross had been away from the flat in Dolphin Square for a couple of days. Joan was relieved to see him back at the stove the evening of the sixteenth, doing something with eggs and butter.

'I'm making an omelette. Would you like one?' he asked.

'Will there be enough?' she asked.

'Plenty. I brought half a dozen eggs back from the country. And I picked some herbs in the garden over the weekend. It's an Italian recipe, to go with this wine.'

Joan looked at the bottle he indicated on the counter, which had Italian writing and a picture of a black cockerel on it. The wine itself was dark red in the glass Hector had poured for himself beside it. It looked inviting. She wondered if he had spent some of his war fighting up through Italy.

'Thank you.'

She let him pour a glass for her and watched him at work. The timing of what she was about to say was good. It was always easier when you didn't have to stare someone in the face.

'By the way.' She was as casual as could be. 'I saw one of the secretaries in a flap about a letter recently. I only saw it from a distance, but I wondered who it might be from. She was terribly flustered by it.'

'Oh?' Hector paused to check the omelette he was finishing. It looked rich and golden. The sizzle and the smell were surprisingly good from such simple ingredients. 'What did you see?'

'There was a crest. Might you know it? I'm still learning.'

'I might.'

'It was quite small. A blue hexagon with a crown on top and writing round the edge. And some sort of symbol in the middle.'

'Hmm. Was that all?'

'Yes.'

'Might the symbol have been a letter? An E, perhaps?' he asked.

Joan thought about it. 'Yes, possibly. If it was angled to fit the hexagon.'

He nodded, lifting the frying pan and sliding the cooked omelette onto a waiting plate. He placed another plate over it to keep it warm, while he melted a fresh pat of butter in the pan. 'That would be the Duke of Windsor. Edward – though he was only officially Edward for months, I suppose.'

'Yes,' Joan mused. 'He's David, really, isn't he?'

'Hard to know *what* he is now. Except *persona non grata*. He must have been writing from Paris. I wonder what he wanted. I didn't think they were speaking to him.'

'Mmm.'

Hector whisked two more eggs in a mug with a sprinkle of salt and pepper. He poured the mixture into the sizzling pan.

'Of course, Wallis had a similar cypher made to match. It didn't have the writing round the edge, I believe. The central letter couldn't have been a W, could it?'

'I'm not sure,' Joan said airily. 'Shall I lay the table?'

'Go ahead.'

She retrieved knives and forks from one of the drawers, and water glasses from a cupboard.

She did know which letter it was: definitely the 'E', not the 'W'.

It worried her a little that Hector hadn't even glanced round to face her as he spoke to her, despite being so helpful. It was as if he could tell she was trying to avoid making too much of the question, and therefore was mirroring her.

Anyone who had been at Longmeadow Hall at the time of the ill-fated Brigadier Yelland had a brain as sharp as a tack, and a chess-player's ability to see several moves ahead. She had a lot to hide, and sensed Hector had just seen through most of it. Her only hope was that he didn't care, or wasn't in a position to do much about it.

CHAPTER 36

Daphne Du Maurier arrived at Balmoral in the dying days of August, along with a West Highland terrier, two large trunks of well-cut clothes and a sense of dread, the last of which she carefully hid from her hosts. Her beloved husband, Boy, wasn't at all well – his busy life had been taking its toll. She was very worried about him, but had left him at home in Menabilly along with the children, the nanny and a team of, she hoped, reasonably competent nurses, and travelled the length of the British Isles because you do, don't you, when your sovereign asks?

Balmoral would be dire. Absolutely beautiful countryside, but Daphne's idea of enjoying it involved personal freedom and solitary walks. The thought of changing outfits several times a day and negotiating small talk with dozens of courtiers filled her with horror. Lord Altrincham had captured the Queen's life perfectly. Daphne liked the young royal couple themselves very much, but the world they lived in was undeniably stuffy. However, it seemed they had asked her to help out with precisely this problem, so there was a glimmer of hope.

They greeted her enthusiastically. The Queen said gleefully that she had reread *Rebecca* in honour of Daphne's coming and had forgotten how chilling it was, and wasn't she clever? It made one think about housekeepers in an entirely different way.

In the first forty-eight hours alone, they laid on a picnic and a barbecue (outdoor clothes) a ride with the children (riding clothes), two jolly evening meals (smart clothes) and a dance (party clothes). Still, Daphne sensed something in the air: a rustle between the couple, something off-centre and wobbly, like a spinning top that had lost its centre of gravity.

It didn't really surprise her. Ten years of marriage will do it to you. God knew, her own marriage wasn't perfect, what with Boy shuttling up and down between Cornwall and London and in danger of drinking himself into an early grave. That wasn't all he'd been up to in London, either. Had Philip really done all those things the papers accused him of in the South Pacific? Whatever it was, he and Elizabeth both seemed uncertain how to put it right. And, of course, nobody spoke about it, directly or even obliquely. Instead, they talked about facing the cameras at Christmas and in Canada, and what the Queen was going to say, and how not to make her sound like the well-meaning captain of the netball team.

'I'm not sure what I'm doing wrong,' the Queen said, more bewildered than upset. 'I know how difficult things are for everyone, especially after Suez. I try to be encouraging.'

'They don't want a pat on the head,' Daphne explained. 'They want to know that you feel what they're going through.'

'But I do! Of course I do.'

'Do you, really, ma'am?'

Daphne said it gently, but the Queen looked shocked to have her empathy questioned. She went very quiet, not sulking, but thinking. She was a good listener, Daphne thought.

'I mean, look at Marilyn Monroe,' Daphne suggested. 'Did you see *The Prince and the Showgirl* this summer?'

'Yes, actually, we did.'

'What's lovable about her are the moments when she's unsure. If you want to connect, ma'am, you can't be strong all the time. Sometimes, you have to admit you're vulnerable. You're a wife and mother, with all that entails. It may seem like a disadvantage, God knows – I certainly do. But it's part of your charm.'

'But I . . .'

The Queen fell silent again. Yes, it seemed wrong-headed to suggest that a monarch couldn't be strong all the time, but Daphne knew what made a character connect with the reader, and they'd asked her opinion, after all.

'I'm thinking of the first Queen Elizabeth,' Daphne explained. '"I may have the body of a weak and feeble woman, but I have the heart and stomach of a king."'

'Well, exactly,' the Queen said. '"The heart and stomach of a king."'

'What you're missing, ma'am, is the first part. The "weak and feeble woman". That's what drags you in, as a listener. That's what makes you sit up and take notice, and believe her, and take her seriously. She builds from there.'

'Oh.'

'What frightens you?' Daphne asked. 'Honestly.'

'Honestly? The television cameras themselves. All this new technology. The idea of being seen by two million people when I can only see two.'

'That's understandable,' Daphne agreed.

'And . . . and I suppose . . .'

The Queen gave Daphne an anguished look, followed by a sweet, shy smile, and was quite adorable in that moment. If only *that* could be captured on television . . .

'Yes?' Daphne prompted.

'I suppose . . . There are people who are very good at imagining the future, you know, and reaching for it, but I find that I . . . well, I lean a little bit into the past. I need tradition, and religion, you know, and old-fashioned ideals like morality and self-discipline. Peace. Love thy neighbour. Truthfulness. They get me through . . . That's not too boring, is it?'

'Not at all,' Daphne said. 'Perhaps we can work it in. Start with home and hearth – there you are, welcoming people into your home, but you're doing it through the modern medium of television, and the new technologies can be rather frightening, but to deal with them, people can draw on . . . oh, I don't know exactly, but something to do with what you said. Traditional values.'

'Oh, all right. The old and the new. I can see that.'

'The question is, can you *feel* it, ma'am?'

The Queen thought about it and her face lit up at last. 'Yes! I really can. I think you have something, Daphne. I know people who feel as I do. Slightly frightened, I mean. Not wanting to let go of everything that's got us this far. But we must look forwards, mustn't we? We must.'

'Wonderful, ma'am. That's the first six minutes practically in the can. Let's work on it tomorrow. Right now, I could do with some gin. Couldn't you?'

CHAPTER 37

They had two gin and tonics, followed by quite a lot of champagne, a glass of wine with dinner (Daphne had three), and a little whisky to round off the evening. There was no more talk of speeches, or television, and Daphne thought the Queen looked infinitely more relaxed.

They had been joined for dinner by a couple of local landowners, an artist friend of Philip's and the Queen's racing manager. By the time they got to charades in front of an unseasonal fire, the party was raucous. Hair was let down; jokes were blue; even Daphne relaxed, and Philip was in his element.

After a few rounds of charades, someone suggested Nebuchadnezzar. It was explained to one of the younger equerries that this was like charades, but involved whole scenes, with each team dressing up to present them. They raced around the house gathering tablecloths and coal scuttles, performing silly skits and getting gradually drunker.

'The Ascot Races' was a popular one, with one of the ladies-in-waiting holding up two coffee cups as binoculars and miming agony, ecstasy and then agony again as a viscount, Sir Hugh and Daphne herself galloped by on all fours.

'Oh, it's me!' the Queen shouted with delight. 'Winning the New Stakes and then losing the Gold Cup! Atlas was pipped at the post. It was ghastly! You *are* clever. Hugh, were you Lester Piggott or Zarathustra?'

'The horse, I think,' Sir Hugh said, straightening up with difficulty.

It was the Queen's turn next, and Daphne was the one to get it. Her Majesty stood to face the audience and waved her arms around. She held her fist to her chest. Her diamonds glittered in the lamplight.

Was it champagne, or something more fervent behind her eyes? Her cousins and Philip's artist friend, sat cross-legged on the floor in front of her, looked on, pretending to be mesmerised.

'Billy Graham! Launching his crusade at Madison Square Garden!' Daphne called out.

'Oh, really?' Philip said from beside her. 'Well done. I thought it was Joan of Arc.'

Two equerries were next. At first, they pretended to play tennis in a dainty, ladylike way, and then one put on a big straw hat and presented the other with one of the dinner plates.

'Me again!' shouted the Queen. 'At Wimbledon.'

Daphne, who had grown up in the theatre, felt that the equerry playing the Queen had made a decent fist of presenting the Rosewater trophy, but the one playing Althea Gibson, the winner, had been disappointingly unimaginative. He had played tennis like a ten-year-old schoolgirl, whereas Althea was a true athlete, better than any man in the room right now. A black woman, too – a real record-breaker. Daphne had watched the highlights of the match on a newsreel and wondered what dizzy heights of fame Althea would reach one day . . . or whether her achievement would be consigned to a footnote in history, as women so often were. Then it was her team's go again.

'The news, is it?' one of the cousins muttered, slurring his s's, as they gathered in a huddle to decide what to do. He made a suggestion that Daphne found in equal parts distasteful and fascinating, but the others agreed to it. All except Sir Hugh who, she noticed, made his excuses and disappeared. Was he horrified by the idea, she wondered, or did he simply need the lavatory? Roles were assigned among the others, and they did a quick prop hunt and rehearsal in the hall.

When they were ready, a sheet was held up by the equerries as a screen, facing the audience. The racing manager and the viscount arrived arm in arm, the latter being dressed in a tablecloth (the airing cupboard must be practically bare by now, Daphne thought) with a headband with cutlery stuffed into it, and clutching one of the flower arrangements from the dining table. They went behind the sheet, then Daphne and the lady-in-waiting sat down to play cards at the front. Each got up to disappear briefly behind the sheet. Then they moved to one side and the screen was lowered, to reveal the viscount lying supine on a velvet chaise longue, in a vest and white tennis shorts, the flowers clutched tightly to his chest, while the racing manager lay sprawled on the floor beside him with a hideous expression on his face and a red scarf wrapped around his neck. His acting was terrible – he would keep blinking and his grimace tended towards a smirk – but the effect was still startling.

There was a collective gasp from the audience.

Looking out, Daphne happened to catch the Queen jerk her head sharply towards her husband, so she glanced over to see why. It wasn't obvious. Philip was frowning, but then, so were several other people.

'Bad show!' Philip called out.

'Is it *Hamlet*?' one of the cousins asked. 'Or *Othello*? I always get those two confused.'

Someone shouted, 'Chelsea murders!' There was a smattering of applause, more for form's sake than anything, and the viscount got up to take a bow.

'Oh, forks in his hair!' the cousin said. 'The tart in the tiara! I get it now.'

The next five minutes were rather awkward as the murder scene seemed to have sobered a lot of people up and nobody felt like Nebuchadnezzar any more. Daphne saw that, under her powder, the young Queen was still pale. She went to sit beside her.

'Is everything all right, ma'am?'

'Absolutely, thank you, Daphne. Are you having fun?'

'Absolutely,' Daphne said, with the same level of truthfulness.

The Queen put on a sociable smile. 'I thought William, who played Althea Gibson, was shockingly bad, didn't you?'

Daphne relayed what she'd been thinking earlier about women being consigned to footnotes in history. 'Our stories are usually told by men. I wonder how often they do us justice.'

'Yes. I suppose mine will be, too,' the Queen said ruefully.

Daphne had forgotten that she was talking to a historical figure. She realised that the Queen never really forgot that she was one.

'They make an exception for queens,' she suggested.

'Perhaps they do. I'm often told I'm an honorary man. It comes in useful sometimes. I'd ask you to do it – write about me, I mean – but your stories are so dark. I'd end up dead in the second chapter.'

'I'm not a historian,' Daphne said. 'I could never write *that* dark.'

The Queen smiled, but it was clear she wasn't really listening again. She was looking at the chaise longue, where the viscount had been lying. Daphne was curious about that.

'I'm sorry our scene upset you,' she said.

The Queen looked at her sharply. 'Oh, it didn't at all.'

Daphne realised she had made a faux pas, to talk to the sovereign about her feelings. She tried quickly to make up for it.

'It was just so theatrical, wasn't it? Much too theatrical, if you ask me.'

'What d'you mean?'

'A classic case of misdirection. My father used to do it all the time when he wanted to divert attention. There's the girl, the beautiful innocent, clutching her flowers, and the man at her feet, the victim of a hideous crime. They set it up like something out of Victorian music hall. I do it in my novels sometimes, when I'm trying to slip something past the reader. The question is, what didn't they want us to see?'

'I'm sure the police are working on that.'

A footman approached them, offering to replenish their drinks.

The Queen lifted her glass reflexively, but she was still looking at the chaise longue, and frowning now.

Daphne glanced over towards Philip, standing in a group of men all raucously laughing. Whatever the Queen was worried about, he either didn't know or hid it well.

'But William was really shockingly bad,' the Queen muttered to herself.

'I'm sorry, ma'am?'

The Queen turned to Daphne and gave her the full force of her open smile. 'I'm repeating myself. Don't worry, it's nothing. Mis— what did you call it?'

'Misdirection.'

'What do *you* think really happened, Daphne?'

Daphne, whose own ideas had covered orgies, psychopaths, satanists and devotees of the Marquis de Sade, decided to share none of these with Her Majesty. She was trying to come up with something suitably anodyne when she realised the Queen wasn't listening anyway. She was looking back at the chaise longue again, in a world of her own.

PART 3

A WOMAN OF EASY VIRTUE

CHAPTER 38

It wasn't that the Queen didn't trust the members of her own household: it was just a simple fact that it was possible for someone to listen in to conversations over the internal palace telephone system without the caller knowing. She assumed that the operators didn't, but it wasn't a chance worth taking, so she and Philip had worked out a sort of code between them ('The Oaks' meant 'I need to talk to you urgently in private' and 'Pall Mall' meant 'I love you' and . . . other things).

Now that she knew not to trust someone in her Private Office, the Queen needed a written code for working with Joan too. With her APS back in London, she couldn't be absolutely sure that her written memos wouldn't be read by someone else.

The answer hadn't taken them long to come up with: private messages were included in instructions about frocks and gloves. Any of the men in moustaches would run a mile at the details of waist measurements and corsetry. The Queen handwrote her notes and put them in envelopes casually paper-clipped to a memo about her wardrobe, as if they contained scraps of fabric or suggestions for embroidery.

The note in front of her was difficult to write. Not because of the content, which was straightforward, but because it meant doing something she hadn't done since she was a teenager – trusting someone outside her inner circle with her most personal thoughts about a crime and its possible solution. And when she was a teenager, that hadn't gone to plan. Not at all. She had learned self-reliance the hard way.

It was talking to Daphne after the ridiculous game of Nebuchadnezzar that had made her change her mind this time. She carved out ten minutes before tackling the remains of her boxes after breakfast to put her thoughts on paper. If Joan wasn't already helping her out with the matter of the sabotage, she didn't know what she would have done. The next steps weren't ones she could take for herself. Little girls, picturing one as Queen, often assumed one had infinite powers, and would be horrified, she judged, to discover how very much she could not do. Talking to prostitutes and their associates, to take one example. Questioning a police inquiry, for another. She could *do* it, but the consequences would be severe.

The thing about the sabotage of her state visits was that it was an act against her job. It was a job she had sworn to do for the rest of her life, in Westminster Abbey, surrounded by the great and the good and watched by millions on television and, more importantly, God, and nobody on earth could take it more seriously than she did.

But it was a job.

And this was different. Being used as an alibi in the case of the Chelsea murders was personal. If anything went wrong, it would affect her marriage . . . Her role as head of state, too, in consequence, but it went deeper than that. As she crafted each line, she was careful not to mention exactly why she was so concerned about what happened to the couple in Cresswell Place – but she was writing to Joan in part because her APS was the most perceptive, quick-thinking woman she knew right now, and it wouldn't take her long to work it out.

It would be so much easier just to sit back, go for some lovely dog walks and picnics, and let Inspector Darbishire deal with this. But he wasn't dealing with it. Or rather, he was making glacially slow progress. And why was he in charge of such a high-profile case at all? What about Chief Inspector Venables? The Queen hadn't forgotten that Chelsea's police division had failed to roll out its star.

With this in mind, she was struck by what Daphne had said about women and history, and by William being so shockingly bad at imitating Althea Gibson. Men were not good at telling women's stories.

What if this was a woman's story?

Darbishire was focusing on Nico Rodriguez. It was understandable, given his gambling, his dirty trading, his possible involvement with London gangs. But what about the girl? The poor 'tart in the tiara', laid out on the bed in her underwear? Having failed to prove that she was involved with Lord Seymour, who owned the diamonds in question, the inspector seemed to have lost interest in her. She had become a footnote.

The Queen found women endlessly interesting. She found women who dressed as princesses and were then murdered within walking distance of Buckingham Palace worthy of her full attention. Then there was the *other* thing Daphne had said about misdirection. There was something about the way Gina Fonteyn was lying on that bed that Darbishire hadn't fully understood yet, she felt sure of it. She also knew that women talked to other women in ways they didn't talk to men. If senior police officers could be female . . . just imagine what they might uncover. It was certainly a novel idea.

At last, she felt there was something she could do.

She wrote her list of instructions to Joan and knew she had taken one of the biggest risks of her reign so far. With a deep breath and a sense of purpose, she folded the note in half and slid it into its envelope, which she labelled 'US and Canada accessories, etc.', and put with the rest of her correspondence, to go to London that afternoon.

CHAPTER 39

Joan took the note out of its envelope while sitting on the lavatory in the ladies' bathroom in the North Wing corridor. It was the once place she could be assured of privacy.

The first page was a discussion of gloves and covered buttons. The second, written in pencil in the same confident hand, was very different.

> I trust the question of my first speech is progressing. We can talk about it further on my return.
>
> In the meantime, I have a request. If you can't do it, I will trust your decision. It is a matter that requires great diplomacy, but my concern is simple: I wish D. to make progress in Chelsea. Please can you find out more about the princess? I believe a woman's touch may be required. Full privacy is essential.
>
> There is also the matter of the Diana, as we discussed. I fear you might have been mistaken. Please rectify.
>
> ER

Joan sat quietly for several minutes. On first reading, the note made no sense to her. It was written as if she knew exactly what the Queen would be talking about, but she certainly did not. Who was 'D'? What about 'Chelsea'? And which of the many, many princesses Joan had recently read about in the course of her new job was the Queen referring to? That was all odd enough, but the last lines were simply wrong. 'Diana' had never come up in their brief conversations. What was Joan supposed to be mistaken about?

However, it didn't take long for her to switch into Bletchley mode. Don't focus on what you *don't* know, look at what leaps out at you. Joan let the words swim in front of her, and her mind relax. Her instinct soon told her that the first paragraph was in fact familiar. The 'first speech' must be the first one they had talked about together: the one that went missing in France. The Queen hoped Joan was making progress with the men in moustaches. Yes, she was.

The second was familiar too, though in a way that didn't fit. She had never discussed Chelsea with the Queen, but it had been in the newspapers a lot recently. Could Her Majesty be referring to the murders? Surely, they weren't connected to her? . . . But she *had* requested the police reports. Joan had overheard Sir Hugh expostulating to Miles Urquhart about them. *She's getting involved where she has no business to be. Sympathy for the lady victim, no doubt. Sometimes, I think we need to rescue her from her better nature.*

The reports would be in the windowless office next to Sir Hugh's, which contained several filing cabinets of sensitive documents and was always kept locked. Joan, as the 'filing fairy', as Urquhart had somewhat horrifically named her, was one of the few people with a key. Finding the documents would be the least of her problems. The latest updates would be missing, because the Queen would still have them in Balmoral, but Her Majesty knew that, and so must mean that Joan could get what she needed from the ones that were still in London.

After that, other details settled roughly into place. 'D' would make sense once she read the reports, presumably. Was that connected to 'Diana', below? Perhaps. The 'princess' might just be – and Joan realised it had been her very first thought, which she had automatically dismissed as too unlikely – the prostitute, or the 'tart in the tiara' as everyone called her. Newspaper speculation was that she might have been dressed as Grace Kelly, who was now Princess Grace of Monaco. Or perhaps just the fact of the diamonds made her look princess-like. The 'woman's touch' might involve talking to her friends or fellow workers. And yes, Joan could imagine them talking more easily to a woman than a man.

All of this would be easy to prove or disprove once Joan unearthed the paperwork. But it didn't help with those last lines.

Joan racked her brain, even though her memory was excellent and she knew she wasn't missing anything. She and the Queen had never

S. J. Bennett

discussed a Diana – not in literature or art, nor as a friend or relative of Her Majesty, or of Joan herself. They might easily have done in any of those guises, which was why she felt Her Majesty was clever to use it. If asked, Joan could make up a dozen false explanations without thinking. But they *had not* done so. She couldn't have been mistaken about something that never came up.

And why 'the Diana', and not just 'Diana'? Nothing in this note was accidental.

Joan closed her eyes and trusted to her subconscious again, but this time, it had nothing to offer.

Never mind. She tucked the note into her handbag, refreshed her lipstick in the mirror at the basins and went back to her office. On the way, she paused at the low bookshelf in the corridor containing a full, leatherbound set of the latest *Encyclopaedia Britannica*. She picked out the volume 'DAMASCUS TO EDUC' and took it with her. Once back at her desk, she flipped to the page on 'Diana' and skimmed through the entries.

It didn't take long.

One of the descriptions ran '*in the Roman religion, goddess of wild animals and the hunt, identified with the Greek goddess Artemis*'.

There it was. The Artemis Club had been in the newspapers a lot recently. It was regularly mentioned in the Private Office. That would explain the 'the' before the name. But she and the Queen had never discussed the Artemis Club either. That was Prince Philip's domain. He attended often, the newspapers liked to speculate what he and his friends did there, and he had even been there the night of the . . .

Oh God.

He had been there the night of the Chelsea murders, as had the suspects in the case. But he had come back to the palace before the murders were committed. That was what the papers said.

Oh God, oh God.

She wasn't mistaken. *They* were.

Joan watched as her skin formed goosebumps. This would call for more than the 'diplomacy' the Queen had so lightly mentioned. It was as delicate and dangerous as anything she had done at Bletchley.

She was terrified at the level of trust and responsibility.

And her body thrilled with it.

CHAPTER 40

The woman in the black silk cocktail dress and matching opera coat looked as if she would be more at home in Mayfair than the run-down streets behind Clapham Common in South London. She was looking for one of the Victorian houses that had long since been converted into flats. When she found the right number, she negotiated the cracked basement steps carefully in her patent heels, dodging the coal sacks and the line of empty milk bottles by the bottom door. She rapped on the knocker and waited.

Eventually, it was opened by a younger blonde, with the bone structure of a movie star and her hair in curlers. She was in the middle of doing her makeup: one lid a perfect cat's eye, the other bare.

The visitor smiled politely. 'Are you Beryl? Beryl White?'

'Who's asking?'

'I'm here on behalf of a friend.'

The blonde looked the other woman up and down. 'Oh, you are, are you? Anyway, she's out. Can I take a message?'

The woman in black knew that she was talking to Beryl herself. The other woman's inability to lie convincingly had been noted. 'It's about Gina,' she said.

Beryl went rigid with fear and suspicion.

'Look,' she said, catching her breath, 'I don't know anything about anything, OK? I haven't talked – I know how to keep my mouth shut.' She made to shut the door. 'So, whoever you're from, you can put that in your pipe and smoke it.'

The woman in black planted her patent shoe firmly inside the door frame. She talked fast and low.

'I'm not from whoever you think. In the press, everywhere, Gina's just been "the tart in the tiara". I think she deserves more, don't you? I know she does. This . . . person I'm working with thinks they can help. It can't bring her back, but it might get justice for her.'

Beryl kept up the pressure on the door. 'Gina's dead. There's no justice for girls like her.'

'Like *us*,' the woman in black said. She held Beryl's gaze.

Beryl seemed surprised and looked her up and down. Suspicion turned to curiosity.

'Well, there's no accounting for taste.'

'I assure you, I work in the highest circles.'

'Do you, now? So, your "friend" was a friend of Gina's, too?' she asked.

'Like I say, I have friends in high places. So did she.'

The door opened a fraction wider. 'Come in.'

★ ★ ★

Joan walked down the small, cold, dark corridor behind Beryl with a mixture of pride and irony. If Tony Radnor-Milne could take her for a woman of easy virtue, then so, it seemed, could one of the star escorts of the Raffles agency. It had its uses.

The flat smelled of damp and fried bacon. They passed a tiny kitchenette that wasn't much more than a gas ring and a cupboard, and a dining area piled high with boxes and lined with racks of hanging clothes. After these, when Beryl opened the door to the room at the back, it reminded Joan of the attic in *A Little Princess*.

The bedroom was unexpectedly large, and festooned with colourful silks. It was lit by lamps draped with sari fabric and the walls were a patchwork of pasted pages from fashion magazines. A two-bar fire took off the worst of the chill. Joan perched against a chest of drawers stuffed with towels, clothes and makeup boxes, while Beryl indicated the little bathroom opposite the open door.

'I'm busy. I've got to be out of here in fifteen minutes. But we can talk.'

She worked on her makeup in the bathroom mirror. Joan didn't mind at all. It was easier to talk if they weren't facing each other anyway.

'I already told that stuffed shirt from the police what I know,'

Beryl said. 'But he didn't believe me. Of course he didn't. I'm just a tart, aren't I?'

'What did you tell him?' Joan asked. Beryl mustn't know that she had access to the reports – which by the way included her address, which Joan was absolutely certain she wasn't allowed to use for encounters like this. If she was ever caught, 'gross insubordination' would be the least of it.

'Well, I made up a little white lie that I had a headache and I asked Gina to stand in for me,' Beryl admitted. 'But it was true that she didn't mind. She *wanted* to. That policeman had it in his head that I set her up, but I didn't. He wouldn't listen.'

'They never do,' Joan called out. She was enjoying her new persona. It was liberating.

'I *told* him I only went to my sister's because I was in a panic and missing my friend. He was positive I'd arranged the whole thing on behalf of the Billy Hill gang or something,' Beryl said. 'I got the idea that maybe a gang *was* involved, and they'd come after me. I s'pose just now I thought you were one of them, maybe. But I've been thinking. Gina wasn't mixed up in anything dodgy like that. She *wouldn't*. Nor would I. So, that policeman can go hang himself.'

Joan was struck by something Beryl had said earlier. 'You told him Gina wanted to stand in for you. So it was *her* idea to swap places?'

Beryl popped her head round the door. The other eye was done now. She looked magnificent.

'Definitely. She asked, and it was no skin off my nose. I pointed out he needed a blonde, and she said she'd dye her hair. It wasn't a bad idea. She could make more money that way. Gentlemen prefer them, et cetera.'

'Don't they just!' Joan rolled her eyes.

'I warned her Perez . . . Rodriguez . . . whoever the papers say he was . . . had a reputation for not being kindly, shall we say? Gina said she knew.'

'Why did she do it? Choose him, I mean. Did she, um, like that sort of thing?'

The woman in black had a much broader imagination than the original Joan, she realised, to her own surprise. She was developing a persona for herself. 'Elaine', who was worldly-wise, well travelled and largely unshockable.

'What? Are you joking?' Beryl scoffed. 'Gina liked champagne and roses. She liked to go dancing. Blokes like him? You grit your teeth and get on with it. Maybe she just wanted to go blonde and this was the start of it. He was some sort of VIP. Not like the posh ones, but he got what he wanted. She was always very ambitious, was Gina. I mean, *really* ambitious. She wanted to hook a prince or something. She seemed to think she could get one, too.' Beryl turned back to the bathroom. 'And look what happened.' She went back to her bathroom mirror.

'Weren't you worried when you didn't hear from her afterwards?'

'Of course! I was going spare with it. I called the hotel where they were supposed to go, but they didn't know anything. I thought he might've actually taken her to the Dorchester, and maybe he'd paid for more time with her, but those posh hotels pretend nothing like that would ever happen. Nothing under their snooty roof. They wouldn't talk to me.'

'You had no idea she'd gone to Cresswell Place?'

'Why would I? I didn't even know she had a key.'

'Where was she supposed to go?'

'A cheap place in Earl's Court. I'm not surprised she changed her mind. She'd been to Cresswell Place before. A few of us had. It was nicer. She'd probably kept the key from back then.'

'Wouldn't the agency have noticed?' Joan asked.

'I doubt it. We lose keys all the time. They just get replacements made. It's not a problem.'

Joan pushed from her mind the sympathy for the poor tenants who knew nothing about the free use of their front doors. 'Elaine' didn't care about such details.

'And it was definitely Gina's idea to go there, not his?'

Beryl looked in and now her eyelashes were twice as long. Her cheeks were brighter too. 'I s'pose. If the agency didn't send them, that brute wouldn't've thought to go. He wasn't a real VIP, however much he liked to think he was. He got mates rates for some reason, but he was nobody special.' She disappeared again.

'Why didn't you tell the police? About Gina coming to you in the first place? Why say you had a headache?'

'Because she had a secret, didn't she?' Beryl said in slightly muffled tones. 'Why else would she want to swap for a slime-ball like Perez?

There was something she didn't want anyone to know, not even me. I wasn't going to tell *them* that.'

'Why not?'

Beryl snorted derisively. 'Wouldn't trust those bedbugs as far as I could throw 'em.'

So the Queen had been right. Women talked to women more easily than they talked to men.

'I saw the inspector on the news,' Joan called out, truthfully. 'He looked all right.'

'He means well enough, but . . . he's one of them, isn't he?'

Beryl popped back again, lipstick done. Her face had more definition, but it had lost a certain softness that Joan actually preferred. She wondered if 'Elaine' swung both ways. Goodness.

'"One of them"?' she repeated.

'They make it pretty clear what side they're on. You go to them 'cause someone's roughed you up, or not paid up, and next thing you know, you're the one in the clink. Why bother?' Beryl shuddered 'Take that weasel, Willis, he's a right one.'

'Willis?'

'Copper from the Vice Squad. Looks like a Boy Scout. You must know him.'

'Oh, him!' Joan said, nodding as if she did.

Beryl warmed to her theme. 'Makes out he's like your big brother in public. He's all, "Can I help you, miss? What seems to be the problem?" And the minute you're in private, he's all over you like a wet cloth. He's got cold fingers and all. Lets you know there's nothing he couldn't do to you if he was minded. Evil sod.'

'Bastards,' Joan said, with relish.

Beryl shrugged and looked briefly wistful. She started expertly removing the curlers from her hair, untwisting them by feel and depositing them in a heap on the chest of drawers beside Joan.

'They're not *all* like that, to be fair. There's one I met. Tall bloke. A sergeant, I think. Very kindly-looking, but strong, too. Massive shoulders. I wouldn't've minded him taking care of me.' She laughed. 'But his guvnor hardly let him say a word. He was too busy telling me about "dangerous characters" who wanted to cut me up. I was so scared I didn't know *what* to think. I wasn't going to get involved.

Besides, it was too late for Gina.' She bit her lip and welled up, reaching for a tissue so she could carefully remove tears before they did any damage.

'I'm so sorry.'

'Why? It's hardly your fault. Anyway, it's not me you need if you want to know what she was up to. It's Rita, her flatmate. Best buddies, those two. If anyone knows anything, she would.'

Joan remembered the reference to an interview with the flatmate in Darbishire's report. It didn't contain any useful information, other than confirming what Beryl had already told them and adding a little bit about Gina's background. But it also mentioned that Rita had been arrested twice when the club where she worked was raided, which made Joan wonder how cooperative she would have been.

'Where would I find her?' she asked.

Beryl looked at her watch.

'She'll be onstage at The Cat's Pyjamas in a couple of hours. In Soho. She's a dancer. Rita Gollanz. The best legs in the West End. Say I said hello.'

'Thanks.'

'And . . . Bed of Roses,' Beryl said firmly, peering at Joan again.

'I'm sorry?'

'You're wearing the wrong lipstick. Bed of Roses by Helena Rubinstein. It's more subtle, less orange. It'll suit your hair better. And get someone to show you how to do your eyebrows. If you're ever this way again, I can.'

Joan grinned. 'Thanks. I will.'

* * *

The Cat's Pyjamas in Brewer Street was a doorway between a Soho pub and an ice-cream shop, leading down to a dim-lit room where bored-looking girls with beautiful bodies gyrated for tired-looking men nursing their drinks at little tables. The music, provided by a trio consisting of piano, double bass and drums, was surprisingly good. Joan knew she looked out of place as she sat alone at a corner table in her evening dress, drinking bitter lemon. She had half expected to be accosted, but she didn't even attract a second glance. Given recent experience, she felt safer here than at the Ritz.

'Rita the Cheetah' came on as the third act, and did indeed have impressively shapely legs. She danced with rhythm and a sly smile that made her much more popular with the punters than the other girls. Over the course of the number she shed a scarf, a pair of animal-print shorts and a little top, ending up in fishnets and robust black satin underwear.

Outside, Joan waited at the performers' entrance for her to appear. Under the harsher street lights, Rita's bright red lipstick and kohl-dark eyes made her look unwell. She was also painfully thin under her cotton jacket. She eyed Joan suspiciously.

'I saw you inside. What do you want?'

'Beryl sent me,' Joan said. 'I've got some questions about Gina if you—'

'Well, you can sod right off,' Rita retorted, clacking rapidly down the street in high heels.

Joan chased after her. 'I'm not from the papers.'

'That's what they all say.'

'I'm . . . I work for one of her gentlemen,' Joan said. She had been coy about it with Beryl, but 'Elaine' was getting more confident.

'And Beryl sent you?'

'She said to say hello.'

Rita paused. 'Look, I've got twenty minutes. D'you want to grab a drink? There's a jazz club that'll let us in. I know the doorman.'

The club was perfect: busy and loud, making it hard for other customers to hear their conversation. Joan paid for gin-and-it cocktails for them both and they settled into a red velvet banquette together.

Rita narrowed her eyes. 'Swear you're not just writing more tosh about those bloody diamonds?'

'Guide's honour,' Joan said, holding up her hand in the salute, with thumb and little finger touching. 'I promise I'm not wasting your time. My "friend" is somebody influential. A private detective, you might say.'

'Like Hercule Poirot?'

Joan grinned. 'If you like.'

'And he wants justice for Ginette? Ha! That never happens.'

'It's worth a try though, isn't it?' Joan frowned. 'Ginette, did you say?'

Rita nodded. 'Nobody called her that, though, except me. Ginette Fleury, she was, really.'

'I thought she was Italian.'

'Most people did,' Rita said with a shrug, 'so she went along with it. She was from Normandy, really. But one of her boyfriends called her Gina years ago and she thought it sounded nice. Like Gina Lollobrigida. So, it became her stage name, while she danced. She made out she was from Napoli.'

'What about the accent?' Joan asked. 'Wasn't it all wrong?'

Rita laughed. 'You think anyone noticed? In our line of work? She could've been Portuguese. It was French, really, very saucy, but she spaghetti'd it up, you might say. *You are-a so incred-i-bee-lay. Tee armow.* Ginette used to listen to Italian songs and watch their movies. And if she had an Italian gentleman, she'd just say she grew up in France. They didn't care. As long as she jiggled.'

Joan pictured the sticky, dim-lit stage where Rita had just performed. 'How did she end up dancing?'

Rita cocked an eyebrow at her. 'She *started* dancing. Don't look at me like that. And don't pretend you weren't. How'd you get into it?'

Joan looked as 'Elaine' as she could. A hint of Marlene Dietrich. 'Long story.'

'Well. Ginette was a very good dancer. She worked hard, and she knew what she wanted.'

'Which was?' Joan asked.

'A leg up. Via whatever means worked.' Rita gave Joan a knowing look and took a sip of her cocktail. 'When Raffles said they'd take her, she was made up. It was the next step for her. Meeting classy gentlemen.'

'Mmm,' Joan agreed. 'The money's better.'

Rita looked unimpressed. 'It wasn't the money. She wanted to meet people. Important people. The agency had the best, and she gave them what they wanted.' She looked down at the table. 'They were lucky to have her,' she muttered.

Joan reached across and placed her hand over Rita's. 'I'm sure you're right.' They sat like that, for a while. 'And yet, she asked for Perez,' Joan prompted gently. 'I wouldn't have said he was classy.'

'No.' Rita shook her head. 'Not from what they said in the papers afterwards. Ginette just said she'd seen this man at the agency when she was popping in to sort out some cash. And she was going to see him again and she needed to dye her hair. I helped her do it.' Rita looked stricken. 'If I hadn't . . .'

'There's nothing you could have done,' Joan soothed. 'Gina sounds like a very determined lady. Ginette,' she corrected herself.

'Short for Genevieve,' Rita explained. 'Her sister called her Ginette.'

'Oh? She had a sister? Is she in London too?'

'No. She's dead. Marianne, she was called. She was a Resistance fighter in Paris in the war. She was caught and tortured by the Gestapo. She died in a camp somewhere – I don't remember the name. One of those . . . you know. People didn't come back. Ginette was fifteen at the time.'

'Oh my God. Were they close?'

'Marianne was like a mother to Ginette. She said there was nothing in Paris for her after that. She came to England as soon as she could find a way.'

'How?' Joan asked.

Rita shrugged. 'I don't know how, exactly. She didn't talk about it.' She gave Joan a sideways look. 'I should imagine gentlemen were involved, knowing Ginette. She was a grown-up girl. She knew how to look after herself.'

And yet, she hadn't.

Which brought Joan back to that night in the mews house.

'Beryl said Gina . . . Ginette . . . asked to swap with her. Do you know why?'

'No. She seemed excited. Like something really good was going to happen, you know?'

'How did it show?

'It was just her mood. When we were dyeing her hair. Sort of feverish, if you know what I mean.'

Joan thought she did. She was reminded of fellow Wrens from her wartime digs again. Sometimes, going to meet a new man, they'd had a certain look about them. It was a heady mixture of anticipation, uncertainty and bravado. They were about to do something they would never get away with in peacetime. Fun, with a hint of danger. But those wartime girls had been going to meet lovers. And Rita had been clear, Rodriguez wasn't that.

'Did she talk about him? Rodriguez, I mean? Perez, as he called himself.'

'No. Just her hair. That it had to be perfectly "princess" and very blonde. She looked a dream.'

'Did she say where they were meeting?'

'No, the silly pet. If she'd told me about that mews place, I could've told the police as soon as I started to worry. She normally did tell me, too, in case anything went wrong, you know. She'd leave a note next to the kettle. But not this time. The police assumed I was the person who rang up, but it wasn't me. I kept telling the sergeant who talked to me, but he wasn't listening.'

'And what about the diamonds? Do you know why she was wearing those particular ones?' Joan saw Rita's eyes narrow. 'I'm not from the papers, I promise! But I have to ask.'

'No,' Rita said harshly. Joan sensed she didn't want to think of her friend being reduced to the 'tart in the tiara'. 'I never saw them. She went on about her hair, and about the dress. It was a beautiful white chiffon thing she found in Debenhams. She looked like a goddess. But her hair was just in a chignon. She never even mentioned diamonds. When I heard about . . . what happened . . . I never thought of Ginette. I was sure it must be someone else . . .'

'Did she know Lord Seymour?' Joan asked.

'N-no,' Rita said. 'The copper asked me that too. She didn't.'

Joan caught her hesitation. 'You don't sound sure.'

'Oh, I am. It's just that he asked for her once. He went for Jean Harlow types. Really old-fashioned blondes, you know, so she didn't fit back then, being brunette as she was, but he'd heard good things about Ginette. This is ages ago. Anyway, she said no *way*. She was very fierce about it when she told me, but laughing too. I don't know what it was, but she didn't want anything to do with him. He's the last person who could've given them to her.'

And yet, someone had. And for some reason, Gina – or Ginette – had worn them to an assignation in a place she'd told no one about, with a man she knew to be violent, whom she seemed excited to meet. Joan couldn't make sense of any of it, but she had a lot to tell Her Majesty.

CHAPTER 41

Joan's letter to the Queen was marked 'Hartnell embroidery: notes for Canadian state visit' and contained several sketches of maple leaves . . . followed by a detailed account of her conversations with Beryl and Rita. She left out the bit about pretending to be an escort herself. Some things weren't meant for royal ears, or eyes. But she thought Her Majesty might be amused if she knew.

The Queen tucked the sealed envelope containing the letter into the pocket of her tweed jacket, and announced that she was off to visit her mother's fishing lodge on the estate.

'It may well need repairs. I want to give it a thorough inspection,' she told the page who fetched her wellingtons.

She took three of the corgis with her, loaded into the back of a sturdy Land Rover that she drove herself, headscarf knotted firmly under her chin, with her two protection officers travelling at a respectful distance behind her on the winding, pine-clad road through the estate.

The lodge was built as a log cabin with a long porch along the front, facing a deep, salmon-friendly pool in the river, and it looked as if it would be perfectly at home in Canada, amidst forests, snows and bears. This thought briefly made the Queen wince as she pulled up outside, remembering the live, televised, bilingual speech she had agreed to give there in less than a month. What a fool she had been!

She put on the handbrake and took a deep breath before getting out to let the corgis out of the back. They were thrilled to be in this smorgasbord of new smells and quickly set about examining as many of them as they could. Watching them fondly, the Queen found she was leaning against the Land Rover and was reminded that she had learned to fix the engine of one of these workhorses when she was a teenager at Windsor. She was proud of her achievement then, and still proud now. If she could master a Land Rover, she could certainly say a few words in front of a television camera. It would just take practice and patience, and practice and patience were both things she was good at.

Feeling better, and calling the dogs to her, she had a brief poke around inside the cabin, and then sat down on the porch. Her protection officers had parked their vehicle at a suitable distance and were only just visible through the trees. The sound of doggy snuffles and the splashes of river water running over rocks and stones provided the perfect backdrop for concentration. She took Joan's letter out of her pocket and read it, undisturbed.

So, Gina was in fact Ginette, and she was the one who set up the assignation at Cresswell Place. Her fellow escort had always said as much, but the policemen never believed her story. The Queen did, especially given the new detail that Ginette might have chosen the dean's house because she happened to have the key.

The more she looked over the letter, the more she was convinced that Ginette Fleury was not some poor unfortunate, caught up in the wrong place at the wrong time: she had wanted to be there. She had made it happen. Just as the Queen suspected, she was at the heart of everything.

Ginette knew that Dino Perez (or Nico Rodriguez, as the more recent police reports referred to him) could be violent, and yet she was excited to meet him. She had gone to the house willingly, and gone to great lengths to be the sort of girl he was looking for. The Queen searched for proof in Joan's account that this person was Princess Grace, but to her nagging concern, the proof wasn't there. Beryl White and Rita Gollanz only knew for certain that he had specified 'a princess'. Having been one herself, and with a sister who was the most famous princess in the world at the moment, the Queen found this disturbing. But something else nagged at her, like a cross-current in the stream.

Despite her concerns, the princess theme, the diamonds, the torn white dress from Debenhams, all felt like distractions – a means to an end. Everyone went on and on about what one wore oneself all the time, but to the Queen, it was just about being appropriate for the occasion. Her favourite outfit was the one she was wearing now: tweed breeches tucked into ancient wellies, a comfortable tweed jacket she'd had since she was twenty-one, and a scarf to keep her hair in check. She'd wear it every day if she could. Her diamonds were precious to her because each piece was a treasure trove of family stories, but in themselves, they were only stones, heavy to wear and difficult to keep clean. Daphne had talked about misdirection. What if the girl was important, but the diamonds weren't the point? What was the other nagging thing?

The Queen sat quietly for several minutes, listening to the running water. A face was hovering in her mind – an old man's face, and as she thought about it she saw that it was contorted into fury. And something about Argentina. And . . . Paris.

Ah yes! Paris! Ginette was French, so perhaps that explained it.

But the face she saw was that of the Comte de Longchamp, who had been scowling at the German ambassador that fateful evening at the Louvre. It was a glare of pure hatred – understandable, she thought, given what had happened to his Jewish wife and his family. The war might have ended twelve years ago, but by no means everyone had forgiven and forgotten. Some tragedies were too hard to bear.

Ginette had an older sister who worked in the Resistance, who was captured and tortured by the Nazis, and sent off to a concentration camp. Perhaps it was Ravensbrück, near Berlin. The Queen had heard of many Frenchwomen – and brave women from Great Britain too, sent by the Special Operations Executive to help the Resistance – who had suffered and died there.

What *was* it about Argentina? Something recent, something connected . . . something she had read not long ago. Then she remembered. It was a top secret memorandum from the Foreign Office, informing her that a senior Nazi officer was known to be living in Buenos Aires, and many others – quite possibly hundreds, or even thousands – were thought to have taken refuge in South America.

Could Rodriguez have been one of these men, who escaped across the Atlantic and reinvented himself?

There was something else . . . He liked to gamble in places like Monaco and Tangier, where French was a common language. Was he a Frenchman, perhaps? One who had worked for the Gestapo? That might explain how Ginette knew him.

If he *had* tortured Marianne Fleury, and if Ginette had somehow recognised him in London, her desire to see him, to be alone with him somewhere quiet, would make perfect sense.

She would have wanted to kill him.

Perhaps she had tried, and failed. Or did she succeed? Was she the one who used the garotte on him? Was she knifing him in the eye when somebody else came in and . . . what? What happened then? How did Ginette end up a victim too? The Queen couldn't picture it. She was missing something important.

Anyway, all of this was absolute conjecture, made up of Ginette's last known movements, her family history, Rodriguez's reputation for physical violence, a face in the crowd, a secret memorandum in her red boxes and . . . little more.

As she had done in the limousine on the Place de la Concorde, the Queen reflected that she would seem quite unhinged if she shared this half-formed theory with any of the men in moustaches. They would think her mad, and interfering in ways that were quite possibly dangerous to the Constitution. They would want to know why she cared so much in the first place. It wasn't as if she tried to solve every violent crime in London. And then they would wonder what else had gone on in Cresswell Place that night, and even though she didn't exactly know herself, that was the last thing she wanted them to think about.

She needed to talk to Joan. And she needed to do it privately and face to face.

It was now the second week of September. They would be back in London in less than a fortnight, at which point Charles was going off to boarding school at Cheam, as his father had done. What a lucky boy, the Queen thought, to be surrounded by pals his own age, running about outside and learning Latin together, not stuck in a stuffy schoolroom, as she had been with her sister, and every heir to the throne before her. She would miss him terribly, and her heart ached at the thought. But then again, she and Philip were off on their next state visits soon, and wouldn't he have more fun with his new friends than moping about the palace?

Once she'd safely delivered him, she could focus properly on the contents of this letter and decide what to do about it. Another week wouldn't make much difference, would it, after all these months? She would have to be patient. Which, fortunately, was one of those things she was good at.

Meanwhile, there had been more to her original instructions to her APS. Had Joan understood the reference to Diana? It was rather recherché. Joan hadn't mentioned any progress in that sensitive direction in her letter. As the Queen got up and dusted off her breeches, she wondered how she was getting on.

CHAPTER 42

Standing at the end of the little cobbled street, Joan could see why the Dean of Bath might have chosen Cresswell Place for his London pad. Given what had happened there, she had pictured the mews as somewhere gloomy and unsettling, but in the late summer sun, it looked like one of the jolliest streets in London.

The low rows of houses were the colours of sugared almonds, except for a few that were hung with red tiles. Joan liked the look of these the best. They were slightly larger than the others. One had a pair of newish windows set into its roof and, glancing up and shielding her eyes from the sun, she wondered who had put them there. For an instant, she thought she saw the figure of someone behind the glass, looking down on her. She realised she might seem rude for staring, and looked away.

She was here to see if she could make any more sense of the witness reports from the police file. The Queen had said she wanted 'D' to make progress in Chelsea. Having read the reports, which she had fished out of a cabinet in the Private Office filing room, Joan didn't think that Inspector Darbishire was particularly slow. Nevertheless, he was stumped, and had been for months. Despite all the male victim's nefarious activities, there was still no evidence of anyone entering the house other than the victims themselves, the dean and his friends; and Darbishire was still convinced none of them could have done it. Nor did he have a robust theory that threw a spotlight on Lord Seymour, or one of the London gangsters on his list.

Joan had the feeling of anyone coming fresh to an inquiry that her quick mind might solve the case. She looked for the house numbers. Number 44, the dean's house, looked unremarkable but rather sad.

The curtains were drawn at the dusty windows. A little bay tree in a pot outside was brown and dead. The dean, presumably, didn't want to live there any more and the landlords must have decided not to try and find anyone else. Darbishire still hadn't managed to find out who owned the building, exactly. He had the company name, but had made no progress on who owned the company.

Number 43, by contrast, was bright and clean, with open windows, fresh gingham curtains and a young rose plant being trained around the door. It had lain empty back in March, but it was cheerfully occupied now. To its right was the house where Mrs Pinder and her husband had been living. A witness further down the street had guessed that the supposed gunshot might have come from here, or the once empty house beside it.

Joan couldn't tell if the Pinders were still in residence at number 42. A large Rover saloon was parked in front of it, obscuring much of the view. Darbishire's report mentioned that there had been a falling-out with the academics who lived opposite at number 22, but gave no reason for it. Joan turned to see that this was the red-tiled house with the new-ish windows. The academics had left, according to the report, but someone was in there now. Meanwhile, the house to the right of that one, where the suspicious 'Gregsons' had lived, sat with windows and front door wide open. The ground floor had been gutted and a pair of plasterers were working on the inside, whistling loudly.

A low-slung Jaguar sports car came rumbling up the street and Joan stood out of the way to let it go by. She took one more look at all the houses, waiting to see if she could spot what the police had missed, but right now, the mews looked an impossible place for murder.

A walk around the nearby stucco villas of the Boltons taught her only that this was where she would want to live if she ever married a very, very rich man, and that it would be easy to escape from their gardens into the lovely square where she was standing via one of the side passages that ran from front to back.

Yes, getting away wouldn't have been particularly difficult for whoever had done it. It was getting in that was the trouble.

★ ★ ★

Back at home, Joan considered her next task, which was to find out about what really happened at the Artemis Club. She felt disloyal doing it, but knew that the Queen wouldn't have asked unless she was absolutely certain it needed to be done. Presumably, if Prince Philip hadn't come home from the club when he claimed, the Queen must have known this for months. Joan had a strong feeling Her Majesty needed an innocent explanation. But what if she couldn't provide one?

She would cross that bridge when she came to it. First, she had to find someone who would talk. She spent several days researching the club as discreetly as she could, collecting various items that Auntie Eva had sourced for her from a theatrical costumier friend, and watching the staff going in and out of the back entrance after dark.

The following Saturday, under glowering skies over Piccadilly, a forgettable pot-washer showed up with mud-brown hair, thick glasses and hands rubbed red raw from washing dishes. She entered the club at seven thirty behind a couple of sous-chefs, back from a ciggie break, wound her way up the sticky, badly lit servants' stairs, and found the manager's office without too much trouble.

'The agency sent me,' she said, staring down at the cracked lino floor. The club rooms, she imagined, were lavishly carpeted and lit with crystal lamps, but here, every expense was spared.

'What? Trumptons? Just now? Why?'

The harried manager barely looked up from the paperwork he was doing.

'I dunno why,' Joan said. 'Only that you were three down and could I make it, sharpish, time and a half?'

The manager looked up properly at this. 'Ha! Time and a half? You must be joking. We're two down, not three, but . . . Normal agency wages. Tonight and tomorrow, yes? Give your name to Mr Holland in Accounts. No going past the baize door.' This suited Joan. 'You know where the aprons are?'

'I'll manage,' she said.

She shut the office door and looked down the dingy corridor towards the sound of shouting and clanging pans coming from the club kitchen. She had no idea where the aprons were, but she would work it out. At the palace, they were always having trouble finding enough kitchen staff for big occasions. Joan had rightly guessed that on a Saturday night the club would be keen for whatever help it could get. And it would give her sore hands (she had rubbed salt into them at length) the weekend to recover. In the school holidays, she had occasionally helped out in the college kitchens at Cambridge. It was hot, busy, hard-going and thankless work: ideal for her purposes.

She headed down the corridor and into the kitchen.

'I'm 'ere from the agency,' she said again, in her best Cockney accent.

A tall, aggressive-looking man in chef's whites looked at her through a gap in several piles of unwashed plates.

'Thank God.'

He gestured towards a door that turned out to be the cupboard with the aprons. Joan put one on, wrapped her hair in a scarf and set to work, humming cheerfully to herself. The pressure-cooker atmosphere of the kitchen at peak service time took her back to her days in Cambridge. Soon she had reduced the teetering piles of dirty plates to neat stacks of clean ones, ready to go. She was quick at buffing glasses to a shine and good at taking on new greasy piles without complaint. The chefs de partie and even the front of house manager were grateful for her ability to get on with things without making a fuss.

Joan felt no need to ask questions at this point. As the evening wore on and service slowed a little, she joined in whatever kitchen chat there was. Her job tonight was all about teamwork, being amenable, suggesting she had a bit of money in her pocket and making friends.

Towards the end of service, when they were all looking forward to clearing up and clearing out, a harried house manager pointed at her.

'You – wassyourname?'

'Jennie, sir. Can I help?'

'You certainly can. There's been an incident outside the second floor lavatories. Somebody overindulged. Massive spew, all over the floor tiles. He didn't make it to the porcelain in time. I've got Frank on it, but he needs a hand. Grab a mop and bucket and—'

'But—'

'But nothing. Get on it, woman!'

'I'm not supposed to go beyond the—'

'Now! I'm not asking!'

She didn't have a choice. She found the required equipment, filled the bucket with hot water and asked one of the waitresses in the corridor where to go. With her backside, she pushed at the heavy baize door, insulated against the noise of the busy kitchen, that marked the entry to the carpeted quiet of the members' side of the club. She hadn't expected to come this far, but as long as she kept her head down, it couldn't do any harm.

Upstairs, the scene that met her was disgusting. The smell of it assaulted her from several feet away. Her stomach lurched. Frank, one of the dogsbodies like her, was doing his best, but he clearly needed help.

'Do what you can,' he said gratefully. 'I'll get another bucket.'

He disappeared upstairs, where Joan assumed there must be a service cupboard with access to running water. Sure enough, he came down a couple of minutes later, his bucket freshly filled, just as she needed fresh water of her own.

She took her bucket to the top of the third floor stairs and glanced around to find the cupboard. It wasn't easy in the dim light. There were two figures in evening dress, deep in conversation at the end of the corridor, slightly silhouetted by a Lalique lamp behind them. Joan started down the corridor trying each door in turn, hoping to find the door before she reached them, and not to put them off with the stinking contents of her bucket.

But before she found it, the taller of the two looked round with a wrinkle of nausea on his face.

'I'm sorry, sir!' Joan called out.

He continued to stare at her. She indicated the doors.

'I'm just looking for . . .' Oh.

She managed not to say the last word aloud.

The tall man looking at her was Tony Radnor-Milne. Dammit! Of all the people! Her wig was not a world-class disguise, because she had fully expected to stay on the servants' side of the baize door. Her bare-faced look was designed to stand up to the scrutiny of strangers, not men she had spent a long and traumatic evening with. But the corridor was dim and this was the last place he'd expect to see her. For the second time, she beat a quick retreat from his company.

'Excuse me,' she muttered, heading swiftly back the way she'd come. She went all the way back to the kitchen and left poor Frank to finish the mopping on his own.

★ ★ ★

A couple of hours later, Joan left with the last of the staff. While mucking in with the dirty jobs, she had nevertheless let it be known to

Frank and others that she was a little bit unusual for an agency temp: a bit older, with a nice wage as a shopgirl, just doing this for extra pin money. So when she said afterwards that she was stopping off at the café on the corner – one that stayed open all day and night to cater for people like them who worked all hours to be at the disposal of the toffs – Frank half-jokingly asked if she'd be paying. She assured him she was. Instantly a tired sous-chef and two waitresses showed eager interest. Joan bought a round of tea and toast with margarine for everyone.

They'd been through a long, hard Saturday night together, which formed bonds that might not last long, but felt real enough right now. There was plenty of sympathy for Joan, Frank and the 'sea of sick' outside the lavatory, and much gossip about the stripper who had allegedly been brought in for a private birthday party on the second floor, although none of those present had actually seen her. Joan let the conversation run its course before she glanced across the street and said,

'Ooh, the Reform Club. I was working there the night of those murders. Could 'ave sworn I'd seen that man, wot's 'is name? Perez—'

'No, Rodriguez, they say it is now,' the sous-chef said.

'Oh, is it? 'Im, then. I could've sworn I'd seen 'im at the club the night before. Sworn blind. Gave me the shivers.'

'Not that you can really tell, I suppose,' the waitress sitting opposite her said, 'when he'd had his throat cut and a knife in his eye.'

'Well, no,' Joan agreed. 'But there were the pictures of 'im before, you know. 'E looked exactly like this gentleman I saw in the street outside. Right there. 'Ave they found who did it yet? I 'aven't seen anything.'

'No, they 'aven't,' Frank said gloomily. 'And they won't. One of 'is criminal associates, no doubt. Fled the country. Surprised they're still bothered looking.'

A thought seemed to strike Joan. 'Oo! Weren't you lot in the papers too? The club, I mean. Wasn't it some of your members that probably did it?'

'They couldn't have,' the waitress beside Joan said with a shrug. 'The police don't seem to think so, anyway. Nobody was arrested. They've all been in since.'

Joan lowered her voice. 'But do you think . . . ?' she asked, eyes wide. 'I mean, between us, did one of them . . . ?'

'No!' the first waitress responded firmly. 'I mean, there's a few I wouldn't trust as far as I could throw them, fair enough, but I know all those three, and the dean too, and if anyone thinks they could have stabbed a man in the eye, they need their head examined.'

Joan kept her voice low, and her eyes as wide as they'd go, as if she was a fiend for gossip. 'I heard a rumour. That same night . . .' She let the line dangle in the air. If she was right, they'd all know what she was referring to. But she didn't want to be the one to say it.

The first waitress sighed. 'Oh, that! Give it up! That's old hat now. You mean the D of E?'

'Shh!' the sous-chef said, obviously worried about even this subtle reference to the Duke of Edinburgh. He raised a hand to his lips, but the waitress beside him batted it away.

'Oh, don't be silly, Bill. We all know what he was up to.' She rolled her eyes towards her female friend, who rolled them back.

'No! What?' Joan said breathily, leaning forward.

'Shh!' the sous-chef said again, drawing more attention to them as a group than anything else he could have done. But nevertheless, they all instinctively drew together across the table. They kept their voices down and spoke quickly, talking over each other.

'It's only a rumour.'

'No, it isn't! I saw it with my own eyes.'

'You did not!'

'Well, I heard it from Abel, who was right there on the street, putting the empties in the bins.'

'And what did 'e say?'

'He saw the coppers coming back round, circling, trying to see where the hell the duke was. They did it for twenty minutes.'

'Was Abel out there all that time?'

'No, he saw them the first time, and Jake or someone saw them twenty minutes later. Abel fell about laughing when he heard. Good on the duke! Job well done!'

'Hmph.' The women folded their arms in disapproval.

'What job?' Joan asked.

'Giving his security the slip, of course,' Frank said. 'Not the first time. He 'ates having them looking over his shoulder all the time. One minute 'e was in the lobby, calling loudly for his coat, and the next 'e was . . .' He imitated a puff of smoke with his hand. 'Pouf. Ha!'

'How?' Joan asked.

'With one of his friends,' the sous-chef explained. 'He'd parked his car round the corner. Prin—the D of E slipped out down our back stairs and roared off into the night with him. The security coppers were left standing outside the front door, looking like lemons.'

'And where did he go with his friend?' Joan asked.

Four pairs of eyebrows were raised sceptically at her.

'Where d'you think?'

She shrugged.

'Who knows?' the waitress beside Joan said. 'Somewhere he didn't want to be seen in public, anyway.'

'And nobody told the police about it?'

'Why would they?'

The sceptical expressions turned to puzzled frowns. Joan had an answer, which was that Prince Philip had disappeared the night of the murders, and wasn't where he said he was. She certainly wasn't going to say that aloud though.

'I dunno,' she offered instead, with a smile and a shrug.

The others looked serious. It was interesting how they were working as a unit suddenly, even though the men and women obviously felt differently about the getaway, as those folded arms still showed.

'What he does is his business,' the waitress opposite said fiercely.

'We'd never breathe a word,' said her friend, looking shocked at the very idea of it.

The others nodded. Joan could tell from their pointed gaze and the pause that followed that they expected something from her.

'Oh, right. Me too, Scout's honour,' she said, thinking they little knew how dependable she was. With one exception. And what on earth would they think if they knew who she intended to share their secret with?

*   *   *

She spent Sunday relaxing in the flat and rubbing her hands with Pond's Cold Cream to get rid of the worst of the redness. On Monday morning, she got ready for the office while trying to work out the wording of her message to the Queen. Joan could see why Her Majesty was anxious: not only did Prince Philip not really have an alibi for the night, but a worryingly large number of people knew about it. Despite their protestations of loyalty, surely it was only a matter of time before somebody talked to someone in the press. And then . . .

It was a cold, damp day with a hint of autumn in it. Joan unearthed a heavy waterproof coat she hadn't used since May and armed herself with an umbrella, just in case. Outside, the streets still shone from an overnight downpour. Schoolchildren filed along the streets in their fresh September uniforms. Avoiding puddles, she left Dolphin Square, crossed over Lupus Street into the heart of Pimlico, and headed towards Warwick Square.

Just as she reached the corner with Denbigh Street and started to cross, a black van came careering round the square at high speed. Joan spotted it just in time and stepped back towards the pavement to get out of its way. And yet, in slow motion, still it seemed to come towards her. Suddenly it was filling her vision and she could see it was going to hit her fair and square. There was something missing . . . something she should have . . . She was shocked and still trying hopelessly to avoid it when she felt a thump in her side. It knocked her clean off her feet and her head was about to hit the cold, hard ground. She flung out her left arm to save herself, hoping that her hat might somehow cushion her skull.

Then there was an almighty crack and the world went dark.

CHAPTER 43

'Where is she now?' the Queen asked faintly.

'In bed, ma'am. With concussion,' Miles Urquhart explained.

'And Sir Hugh telephoned you just now?'

'He did. I don't have all the details. It was a terrible accident. Wet road . . . hard to stop. I'm not sure she looked before she tried to cross.'

'Do they know who did it?'

The DPS saw that Her Majesty looked white as a sheet. But it wasn't as if the girl was dead. Just a broken wrist and a sore head. Urquhart sought to be reassuring.

'I don't think so, ma'am. As I say, it was an accident. But a very helpful passer-by saw what happened and took her to hospital in a cab. She's at St George's, but she should be out tomorrow.'

'I . . . Goodness me.'

The Queen was normally good with bad news, Urquhart reflected. She generally took it better than some men, remarkably. But not today.

'She'll be right as rain in no time,' he added cheerfully. 'And I'm sure we'll manage without her. We did before. Fiona may be ready to come back soon . . .'

He saw Her Majesty frown. The Queen liked this new girl, for some reason. Even if she couldn't cross a road without mucking it up.

'Thank you, Miles. Let me know if you hear anything else, will you?'

He had done what he could. Urquhart bowed and left.

Alone in her study at Balmoral, the Queen felt a pang of guilt so sharp it was as if someone had stabbed her. She went to the window and put a hand against the cool glass, waiting while it subsided.

She had sent Joan that note. She had made it clear the job might be difficult, and she knew it might even be dangerous, but she had never imagined they would go so far – whoever they were. Now, here she was, five hundred miles away and Joan could have died, and she was powerless to do anything about it. The more Urquhart assured her it was an accident, the more she felt certain that it wasn't.

★ ★ ★

Joan's head hurt like hell. She felt woozy, and dizzy whenever she opened her right eye enough to see out of it. A hank of hair obscured the view from her left eye. When she tried to lift her hand to push the hair away, she found it unaccountably heavy. When she looked down, the plaster cast on her left wrist caught her by surprise. She knew it was there, but kept forgetting.

'Nurse!' she called croakily. 'Nurse!'

The door opened and a head popped round. A male head, with short hair. She could hardly see him through her double vision.

'Please could you get someone to find my painkillers, doctor? I have a god-awful headache.'

'And you're blind!' he said, in a Scottish burr.

There was a hint of humour in his voice. He didn't mean she was really blind. She knew that voice.

'Hector!'

'You're not in St George's now, remember? You came home three hours ago. Your pills are on the side table, here.' He pointed somewhere, but she couldn't pay attention. 'Don't take them all at once.'

'No . . . I . . .'

He saw how out of it she was and took pity on her.

'Look, here you go.'

She took two pills from his proffered hand and he passed her a glass of water.

'Why aren't you at work?' she mumbled.

'Ha! So you don't know where you are, you can't see through that shiner on your eye, but you're worried about my job at the ministry.'

'It's not the ministry,' she said, closing her eyes. That much she knew.

'Yes it is,' he insisted.

She was quiet for a while, letting her closed eyes rest, but she didn't hear the sound of him leaving her room. He was hovering.

'There was a van,' she said eventually. 'Something . . .'

'Yes?'

'Something not . . . something missing. I—'

'Yes? What?'

He sounded genuinely concerned, not as if she was going mad. Joan tried to remember her last thoughts before she blacked out. The walk came back to her in shards and fragments. Crossing Lupus Street. The trees in Warwick Square ahead of her. The clouds overhead. Her hat. The road rising up to meet her . . . She jerked up, opened her eyes and winced.

'There, there,' that gentle Scottish burr intoned. 'Take it easy, girl.'

But she wanted to remember – not all of it – but the bit that had confused her. There was something wrong . . . something that made her frightened . . . And then something else didn't make sense. Too much.

'They said I was hit by a van,' she said, 'in hospital.'

'Mmm,' Hector agreed.

But no. She remembered now, being thumped from the side, like a rough hockey tackle. When it should have been head-on.

'I was on the street . . . and the van was . . .' She closed her eyes at the flash of memory. 'And someone pushed me out of the way. Didn't they? I don't see how I could have . . . The van was . . .'

'Did they?' Hector asked. 'I don't know about that. How very fortunate.'

'The person who came with me, to hospital. The nurses said they didn't leave their name.'

'Good Samaritans like to be anonymous.'

'I suppose . . .' Joan mumbled groggily.

'Go to sleep, girl,' he encouraged, leaning over her to adjust her pillows.

It seemed a good idea, so she did.

★ ★ ★

Joan's sleep was fitful, plagued by nightmares and disturbed by headaches. Her arm ached too, and her back and thighs. When she needed the lavatory, she had to stagger to the bathroom. She would have crawled but for her broken wrist. She lost another day to pain and confusion. But by evening, she was starting to feel less lost and brittle.

She was aware that Hector had been there for some of the time, tempting her with thin broth and cups of tea. He had even given her his arm to lean on when she decided she was well enough to sit in the living room – and again when she felt woozy and agreed that perhaps, after all, she wasn't.

When he wasn't popping his head round the bedroom door to check on her, she could hear him padding round the flat. His presence was reassuring, if surprising. It wasn't the weekend, was it? Meanwhile, as the fuzziness in her brain slowly receded, she worked on putting together what had happened.

A van had come speeding towards her. By extraordinary good fortune, someone had pushed her out of the way, just in time. Somehow – she couldn't imagine how – they had avoided being hit themselves. They had taken her to hospital and quietly disappeared. She remembered a lightning bolt of pain in her wrist as she put her hand out to protect her head from the worst of the fall.

The pain had distracted her from something. Not something that *was* there, but something that *wasn't* . . .

She thought about the van again, though she really didn't want to, and tried to picture the situation from above. It was a technique they had taught at Trent Park. She saw herself standing at the corner of the square and starting to cross the road, the van appearing from nowhere and heading for her, almost as if it was deliberate. No, not from nowhere. If she had paid attention, she might have seen it coming down the long side of the square, but she would never have imagined it to be travelling so fast. If the driver had been paying attention, he should have seen her too, but he obviously didn't, because . . .

Because . . . why? Why was she so sure he didn't?

Because she didn't hear the brakes.

Yes! That was what was missing as the van's metal grille blocked out the light, in the moments before she was shoved out of its path. There should have been the shocking squeal of brake pads and the hiss of tyres trying to grip the slick, wet road, but the engine noise didn't change.

He was heading straight for her. He meant to do it. He could easily have killed her if it wasn't for her Good Samaritan.

Joan juddered at the thought.

Oh, God. Her poor father. He'd never have got over it. And what about Her Majesty, if something had happened? Who else could she turn to? Joan had so much to tell her, not that all of it made sense at the moment. But if the driver had come for her once, he could do it again. She suddenly wondered what would happen if she didn't get the chance.

★　★　★

Hector Ross had been moving quietly round the flat, trying not to disturb his tenant while she slept. He was good at being quiet and unobtrusive. He'd had a lot of practice. However, when he put his head around the door an hour later, he found her sitting on the bed, half dressed, struggling to put on a shoe one-handed, and making a bad job of it.

'What are you doing, girl?' he berated her. 'You can't leave the flat! You need to rest! Och, your brain's gone completely doolally. Here, let me help you put your feet up.'

Joan put her good arm out to send him back. 'No! I need to go.'

'You really can't! You won't last ten minutes. Honestly, Joan, trust me. I wish you would.'

She sat there, pink in the face from the effort and regarding him fiercely.

'I have to get to my desk. There are things I need to do. I may not have much time . . .'

That knock to her head was worse than he thought. She was being silly. He folded his arms. 'Don't be so dramatic. I won't let you go.'

'You can't keep me here!'

'I will if I have to.'

'Look!' she said, rising to stand, swaying, and sitting back down, hard. 'I was nearly killed. Maybe you don't take it seriously, but don't tell me not to be dramatic.'

He put his hands up. 'I know. You've been through a lot. I'm sorry. But someone needs to take care of you at the moment. I . . . What?'

Joan's glare had become a puzzled frown. There was a spark of suspicion in her lovely, intelligent hazel eyes. Hector realised he'd made a rare mistake, but these were emotional times. He hadn't slept much recently.

'I told you I was nearly killed,' she said slowly, 'and you said, "I know."'

'Well, of course you were!' he expostulated. 'A van nearly ran you over.'

'You said it was an accident.'

'Exactly.'

She shook her head. 'It wasn't . . .' She was staring at him again. 'And I don't think you think so, either.'

Her lips were tight. He should have told her not to be silly. The trouble was, he agreed with her and he hadn't thought she'd work it out so quickly, if at all. She had caught him off guard.

The frown line between her eyebrows deepened.

'What do you know, Hector?'

'Nothing!' he protested, with a well-practised look of innocence that didn't seem to assuage her at all.

'Were you there? No. Did someone call in? Were you having me followed?'

'Of course not! I'm not some sort of mad obsessive, Joan. I'm just your concerned landlord, that's all. And I'm worried about those pills of yours. Perhaps you ought to halve the dose.'

Her voice was cold.

'What do you know?' she repeated.

'What *is* there to know?'

She shook her head and winced at the pain of it, and it was worse than the coldness because now there were tears in her eyes.

Her voice broke as she said, 'Stop lying, please. I don't have the energy. Someone's trying to kill me, and you know it. And you know about the suitcase. I saw you glance at it just now. And I know about the Secret Service. Or, what do you call it?' She frowned, trying to remember the official name that was rarely spoken. 'MI5. So cut the bullshit, Hector. Did you have me followed?'

He sighed. This hadn't gone the way he expected at all. *He* should be the one asking questions.

'I'll bring you a tray,' he offered. 'I've been warming up some soup.'

CHAPTER 44

There was more than soup. To Hector's frank amazement, a footman had delivered a hamper from the palace that morning, containing two large Thermos flasks of cock-a-leekie, a loaf of fresh bread, a glass jar filled with handmade chocolates and a box of heather-scented shortbread. There was also a large bouquet of tasteful white flowers from the Queen's favoured florist, and a handwritten note in calligraphic script, saying 'Get well soon'.

Hector showed Joan the message and put the flowers, roughly arranged in a water jug, among the scattered kirby grips and photograph frames on her nightstand. He plumped her pillows and put the soup tray on her lap. She seemed somewhat mollified, but not as much as he had hoped.

'Somebody is concerned about you,' he observed. 'Do you recognise the handwriting?'

She looked at the note blankly and shook her head. 'No.'

'Not Sir Hugh, then? I wondered.'

She raised half an eyebrow. 'Not him. A clerk, I think.'

She knew he was fishing, and she wasn't giving anything away, this girl. Hmm. He badly needed information from her, but even in her weakened state, it wasn't going to be easy to get her to talk.

'Come on, girl, eat.'

Joan did as she was told. He had tried the soup and knew it was perfectly seasoned and quite delicious. Goodness knew, she needed it. In a brief pause between spoonfuls, she looked up at where he stood between the nightstand and the doorway and said flatly, 'So, you had me followed.'

She was understandably miffed.

'You may think that,' he said, 'but you've been in a serious accident. I'm not surprised your brain's all over the place. And perhaps you're right. Perhaps it wasn't an accident. But who on earth would want to hurt you? I don't understand.'

Joan didn't even look at him. She finished the soup, ate some of the bread, put the tray to one side, and said, 'No.'

'No, what?'

'No, I'm not answering your questions until you answer mine.'

'I'm only trying to help.'

Joan closed her eyes and settled back against her pillows.

'Shut the door on your way out.'

Dammit. If only her brain *was* all over the place. He needed to know who had targeted her. It mattered for her own safety as much as anything else. And yet she wouldn't cooperate. Hector could understand why not: she didn't approve of being tailed.

'Even if you *were* followed, I could never admit it,' he offered. It was the best he could do. Surely she could understand?

Joan opened one eye.

'Why?'

'Why can't I admit it?'

'Why did you have me followed?'

This was very delicate. 'You have to trust me. There's only so much I can say.'

He saw her hackles rise as the other eye opened.

'*Trust you?*' she retorted. 'You're spying on me. You think I'm some sort of enemy agent . . .'

'I promise you, it's not—'

There were practically sparks coming off her now. 'You had no right to do this, Major Ross!'

'I assure you, it was for your own g—'

'Get out!'

She found a small, embroidered cushion on the bed and flung it at him with force.

Hector withstood the cushion, but not her fury and refusal to cooperate. It was obvious he wasn't going to get anything out of her if he kept feigning innocence. Besides, the whole situation was so odd he really didn't know quite how to handle it. Hostile forces and deep-cover sleeper agents he could manage, but complicated women in sensitive positions who suddenly started dressing up . . .

'I don't think you're an enemy agent,' he said quietly. 'You were seen somewhere you weren't supposed to be. Questions were raised. The simplest thing was to get someone to check what you were up to. He had no idea he'd end up saving your life.'

Joan glared at him furiously. 'He was tracking me! Don't make it sound as if I should be grateful!'

Hector shrugged. 'When he started following you, it was more out of curiosity than anything. But you must admit, a junior secretary at the palace who hides wigs in a suitcase and dresses up as a little old lady in the ladies' lavatories at Victoria Station . . .'

'What do you mean, "junior secretary"?' Joan cut in. 'I'm Her Majesty's assistant private secretary! It's a totally different thing!'

Hector sighed. This perhaps hadn't been the moment for a throwaway remark. It wasn't at all relevant to what they were talking about.

'Ignore me.'

'No! What do you mean?'

It was a detail, but he sensed he'd get nothing out of her if he kept on avoiding her questions. And this one was at least easy to answer. He held up his hands. 'Your new title may be a different thing, but one wouldn't know. You look like a typist, you go to every length to be treated as one, and then you're angry when you are.'

'No, I don't!'

'You wear dowdy serge suits and sensible shoes.' He'd been brooding on this for a while. 'You have a typewriter on your desk, for God's sake! You told me so yourself. You type up memos and do the filing. You take work from the real secretaries and are surprised when they treat you with suspicion. No wonder they're confused. I would be.'

'I . . . I'm just . . .' Joan struggled for words, and he saw how white-faced she was again. She was still in physical pain, which he'd forgotten momentarily, and he suddenly felt an absolute heel.

'Anyway, that's beside the point,' he amended. 'The fact is, you work with classified information, and you're currently running around London in fancy dress, and going to highly sensitive places. Who are you doing it for? And who—' he was relieved to come back to the nub of the issue at last '—is trying to kill you?'

Joan looked dazed.

'I don't know,' she said, quiet again. She shook her head. 'I honestly don't know.'

Finally. At least they could have a proper conversation.

'What were you doing at the Artemis Club?' he asked more gently.

She gave him a sardonic smile. 'If I was doing something I shouldn't, I couldn't possibly admit it.'

Touché.

'Who are you working for?'

She raised an eyebrow, gathering her forces. 'Well, officially it's the Queen.'

He waved her response away. 'Yes, we know that, but who *really*? Who asked you to go to the club?'

Joan smiled. 'You have to trust me. There's only so much I can say.'

Hector reluctantly admired her loyalty. Whoever she was protecting, it was someone important. Someone in a hole.

'The part about where someone tried to kill you . . .' he reminded her. 'You really do have to trust me a little too.'

She regarded him for a long time, thinking.

'All right,' she said at last, 'there's an individual at the palace who's concerned about what happened on the night of the Chelsea murders. I was trying to find out what the staff at the Artemis knew, but it didn't amount to much.'

'You mean what they knew about the movements of the suspects?'

'Yes.'

'And another individual?' he suggested. It was starting to make sense now.

'I can't say.' Her frank stare was a silent admission.

Hector sighed. Was that all? 'It doesn't explain why—'

'I know!' she said, interrupting him. 'I mean, I didn't find out anything more than you must already be aware of. The staff were bandying it about pretty freely. Why go for me the next day? Why not any of them? I assume they haven't been threatened?'

'Not to my knowledge, no,' Hector agreed. 'There must be something else.'

Joan put a hand over her eyes. He was about to ask her another question, but she motioned him away. It wasn't rude this time: he could tell she was thinking. So he fussed around her quietly, removing the soup tray and straightening her blankets. He was as invested in her progress as she was.

Meanwhile, it was a relief to know that at least one of the young Queen's courtiers was looking out for Her Majesty's best interests. She was right about him working for MI5. It would make his own job a bit more difficult if there was to be interference from the palace, but Hector had been deeply worried for some time about a huge potential royal scandal and it did not bode well that nobody in the Queen's close circle seemed to be aware of it. Now he knew better. Joan might not admit who it was, but Hector had a couple of likely candidates in mind.

He dumped the tray in the kitchen. On his return, Joan looked up and said, 'There was one thing. I saw Tony.'

'Radnor-Milne?'

'Yes, in a corridor at the top of the club. I didn't think much of it. He's a member of the Artemis, I assume, so I wasn't surprised to see him — just worried that he'd recognise *me*.'

'And did he?'

'I wasn't sure, but I think he did. That must have been a bit of a surprise.'

'No doubt,' Hector agreed. 'Who was he with?'

Joan cocked her head. 'That's the interesting thing. I paid no attention at the time. I was focusing on Tony. But it was the Duke of Maidstone.'

'That idiot?' Hector was astonished — not that the duke would be there, but that Joan seeing him there could have had such consequences. 'How d'you know him?'

'I don't, really,' Joan said. 'I happened to meet him a couple of times in the war, because we used the dower house of his home as accommodation when I was training for . . . something I was doing at the time.'

That would have been her work at Trent Park, Hector surmised. She didn't know he knew about that, but he had requisitioned her file from the palace after he recognised her from Longmeadow Hall. He was surprised they had employed her after that blot on her copybook, but Sir Hugh was obviously more liberal and forgiving than his stiff military bearing suggested.

Hector didn't press for confirmation about Trent Park. He liked Joan's tendency to give away no more than was strictly necessary — even

236 ⤺ S. J. Bennett

now, with her life in danger. He liked a lot about Miss Joan McGraw, he admitted ruefully to himself. He would sleep well at last tonight, knowing she was here, safe, and would start worrying as soon as she left Dolphin Square again, knowing that she wasn't.

'You're certain it was Maidstone?' he asked. 'The light would have been dim.'

'It was, but I am,' she said.

'They were in private conversation?'

'Yes.'

'How did they react when they saw you?'

'Only Tony really looked at me. He seemed, confused. I turned away quickly and didn't see what he did afterwards.'

'Do you have any idea what they were talking about?'

'Absolutely none. Honestly.'

He believed her.

'Well, if you or your mysterious partner in crime come up with any conclusions, let me know.'

She nodded.

'I take it you'll be going to the office tomorrow,' he added.

'Of course. I must.'

He sighed. 'I'll order you a taxi. Only get in if the driver mentions my name.'

This time, she agreed without creating difficulties.

CHAPTER 45

The Joan McGraw who got into the taxi the following morning did not resemble the one who had come home from the palace the week before in several ways. First, her arm was in a sling, which was perhaps the most obvious thing, but also, her lipstick was a stronger shade. Her hair was styled loose in careful waves; soon she would have it cut in a more flattering style. Her shoes were patent courts with a noticeable heel. The skirt suit she wore was her Sunday best. As soon as she could commission her aunt to make a couple more, in the style of Pierre Balmain, she would, and possibly some belted dresses to show off her waist . . .

Joan had always thought of women at work who dressed to impress as flirts. However, she had also seen, without really paying attention, that the women who reached senior positions in the Wrens were happy to stand out from the other ranks. She liked it when they did; she had just never thought of herself as one of them. But Hector was right. How much more senior did you get than 'Assistant Private Secretary to Her Majesty the Queen', as she had said to him so stuffily yesterday? It might make her uncomfortable, but she'd better get used to it.

The taxi deposited her safely outside the gates to the forecourt of the palace and Joan strode as confidently as she could in her heels and pencil skirt to the Privy Purse door on the right, which led to the North Wing corridor. Despite the bruising under her eye, and her arm being in a sling, the sentry in his bearskin gave her as much of an up and down as his sideways glance would let him. His facial muscles didn't flicker, but there was something about the way he stood taller to attention. She stood taller, too.

On reaching the secretaries' shared office, she asked one of them to collect her typewriter, and said they could probably make better use of it than she could. They clucked over her bruises and her broken wrist and they asked if she'd want the typewriter back when her hand was better. She told them she wouldn't.

One of the women offered to get Joan a cup of coffee and she accepted as if it was her due. When they asked what had happened to her, she gave them a two-line answer, avoiding all follow-up questions. No attempt at chattiness. Sir Hugh wouldn't chat. Miles Urquhart didn't know how. Jeremy Radnor-Milne only did it when he wanted something. Then she retreated to her desk.

Alone at last, she sat down and smiled to herself. That wasn't so bad.

Meanwhile, Urquhart wouldn't be back from Scotland with the Queen until tomorrow and the peace and silence of the deputy private secretary's office – broken only by the removal of the typewriter and delivery of the coffee – gave Joan the opportunity to think.

She was less worried about Tony Radnor-Milne and his co-conspirators now that she knew MI5 was watching out for her, but when and why exactly did Hector and his friends take notice of her? This had been her first thought when he had talked to her last night, but she knew he would never tell her, so there was no point asking.

It must have been before she started visiting the Artemis Club. He mentioned the 'little old lady' disguise, and she had only used that the first time she visited Piccadilly to stake the club out, so her follower must have already been on her trail at Victoria Station, where she changed and left her suitcase at the left-luggage desk. Ironically, she had used the station to avoid Hector himself encountering her quick change at home. Fat lot of use that had been.

Had they spotted her when she had visited Beryl? Joan thought that was a distinct possibility. She'd been wearing her posh black outfit, which would have looked odd in the circumstances to anyone who knew her. Why would MI5 be watching Beryl's flat? The police might be, she supposed, but would they recognise her? Beyond the senior people she had met through the Private Office, she didn't know anyone in the police.

The same applied to MI5 as the police, surely, when she thought about it: she wasn't famous in any way, and anyone who didn't know her personally was unlikely to clock her face. So either she had just been very unlucky, or she must have been somewhere that made them so nervous they did some research to discover her identity.

Where? After joining the Private Office, Joan's social life had dwindled significantly, even when the Queen was away. Since her return from Balmoral in mid-August, three weeks ago, she had met a couple of old friends for tea in a coffee bar in Soho and gone to the flicks with another to see the latest Dirk Bogarde. One of Prince Philip's equerries had taken her to the Café Royal on what he hoped would be a romantic encounter, but though she enjoyed his company, she had sadly disappointed him – or rather, he had disappointed her. Other than that, there had only been a couple of perfectly unexceptional shopping trips and the abortive visit to Cress-well Place.

She breathed deeply, and took a contemplative sip of coffee.

Cresswell Place: the street where the murders took place. The murders that happened the night Prince Philip went AWOL without an alibi. Joan didn't know what the men in the Security Service looked into specifically – she'd assumed it was mostly Russian spies these days – but the activities of the royals, extra-curricular and otherwise, were certainly a matter of security.

And there she was, a member of the Queen's Private Office, standing literally opposite the scene of the crime, looking around like some sort of foreign tourist. What an absolute fool she had been.

CHAPTER 46

On the journey to Windsor from Balmoral the Queen told Miles Urquhart that she needed to practise her Canada speech with her APS after church the next day, and that he was to let Joan know, so she could travel from the palace, and set aside an hour in her diary.

His eyebrows shot up halfway to the ceiling. 'On a Sunday, ma'am? After a long journey? I hardly think—'

'I need it, Miles,' she said grimly. 'I'll be perfectly all right.' And the problem was, she did need the practice, but she had no intention of getting it with Joan tomorrow. Since the last time they saw each other, Joan had done some dangerous investigating and the Queen had done quite a lot of thinking. They had far too much else to talk about.

★ ★ ★

Joan arrived at the Oak Room at Windsor Castle at the appointed time, and the Queen made it clear to the footman at the door that under no circumstances were they to be disturbed. In the light of Joan's accident, she invited the poor young woman to sit down on one of the comfortable sofas.

The rain fell steadily outside, but the room was warmed by a small electric fire. One of the corgis made herself at home at Joan's feet, and the Queen took this as a good sign. Corgis were an excellent judge of character. They tended to nip the ankles of people they didn't approve of.

Joan brushed off the Queen's solicitous enquiries about her wrist, just as she brushed off Joan's thanks for the soup and flowers. The Queen had wanted to discuss her theories about Ginette Fleury first but, looking at Joan's bright face, she decided it could wait. There was something different about her APS today. It wasn't the fading bruise under her right eye. Was it her new hairstyle or her recent adventures? Whatever it was, it suited her.

'I can see you have news,' she said. She was glad she had decided not to wait any longer. 'Tell me everything.'

'First of all,' Joan said, 'there's something I wanted to tell you last month, but I felt I had to do it face to face. I didn't trust it to a letter, even in code.'

This was alarming. 'What?'

Joan took a deep breath. 'I think the press secretary might be working with your uncle.'

The Queen had been fearing all sorts of developments, but not this.

'The Duke of Windsor?'

'Yes, ma'am.'

'Impossible. He has no role here any more. He knows that.'

Joan held her ground. 'I saw a letter. The contents included the words "plan" and "delay" and "Washington". The letterhead was his. There were two sheets of paper, handwritten, and Jeremy didn't want me to see them. I don't think he knows I *did* see them, by the way.'

'That certainly puts things in a new light,' the Queen said, stiffening.

Her uncle meant trouble, and had done all his adult life. He was a very self-indulgent man, who had chosen his love life over the Crown. It was difficult to forgive the burden he had placed on her father as a result of his decision not to remain as king. Although, given the warmth Uncle David and his wife had showed to Hitler before the war, she had to admit the abdication wasn't altogether a bad thing. She would deal with that thought later.

'Was there anything else?'

'Yes, ma'am,' Joan said readily. 'Tony Radnor-Milne is working with the Duke of Maidstone. I saw them together at the Artemis Club. That's why I was run over.'

The revelations were coming thick and fast. *Bunny?*

The Queen remembered the glee with which he'd told her about the girls at the Raffles agency. She'd been thinking about him in vague relation to the murders, and here he was again . . . but in the context of the plot against her.

'You look surprised, ma'am.'

The Queen sighed. 'Not entirely. Nothing Maidstone does will ever surprise me. He once "hid" a hundred sheep in Canterbury Cathedral for a bet. I'm quite surprised that someone like Tony Radnor-Milne would be interested in him, though. They have shooting in common, I suppose.'

'I don't think they were talking about shooting.'

'Hmm.'

'Could it be something to do with industry, or trade, or finance?' Joan suggested. 'I know Tony's a big investor in rubber. And plastics and aviation.'

'I can't see the duke taking an interest in aviation. But rubber . . . Thank you. I'll think about it.' Joan had obviously had a very educational time at the Artemis. But that wasn't why one had sent her there. Hesitantly, the Queen asked, 'Did you find out anything else at the club?'

She hoped Joan didn't think she had been hinting at anything more than simply *oddness* in her note. She felt certain the explanation would be utterly benign. Reasonably benign anyway. She just needed to hear it.

'I did, ma'am.' Joan shifted uncomfortably in her seat. 'On the night of the murders, the um . . . the person in question . . . left with a friend after dinner and lost his security detail. His whereabouts are unclear after that. That's all I know for sure. But I should add, quite a lot of people know about it.'

The Queen's heart sank. She knew Philip's alibi for that night couldn't be *perfectly* legitimate, but still, every chink in it hurt a little. At least she was sure of one thing: the friend wouldn't be Bunny. Philip couldn't stand the man.

'I see,' she said. 'And when you say, "lost his security detail" . . . ?'

'He did it deliberately, ma'am.'

'Ah. And you don't know where he went?'

'Actually, I think I do,' Joan said.

She explained about her visit to Cresswell Place and her subsequent chat with Hector Ross. Yet again, this came out of the blue. The Queen knew of Major Ross through the papers in her boxes, the ones marked 'Top Secret'. He was responsible for several of them. Thanks to Sir Hugh's well-meaning interference – possibly at the suggestion of

Tony Radnor-Milne – he had become Joan's landlord. Given his solic-
itousness with the provisions from the palace, the Queen was alarmed
to infer that they seemed to be sharing a flat. Not because of any prud-
ishness, but because it could be extremely awkward if news of it ever
leaked to the sorts of people who liked to stir up trouble.

The Queen sighed to herself. This whole business seemed to
involve men and women being together in places they shouldn't be.

'What made you connect the duke's private visit with Cresswell
Place?' she asked.

'I sensed from your note that you did,' Joan admitted. 'And by the
way, I think MI5 are still watching it.' She explained her thought
process for when they started following her. 'Hector . . . Major
Ross . . . said I'd been in "sensitive places". It's possible they were
watching Beryl White's flat, but I can't see why that would be sensitive. At first, when I thought about it, I was furious with myself for
going to Cresswell Place at all, but then I wondered why on earth
anyone was still watching it five months after the murders. And yet it
seems they are.'

The Queen nodded slowly.

'It might explain why Inspector Darbishire hasn't been making
progress. I find that when different services accidentally collide, they
tend to tread on each other's toes.'

'I can ask for the MI5 file on your behalf,' Joan began. 'If we're
right—'

'No, don't.' The Queen raised a hand. 'I don't want you involved
in this. It's easier if you aren't. Everything must go through Sir Hugh.
Just . . .' She caught Joan's eye. 'Make sure you do the filing.'

Joan nodded. 'Do you want me to find out any more about Tony
Radnor-Milne?'

'No. Leave that to me, too. And on that subject, ask the Master of
the Household if he can find you a room in the palace, just for now.
We have plenty of accommodation. I'm sure there's something you
can use.'

'I assure you, I'm perfectly all right, ma'am,' Joan protested.
'There's no need—'

'There's every need. You're not safe,' the Queen pointed out. Not
from potential murderers nor, it seemed, the head of D Branch at MI5,
who fed her soup.

Joan didn't look happy. She shook her head, which people rarely did when the Queen told them something in her 'this is final' voice.

'I can't stay walled up there, ma'am. I'm sorry. There's too much to do.'

She should try being me for a few days, the Queen thought.

'I'm not asking you to stay indoors all the time. Merely to work and sleep there. I'm sure you have errands and visits you need to make. I would say, "Be careful", but I'm sure I don't need to remind you.'

Joan smiled briefly. 'No, ma'am. I'll ask about a room. But, going back to Beryl White . . . My letter about Gina Fonteyn really being Ginette Fleury . . . Was it any help? It doesn't explain the presence of MI5, does it?'

It didn't, but at last the Queen could talk about what had been on her mind since she'd read Joan's letter in August. She had almost lost sight of it, with all this talk of her uncle and MI5 surveillance.

She summarised the idea she had about the possible connection between the victims, going back to the capture of Ginette's sister in the war.

'So Ginette organised the whole thing for revenge?' Joan asked.

'That's what seems to make sense. She had seen the man known as Perez, or Rodriguez, by chance at the agency a few days before. She could have recognised him then from Paris. She happened to have the key to the mews house, which would make a private place to confront him – or so she assumed. She would hardly have known about the dean's dental appointment the next day. She went to great lengths to make sure she, not Beryl, was the one to meet the client, looking the way he had requested, so as not to put him on guard.'

'Did she have any training, though? It seems a crazy thing to do.'

The Queen frowned. 'Doesn't it? If I'm right, she took an enormous risk. That's why I thought of her sister. What you told me about Marianne Fleury being sent to the camps . . . It might drive a desperate young woman to do whatever it took to get justice. Or what she saw as justice. It seems a powerful motive – if he *was* the man she blamed.'

Joan shook her head.

'You don't agree?' the Queen asked.

'I do. But . . . I'm still adjusting. "Nico Rodriguez". I didn't know that about Argentina. That it's a hideaway for old Nazis, I mean.'

'We assumed that most of the worst offenders saw justice at the Nuremberg Trials, but I'm not sure that's the case. My red boxes are rather useful. I do learn a lot of things.'

'Yes, ma'am. But even if Ginette wanted to kill him,' Joan said, 'that doesn't explain how she died too.'

The Queen sighed. 'That's the problem. They couldn't have killed each other and cleaned up the scene. Someone must have followed them there. Someone who wanted one or other of them dead.'

'Someone who MI5 were following? Lord Seymour?' Joan suggested. 'His story about the tiara theft doesn't ring true.'

'No, it doesn't,' the Queen agreed. 'But I don't know why MI5 would be following a Government minister. I haven't heard any rumours about him and I've been listening out for them. However, I note what you told me about Ginette refusing him as a client. She was certainly aware of him.'

'Yes, she was. Could she have been . . . oh, I don't know . . . his daughter? From a secret liaison in France? And he *gave* her the tiara? That would explain why she was cleaned up. Though not exactly how they died.'

'I dearly hope not,' the Queen said with feeling. What an awful thing that would be. 'But it's the sort of thing the police could investigate, if they knew the truth about her.'

'Then he could be the father of Marianne, too,' Joan added. 'He's old enough. Or they could have been half-sisters, I suppose.'

'Wasn't Lord Seymour at the House the following morning?' the Queen reminded her. 'How could anyone sit in a technology briefing after . . . after what he would have endured?'

'I don't know, ma'am. But I've seen people do the most extraordinary things after a traumatic experience. It only hits you later, sometimes.'

The Queen shook her head sadly. 'I hope it's not Stephen Seymour. He's always struck me as a decent man. Anyway, it's really not for us to find out.' She straightened up and became more businesslike. 'Inspector Darbishire should be doing it. All he needs is a little prod to connect the victims. Once he knows where to look I'm sure he can ask all the questions we can't.'

'Yes, ma'am.'

'You did very well while I was away. I trust you can find a way of getting him back in the saddle.'

'I'm sure I can.'

'Without knowing how he got there.'

Joan smiled. 'I think I can manage that. If Major Ross's reaction is anything to go by, it will never cross his mind who's helping him.'

The Queen was pleased. 'Good. That suits us rather well.'

CHAPTER 47

After Joan left, the Queen walked across to a table by one of the windows to examine the photographs in silver frames displayed there: her mother and sister at the races, her beloved father on his coronation day, Philip looking suave in sunglasses and a natty blazer, Charles, who would be off to school the day after tomorrow, Anne on her little pony . . .

These were the people who mattered to her. She didn't know the victims in Cresswell Place, didn't know their families, and feared now, more than ever, that finding out what happened to them would open a Pandora's box of secrets that she would rather not discover.

She closed her eyes. What were MI5 doing there? Given what Joan had told her, it was almost certainly something to do with her uncle or her husband. And most probably the latter, though she still longed for it not to be.

Better to find out now, than be told by Sir Hugh at the start of a national scandal over which she had no control. And those victims deserved the truth, whatever the cost.

As always, the Queen thought of her grandmother, Queen Mary, who had taught her humility and self-discipline. This job was not about her wants, her weaknesses or her feelings: it was about the country and the Commonwealth, and from the age of twenty-one, she had devoted herself to their service. It might seem priggish to some, but she had better get on with it.

She lifted the heavy receiver from the Bakelite phone on the table and played absently with the cord while she waited.

'Sir Hugh Masson, please.'

'Putting you through, ma'am.'

After ten seconds, the line crackled.

'I'm very sorry, ma'am, Hugh's away from his desk. Can I help?' It was the voice of her DPS.

'Yes, Miles, you can. I'd like to see a file,' the Queen said. 'From the Security Service. On Cresswell Place.'

She sounded slightly more confident than she felt that the file in question existed. Joan had suggested that Beryl White's flat was another possible location. But the odds were shorter on the mews. And she had never lost sight of Philip's reaction when it was first mentioned.

'Are you sure, ma'am?'

'Quite sure,' the Queen insisted.

'How, if I might ask, did you hear about it?'

She smiled to herself. Urquhart's voice was so light with casual curiosity it was almost a squeak. He knew exactly what she was talking about. And if he did, Sir Hugh did, and they'd been discussing it among themselves. Joan was right. She could only pray they hadn't mentioned it to Jeremy.

'Oh, I hear things,' she said calmly. 'And Miles, you might enquire as to why I wasn't given sight of this report in the first place.'

There was a brief silence.

'Of course, ma'am. I'll see what I can do.'

★ ★ ★

Three days later, with young Charles safely ensconced in his new boarding school, the Queen was back at her desk at Buckingham Palace when the red boxes of paperwork were delivered for her to review.

Having dealt with the first one efficiently, she found the second to be unusually full. True, the wheels of Government were turning faster again now that September was nearly over, but some of the papers in this box were appendices that didn't really need to be there. Suspicious, she did what her father had taught her, and lifted everything out, to see what Sir Hugh and the minions in the Cabinet Office had buried at the bottom. She was grateful that was where they still put anything they didn't want her to see. It made it much easier to find it.

Nestling under a sheaf of minor memoranda was a slim manila folder marked 'Top secret. For your eyes only', with the familiar markings of MI5. Pinned to the cover was a small handwritten note from

Sir Hugh that read, 'Your Majesty, I believe this is the file you requested. I strongly advise you not to read it. I would be more than happy to apprise you of its contents.'

She looked up with a smile. One of her ladies-in-waiting had gone to a convent boarding school where, she said, there was a leatherbound volume in the library in which the nuns had made a note on the title page, forbidding girls to read 'pages 63, 72 and 147'. Needless to say, these pages were heavily thumbed, and the rest of the book was pristine. Catholic schoolgirls were no fools.

Poor Sir Hugh. He was honour-bound as her private secretary to provide the file that she had asked for, and equally desperate for her not to see it. She unpinned his note and saw that the file was precisely what she had hoped: the record of a stakeout in Cresswell Place covering the night of 31 March. She read through the opening pages with a churning mixture of relief and high anxiety.

CHAPTER 48

The same morning, an envelope addressed to 'The Man In Charge Of The Chelsea Murders' arrived at the police station in Lucan Place.

Darbishire stared at the letter in front of him for the hundredth time. He picked it up, sniffed it and handed it to DS Woolgar, who was currently taking up most of the space in his office.

'What do you think? Can you smell something on the paper? I'm sure I—'

'L'Air du Temps, sir,' Woolgar said happily. 'Nina Ricci. My mother likes it, sir.'

Darbishire's forehead crinkled. 'Did they *spray the letter* with it? Why on earth . . . ?'

'Smells nice, sir, doesn't it? I wish more women would think of it.'

'When writing to a detective inspector at the CID? About a murder?'

Woolgar shrugged. 'At least it tells us something, sir.'

'What's that, Sergeant? Do explain.'

Woolgar was still keen as a puppy, even after the Seymour debacle, which had kept him down for about fifteen minutes. If hard police work was required, he was less interested, but if it was just a matter of 'the little grey cells', he was all over it like a rash.

'She's a tart with good taste. And we know she's not stupid. No fingerprints on the notepaper. And she can type.' Woolgar nodded approvingly.

'I give up,' Darbishire sighed. He had been niggled by the Seymour incident because he had actually listened to his sergeant's lurid fantasies, and now he felt a fool. 'No, Woolgar, we don't know she's a tart. Your suggestion she has good taste is subjective. She might even be a "he".'

'Oh, no, sir,' Woolgar said confidently. 'Definitely a "she". And what she says about DS Willis at the end, sir, well . . .'

His confidence was, in the inspector's considered opinion, misplaced. For now, all they knew was that someone had written them a typed, anonymous, scented letter consisting of three short paragraphs, on the sort of cheap paper you can buy for half a shilling in Woolworths, and they'd posted it near the sorting office in Oxford Street, which means it could be any one of ten thousand people. (Darbishire gave Woolgar one thing: whoever it was wasn't stupid.) And that person knew Gina Fonteyn.

Or Ginette Fleury, as he must now think of her. Everyone who spoke of her had been so confident that she was Italian. Darbishire served in Italy, and he recognised how different the languages were. It made him despair.

'It may all be pie in the sky,' he said, 'but we can't ignore it. I'll contact my friend at the Sûreté, and see if they've got a record of Ginette and Marianne Fleury in Paris. If Marianne was captured and sent away, they should know about it. And if "Rodriguez" worked for the Gestapo, they might have a record of him.'

'Bound to, sir.'

Darbishire tapped his pen on the letter. 'Don't forget, Sergeant. A critical eye.'

'Yes, sir,' Woolgar said, with a grin that made it clear he already believed all of it. 'So they *knew* each other! Fleury and Rodriguez.'

He'd learned nothing. Absolutely nothing.

'Perhaps they did.'

'They could have been lovers, and he let her down. Or ran away, sir.'

'She was fifteen at the time, according to this letter!'

Woolgar shrugged. 'You never know.'

Darbishire had little girls at home and shuddered at the thought. 'Surely if her sister was in the Resistance, it's more likely that he betrayed them somehow? If anything, they were mortal enemies.'

Woolgar seemed pleased by this response. 'You see? Not pie in the sky at all, sir. She killed him, and then one of his old mates came in somehow and found them there, and killed her.'

Darbishire leaned back in his chair and folded his arms. 'And washed her, and laid her out all neatly? Because . . . ?'

'Because he was secretly in love with her. Which is why he'd followed them there in the first place. To save her from herself. Or because he was jealous. Maybe both.'

Darbishire didn't know that there was a comparison to be made between himself and Her Majesty, but he was less tolerant of his subordinate's speculations than she was. He had learned his lesson. This sounded to him very much like romantic tosh.

'Can I ask, Woolgar, are you a secret devotee of Mills & Boon? Georgette Heyer?'

'I quite like Barbara Cartland, sir. My mother has a collection.'

'It follows.'

'Is that all, sir?'

'No. You can get in touch with whoever has the archive for Ravensbrück concentration camp. No, I don't know how. Just work it out.'

But Woolgar didn't move.

'Yes?'

'Can I just ask, sir, are you going to do anything about what she said about DS Willis? About him scaring women, I mean. And touching them up and . . .'

'No, Woolgar, I'm not.'

'Right. Because you don't believe her, or . . . ?'

'Because that person, who may be male or female, has chosen to remain anonymous,' Darbishire pointed out wearily. 'Because they may well be lying, or have a private grudge. Because to the best of our knowledge, Willis is a highly regarded officer in the Met, with a spotless record, and I don't want to be the one to tarnish it unless I'm absolutely, rock-solid certain that it's fully deserved.'

'Yes, sir.'

'If you tarnish one man, you tarnish us all, Woolgar.'

'Right, sir.'

Privately, Darbishire thought he might in fact have a little word with DS Willis, let him know there had been talk. That should be enough to clear things up, he judged. Put the wind up the man if any wind, indeed, needed to be put. Darbishire had his doubts about a few senior people, but on the whole the officers of the Metropolitan Police were fine, upstanding men. He was proud to be one of them. It made him sad to think that DS Woolgar – the fan of trashy female fiction – might be so easily persuaded to imagine otherwise.

CHAPTER 49

The Queen closed the file on her desk, got up and walked to the window of her office. A detachment of the Life Guards was riding down Constitution Hill on glossy black horses. She observed the plumes of their helmets swaying in time to the horses' tails without really taking them in.

Now she knew what she had long suspected, and everything was better, and worse.

According to the report from MI5, a team of officers from their surveillance department, known as A4, had indeed been watching a house in Cresswell Place on the night of the murders – just as Joan assumed. It wasn't the dean's house at number 44, but a place two doors down, rented by a certain William Pinder. He was a civil servant who worked for MI5 itself at a fairly senior level.

And possibly the Russians. That's what they wanted to find out.

The Queen hadn't known about this particular investigation. Usually they waited until they discovered something of note before telling her. The fact that they hadn't done so for several months suggested this one wasn't going well. It must still be active, if Joan was right that they had spotted her in the street ten days ago.

William Pinder was suspected of being the Third Man in the Cambridge spy ring, which had been uncovered so ignominiously after Burgess and Maclean fled to Moscow. Another man from MI6, Kim Philby, had also been accused of spying for the Russians. He had robustly and publicly denied it, but a cloud of suspicion still hung over him in some quarters.

Like her father, the Queen occasionally wondered whether she was harbouring yet another of them. More rumours swirled around her Surveyor of Pictures, Anthony Blunt. In his current role, he was well regarded as an expert on the Baroque. It was less well known that, as a British spy, he had done useful work for the family at the end of the war, when her uncle – now the Duke of Windsor – had created some awkward paperwork that needed to be retrieved in a hurry. Erudite and useful as Blunt was, the Queen still wasn't sure about him. He had been a Cambridge man, too. If MI5 told her tomorrow that *he* was the Third Man, or the Fourth or Fifth, she wouldn't be entirely surprised. However, they assured her at regular intervals that he wasn't.

Perhaps it was this William Pinder. The team from A4 were particularly worried about him that night because he had been acting strangely. A footnote in the report referenced lateness at work, increased alcohol consumption and a 'furtive attitude'. The Queen thought that being watched by your own employer might do that to a man, if he was good enough at his job to have caught them at it, but they thought he might be preparing to leave the country.

Instead, what happened that night was that shortly after eleven, an Aston Martin DB2 sports car drew up outside, driven by a man later identified as a gallerist and member of the Artemis Club called Roly Hill, who had beeped his horn once. The front door was opened by William Pinder's sister Abigail, who was staying with him at the time, at which point a second man, referred to as 'Hamlet', got out of the car's passenger seat and strode inside as quickly as he could. The sports car then drove off.

'Hamlet'. The Danish prince. Honestly.

The Queen had a headache. Despite one of her study windows being slightly open to let in the cool September air, she found it difficult to breathe. She didn't know William Pinder, but she knew his sister Abigail, who was still considered a great catch at the age of twenty-seven. She was a lively, attractive, intelligent young woman – the only deb of her year to go to university – popular at polo matches and famously good at bridge.

'Hamlet' was inside the house until well after four in the morning. Like the dean's, this house had two upstairs bedrooms and a living room downstairs. The living room had a window with thin curtains and one person was seen moving around behind them for a few hours, believed to be William Pinder. There was no sign of the other two.

The Queen's head throbbed.

'Hamlet' left, alone, at 4.15 a.m., when he was picked up by a man later identified as Captain John Macbride of the Grenadier Guards in his two-seater MG. Abigail Pinder was seen tearfully waving him goodbye through the window.

What the report did not suggest at any point was that 'Hamlet' ever visited the dean's house, two doors down. Perhaps he or William Pinder could have done so round the back, past the empty house, via the little yards these places had. But the report made no reference to it and the Queen remembered Darbishire's note that the dog at number 41 hadn't barked that night, suggesting that nobody had exited the house that way.

That was not what A4 were worried about. It was the simple fact of 'Hamlet's presence on this street for several hours, with the attractive blonde who was a close relative of a man they suspected of being a national traitor.

Which, quite honestly, was probably enough.

Even so, not *all* the Queen's worst fears were realised – not that she had ever really articulated them to herself. She had never thought for an instant that her husband was directly involved with what happened at number 44, or even knowingly mixed up with anyone who was. And yet . . . the coincidence had preyed on her mind for six months. But perhaps that was all it was: coincidence.

She looked across at Constitution Hill and saw that the Life Guards had ridden out of sight. As her breath returned to normal and her headache abated slightly, she glanced round for the corgis, two of whom had been dozing in their baskets. She called them to her and spent a minute crouched at ground level, ruffling their warm coats.

Coincidence! Coincidences happen all the time. But what a strange accident of timing. 'Hamlet' arrived at number 42 less than ten minutes after the watchers had noticed the man who turned out to be 'Nico Rodriguez' being let into number 44.

The surveillance officers, as she suspected, had turned out to be the most important witnesses to the goings-on at the dean's house that night. To Darbishire, these witnesses were the elusive 'Gregsons', who remained a question mark in his reports. There were in fact three of them – two young men and a young woman. They had been positioned in number 22, not number 23 as they suggested (they were also the mysterious 'academics'), and they hadn't been watching the dean's house deliberately: they had simply recorded whatever they saw in the street, which at the time didn't strike them as important or unusual.

What did strike them as very unusual indeed, however, was the arrival of 'Hamlet' that night, at the house they *were* watching, and they spent some time double-checking with each other that it was really him, and telephoning the planner from A1 to ask what to do.

It was easy to imagine that these people had wanted to be helpful a week later, when they realised a double murder had taken place and knew they might have important evidence to share. They had done so, but for the sake of national security they must have decided to get two of them to pretend to be a local couple, to place them in the conveniently unoccupied house next door, and to distract police attention away from what they were really up to. No wonder Inspector Darbishire had been frustrated when he tried to follow up with them.

It certainly was important evidence, the Queen thought, walking up and down her study now, thinking hard. It gave the precise times both victims entered the house and corroborated the alibis of the dean's guests from the Artemis Club – who must have left the club together about half an hour after 'Hamlet' did. *But* the team didn't seem to consider that for a crucial five or ten minutes, they hadn't been concentrating.

Perhaps 'Hamlet's arrival was important after all: he had inadvertently distracted the key witnesses.

If Darbishire could interview them properly, using whatever techniques the police were trained in these days, he might be able to get them to remember something they'd missed. But he wasn't allowed anywhere near them.

She could see why. There was a lot of national security at stake in all sorts of different ways.

But murder was murder, and the secret of the report on her desk was that it was a muddle. It wasn't good enough. She had to do something about it.

CHAPTER 50

Sir Hugh was intransigent.

'I'm sorry, ma'am. We can't.'

'We must, Hugh.'

Her private secretary looked at her dolefully from behind his thick spectacles. 'I admire your commitment to truth and justice, but I'm not sure you've fully understood the possible repercussions . . .'

'It might be difficult for us, yes, but the police need to know—'

'You do understand to whom "Hamlet" refers, ma'am?'

'Of course I do!' she said, irritably.

'The news will leak. It always does. The Met police are the worst. Whatever the truth turns out to be, there will be rumours, there always are. People will say there's no smoke without fire. You may never live it down.'

'I'm sure he had his reasons for being there. Have you asked him?'

'No, ma'am,' he said. 'Have you?'

There was a short silence.

'Not in so many words,' the Queen admitted. 'But I raised it in Scotland. Before I knew where he'd gone.'

'And did he explain himself?'

'No.'

'Ah. There we are.'

'But—'

'Ma'am, if I may say so, it's better *not* to ask. Not to know. Your . . . ahem, "Hamlet" might be aware of that. If asked subsequently, we have plausible deniability. We—'

'What on earth's that, Hugh?'

'Plausible deniability? It was developed by President Truman, ma'am, for covert operations. The idea is that if anyone asks awkward questions, you can honestly say you didn't know.'

'But I *want* to know!'

Her private secretary raised a hand. 'Forgive me, ma'am. What you want and what's good for the country are two different things. I think you might find that if you *did* know, you may wish you'd never asked.'

She regarded him bleakly. What would her grandmother think? What was dutiful and what was selfish? She no longer knew.

He took pity. 'I'm not saying you *would* regret it, ma'am, but it's possible you might. And that if we do nothing, this might all go away in time, and we'll be grateful for stones unturned. You never know what you'll find underneath them.'

'But—'

This time he tapped his fingertips together – a sure sign of exasperation. 'I know you want to do the right thing. But sometimes the right thing – for the country – is not to do anything. Please trust me on this.'

She didn't trust him.

But nor could she be absolutely certain that Sir Hugh wasn't right. If she overruled him, or went behind his back, and talk about Philip got out as a result, true or otherwise, the consequences could be catastrophic. With her visit to North America coming up, the last thing any of them needed were unfounded rumours. She would be doing the traitors' job for them, and doing it better than they ever could.

At this moment, she felt certain that Sir Hugh wasn't in concert with those men in any way. He was trying so very hard to protect her. She trusted *that*.

'All right,' she agreed with a heavy heart. 'At least until I'm back from America.'

'Thank you, ma'am. We can certainly discuss it then.'

'And thank you, Hugh, for looking after me.'

Her private secretary smiled gravely. 'Your best interests are all I ever seek to serve. Shall I take the boxes with me, ma'am?'

'Joan can pick them up later,' she said lightly.

The Queen pictured Inspector Darbishire at his desk, hamstrung by his ignorance of the slim manila folder sitting in the bottom box, like an unexploded bomb. For now, he was on his own. And so was she.

PART 4

THE SINGLE PETAL OF A ROSE

CHAPTER 51

In the privacy of the little filing room, Joan extracted the folder from the top of the second red box, where the Queen had strategically placed it, and read it in the ladies' lavatories while most people were at lunch.

One of the advantages of Joan's memory was that she didn't need to take notes. She read rapidly, and could picture every word on every page if necessary. So she was able to return the folder to Sir Hugh's office and then think about its consequences while sitting on her new bed after work, up high in one of Buckingham Palace's attic rooms.

The timings were important. If somebody *had* got into number 44 Cresswell Place without being noticed by the surveillance team, they must have done so between 11.08 p.m. and 11.20. That was when the A4 team got instructions from their office at MI5 to give the codename 'Hamlet' to the person they had observed and maintain a watching brief.

The report didn't make it clear what they had been doing in the meantime, but they had made at least three calls to HQ. Joan knew from her war experience that it was all too easy to make a small mistake when you were tired, confused and dealing with the unexpected. It only took one minute's lapse in concentration, but if it happened to be the right minute . . .

She mapped those timings against what they knew about the people mentioned in Darbishire's reports. Of these, the dean and his guests were still at the Artemis Club, getting ready to order a couple of taxis to take them to Chelsea. The notorious Billy Hill was at a theatre performance from seven thirty until ten. His whereabouts after that weren't corroborated by anyone outside his gang, but in the last report Joan had access to, the inspector noted that the killings weren't typical of the way he operated.

Lord Seymour was about to leave the Houses of Parliament, to walk to his home in Westminster. There was simply no way the minister could have got to Cresswell Place in that brief window of time. Either he was in the clear, or he had commissioned somebody else to commit murder for him, and that person had had the luck of the gods when they arrived at the scene.

★ ★ ★

Joan explained all this to Her Majesty the following morning.

The Queen nodded gravely. 'I think we should add the Duke of Maidstone and Tony Radnor-Milne to the list.'

'Should we, ma'am?'

'It might sound fanciful, but at least one of them almost certainly tried to kill you.'

Joan was confused. 'Yes, but that was over something entirely different.'

'I know,' the Queen said. 'But I have reason to believe they might be involved in this, too. I wonder whether the duke has a stake in the Raffles escort agency.'

'Really, ma'am?'

'Yes. He was the first person to talk to me about it and it felt as if he was showing off. Then there's the agency's name itself. I know the duke's family used to stay in the Raffles hotel in Singapore. It's the sort of word he would use.'

'I see.'

'And I've been thinking. The police established that the same company had stakes in Raffles and the Chamberlain nightclub in Tangier. At first, I thought of Neville Chamberlain, who seemed very unlikely as an inspiration. Then I realised it must be named after Joseph Chamberlain, who was a great advocate of imperial unity. I've had more than one long conversation about him with Maidstone.'

'Oh!' Joan thought about it. 'And if he owns the Raffles agency, or at least some of it, he might own the mews house, too. The police reports suggest they're probably run by the same people.'

'He might. So he should certainly be on our list.'

'Yes, ma'am. Although, if he or Tony were going to do anything, they'd probably pay someone else and make sure they had an alibi.'

The Queen sighed briefly. 'True.'

'And what would their motive be?'

At this, the Queen's eyes seemed to shine a brighter blue than usual. She picked up her pen and played with it absently.

'I've been thinking a lot about this. I don't know what they had to do with the murders, but I think I know what they have to do with me. They both seem to have stakes in companies based in Singapore and Malaya. I wonder if their profits are bound up with traditional trade routes to the Far East and the West Indies. With goods such as rubber, for example. But our days running an empire are over. We need to cooperate with our old dominions, but the prime minister equally wants us to build relationships with the rest of Europe and the United States. We need to. The USA is a superpower now. They don't trust us and I can see why Mr Macmillan wants me to build bridges . . .'

'But what if the duke and his friends didn't want that to happen?' Joan suggested, following the line of thought.

'Exactly.'

'And you're very good at building bridges.'

'I wouldn't say that . . .'

'You are, ma'am. That's the point.'

'Well, the thing is, I try. I happen to agree with the prime minister, and anyway, it's my constitutional duty to do as he suggests. I'd do it even if I thought it was a terrible idea. But my uncle, the Duke of Windsor . . .' The Queen paused at the very thought of her uncle.

'He doesn't play the game,' Joan said.

'No, he doesn't. I can imagine him wanting to hark back to the past, when we didn't need Europe and America in the same way. He could easily be persuaded that way, certainly. And he wants to be relevant, even if he can't be king. I don't think it would be difficult to suggest to him that if I was incapacitated in some way, he might be the best person to replace me.'

Joan looked horrified. 'As king?'

'No. I don't think even he would go that far. As some sort of roving ambassador.'

'But no one would have him! He abdicated! It's a terrible idea!' Joan objected.

264 ⬒ S. J. Bennett

The Queen smiled grimly. 'I'm afraid the Duke of Maidstone is the sort of man to have ghastly ideas and think they're wonderful. He's been told all his life how brilliant he is, even if, as I told you, that's not entirely true.'

'But what about Tony?' Joan asked. 'He's not an idiot.'

'No, he isn't. It surprises me very much. But perhaps if he thought he had even the faintest chance of succeeding . . . He too, is a man who seems very confident in his own abilities. With a little more justification.'

'And he has a brother in the Private Office,' Joan agreed. 'I suppose that might help.'

'There's a small group called the Empire Club, or something like that,' the Queen said. 'I heard about it on a shooting weekend a couple of years ago. I'm going to find out more about it. I doubt the three of them would be acting alone.'

Joan frowned hard for a while. Then she threw her hands up. 'What silly, dangerous people, if it's true, ma'am. They're opportunistic and incompetent. Hector . . . Major Ross . . . he thinks so too. They don't stand a cat's chance in hell of getting what they want. But they could do some real damage in the process.'

The Queen sighed. 'That's what I've been thinking. They *could* do harm, and all for nothing. Just because they're hopeless doesn't mean we mustn't do everything we can to stop them.'

'If you're sure,' Joan said, 'shouldn't you get rid of Jeremy now, before he does something worse than itching powder in your makeup?'

'That would have been terrible, actually. But no. It's all conjecture. We don't have the letter from my uncle that you saw on his desk. As I said at the beginning, we still need proof. If we act without it, we'll just drive them underground.'

'Will you tell MI5?'

'I think, in a way, you already have,' the Queen said. Joan's familiarity with "Hector" Ross had its uses. 'Now I'm waiting for them to come and tell *me*.'

CHAPTER 52

Oblivious to the fallibilities of witnesses hidden in MI5's Cresswell Place file, Darbishire checked the final wording of his latest report and put it in the basket for his secretary to type. The good news was that he finally had something useful for Her Majesty to read. The bad news was that Woolgar was more insufferable than ever. 'I told you, sir! There *was* something between them. Not pie in the sky at all.'

The male victim at Cresswell Place turned out to be, not 'Dino Perez' or 'Nico Rodriguez' from Argentina, but a Frenchman named Jean-Pierre Minot. A small-time thief from a northern suburb of Paris who became a big-time collaborator and torturer for the Gestapo during the Occupation, working at a notorious apartment in the Rue de la Pompe.

Minot had a specialism involving internal doors and ropes that Darbishire wished he hadn't read about, and now couldn't get out of his head. He could handle death, he was good at it. But even he had his limits.

Young Minot was very popular with his Nazi comrades, and universally loathed in the rest of Paris. When Darbishire showed 'Rodriguez"s picture to his friend in the Sûreté, with the suggestion he might be Gestapo, it took them only a couple of days to come up with a match. It was a shock that he was French, not German. It also meant he was hated even more by his fellow countrymen, for what he did to them.

Minot had done the best he could in South America to disguise his appearance with black hair dye and some form of surgery to his nose.

He had aged by over a decade, but the likeness was still strong enough. 'Something in the eyes', Beryl White had said. It was no surprise that Ginette Fleury had recognised him.

Ginette herself, however, remained elusive. Woolgar had managed to track the sister down to Ravensbrück camp, just outside Berlin, the largest camp for women in the German Reich. Marianne Fleury was taken there in 1944 on one of the last such trains out of Paris, and had died there eight weeks later, already severely weakened by what she had undergone at Minot's hands.

In Paris, there was anecdotal evidence that she had been living with a teenage girl before her arrest, but the neighbours thought they came from Normandy and the records there were patchy. After all the bombs and fires, Darbishire wasn't surprised.

His contact in Paris was still looking for confirmation of who the letter writer said she was. But in a way, it didn't matter. Darbishire had just reinterviewed Rita Gollanz, who corroborated the story about Ginette's real identity. The fact was that Gina Fonteyn, known to Rita as Ginette Fleury, claimed Marianne was killed by the Gestapo, and he had proof that this was true. And the killer – as good as dammit – was indeed the man who was found beside Ginette that night. She told Rita she was fifteen at the time Marianne was captured, so that would make her twenty-eight now, which Deedar agreed was about right for the body he examined. So far, everything suggested by the letter writer fitted. It was a story of revenge.

Darbishire didn't mention the letter in his report. He referred to 'new information' and smoothly progressed to the work that he and Woolgar had done to verify it. They were responsible for finding the evidence, and that's what mattered.

It still wasn't clear what happened after Ginette Fleury and Jean-Pierre Minot met up in Cresswell Place. Woolgar's theory about a jealous lover was obviously pure hokum, but now that they were on the right track, getting to the truth was only a question of time. The momentum was back in the investigation, which made this tired policeman very happy.

The only fly in the ointment – apart from Woolgar's puppyish and unjustified self-congratulation – was the look that Chief Inspector Venables gave them both this morning, when Darbishire was being congratulated on cracking the true identities of the victims. There was a gleam in his eye that Darbishire didn't like at all. It was something he would need to keep a careful eye on.

★   ★   ★

At Windsor for the weekend, Philip was in high spirits. They'd be off on their next royal tour in a fortnight. He loved Canada and was fascinated by America. His personal library was piled high with books about both nations and he was eagerly consulting friends who knew them well. They had even eaten hot dogs for supper one night. The Queen was not convinced, but Anne, who'd had them in the nursery, pleaded for them to be on the menu daily and tried to persuade the nanny to post one to Charles at boarding school.

Philip had persuaded the BBC to lend him an old television camera, so she could practise the speech she was going to give before she opened parliament in Ottawa. He'd set the contraption up in her study there without consulting her – the dogs hated it and one had pissed all over it, which said a lot – and it dominated the room like an alien creature. However, she had to admit, the more one got used to it, the easier it was to imagine talking into it 'like a friend', as everyone told her to. Philip said she still looked like a plank of wood, but willow now, rather than oak.

They were taking a short break between rehearsals.

'I've been meaning to ask you something,' she said. 'Didn't you once belong to something called the Empire Club?'

'Hmm? D'you mean the Empire Society?' he asked, unscrewing the camera lens and peering inside.

'Possibly. The one run by the Duke of Maidstone.'

'"Bonkers Bunny". Yes. I joined for about ten minutes. Bunny invited me to shoot with them out at Enfield. The bag was good, but the guns were ghastly.'

He meant the people, not the weapons. 'Who?' she asked. 'Stephen Seymour wasn't one of them, was he?'

'No, not that day. It's men like old Robbie Suffolk and Quentin Fanshaw at the Bank of East India.'

'Do you know why it's called the Empire Society?'

'Ha!' he said. 'I thought it was a joke, but they seem to have this idea that we still run the empire. Not sure where they've been the last thirty years. They like to bang on about the old days when their

268 ⌒ S. J. Bennett

grandparents rode about on elephants. Might as well be back in the 1850s. They're "frightfully grand, you know",' he said, mocking the upper-class accent of an older generation. One that hadn't arrived as a family of refugees in a boat. 'Grovellingly polite and hideously rude. They call me a Greek and you a Hun, when they think we're not listening. Can't abide 'em.'

'Didn't you say Bunny had interests in Borneo?'

Philip had been tinkering with the camera and now held two rods in his hand that looked rather important. He tried to fit them back in as he spoke. 'Yes, huge ones. Teak and rubber. How d'you think he can afford to keep that shoot going? Why?'

'No particular reason. I wonder what the society will do now there's no empire. He wasn't thinking of changing it to the Commonwealth Society, was he?'

'God, no! He thinks we backed down. Shouldn't be giving places like Malaya their independence.'

'He doesn't appreciate the peaceful handover of power?' the Queen asked.

'Absolutely not! Robbie Suffolk called us bloody cowards.'

'They never said anything to me.'

'They wouldn't, Lilibet. You're the Queen. They want to be invited to the next coronation. Right, are you ready? I've got the lens back on. Let's try again.'

CHAPTER 53

When Sir Hugh told her that the foreign secretary and the new director general of MI5 were seeking an urgent audience with her, the Queen was ready.

'This has nothing to do with the, er, events at Cresswell Place, ma'am,' the private secretary assured her. 'It's another matter entirely.'

'Is it? How interesting.'

'I must warn you, what they have to say is rather disturbing.'

'So, you've spoken to the DG about it already, Hugh?'

'I have, ma'am. And the foreign secretary and the PM have been briefed too. We've needed to put certain measures in place in the Private Office. But I can assure you, we have everything under control.'

* * *

They met on the 5 October, a week before the Queen and Prince Philip were due to fly to Canada. Palace luggage rooms were filling up with bags and boxes. Last-minute telephone conversations were winging backwards and forwards across the Atlantic. The atmosphere was rather fraught. But the Queen herself was calm. She had done this before. And now she didn't have to shoulder the burden of a conspiracy of fools all by herself.

She held the audience in her blue sitting room between a meeting with the head of the armed forces and a delegation from the Women's Institute.

For once, she was not the only un-moustached person in the room. Both the foreign secretary and the director general of MI5 were bare-lipped. The Queen thought to herself that times were changing as she made them comfortable and deftly prevented Susan, her favourite corgi, from nipping at the foreign secretary's ankles. When the dogs and men were settled, she asked what the news was.

The DG spoke first.

'There's good news and bad news, ma'am. The good news is that we're in full control of the situation. Our director, D Branch, Major Ross, has played a bit of a blinder.'

'How wonderful!'

'He's been pulling together information from various sources. It's very troubling, and I might say, quite shocking, but I'm afraid to have to tell you . . . this is the bad news . . . that there has been a conspiracy against you at the highest level. Why exactly that might be, we're still not sure yet, but there's no doubt that these individuals mean you harm.'

'Can you tell me who they are?' the Queen asked, making sure to look suitably alarmed at the idea, rather than relieved that someone else was taking care of it.

'The ringleader is the Duke of Maidstone, ma'am. With the support of Tony Radnor-Milne.' The DG looked very grave. 'His brother's been working as a double agent in your Private Office.'

'And how did Major Ross discover this?' she asked.

The foreign secretary smiled and cast an eye in Sir Hugh's direction. 'You have a guardian angel, ma'am. Somebody who doesn't want to be recognised, remaining in the shadows, looking after your best interests.'

'You have no idea who it is?'

Another glance towards Sir Hugh, who remained impassive.

'No, ma'am. But I'm afraid there's one more thing.' The foreign secretary looked grave too. 'Your uncle, the Duke of Windsor, is involved. I realise that must be a particular shock.'

Not really, the Queen thought. She was silent for a while.

'I've been thinking,' she said eventually. 'Or rather, it occurs to me, now you've told me about it, that Maidstone and Radnor-Milne both have trading interests in our Commonwealth countries. The duke runs the Empire Society – d'you know it?'

They all nodded, although she strongly suspected only Sir Hugh had heard of it.

'It's an antiquated celebration of our colonial past,' she went on. 'I suppose if we tighten our friendship with America and Europe, as the prime minister wants us to, they might feel slightly threatened.'

'Threatened?' the foreign secretary asked.

'The old trading routes are changing. I don't know how well that suits them.'

He brightened. 'I see what you mean, ma'am.'

'It's quite a closed little club,' the Queen added. 'Not secret, but exclusive. The Marquess of Suffolk is a member, and the head of the East India Bank. I think there are about a dozen of them. My uncle may share their views more closely than I do.'

The director general smiled reassuringly. 'I doubt we need to worry about them, ma'am. But we have eyes on Radnor-Milne, and Maidstone, and your uncle, too. As soon as we have firm proof of what they're up to, we'll step in. You may wonder why we haven't done so already.'

'Not really.'

'It may seem unnerving,' he breezed on, 'but if we were to pounce now, we'd only drive them underground and the situation might become more dangerous. It's better to let them think they're safe.'

'I see that.'

'I know you must be alarmed to think of someone in your own Private Office acting against you, but rest assured that no move he makes will go unnoticed by Sir Hugh. If he tries to do anything—'

'I'll make sure it doesn't happen,' Sir Hugh cut in.

The Queen gave up trying to point out that this concept wasn't new to her.

'I'm glad you've thought about it so carefully,' she said. 'I take it you have no idea what they might be planning?'

'Not yet, ma'am. But after yesterday's events, your trip to America is more pressing than ever.'

'Yesterday's events?'

'The Russian launch of a satellite, ma'am. Called Sputnik.'

'Ah yes, I heard about that. My husband was very excited. They've successfully launched a transmitter into space. He was looking for it with his telescope.'

The foreign secretary leaned forward with an anxious look. 'It's all very well, ma'am. The trouble is, the Americans have realised it's much bigger than they thought. A more impressive object all round. And

272 ⟨ S. J. Bennett

their own launch isn't for a few weeks, and will be smaller. We mustn't let the Russians get ahead, ma'am. We must all pull together. Sometimes the Americans forget how much expertise we have to give . . . How much we've given them already . . .'

'You think they need a little reminder, Foreign Secretary,' the Queen said, raising an eyebrow.

'If you wouldn't mind, ma'am. Of course, Lord Seymour will try and do his bit too . . .'

'Stephen Seymour?' she checked. 'That's very surprising. Is he still going on this trip? He hasn't been excluded from the murder investigation, has he?'

'No, ma'am. He offered to stay behind, but he'll be very useful to the delegation in Washington and New York. He's been rather diligent about getting to know our leading scientists in terms of space technology and so on.'

'Oh, I see.'

The foreign secretary threw a superior glance at the director general. 'And we need all the help we can get with the Americans, after the catastrophe with Burgess and Maclean. They assume we simply feed all their secrets to the Russians now.'

The director general's lips formed a thin, hard line. 'That's all water under the bridge, ma'am. We're establishing new lines of communication . . .'

'Is it, though?' the foreign secretary asked, at which the director general gave him a filthy look. 'What about . . . ?'

'William Pinder's clean as a whistle. We're winding that operation down,' the director general said through gritted teeth. 'He'll be back at his desk after a little rest cure. The file is being archived.' He threw the Queen a brief, meaningful glance.

She felt sorry for William Pinder. The poor man had been closely observed for months, and now it seemed he was expected to carry on with life as normal. It couldn't be easy for him. No wonder he needed a 'rest cure'.

'I hope it's being buried,' the foreign secretary said, referring to the file. 'The last thing the Yanks need is more ammunition that we're a breeding ground for communist spies.'

The Queen thought of Inspector Darbishire again. Would he ever be allowed access to those few, crucial pages? She would have to try and find some other way of letting him know what he didn't know about that night in Cresswell Place. But it would have to wait. What with rogue dukes and Russian satellites, they all had enough to worry about for now.

CHAPTER 54

The Queen Mother moved into the royal apartments in Buckingham Palace to help look after the children while their parents were away. Except that most of the time it would only be Anne, because Charles was safely at boarding school, having – his mother assumed – heaps of fun.

'Don't worry about us,' her mother assured her. 'We'll have a lovely time without you. I'm going to set up a little cinema in the Ball Supper Room, so that we can watch you on the news.'

Margaret insisted on a little fashion show, so she could see all the finished frocks from Hardy Amies and Norman Hartnell. Both designers had surpassed themselves this time, knowing how important the visits were. And, the Queen had to admit, she had mentioned to both of them that her sister thought she should look more 'modern'. The resulting shapes were fluid and more simple, making use of new materials and techniques. This *femme de trente-et-un ans* was determined not to seem too last-century. It was time to stop dressing like her mother – even if her mother looked very good in what she wore.

The results pleased even Margaret, and gave the Queen a boost of confidence she felt she really rather needed. She had never had to give a live, bilingual televised speech *and* counter the effects of an unwise invasion and a spy scandal before. With more riding on the next ten days than she would ideally have liked, she and Philip set off by plane for Ottawa.

Jeremy Radnor-Milne informed the waiting press that Her Majesty was 'very excited' about this trip.

★　★　★

At the Moulin de la Tuilerie, his country home just outside Paris, Edward, the Duke of Windsor, came in from a game of golf with friends and called out to his wife. There was no answer. She was probably out shopping. She shopped a lot, poor darling, because there was little else to amuse her in the countryside. He loved his little garden here, but she was more of a city girl.

Alone – apart from the servants – he wandered aimlessly through the gracious reception rooms. It struck him for the ten thousandth time that he should be somewhere important, with *people*, making things happen, as he was born to do.

God, he was bored. Unutterably bored. When would Wallis be home?

The sound of padding paws on a tiled floor announced the arrival of her three pugs. They were missing her too. The fourth – named Peter Townsend after the man Margaret had tried unsuccessfully to marry – they had given away. Edward loved Wallis's wicked sense of humour. It was one of the things they had in common.

God, he was bored.

He strode on to his study and sat down to read *The Times*, but got distracted. Surely they should have contacted him by now? Elizabeth would be in Canada any minute. He'd originally assumed he'd be there himself, but now they were talking about next year, or possibly the year after. That couldn't be right, surely? His talents were being wasted. Bunny Maidstone had practically promised . . .

He reached across to the letter rack on his desk and fished out a sheet of paper with his cipher. A quick note to Bunny, to find out what the hell was going on. Jeremy Radnor-Milne had said something about keeping a low profile recently, but the man was a proletarian prig and this was only a little note to an old friend. He dashed it off, addressed the envelope himself and took it to the hall, to leave on the table for someone to take to the post.

At that moment, the swish of tyres on the gravel outside announced the return of his darling wife.

'Look what I picked up in town!' she said. 'They just finished framing it for me.'

She reached into her capacious shopping bag and pulled out a package, which she unwrapped in front of him. It was a little sign that read 'I may not be a miller, but I've been through the mill'.

'From "Le Moulin" – "the mill", remember?'

'Oh, yes, very funny,' he said. And felt dreadful about this deadly dull life he was giving her at the moment, and hoped a reply from Bunny would bring him better news soon.

His letter was picked up by one of the white-gloved servants, a man who hadn't been with them long, and spoke much better English than some of the rest.

'Take care of that, would you?' the duke asked.

The man promised he would.

★   ★   ★

On a friend's grouse moor in Scotland, the Duke of Maidstone was having a miserable time. Tony Radnor-Milne had come up for the weekend and, for reasons Bunny couldn't fully comprehend, he was furious about something and held Bunny responsible. Bunny wasn't used to being glowered at by the lower classes, and he didn't appreciate it. Tony could get above himself, sometimes. He thought he was better than everyone, and that was a dangerous trait, in Bunny's view.

'Out with it, man,' he said, when they were alone, having hung back from the other guns between drives. 'What's got you so hot under the collar?'

Tony stared at the horizon for a minute as they walked along. When he spoke, it was through gritted teeth. 'I heard about what happened to the trollop at the palace.'

'Oh, her. I thought you were rather keen on her?'

'A van, heading for her at speed?' Tony spat. 'Are you insane?'

'What makes you think I had anything to do with it?'

'She sees us together; I tell you who she is; three days later she's hospitalised. I'm not *stupid*.'

'Nor am I!' Bunny protested.

'Oh, really? And nor are MI5. D'you know she shared digs – and God knows what else – with the head of D Branch?'

'No, I didn't know that,' Bunny admitted. He didn't know much about the girl at all. She was a friend of Tony's, for God's sake. That was the whole problem.

'And they've got her living at the palace now, instead of with him, so they obviously suspect something.' Tony stopped and turned to Bunny with spittle coming out of his mouth. It was quite disgusting. The man needed to get a grip. 'You *stupid, stupid* man.'

'I resent that! And I don't like your attitude. I'm warning you, Tony . . .'

'You're warning *me*? They had nothing. The girl saw the two of us together at the Artemis, so what? I admit, I was alarmed at the time. What the bloody hell was she doing there? I think I can guess.' His lips curled into a brief, lurid smile. 'But that needn't involve you and me.'

'Except that it does, though, doesn't it?' Bunny said.

Tony scowled. 'Nobody knows about that.'

'And that's how I intend it to stay.'

'But they'll work it out. That bloody van was a big, black sign saying, "Look at me!" What were you thinking?'

Bunny had had enough of this. If Tony hadn't befriended the palace tart in the first place, none of this would have happened. He, Bunny, was merely taking care of things. Or, rather, getting a couple of his 'associates' from the casino business to do it at arm's length. They were better at that sort of thing, and they wouldn't talk. True, they hadn't actually managed to kill the girl, but in a way that was a good thing, wasn't it? With luck, they'd scared her off.

Bunny didn't want to think about what Tony had just told him about the man from MI5. He'd had no clue about that, or he'd have factored it in.

'I'm pulling out of Raffles,' Tony said abruptly. 'And the club in Tangier. Thought I'd let you know. The less we have to do with each other, the better.'

At this moment, Bunny agreed. 'Fine. Do it. We have a queue of investors.'

'And that business next week. Call it off. We can't do it with MI5 breathing down our necks.'

Bunny was haughty. 'I'll see what I can do.'

'See what you can do?' Tony jeered. 'Call it off, man. That's an order.'

'It's not that simple. I put Robbie Suffolk in charge. He has contacts who can do that sort of business and, frankly, I didn't want to get my hands dirty.'

'So? Call Suffolk off.'

'He's in India. With some sort of yoga wallah.'

'What the hell? Contact him in India then! They have the telegraph.'

'I'm not exactly sure which state. Don't worry! I'll look into it. I'll talk to him when I—'

They were interrupted by one of the ghillies, who had somehow walked up behind them without either of them noticing.

'Can I help, Your Grace?' he asked. 'I saw you'd fallen back a bit. I think you're needed at the next drive.'

'I can manage perfectly well,' Bunny said stiffly. 'Take my guns. I can walk faster without them.'

'And mine,' Tony said, handing over the eye-wateringly expensive pair of shotguns he had been showing off last night.

Bunny was quite glad to see him stride off without them. Given the look in Tony's eye, he wasn't sure he'd have trained them on the grouse.

★　★　★

Lord Seymour paced up and down the deck of the *Queen Mary*. The weather over the Atlantic was dire, and this was a brief break in the rolling seas. Another three days of this. Government ministers didn't usually have time to potter across the ocean when a fleet of jet planes was available, but his wife had insisted. She liked the luxury of the liner and it was actually easier to travel this way than to transport her inordinate amount of luggage by air.

He didn't know how much longer this life would last. Already, he was being treated as a pariah in the party, by men who had done everything he had done, and much worse. There were meetings he wasn't invited to, statements that were made without his approval. Once this trip was over, he wasn't sure what would happen next.

What would his wife make of Scotland? he wondered. She used to love it, once.

Lady Seymour was several yards ahead of him, standing stock-still at a railing, looking out impassively over the endless waves. Even now, he couldn't help but admire her profile, and the couture cut of the slacks she wore. His wife was the best-dressed woman on the ship, he was pleased to note. She usually was, wherever she went, but the competition on the *Queen Mary* was fierce.

He strode up to her. 'You look lovely, darling.'

She didn't turn to him or say a word. She had hardly spoken to him for days.

In fact, she had hardly spoken to him since April. It was as if a veil had descended over her – and not the bridal sort. She fulfilled her duties, she remained as exquisite to look at as the day he met her, but there was something robotic about her now. He didn't know what he could do to get her back.

They hadn't spoken about the tiara. Not exchanged a single word. He'd got it back from the police now, but she wouldn't wear it. She'd arranged to borrow something from Bentley's for the ball in New York. Her dress was by Givenchy and had cost him an arm and a leg. As he'd told that police inspector, she would look magnificent. But he doubted she would talk to him that night, either.

Seymour went back below deck to change for dinner. Last night, he had got hammered and that had felt a little better. Tonight, he intended to get hammered again.

CHAPTER 55

The good thing about a royal tour, if one was worried about something, was that there was almost no time to think about it at all. The Queen's first day in Canada was typical of her schedule: meeting, travelling, paying respects to the war dead, endless waving . . . And then there was her live speech to the nation, which she only managed because Philip got her to laugh a minute before, and relaxed her enough to be able to speak.

The following morning, the men in moustaches were lined up as usual, to tell her how well it had gone yesterday, and how pleased everybody was. Sir Hugh was fulsome in his praise, but nobody was more enthusiastic about applauding her than Jeremy Radnor-Milne.

'What a historic day, ma'am. You've mastered the new medium as if to the manner born. And in French! *Tellement impressionnant, madame. Épouvantable!*'

The Queen was about to cut him off herself when they were interrupted by a footman announcing that the private secretary was needed on the phone.

'Can't it wait?' Sir Hugh asked irritably. 'Can't you see we're in the middle of—?'

'It's the Assistant Private Secretary from London, sir. She says there's news.'

'Excuse me, ma'am,' he said. 'I'll be five minutes.'

★   ★   ★

In fact, it was more like ten. Her Majesty and the remaining men stood together, making stilted conversation. When Sir Hugh returned, he was smiling broadly.

'Jeremy,' he said, 'can you go and wait in our office? I'm expecting another call.'

The press secretary had no alternative but to leave them. As soon as he'd gone, Sir Hugh announced, 'We've got 'em! Absolute proof, and links between them all. Traitors, the lot of 'em.'

'Who?' Urquhart asked.

'This group called the Empire Society. I don't know if you remember it, ma'am. The DG of MI5 was telling us about them. They've been keeping below the radar, but they flew too high this time. Tried to kidnap Prince Charles from his prep school! Utterly outrageous. The idea was . . . Are you all right, ma'am? Do you need a glass of water?'

The Queen had sunk into the nearest chair, her knees having given way. For a moment or two, she couldn't see. When her vision returned, the men were leaning over her, solicitously. A glass of water was provided.

'Is he safe?'

'Prince Charles?' Sir Hugh asked. 'Oh yes, ma'am. Right as rain. The boy has no idea anything even happened. They had this plan to send someone in dressed up as a schoolmaster and catch him on the way back from games, and tell him he had detention, or a letter, something of that sort, and lead him to a place where they could shove him in a car. MI5 had eyes on them all the time. The thing was organised by the Marquess of Suffolk, would you believe? I had no idea the man had two brain cells to rub together. Apparently, he didn't. He entrusted it to a couple of likely lads, well known to the police, and carted himself off to Kerala, so he'd be out of the way.'

'How close did they get?'

'They got to the school,' Sir Hugh admitted, 'but only because the surveillance team let 'em. As soon as they emerged from the car, dressed up in their tweed jackets and whatnot, they pounced. It was undeniable, what they were up to. The boot of the car was full of—'

The Queen raised a hand sharply. 'I don't want to know what it was full of. Thank you, Hugh.'

'Ah. Yes, of course. But as I say, the young prince is perfectly unharmed. We would never let anything happen to him. But you can see what they were trying to do.'

'Yes, I can,' she said heavily.

'What?' Urquhart asked Sir Hugh.

'They were going to hold him for a few days in a farmhouse somewhere. Naturally, Her Majesty and Prince Philip would want to fly back to England. Even if they didn't, they wouldn't be able to continue with the schedule. And if they did, all the press would be about the kidnap anyway. Doesn't bear thinking about. So then everyone starts saying, "young family, parents can't go away, too dangerous" . . . And along comes the Duke of Windsor and his wife – unencumbered – and off they go. That was the intention.'

'But . . .' Urquhart blustered, 'but . . .' His ruddy face clouded with incomprehension. 'What about the Queen Mother? She's perfectly good at doing this sort of thing. She did it in Africa just now. Or Princess Margaret? Why on *earth* would we ever get back that man and his monstrous . . . ?'

'Miles!' Sir Hugh glared at his fellow courtier, who was in danger of saying something very rude about a member of the royal family.

The Queen said nothing. Sir Hugh was full of delight at the foiling of the kidnap plot, and Urquhart was doing a good job of pointing out how utterly futile it would have been. Futile, but quite terrifying. The thought of her little boy in a farmhouse, locked away . . .

Sir Hugh rattled on. 'It was a fantasy, the whole thing. That's what these plotters are: sheer fantasists. They wanted someone malleable, rather than someone popular. As long as he was *their* man.'

If MI5 hadn't been watching . . . the Queen trembled at the thought. If Joan hadn't seen Radnor-Milne and Maidstone together, and helped them connect the dots . . . If *she* hadn't told them about that treacherous bastard, the Marquess of Suffolk, even if they had conveniently forgotten where the information came from . . .

'And they seemed to think the PM wouldn't notice if the man continually went off-piste . . .'

The police and MI5 would have found Charles. They would have got him back quickly. It would have been a damp squib for the traitors. But for her little family . . . The trauma of it all . . .

'I'm terribly sorry,' she said. 'I'm still feeling rather faint. I need some fresh air.'

Sir Hugh looked surprised. 'There isn't time, ma'am. You're open-ing parliament in a couple of hours. You'll need to get changed . . .'

'I can change quickly. Can someone please show me the way to the gardens?'

For fifteen minutes, walking among the paths and borders of Gov-ernment House, she didn't think she could do it. How could she put on her coronation dress and make a historic speech – the first monarch to do so in this place – when she could hardly stand?

It took every ounce of will to summon the spirit of her grand-mother. It wasn't about her, it was about the job. As a mother, she couldn't do it; as monarch, she must.

By the time Philip came to find her, she was ready.

'Are you all right, Cabbage? Somebody said you had a fainting fit.'

'I didn't. Perfectly all right, thank you. D'you know where to go?'

★ ★ ★

The opening of the Canadian parliament went without mishap. The Queen felt exhausted, but tried not to let it show. On their return, and before the evening banquet, Sir Hugh managed to update her with the whereabouts of the conspirators.

'I'm afraid we let the ball drop a bit there, ma'am. It was important not to let our hand show. In the meantime, I think Tony Radnor-Milne might have got a whiff of something. He's gone to South Africa, of all places. The second he sets foot on British soil, he'll be arrested for treason.'

'Let him stay there. What about the Marquess of Suffolk?'

'In prison in India. Not quite the yoga retreat he had in mind. The others know we know, if you know what I mean. The PM doesn't want everyone arrested, or it will look as if there was some sort of coup. It might spook the markets.'

Not as much as it spooked me, the Queen thought. She had been worried about the children in case something happened to *her*, but she had never seriously considered something might happen to *them*. How-ever, she was feeling slightly better.

'And Maidstone?'

'Ah.' Sir Hugh adjusted his spectacles. 'He, too, seemed to have got wind of something. He was last seen on a jet to Chicago.'

'America!'

'Ironically, he has friends there. I doubt it'll take long to track him down. Meanwhile, there's the question of Jeremy, ma'am.'

'Yes, there is,' the Queen said.

'We've been letting him work in a room without a telephone. He knows something's up, but doesn't know what. I thought you might like to deal with him yourself, ma'am.'

The Queen looked up. 'That's very kind of you, Hugh,' she said warmly. It was a thoughtful gesture from a busy man. 'I would.'

★ ★ ★

Jeremy Radnor-Milne could feel in his bones that the game was up.

He had suspected for a week, now, that Sir Hugh knew something. There had been conversations in the North Wing that he was no longer included in. Editors who seemed to be re-briefed after he briefed them. Little conversations with his one or two allies among the household staff that were interrupted before he could give useful instructions. Nothing obvious . . . but then, Jeremy liked to think of himself as the master of 'nothing obvious'. So he was sensitive to it happening to him.

He had got his wife to warn his brother, using a code word they'd agreed. If he was right, they were probably tapping his phone. But all he could do was carry on, meanwhile. Where else could he go?

When the Queen asked to see him in the private sitting room she had been allocated in Government House, he knew he was right. She looked tired, and low. Usually, she was energised by visits like this; she'd display more energy than all of them put together. But today, she was deflated.

She was sitting in a chair with the light behind her, and he was forced to stoop a little to see her properly.

Looking at her pale face and the dark circles under her eyes, he suddenly realised what he had done. He'd always assumed that she'd carry on regardless, even if her uncle took on some of the trickier visits. He was really very fond of her. A huge fan. That wasn't an act. But recent events seemed to have changed her, which wasn't the plan at all.

'Ma'am? You asked to see me?'

Her voice had an unaccustomed edge.

'Sir Hugh and I have agreed that you've served us enough in your present capacity.'

'I . . . I thought so, ma'am. I realise that I . . . If I can just explain.'

'I think you've earned a very particular next assignment. Sir Hugh has arranged for you to act as our liaison with the local authorities on Ascension Island. It's a one-year posting, but we've extended it to three.'

'Ascension Island, ma'am?' Jeremy tried to sound polite and conversational. 'I don't think I . . .'

'It's a refuelling post in the middle of the Atlantic. There's a small RAF squadron and the navy come and go. It has plentiful sea life, I understand. The birdwatching is also excellent.'

'Did you say the Atlantic? Not the Pacific?'

'No. And if that works out well, there's a position in the Falkland Islands that might suit you.'

'Where are they, ma'am?'

'Near Antarctica.'

'I have to say, I'm not a birdwatcher,' he said, with a nervous chuckle.

'You will be.'

He had always thought of Her Majesty as soft and feminine. There was that impressive bust, that smooth, clear skin. But today she was implacable. She reminded him a bit of Queen Elizabeth I, as he imagined her. Queen Elizabeth I, dealing with one of the traitors against her, he realised. Except, *that* Queen would have sent him to his end at the Tower.

Perhaps Ascension Island was better. Presumably they had women on Ascension Island? Would his wife be able to come with him?

Would she want to?

'I'm . . . I'm very sorry, ma'am. It was nothing personal,' he said with feeling. 'I think of you as—'

'I think of you as gone,' she said. 'Goodbye, Jeremy.'

'Can I just say—'

'No, you can't.'

'But if I just—'

The military equerry at the door, whose presence Jeremy hadn't even been aware of, stepped forward, gripped him by the arm and dragged him unceremoniously from the room.

Within twelve hours, he was on his way to the mid-Atlantic in a cold and noisy military plane. At least it wasn't jail, or the Tower – but then Sir Hugh would have had to explain why to the press, which Jeremy knew he would strain every sinew not to do. His luggage would be sent on, he was told, but his wife and children wouldn't. All he had was the clothes he was standing up in, and a box that Miles Urquhart had handed to him as he was led from Government House. Opening it on the flight, he discovered that it contained a pair of binoculars and a doodle of a seabird. He shivered.

CHAPTER 56

Ironically, the Radnor-Milnes and their co-conspirators hadn't targeted the rest of the Canada trip at all, and yet it was still difficult. The Queen never quite recovered her equilibrium. The crowds were large and happy, but Sir Hugh couldn't hide from her that there were voices that loudly questioned whether Canada should have a queen at all, especially if she cost the country so much money.

The Canadians were still hurting, like the British, after the war. But they felt they were hurting more. Knowing this, Sir Hugh and his team had done everything they could to make the visit as low-key as a historic opening of parliament could be. The Queen worked hard, but wasn't sure she was quite connecting the way the people wanted. She thought of Joan's aunt again. She didn't *try* to be distant, but sometimes it just happened.

Everyone, however, loved her frocks. So at least there was that. And they were dazzled by her diamonds. So there was that too.

★ ★ ★

After four days, which felt more like fourteen, they flew to Virginia. She was very nervous now. She could hardly forget that a huge amount depended on this visit. But also, she was a mere guest in a country that had definitively and triumphantly got rid of her great-great-great-grandfather.

The Queen was good at history, because often it was personal. She knew she was only the second British monarch to visit the USA. The first was her father in 1939, but that was in the build-up to the war, when diplomacy was all about defeating Hitler. And it was impossible not to fall in love with her mother, which naturally, the Americans had. Since then, there had been the Suez crisis and all the rest.

Would they use the trip as an opportunity to belittle the United Kingdom? She knew the president wouldn't, because he was a friend. But what about the press? Could she live up to her mother's success? You could never underestimate the American news machine, or be entirely sure what it would do.

Philip tried to calm her down. He was good at it, making jokes on the flight and laughing at his own very terrible impersonation of an American accent. He knew about Charles, and assured her that 'what the boy doesn't know won't hurt him'. And then suddenly the plane was landing, and Sir Hugh was reminding her of her schedule. And there was really nothing more she could do.

★　★　★

In a life that largely consisted of travels and tours and being seen in public, this became a visit she would never forget. It started with a visit to Jamestown, which was celebrating 350 years since its foundation – just like Romsey in England, whose charter she had presented the day before she left for France in April. This was 'old America', and forty thousand people came out to see her that day, followed by thousands more wherever they went.

By the third day, her fears about this trip had become one of Philip's standing jokes.

'D'you remember how jittery you were before we got here? Look at 'em!'

They had been practically mobbed in Virginia and now they were staying in the executive wing of the White House, where Washington had rolled out the red carpet as only the Americans could.

In short, she needn't have been nervous. It was going well. The Eisenhowers had been tickled when she told them the story of hiding under the tablecloth at Windsor Castle during the war. Bonhomie reigned and the prime minister was 'ecstatic'. In fact, if she could stay a little bit longer, and if she wasn't missing the children, she would.

They were getting ready for their final banquet in Washington. The Queen knew it was ungrateful to long for a nursery tea in front of the fire, and tried to put the thought from her mind as Bobo helped her climb into the sequinned net dress that Mr Hartnell had designed for her. Philip came in, looking divine and adjusting his cufflinks, and told Bobo to 'buzz off' so that he could 'appreciate Her Majesty privately for a moment'.

Bobo complied.

'Not everybody gets to kiss the Queen of England,' he said, before doing so. Then he stood back to admire her dress. He was learning.

'Just heard a terribly funny thing,' he said. 'My valet told me. There was an actress who tried to get into my room last night. Absolute bombshell, apparently, all glitter and zips. Not like you, Lilibet, you know, very racy.'

The Queen didn't know whether to be flattered or offended. 'And?'

'And she insisted I'd told her to wait for me upstairs, because there was something I needed to give her. Can you imagine? Swore blind we'd met. Even produced a note with my handwriting on it, except it wasn't, obviously. Ha! Poor girl. Obviously, I was in here with you so it would have been a wasted evening.'

'For you or for her?'

'For her, Cabbage! Don't be ridiculous!' He frowned. 'You're not finding this funny.'

'You know about Charles,' she said. 'Don't you think this might be part of the same plot?'

'Well, good luck to 'em. I think I can spot when a gold-digging blonde tries to worm her way into my affections. You're right, it sounds just like the tomfool, half-cocked sort of thing they'd try and do. Presumably they couldn't call her off. Anyway, she got ejected PDQ, poor thing.'

Philip chuckled as he fiddled with his cufflinks again. The right one always took a little more work, left-handed. His valet could do it for him, of course, but cufflinks were one of the areas where her husband liked to maintain a modicum of autonomy.

She was thrown back to the ambassador's residence in Paris. The broken chain at the mention of Cresswell Place.

She realised that she was tired, and hadn't had enough to eat today, and it probably wasn't Philip's fault that she felt suddenly dreadful, but something in her cracked. She went over to her dressing table and sat down. She was tearful, which was rare and dreadful, so she turned her head away so he wouldn't see.

'What is it, Lilibet?' He'd stopped laughing. He sounded confused.

'It's . . . been a busy day, that's all.'

'Do you want me to get Bobo?'

'No.'

She grabbed a handkerchief and wiped her eyes quickly. Philip rushed over and knelt in front of her, which was the last thing she wanted. She wanted him to go.

'What's happened? What can I do?'

'There's nothing you can do.'

He smiled nervously. 'This sounds serious. It's not like you. Is someone hounding you? More of that bloody plot? I can protect you, you know. It's what I'm here for.'

He reached out to hug her, but she pulled back.

'I'm not a frigate, in need of a flotilla.'

His expression clouded. 'Of course you aren't. What are you talking about?'

'I'm your *wife*.'

She glared at him through tear-filled eyes, feeling that she knew how to say what she didn't want, but not to ask for what she needed. *Wife* said it all to her. The vows they'd made, the life they were trying to build. The children.

'It hadn't escaped my notice.'

He was gritting his teeth now, clearly offended at being pushed away. The Queen could feel it all falling apart, this tour, herself, them both, everything that was personal to her. She could do the job. She would do it always. But what would it be like if the soul had gone out of it? If she were entirely alone?

'Lilibet! You're really crying. You never cry. Has somebody hurt you? I'll bash the bastard's head in. I'll kill him, God help me. Who did this?'

'You did this!' she shouted, exhausted and too furious to hold it back. '*You* did this! You lied to me!'

'When?'

'You told everyone you were at the palace the night of those murders. You were with a woman. MI5 know all the sordid details . . .'

'A woman? What woman?'

'Abigail Pinder. William Pinder's sister.'

There. She'd said it.

'What? Abigail isn't a woman,' he said, frowning. 'I mean, she's a *woman*. But, you know what I mean. She's a friend.'

'Oh, Philip.'

'I never lied to you,' he said more gently. He looked hurt and confused.

'You said you were at the palace,' she repeated.

'Yes, well . . . that's what I told the busybodies who were asking about my whereabouts. It was none of their business. You might have overheard me . . .'

'You used me as your alibi!'

He frowned and looked less certain. 'It stopped them prying. You didn't mind, did you?'

'Of course I minded!'

'You should have said so!'

She turned to the mirror and started fixing her tiara in place, to give her hands something to do.

'I asked you about it at Balmoral,' she told him, as calmly as she could, looking at his reflection, 'and you lied again.'

'Did I? I didn't think it mattered. It was only to protect a friend. I was doing it out of decency.'

'Decency? Protecting Abigail Pinder?'

'Not Abigail,' he said, frowning. 'William.'

'What?'

'Her brother.'

The Queen turned round to face him properly again.

'How does he come into it?'

'Oh, for Christ's sake! All right.' Philip threw his hands up. 'If you must know, I met up with Roly Hill at the Artemis. He was called to the phone because Abigail was trying to get hold of him. She said she was with her brother and she was desperate. She wanted Roly to go over and talk to Pinder about the state he was in, but Roly couldn't. His wife had a new baby and she'd have divorced him if he didn't get home by midnight. Then he pointed out I knew Pinder pretty well, too.'

'Did you?'

'We served together in HMS *Valiant* during Matapan. Brave man. Exceptional sailor. That's how I met Abigail. According to what she told

Roly on the phone, Pinder's wife Marion had effectively left him. Abigail was on her own with him and he wouldn't talk to her. He was threatening to . . . Well, as I said, he was in a bad way. Roly was stuck, so I said I'd go over. It involved a certain amount of subterfuge, of course. Nothing in this life is bloody simple. Obviously, it wouldn't do for anyone to know I was going to a house at night with a very pretty blonde in it. I took precautions not to be caught in the act. I'm not stupid.'

Oh, if only you knew, the Queen thought. She said nothing.

'So I gave my security the slip and we hightailed it to the mews in Roly's Aston Martin. The street was dark and quiet, nobody about. He dropped me off right outside and headed home. Abigail let me in and explained about Pinder.'

'What about him?'

'He'd locked himself in the back bedroom with a bottle of whisky and a gun.'

'*What?*'

'Quite. Abigail caught sight of the barrel just before he locked the door on her. An old service pistol. He was being hounded by MI5, did you know that?'

'Yes.'

'He'd been working for them for ten years, and they'd got it into their heads, because he knew a couple of Russians socially, that he was the Third Man.'

'I'd heard.'

'Preposterous, of course, but they wouldn't let it go. The poor sod was suicidal. It took me a good hour to talk myself into the room, and three more to talk him into handing over the gun. I took the magazine out, but it wouldn't clear so I fired into a pillow, just to be sure. The thing went off and practically deafened us. I'm amazed no one else heard it. Anyway, by then it was the early hours. Abigail joined us and we finished the bottle, the three of us, sitting up against the bedroom wall, listening to Grieg on Pinder's gramophone. Very soothing, Grieg, if you're in a certain mood. Then I called my equerry, who called his brother in the Grenadiers, reliable chap, who came to pick me up in his car.' He shrugged. 'And that's it. The whole story. Hardly a night of unbridled passion, or whatever you were thinking.'

'I didn't know what to think.'

'No need to think anything.'

'Why didn't you tell me?'

Philip raised his arms again in a gesture of helplessness. 'Not my story to tell. Pinder was in a very bad way. He doesn't want half the country knowing his business.'

'I'm not half the country!' she pointed out, raising her voice again.

He looked grumpy, and only slightly apologetic. 'Officers' code. I assumed you'd understand.'

'Well, I didn't.'

There was a pause. Philip had said that was the whole story, but of course it wasn't.

'And what about Abigail?' the Queen added quietly. 'You say she's a friend.'

'Exactly!'

She looked at him very steadily. 'What sort of friend?'

'The best sort! For God's sake, Lilibet. The sort who's interested in Jung and Heidegger. Don't tell me you are too, because unless Heidegger was running in the four thirty at Newmarket, you wouldn't give a damn. Abigail's studying psychoanalysis. She's very interesting on the subject.' He reached out a hand and laid it on her arm. His voice was softer. 'I don't bore you with Jung, Lilibet, and you don't, thank God, bore me with your breeding programme for the Derby. But I'm yours, you know that. Body and soul.'

He didn't say such things to her often, but every time he did, they sung through her like electricity down a wire. Nobody could be as serious about love as Philip could. Or as serious about *anything*. Or as funny. Or as damned complicated. Her mother was right.

He brushed a tear away from her face. 'Now, stop fretting. It doesn't suit you.'

After an argument like that, and all those weeks of tension, and the sudden clearing of the air, there was only one thing to do – but it would have to wait. Bobo was knocking at the door and there was more than a hint of urgency in her voice as she pointed out the time.

★ ★ ★

Much later, in the middle of the night, Philip had gone back to his room and the Queen lay wide awake. Jet lag, she supposed. It reminded her a little of the night Anne had had toothache, but that had been fraught, and now she felt more relaxed than she had in months.

She thought about poor William Pinder, who turned out to be a loyal servant of the Crown, but had been hounded by his own organisation. How awful that he had felt so desperate he had armed himself with a service pistol.

And then there was Boy Browning, back home in Menabilly. Philip had blithely said his head of household was taking the summer off for a bit of a health cure, but Daphne du Maurier had told her at Balmoral that the general was very unwell, mentally and physically, and she wasn't sure if he would return to work.

It occurred to the Queen, not for the first time, that women were treated like delicate flowers, cosseted and protected at every turn. Men were always leaping forward to throw their cloaks over metaphorical puddles. But she was quite as strong as them, if not stronger. Men were like oak trees: they fell hard when things went wrong. She thought of herself more as a willow, bending in the wind and weather.

Willows reminded her of the river near Windsor, and of the lake at Buckingham Palace. What would Anne be doing? she wondered. It was morning already in England. Would she be at her schoolwork, or outside in the fresh autumn air? And what about Charles? Would she ever tell him about the plot that never happened? Probably not.

Thinking about her children, she finally fell asleep.

CHAPTER 57

The Americans made it plain at every turn: they didn't want a monarch of their own again, but they were absolutely delighted to welcome this one as a guest.

They weren't enthusiastic in the same way that English people were. Everything was bigger, bolder, louder. They pressed against barriers, requiring police officers to restrain them. They shouted and hollered. They thronged the streets for miles, wherever the royal couple went.

After three days in Washington, it was time for the final leg of the journey. This time, they took the train up the East Coast to New York.

The Queen had been quite specific about the way she wanted to see this city for the first time, because she had envisaged it so clearly. The train took her all the way to Staten Island, from where she and Philip could take the governor's launch past the Statue of Liberty to the tip of Manhattan.

The view of the looming skyscrapers was everything she had imagined – as long as one ignored the helicopters circling overhead, taking pictures. She was as excited as any tourist. It was only a shame that they could carve out a single day for her to visit.

She and Philip would have to make the most of the hours ahead, because their plane left tonight.

* * *

To call those next few hours a whirlwind would be an understatement. If Washington had rolled out the red carpet, New York flung it far and wide across the city.

Sir Hugh told her the television channels were proclaiming that there were a million people on the streets. Fifth Avenue was packed with faces and flags at every window of its multi-storeyed buildings, which were almost obscured by the blizzard of ticker tape. An elevator swept them up to the top of the Empire State Building, from where Manhattan lay spread out at their feet, as wonderful and extraordinary as she had imagined. This was 'new America', and to her own surprise she thought it the most beautiful thing she had ever seen.

The royal couple's base was to be at the Waldorf Astoria. They were supposed to have the Presidential Suite, but King Farouk, who was there before them, had been taken ill and couldn't be moved. Instead, she and Philip were given a thousand unnecessary apologies and Suite 42, which had undergone a very rapid makeover in their honour.

Looking down from one of the highest windows in New York as she changed for lunch, she saw the city fall back into its normal rhythm, as traffic began to clog the roads that had been cleared for her parade.

'I could stay here all day!' she called across to Philip, who was getting changed in the bedroom across the suite's hallway.

'Well, don't! They've laid on a banquet.'

They had, and after that expansive lunch they whisked her – as much as anyone could be 'whisked' in this city – down wide avenues to the United Nations, where she made a speech in praise of the ideals of peace and cooperation that drove the new Commonwealth.

Now, evening was approaching. Their only evening in the city, and with it a ball, which she would be hosting. The Queen retired to her bedroom in Suite 42 to rest, but couldn't, and found herself looking out of the window at the little lines of tiny yellow taxis, far below.

Knowing she would want to capture the moment, Bobo had set her camera on the dressing table, so she could take pictures of the scene to show the children later. The day had been astonishing from start to finish. The train, the Statue of Liberty, the United Nations, the ticker-tape parade . . . And now here she was, in the world's tallest hotel, and it was about to be full of fun and dancing.

She remembered a Cole Porter song that she and Philip had danced to in the moonlight at Cliveden: 'I Happen to Like New York'. It made perfect sense now.

Her evening gown was hung out, ready for her to change into. In a minute, she would get Bobo to draw her a bath. They had allowed ninety minutes in her schedule to get ready. She would need less than half that time, which left a few precious minutes for relaxation and reflection.

The parade! All those happy, excited people, so keen to see her they had to be held back by the police. The ticker tape rising so high on the wind they could still see it whipping around at the top of the Empire State Building. What a view that had been! She hummed to herself.

I happen to like New York.

Feeling almost guilty with self-indulgent enjoyment of this private moment, she sat at the dressing table, where Bobo had laid out everything she would need. There were the earrings, the necklace, the diamond tiara, her lipstick from Helena Rubinstein, her scent, her powder . . . She pictured all the other ladies in the hotel, and in other hotels and apartments in New York, getting ready for this evening too. They probably took longer over it than she would. She was so used to it by now. With experience, she could adjust her hair and put on her tiara in under two minutes.

Regarding herself in the mirror, she lifted the tiara and positioned it on her head, for effect. All her pieces of jewellery had titles, and this was Queen Alexandra's Kokoshnik tiara – a great wall of diamonds commissioned by her great-grandmother when she was Princess of Wales. The Queen had already worn it in Canada and knew exactly how she would fit it into her hairstyle later. It took practice. Only one way was truly reliable in the end.

And suddenly it all came together. Who committed murder in Chelsea that night in March, and how, and almost certainly why. When you thought about it, it was obvious.

'Ma'am?'

She looked round to find Bobo hovering in the inner doorway.

'Shall I draw that bath for you now?'

The Queen shook her head. 'I need to talk to someone first.'

She gave her instructions. It was time to come face to face with a murderer.

CHAPTER 58

Lady Lucie Seymour followed Bobo into the bedroom. She was already dressed for the dinner and ball in ice-blue silk trimmed with tiny glass beads and looked, as her husband had anticipated, magnificent.

She dropped into a curtsey and murmured 'Your Majesty.' Then she glanced up, puzzled. 'You wanted to see me?'

'I did,' the Queen said. 'Please sit down.'

Her name was Lucie, not Lucy, as the Queen had originally assumed. She had seen it written on the list of guests for this evening. She hadn't realised the full impact of that spelling at the time, but now she knew.

She indicated two armchairs placed conveniently by the window, and chose one of them while her guest sat opposite her in the other. Bobo left them to it. The distant traffic honked and hooted far below.

'Your dresser said it was about my sister,' Lucie said. She shook her head. 'I'm afraid I don't have one.'

The Queen sighed deeply. 'I'm very sorry. But I think you did.'

Daphne had been wrong in Balmoral, though she was on the right lines. The layout of the bodies hadn't been misdirection: it was love.

She had anticipated that Lucie might lie about her family, and she wasn't entirely sure what she would do at that point. Instead, she watched as a single tear appeared in the inner corner of her visitor's right eye and made its way very slowly down her powdered face. At that moment, she seemed to turn from marble into something as fragile as an eggshell. Her voice was almost inaudible.

'How did you know?'

The Queen held out a hand in a gesture of reassurance. One needed dogs at a moment like this, she thought. Even a horse would do, or in extremis a cat, though she was allergic to them. But the Waldorf Astoria didn't have them on tap. She clasped Lucie's cold fingers briefly with the warmth of her own.

'I realised as I was trying on my tiara,' she said. 'Of course, you'd have tried yours on too. It's impossible to get it right unless you've worked out how to wear your hair. You were going to wear it on your birthday, so Stephen gave it to you early so you could practise.'

Lucie nodded slightly. 'Yes, he did.'

'You had it out of the safe. But Ginette took it.'

Lucie just looked at her. Another tear followed the first.

'You were very close to her,' the Queen said quietly. 'It suddenly occurred to me that if Ginette had an older sister in Marianne, there was nothing to say Marianne didn't have an older sister too. One who helped Ginette out when she came to London.'

Lucie nodded, staring down at her skirts.

'One she didn't talk about.' The Queen's voice was gentle. 'Perhaps because she didn't want to embarrass her relative in high society.'

But this time Lucie shook her head. She stuck out her chin as she looked the Queen in the eye.

'Because of what she did for a living, you mean? You don't understand, ma'am. How do you think I met my husband?'

'Ah,' said the Queen, after a tiny pause. 'I see.'

'Stephen always likes to say we met in Geneva, but it was in Paris. And not at a diplomatic dinner party. That's what gave Ginette the idea, *la pauvre*. Before the war, she wanted to be a milliner, like Marianne, not like me. Marianne was the talented one. She was friends with young Monsieur Dior, they wanted to work together, they both had such plans. She made hats for the Nazi wives during the Occupation and carried messages for the Resistance as she delivered them. And then . . .'

'And then along came Jean-Pierre Minot.'

'Yes.' Lucie swallowed, but her gaze didn't waver. 'He was a star of the Gestapo by then. Marianne was taken to the Rue de la Pompe. They say he worked on her hands first. As soon as the war was over, I hurried home for news. I was hoping to find her alive, but of course I did not. I found out exactly what Jean-Pierre Minot had done – what Ginette already knew. He was famous in those days. Any woman in Paris would have killed him, but he'd vanished. After that, Ginette could never look at a hat. But she had such *life*, ma'am, despite it all. She wanted success. She saw my life in Westminster. She wanted to follow me and marry a rich man who wanted her. I told her that was only in fairy tales but . . .' Lucie waved a gloved hand.

'She had your example,' the Queen suggested.

'Not only mine. There are others. More than you might think.'

'I'm learning fast.'

Lucie cracked a smile. 'Not every duchess was a debutante. And so yes, I tried to help her whenever I could. I didn't see her much, usually when she needed money. But she came to me that night to tell me she'd seen the man who tortured Marianne in the Rue de la Pompe. She was dressed in white, her hair had changed. She looked quite different – in her face, too. Her eyes, you know?'

The Queen listened quietly.

'She said she knew him instantly,' Lucie went on, 'and she was going to watch him die. I told her not to be ridiculous. To my shame, I didn't believe her. Not at all. We were talking in my bedroom so the servants wouldn't hear us. I went to order a tisane from the kitchen to calm her down and talk sense into her, but when I came back, she wasn't there.'

'And nor was the tiara.'

Lucie gave a hollow laugh. 'That was the first thing I saw. I was furious! Imagine! For half a minute, I cared about the diamonds she'd taken for her hair. I didn't understand her plan. By the time I realised what she'd done, she was halfway there. I was frantic!'

The Queen gave her a freshly laundered handkerchief from her handbag.

'Ginette was only a girl in the war,' she suggested. 'But you were not. You were in your mid-twenties at the time, yes?'

Lucie nodded.

'My mother mentioned to me that you and your husband knew the Arisaig estate,' the Queen explained. 'That's where SOE agents who went to France were trained in combat. I assumed your husband had been stationed there, but I now realise it was you, wasn't it?'

Lucie nodded dumbly.

'You spoke French as your mother tongue. Were you training to be an agent yourself? No?'

'I helped to train them,' Lucie said. 'They needed women as well as men to practise combat with. I was a driver, but I did everything. I learned quickly.'

The Queen nodded to herself. 'So you knew how to kill a man, but your sister didn't.'

'How did you guess Ginette was my sister?' Lucie asked. 'Even Stephen didn't know for a long time. I'm certain he didn't tell anyone.'

'*That's* why she wouldn't see him,' the Queen murmured, as much to herself as to Lucie. He presumably didn't know of her relationship to his wife at the time he asked for her, but Ginette would have done. The Queen went on, 'When I realised Minot's killer was a woman, I doubted anyone but a mother or a sister would have done what you did, and you're not old enough to be Ginette's mother. You found out her plans for him, that she wanted to kill him that night. You couldn't let that happen.'

Lucie's eyes were wide. 'She was mad! He was Gestapo! He was good at it! Ginette thought she was grown up, but she was still a child. It's why I truly didn't believe her craziness until it was too late.'

'How did you know where to follow her?' the Queen asked.

'She left a note under my pillow. It gave the address, so I'd know where to find her if she didn't contact me in the morning. For some strange reason she thought I wouldn't look for her until then. She was *dingue, dingue* . . . I wasn't supposed to see the note until I went to bed, but she'd left my pillow crooked.' Lucie smiled again, fondly, her face blotchy under her makeup, her lipstick smudged, mascara running. 'Ginette always, how do you say it, *faisait à la va-vite.*'

'She was slapdash? I think that's it.'

'Yes!' Lucie nodded. 'Except about her appearance. So I noticed the pillow straightaway. As soon as I read the note, I realised why she had really come to see me.'

'Oh? It wasn't the diamonds, was it? They just happened to be there.'

Lucie nodded. 'It was in part to say goodbye, just in case. And she knew I kept a flick knife in a jewellery roll in my dressing table. A memento from Arisaig. One of the trainers gave it to me – a trophy he'd picked up from a German soldier in the desert. It was quite small and easy to hide, but well made. Deadly – in the right hands. I looked. It was gone.'

'But your sister's weren't the right hands,' the Queen said, pursuing the thought she'd originally had. 'You no longer had the knife, so you armed yourself with cheese wire.'

'I know how to kill a man. Ginette thought she did, but it's different when he's fighting for his life. It wasn't cheese wire, ma'am, it was flower arranging wire. I used bamboo struts for the handles.'

'Does that work?'

'It did,' Lucie said, flatly.

'And so you disguised yourself and went after her, to Cresswell Place.'

Lucie's face was taut with pain. 'You make it sound easy. It seemed to take forever. I pulled a pair of Stephen's trousers over my dress and took his boots and driving gloves, and a spare mackintosh and hat. I thought I'd save Ginette and we'd get away looking like a couple, a man and a woman. Nobody would guess it was us. I just wanted her to be alive and free, that's all I was thinking. But I'd need to get into the house, so I had to find something to pick the lock. And I needed a cosh to knock him out.'

'Did you have one of those at home?'

'In a way. I stole one of Stephen's shooting socks and put a paperweight in the toe. Once I'd stuffed the coat pockets with what I needed, I caught a cab to the Old Brompton Road and ran from there.' Lucie winced with frustration. 'I laced up the boots as tight as I could, but they still slowed me down.'

'How did you know how to find the address?'

She looked surprised. 'I looked it up in the *A to Z*.'

'Oh,' said the Queen. This was not something she had ever needed to do, though she knew of the book of London maps that Lucie was referring to. She quietly decided to get Joan to show her how one worked.

'And you happened to get there at eleven fifteen, or thereabouts – half an hour after Ginette, and ten minutes after Minot joined her.'

'Did I? I lost track of time.'

At this point, the bedroom door opened without ceremony.

'Darling, what do you think of this . . . Oh!'

Philip stood in the doorway in a white dress shirt with a wing collar, evening trousers and white braces, staring at the two women in their armchairs by the window.

'Having a chat? I hardly think we have time. Hello, have we met?'
Lucie stood up and curtseyed.

'Your Royal Highness,' she said with a smile that seemed polite,
but, from close to, had a touch of hysteria about it.

'This is Lady Seymour,' the Queen told him.

'Bloody hell. Your husband's been in hot water, hasn't he? Is he
here tonight?'

'He is,' Lucie said.

'Brave man. I'll look out for him. Don't keep Her Majesty too
long,' he added cheerfully. 'She's got a ballroom full of people waiting
for her downstairs in . . .' He checked his watch. 'Twenty-seven
minutes.'

'I won't, sir.'

'Anyway, Lilibet, what d'you think of this bow tie? Chap gave it to
me in Washington. Says it's the new American style – much softer, see?
But my valet hates it. Shall I go Yankee this evening?'

The Queen peered critically at his neckwear. 'I think we should
look as British as we can,' she said. 'That's what they've come to see.'

'Oh, all right then, dammit. If you think so. Aren't you going to
have a bath? Shall I call for Bobo?'

'I'm just sorting something out with Lucie.'

'Can I help?'

'I don't think so.' She gave a little grimace to put him off. 'Women's
business.'

'Oh God! Count me out. See you later. Cheerio.'

He went out, banging the door behind him.

The Queen caught Lucie's eye. The blonde woman's perfectly
sculpted lips wobbled. Then her shoulders shook. She laughed raggedly
for about ten seconds as the hysteria found its way to the surface, after
which the shaking turned to sobbing. This was, all round, a difficult
evening.

'I'm so sorry,' the Queen said. 'Awful timing. You were about to
go to the mews house. But you got there too late, I think.'

Lucie glanced out of the window, where the lights were coming
on and New York was turning from day to night. She sighed.

'All that time I had spent looking for something to pick the lock,
and I didn't need it after all. My sister must have left the door on the
latch for that . . . monster. All I had to do was push, but I made sure the

door locked behind me. I couldn't hear anything, so I thought perhaps everything was fine. That she'd changed her mind. I tiptoed upstairs so that if she was . . . doing what he came for . . . then I wouldn't disturb them. But . . .'

'She hadn't changed her mind,' the Queen prompted gently.

'No. Ginette was lying face up on the bed and he was bent over her, with his back to me. I could see she'd tried to surprise him with my knife. It was still sticking out of his side. He was strangling her with one of her own stockings and he didn't hear me come up behind him. When he started to turn round, I swung the cosh.'

The Queen turned pale, but gestured to Lucie to carry on.

'With practice, you can do a lot of damage,' Lucie said, 'but I hadn't practised for years. He collapsed on top of Ginette, but I didn't trust him. Men like that get up again and again, so I rolled him onto the floor. I got out the garrotte and did what I had to do. Then I went to Ginette. The nylon stocking was still there because he'd pulled it so tight around her neck. I took it off but it took time. I kept hoping . . . I tried to save her, but it was too late . . .' Lucie shut her eyes. 'She squeezed my hand. I kissed her. She breathed her last breath.'

'You didn't call a doctor.'

'She was dead within a minute. What was the point? They would have put her in a bag and taken her away.'

Lucie gave the Queen a look that was both devastated and cold. This was a woman who knew how to kill a man with an improvised weapon, and didn't hesitate to do it. She was tough and unsentimental, grief-stricken and worn out.

'You washed your sister as an act of love,' the Queen said.

'*Oui.* I didn't want that bastard's blood on her. It was on the silk *jarretière* – what's that word?'

'Garter?'

'Garter, yes, that I think she used to hide the knife under her dress, so I took it. The dress was torn and dirty, so I took that off her too. Then I used the other stocking on him, because I wanted him to know how it felt.'

Even though he was well and truly dead by then, the Queen thought.

'And the knife?'

Lucie remained impassive. 'I planted it in his face. Then I walked into the other room. I found lilacs. Ginette always loved those flowers.

I was just putting them in her arms when I heard the sound of men's voices downstairs. I waited. They were there for ages and then one of them came upstairs. Then another, and another. I was stuck in that goddam room, but I didn't mind. In the end, I spent the night with her. It was nice. Peaceful.'

'I suppose so,' the Queen said. She couldn't begin to imagine what this must have been like, but she did know sisterly love.

'We hadn't spent so long together in years,' Lucie went on softly. 'I took the gloves off and held her hand. I lay beside her and told her stories about France, while this other man snored like a pig across the landing. I could have gone while he slept, but I didn't want to leave her . . . I assumed I'd tell him what had happened in the morning. But I wasn't really thinking about the morning.'

'And when it came, what did you do?'

'I waited until dawn. Then my training took over. I don't really remember, but I got outside with the dress under my coat. I didn't feel as if I was in my body. I climbed over a wall, crept through a garden and came out in the Boltons, where Deborah Fairdale lives. Do you know it, ma'am?'

The Queen half smiled. 'I do.'

'From there, I walked quickly to the King's Road. I found a telephone box and called the police. I can't remember what I said, but I assumed they would find the bodies in five minutes. Then I went home and hid the dress and gloves and boots in an old suitcase and slept for twenty-four hours. But there was no news of the bodies that day, or the next. Every minute since has been a dream. A nightmare.'

'I assume your husband knows what you did,' the Queen said.

'I imagine. The diamonds . . . His gloves and boots gone too. He must have recognised my old knife in the newspaper. We haven't talked about it.'

'He must love you very much.'

Lucie shrugged. 'I'm a lovely ornament. He's a generous admirer. C'est tout.'

'He's allowed many people to assume he's a killer to protect you. I doubt his political career will recover.'

Lucie shrugged. 'Perhaps.'

The Queen saw how unmoved she was by what was surely an act of selflessness. Lady Seymour seemed unmoved by her husband altogether. She sat there, ramrod straight, her alabaster beauty unaffected by the ravages to her makeup, her slim shoulders rising from the beaded perfection of the evening gown he had paid for.

Lucie's face had only truly come alive when she talked of Scotland, and the work she had done to train agents to work with the Resistance. The Queen knew several women who had lived extraordinary lives in the war, at all levels of society. Many of them continued to do so, in one way or another, taking what they had learned and applying it in charities, schools, hospitals and military units. It had changed their lives; they had an energy that sparkled. By contrast, she could see that the return to life as a 'lovely ornament' had done Lucie no good at all. Perhaps it didn't help that her loving husband was unfaithful. Meanwhile, it must have cut her to the quick to have found out what happened to her sister Marianne. She had become hollowed out by boredom and grief.

Those wartime experiences were still inside her, though. Lucie was a woman who could escape from a murder scene without leaving a trace, and without really trying. Luck had played its part; she might so easily have been spotted going into the mews, or escaping through the Boltons later, but she wasn't.

However, her luck was running out. If the Queen could work out her part in the murders from the tiara, perhaps Inspector Darbishire would get there one day. Lucie never had an alibi to speak of – he had simply never asked.

'Was there any other way . . . ?' the Queen asked.

'To stop the man who was murdering my sister? No. If I'd hesitated for one second, he'd have killed us both.'

'The police might understand, you know. It was self-defence, of a sort.'

'They wouldn't,' Lucie said decisively. 'It never ends well when a woman kills a man. But I understand – my time is up. Thank you.'

'Thank you for what?'

'For warning me.'

Was that what this was? A warning? The Queen hadn't thought of it that way – more as a prelude to the inevitable consequences. But perhaps Lucie was right.

She stood up and Lucie did too.

'I'm so very sorry about your sister. Both your sisters.'

They faced each other, and Lucie noted that the Queen was not calling for help. She smiled.

'And now I really must get ready,' the Queen said, apologetically.

'You've missed your bath. *Je suis désolée.*'

'I'll manage,' the Queen assured her.

Lucie hesitated.

'I don't think we'll see each other downstairs.'

'No, I doubt we will. Goodbye, Lucie.'

The other woman dropped into a deep curtsey, just as Bobo bustled into the room, making anxious noises about 'The time! The dress! The hair! Your bath, Lilibet! Oh!'

'Goodbye, ma'am.'

She let herself out.

CHAPTER 59

The ball seemed to go by in the blink of an eye. Everyone loved the Queen's dress, which combined a slim, sequinned column made of cellophane lace with a wide tulle fantail that swept behind her with a reassuring swish. Many people commented. Even some of the men, which was almost unheard of.

It took a while for the Queen to get the image out of her head of what Lucie must have gone through that night in Chelsea. But the champagne helped, and so did the Queen's sense of duty, which demanded that she pay close attention to everyone she met, and laugh whenever a joke was attempted, and laugh loudly if it was attempted by the Governor of New York.

A very good band played very good jazz, and Philip had a brief dance with her, wearing his much-admired, very British, stiff bow tie. New Yorkers certainly knew how to party. By the end, she was sorry they couldn't stay all night. Like Cinderella, she had to leave by midnight – although this Cinderella ran to the plane with her prince beside her, the skirts of her ballgown caught by the runway's Krieg lights as they floated in the wind.

MISSING IN NEW YORK

Page 7. After the grand banquet at the Waldorf Astoria for HM the Queen last Monday, it was discovered that one of the guests had vanished. Attractive socialite Lady Seymour, 40, wife of the UK's Minister for Technology, has mysteriously disappeared. The

NYPD has been alerted and so far there is no sign of her. Pressed for comment, Lord Seymour said his wife must have suffered a sudden health crisis, and has made an impassioned plea for her return. The minister was briefly a suspect in the Chelsea murders, as the owner of the diamond tiara found on one of the victims. The Metropolitan Police say their inquiries are still ongoing.

Norman Hartnell among British designers paying tribute after the sudden death of couturier Christian Dior at 52. France in mourning. See page 9.

More coverage of the Queen's unforgettable fifteen hours in New York on pages 2, 3, 4, 11 and 12. Full colour pull-out in this weekend's Sunday supplement.

'How long had you known for?' Joan asked.

The Queen was back at her desk, beside the bow window in her Buckingham Palace study, surrounded by paperwork.

'Oh, minutes before she appeared in my suite. For ages I thought Tony Radnor-Milne must be connected, and I still think he knew Rodriguez through the casinos and the agency, but I realised he wasn't connected with who Rodriguez really was. Whereas Ginette . . . I quite accept I hadn't thought it through properly. I'd just realised that Lucie had access to the diamonds and she might possibly know how to garrotte a man at short notice. But I thought she must have done it to try and save her sister. It was suddenly clear to me that they were sisters. I was sure Lucie hadn't done it to save herself.'

Joan raised an eyebrow and the Queen sighed.

'I got caught up in the moment,' she admitted. 'I just needed to know that I was right.'

'Did Lady Seymour regret it?' Joan asked. 'It must have been terrible, that night . . .'

'Oh, it was,' the Queen agreed. 'Lying beside her sister's body. But she didn't seem to regret what she'd done for a moment. Only that she was too late. I don't think she realised quite how lucky she was that she wasn't caught at the time.'

Joan didn't point out that she was equally lucky not to be caught afterwards, in New York. She only knew that if *she* had been put in the same position, that night in Chelsea, she'd have done exactly what

Lady Seymour did. Now it was up to the police to find her, if they could.

The Queen swiftly changed the subject. 'Do you see much of Major Ross?' she asked. 'You're back in Dolphin Square, I understand.'

Joan tried to keep her face neutral. She could, if she wanted, tell Her Majesty that Hector Ross no longer stayed at his club; that he was teaching her about whisky; that he was very fond of her kimono, and when he was tired, he liked to run his fingers along the silk. But these topics didn't seem appropriate for the royal study. Instead she said, 'Not much, ma'am. He spends every evening out now, being feted for uncovering the kidnapping plot.' This much was true.

Fortunately, the Queen focused on what *was* said, not what wasn't.

'I didn't think many people knew about it.'

'Oh, enough do in his circles, ma'am. I hear rumours that you're going to give him a medal. Are you?'

The Queen gave a little shrug. 'It's not entirely up to me. But I think he deserves one, don't you? He didn't have a huge amount to work with, but he put it together very fast.'

'He did,' Joan agreed. 'With help.'

'Does he have any idea where that help came from?' the Queen asked anxiously.

Joan knew Her Majesty liked remaining in the background. She didn't want the DG of MI5 worrying that she was trying to do his job for him.

'He does, actually,' Joan said with a smile.

'Oh?' The Queen looked alarmed.

'Major Ross knows I answer to someone important. He was absolutely sure it was Sir Hugh, so he collared him at the club one day and asked him outright, and Sir Hugh categorically denied it. I wouldn't say anything, of course, so then he decided it must be Sir Hugh's deputy, and when he asked the DPS . . .'

The Queen grinned. 'Miles *didn't* categorically deny it.'

'Not categorically, no. And I share an office with him, so it all makes sense.'

'How perfect.'

'Now everybody's buying Miles drinks at *his* club – even people who have no idea what it's all supposed to be about – and he comes in slightly hungover each morning, but very happy.'

'I don't suppose *he* has any idea who . . . ?'

'I don't think so, ma'am,' Joan said confidently. 'I'm just an ex-typist, and you're the monarch. He might suspect the Master of the Household, but he's not saying.'

The Queen nodded happily. 'Well done.'

CHAPTER 60

'Sir?'

'Yes, Woolgar?'

'Somebody rang from the shorty while you were out. Said to tell you that someone's been in touch about that missing woman in New York. Lady Seymour, sir.'

Darbishire took off his coat and sat at his desk. 'What's the shorty, Sergeant?'

'You know, sir. You've been in touch. In Paris. The Frog police.'

'The Sûreté?'

'That's what I said.'

Darbishire sighed. 'Go on.'

'This chap rang them a couple of days ago and said he'd seen a newsreel about the Queen. They're showing them in Paris too. And it had this bit at the end about Lady Seymour, saying she was missing and everything. And this chap said the police had been in touch with him recently, asking about Marianne Fleury and what happened to her in the war, because, you know, we were asking . . .'

'Yes, I know.'

'And he realised that this woman had been around years ago – ten years ago, in fact – to ask the same thing. Because she was . . . and you're never going to believe this, sir . . . Guess.'

'I'd rather not, Woolgar. Not a spurned lover, I presume?'

'Ooh, saucy, sir! No. Her sister!'

'But surely . . . ?'

Darbishire stopped and thought about it. He had assumed Lucie was Swiss, but he hadn't paid it much attention; he just pitied her as the cuckolded wife. She would be about six years older than Marianne, which would make her a dozen years older than Ginette. He had cousin siblings who were a dozen years apart.

'How on earth did this man remember her after a decade? Surely he could be mistaken?'

'He said he'd never forget a face that beautiful. He was very French about it.'

'Was he? And did he have any idea where she might have disappeared to?'

'No, sir. At least, the man I spoke to didn't say. I said you'd call him back.'

Darbishire would.

He was rapidly reconsidering the alibis. He had never trusted Lady Seymour's assurance about her husband's whereabouts, but nobody had thought (he hadn't thought) that her husband and the butler might equally be lying about hers.

If Darbishire's chap was right, did Seymour kill Minot in revenge for what happened to his wife's sister?

Possibly, but Seymour wasn't missing.

Would Seymour protect a murderess?

If his wife had killed a monster to try and save her sister he would, if he was any kind of man at all. How she might have killed Minot, Darbishire had no idea, but he knew that murder wasn't always a man's prerogative. Darbishire's job was to bring killers to justice, but privately, he thought some acts were fully justified. He would try and find her, of course, but if any of this new information turned out to be true, he rather hoped he wouldn't.

★ ★ ★

But he didn't get the chance to look.

A couple of hours later, the chief superintendent stopped by Darbishire's office – something he never normally did – and announced that George Venables was finally free to take on the Cresswell Place case.

'He's been snowed under with this and that. We're grateful for everything you've done, Fred. Good, diligent police work. It's a shame you didn't make more progress early on, but I think with George on board we can really crack this case. I'm sure we can rely on you to give him the full support you're famous for. Anyway, well done, as far as you got.'

'No hard feelings, I hope,' Venables said later, giving him a manly pat on the back. 'I know it's been a bastard of a case. Unreliable witnesses . . . no leads . . . You're probably glad to see the back of it!'

This week, Darbishire had noticed they'd added another storey to the eyesore across the river from the Yard. He was glad he wouldn't have to keep going into that office to smarten up his royal reports. When Woolgar tried to commiserate about Venables, Darbishire talked instead about the new building, and the skyline he was starting not to recognise any more.

'D'you want to come for a beer, sir?' Woolgar asked. 'A few of us are going to the pub.'

The inspector declined gracefully. He wouldn't be the best company. He shrugged his coat on and went home to his wife and girls.

★ ★ ★

In the sunny morning room at Clarence House, the Queen Mother was not happy as news emerged of Chief Inspector Venables's fascinating new discoveries.

'But, darling! They're saying Lady Seymour might be the murderer! She was the victim's sister! And Philip tells me you were alone with her for half an hour!'

'I was perfectly safe,' the Queen assured her. 'Philip was next door, and Bobo was just around the corner.'

Her mother was slightly mollified. 'Bobo would never let anything happen to you. But did you have any idea?'

'None at all. Why would I?'

'What were you talking about?'

This was tricky. Philip could easily be put off by the notion of 'women's business', but her mother would only be more intrigued.

'Lady Seymour heard rumours about a spy ring,' the Queen improvised. 'Nothing concrete, but she didn't trust anyone and she was desperate for me to know. I said I'd sort it out with MI5. The poor woman . . .'

'A *spy* ring? How exciting!'

'But it was all in her head,' the Queen insisted.

'And did this have anything to do with the murders?'

'Did what?' Margaret asked, walking in with a couple of frisky little dachshunds at her feet.

'A *spy* ring, darling!' the Queen Mother said.

'No, it absolutely didn't,' the Queen said firmly.

'I *told* you it wasn't Clement,' her mother remarked happily, changing the subject.

'Who's Clement?' Margaret asked.

'The Dean of Bath – you remember, darling. He saw some terrible things in the war, but we talked about it once and we agreed you can't keep fighting on forever. You only end up wounding yourself. That poor woman, the one on the bed, I mean. She wanted revenge, I gather. I can see that, but *murder* is never the way. Especially if you're not very good at it. How did she end up with the diamonds again?'

The Queen hesitated and Margaret sighed audibly as she inserted a cigarette into her holder. This obviously wasn't the first time since the news broke that she had been called upon to explain.

'Lord Seymour gave them to his wife, Mummy. *She* gave them to her sister. Then, she must have realised her sister was in danger and followed her to Clement's house.'

The Queen didn't correct her about the gift of the tiara. Without Lucie around to explain what really happened, nobody had the full story. What they knew was close enough.

'*Such* a nice tiara,' the Queen Mother said sadly. 'Nobody will want to wear it now.'

'I certainly don't,' Margaret assured her.

'I'll buy one for you one day, darling.'

'D'you know what?' Margaret said, through a plume of cigarette smoke. 'It's the twentieth century, for God's sake. I think I might just buy one for myself.'

CHAPTER 61

The deputy private secretary had become very grand. Now that Joan no longer did secretarial duties, she had been moved to a much smaller office of her own, so Urquhart could share his with Sarah, the typist, who could help him out properly. He also had a dog: a black Labrador puppy called Nelson, who ate everything in sight and was adored by everyone in the office. He had given up on the hope of Fiona's return, so this was the best replacement he could find.

Sarah was good, but she often came to Joan for advice. One day she brought in a large, square box that had come all the way from America, marked 'FRAGILE'.

'It says, "For the Queen's eyes only", but it can't really mean that, can it? I mean, it's not from the CIA or anything. That's not how they write things.'

'I'll take a look, if you like,' Joan offered.

'Would you? Thanks ever so.'

Inside, buried in excessive layers of packaging, was a single vinyl record in a cellophane-covered presentation box. Its label read 'The Queen's Suite'. There was a note with it, which Joan read with growing amazement. She took it to Her Majesty that afternoon.

'It's from Duke Ellington, ma'am. He said he met you in the spring, and he wanted to write something for you.'

The Queen smiled brightly. 'Yes, he did.'

'Well, he wrote this piece, and he got his orchestra to record it. But they only made one pressing, ma'am.'

'What d'you mean?'

'This is the only record. And he's paid Columbia Records for the copyright so no one else can make one. He wanted it to be a gift for you, personally.'

At this, the Queen's face lit up in a whole new way. 'Did he really? May I see the note?' She stood up. 'Let's go to the Ball Supper Room. There's a gramophone there.'

The music was quite beautiful. The Queen announced it was one of the nicest pieces of jazz she'd ever heard. So did Philip, when he wondered what all the fuss was about and came in to listen.

'Dance with me!' he instructed.

'What? Here?'

'Where else!'

He took her in his arms and the staff left them to it as they twirled around the room.

★ ★ ★

November gave way to December. The Duke of Maidstone came home, miserably, from his short exile in Chicago. He had been stripped without warning or explanation of almost all his family's ancient roles in the pageantry of the monarchy. The best he could do was ask, tremulously, if his son might be able to resume them again when he inherited. But the jury was out. His shooting invitations were rescinded. The duchess started to worry about his heart.

In Johannesburg, Tony Radnor-Milne tried to give the impression that he had always wanted a life of wine-making and investment, five thousand miles away from his businesses, his soon-to-be-ex-wife's abbey, and two mistresses he was very fond of. He had asked them to join him, but each had politely declined. There was no explicit reason why he couldn't return to England, but nor did it seem wise to try. Treason was still treason, and his brother seemed to think his arrival at London Airport wouldn't be looked on kindly.

It was the not exactly knowing that cut deep. It made him feel as if he was doing this to himself, and he sensed that was intentional. He had no idea Her Majesty could be so calculatedly cruel. He didn't think she had it in her.

★ ★ ★

As Christmas approached, it was traditional for people who were going to receive medals in the New Year's Honours List to be told privately a few weeks before, so they could prepare for the congratulations that would follow.

To his astonishment, Fred Darbishire was on that list. He was being given an MBE, 'for services to the Metropolitan Police'. He had no idea what services those were, specifically, but he liked to imagine the look George Venables – who had no such ribbons on his dress uniform – would give him. His wife was thrilled and that was what really mattered. She would get to watch him receive his medal at Buckingham Palace. They would make a day of it.

Meanwhile, the royal household decamped to Sandringham in Norfolk, to spend the festive period by the sea. On Christmas Eve, a postcard arrived addressed to Her Majesty, with a postmark from Cuba. It read simply, *'Am nursing now, at last. Feliz Navidad.'*

'I guess that's where she went,' Joan said, having made sure it was at the top of the basket containing the Queen's private correspondence.

'Nursing,' the Queen observed. 'Good.'

She was feeling nervous, because in forty-eight hours she would be addressing millions across the nation and the Commonwealth, live on television, and she knew she had to connect with them. She would welcome them into her home, the first time they would see her there, and talk about being frightened – of the future, of technology, of rapid change – and about the deeply held values that got her through. She hoped Daphne was right about it, but regardless of what Daphne thought, it was what the Queen wanted to say.

She had had moments of feeling enormously frightened this year, but she had worked through them and done the right thing, or at least, she hoped she had. Promising a life of public service made everything straightforward in the end: you knew what you were supposed to do. Nursing, in that context, sounded like an excellent choice for Lucie Seymour.

'I have something for you,' the Queen said to Joan. She opened her desk drawer and took out a narrow, wrapped box.

'Shall I open it now?' Joan asked.

'Why not save it until you're at home with your father?'

★ ★ ★

Joan travelled to Cambridge by train that evening, and unwrapped the box on Christmas morning, in her father's rooms at St Anselm's. It was a blue cardboard affair, bearing the name of one of the royal jewellers. Inside, was a smaller box made of silver and blue enamel, with the royal cipher engraved below the clasp.

'That's very nice,' Vincent McGraw said approvingly. 'What's it for?'

Joan smiled at her father. 'I think it's for keeping secrets.'

'No doubt. I mean, what are you actually going to keep in it?'

Joan thought about it. Hector Ross had given her a single string of iridescent, perfectly matched, absolutely illicit pearls before she left for Sandringham. 'You need these,' he'd explained briskly, sweeping her hair aside to attach them around her neck. 'Office uniform.' She was wearing them now.

'More secrets,' she said.

AFTERNOTES

Sharp-eyed readers may recognise number 22, the Arts and Crafts house in Cresswell Place where the dubious academics stayed, as the mews house of Agatha Christie. She was one of the first people to do up a traditional servants' house in the 1920s and set her short story 'Murder in the Mews' there. With admirable generosity, she lent the place to a couple of friends, who ended up introducing her to her future husband, Max Mallowan. Sometimes good deeds *do* go unpunished. The other houses are invented.

* * *

Duke Ellington actually met the Queen at a white-tie event at the Leeds Music Festival in 1958, so I have borrowed their exchange for a private event a year earlier. This is what he said about meeting the royal couple:

'You are astonished by the applause and then struck speechless by the grace of the beautiful Queen . . . HM's general tone reflects the contentment of a normally happy married life, in contradiction of all the rumours and accounts of monarchs, which restores your faith in people as people. A handsome couple with careers. Two young people trying to get along.'

He did indeed write a suite for her after that meeting, and had a single copy produced to give her as a personal gift. *The Queen's Suite*, now recognised as among his most beautiful compositions, remained hidden from the public until after Ellington's death in 1974. I listened to the centrepiece of the suite, a song without words called 'The Single Petal of A Rose', many times while I wrote this book. The Queen remained a fan of Ellington's music all her life.

Daphne du Maurier really was married to General Boy Browning, who had also been Princess Elizabeth's head of household and then worked for Prince Philip. As a couple, they went to Balmoral, which Daphne hated because of the stuffiness of court life. But not, as far as I know, in 1957. However, she was asked to work on the Christmas message that year, which is how I got to find out about this – to me – extraordinary association with the Queen. And yes, Prince Philip was a fan, with a love of sailing in common (though not, I imagine, her novels). He was rumoured to have asked her advice before he married. I like to think the author of *Frenchman's Creek* would not have advised in favour unless she thought he was deeply in love.

Billy Hill was unimpressed about having his phone tapped by the police. He retired to Spain, but bought a nightclub in Tangier in the late 1950s, which his partner, Gypsy, ran for many years. I wonder where he got the idea from . . . His place in the London underworld was taken by his protégés, the Krays.

My story contains echoes of scandals that would eventually happen in the 1960s – the Profumo affair, featuring the swimming pool at Cliveden; the Third, Fourth and Fifth men of the Cambridge spy ring – one of whom, Kim Philby, announced his (disproven) innocence in a house that happened to back onto Cresswell Place; and the 'treacherous' coup that Harold Wilson feared in 1968. Powerful men with an excessive regard for their own intelligence have been known to make stupid decisions. Truth is always stranger than fiction.

I invented a lot, but not the way the Queen was received in France or the USA. From Eleanor Roosevelt's diary, 26 October, 1957:

> Queen Elizabeth's visit to the United States, I think, has done much to eliminate some of the bitterness that resulted when this country allowed the Suez crisis to occur and then said we knew nothing of what our allies were doing.
> It always seemed to me that this was a rather lame excuse, since Great Britain and France were our allies and it indicated that our communication must have deteriorated to a point which

is not permitted among friends. I hope we will never again indulge in such negligence.

Now that the Queen has done all she can to repair the damage, I hope we will do what we can to restore the warmth of the British-American relationship which is, I think, essential to the strength of the West.

As I looked at the young Queen and her husband, Prince Philip, on their visit to New York, it seemed that she was filling her role with great dignity but also with some weariness. How very young this couple looked – and how we do make our visitors work!

In 1959, Princess Margaret bought the Poltimore Tiara at auction. She wore it on her wedding day in 1960 to a society photographer called Anthony Armstrong-Jones. He had taken the official photograph of the Queen and Princess Anne reading together, to mark the young princess's birthday in 1957. The print was made on 10 October, shortly before the Queen left for her trip to Canada and the United States.

Readers of the same vintage as me may have grown up with the Jennings stories of Anthony Buckeridge. Long before the days of Harry Potter, they recounted the adventures of a (very non-magical) boy at a British boarding school. Growing up far away in Hong Kong at the time, I devoured them. And so, I have borrowed the names of Jennings's friends Darbishire (spelled this way) and Venables, in honour of the real Chief Inspector George Jennings of the Kensington division, whose team solved the Rillington Place Murders in the 1950s. His subordinate, Inspector James Black, successfully led the early part of the investigation and it is in Black's honour that Darbishire is a mere DI, but the relationship between my inspector and Venables does not reflect the far more respectful one between the real Metropolitan Police officers.

As I researched the Special Operations Executive, and also murders in and around Chelsea and Kensington in the 1950s, I discovered that two female wartime heroines were murdered there, one by a stalker, one unsolved. The first was Krystyna Skarbek, known as Christine Granville, a Polish agent in the SOE with an extraordinary war record, who was reduced to menial jobs afterwards, before being killed in Earl's Court in 1952 by a jealous man who had worked as a fellow steward on an ocean liner. The second was Teresa Lubienska, a seventy-three-year-old Polish countess who had been in the Polish Underground Army and survived two concentration camps, and was stabbed by an unknown assailant at Gloucester Road tube station in 1957. Both should have been hailed as heroes. Instead, they led difficult post-war lives and only now is their heroism being fully appreciated, as female historians and writers take on the task of bringing to light what they did. I learned a lot from *Mission France* by Kate Vigurs, first published in 2022.

The tale of the fictional Marianne Fleury was inspired by my reading of *Miss Dior*, by Justine Picardie, first published in 2021, which tells the extraordinary story of Christian Dior's sister Catherine. She was a young Resistance fighter, captured and sent to Ravensbrück concentration camp from Paris. She returned after the war, almost unrecognisable after all she had suffered, but continued as her brother's muse and became a successful rose farmer in Provence, whose flowers were used in his perfumes. Christian died in the time frame of this book, in 1957, but Catherine died in 2008, at the age of ninety. Justine's book captures the joy and terror of those war and post-war years. It also describes the importance of couture fashion in the rebuilding of post-war France. I recommend it.

S.J. Bennett, August 2023

ACKNOWLEDGEMENTS

As always, I must thank the late Queen Elizabeth II for a life of service, a sense of fun, and for preserving the mystery of the monarchy enough to let a novelist imagine this secret fictional string to her bow.

I have been lucky to see this series, like the Queen, travel around the world, and I want to take this chance to thank Sam Edenborough, the team at ILA and all my editors, translators and marketing teams in countries from France and Germany to Australia and Japan. It's a privilege to see your support for the stories and the wonderful covers you give every book.

At home, I'm ever grateful to Ben Willis at Bonnier Zaffre, who is the best editor I could possibly hope for. Thank you, too, to Nick Stearn for the covers, to Iker Ayesteran for the wonderful illustrations (especially the corgis), to Isabella Boyne for making everything run more smoothly than I have any right to ask, and to Elinor Fewster for making sure people know about the books.

Charlie Campbell at Greyhound Literary remains the best agent in the business. I still feel as lucky as I did when we started out together in 2020. And here we are, four books down the line. Meanwhile, Grainne Fox at UTA has transported the series to America not once but twice. Thank you, Grainne. Melissa, Thai and everyone at Crooked Lane Books, I'm delighted to be working with you on this new adventure.

The Transatlantics: thank you for all your encouragement and sage advice. Bonnie MacBird, you are a great Sherlockian and a treasured friend. Vanessa Harbour, I couldn't have done it without you this time; those Friday morning crit sessions were times well spent.

To all the writers in the crime community, thank you for being such a supportive and creative bunch. Especially Vaseem Khan, for your generous encouragement, and Ruth Ware, for being the ideal person to bounce ideas off if somebody needs to be killed in a way a police pathologist might not be able to reconstruct. Don't get on Ruth's bad side, is all I can say.

The Queen's year of state visits in 1957 was a busy one and I sourced the finer details of her schedule from many places, not least the Pathé newsreels of the day. But a favourite resource for its (rare) reliability on exactly where the Queen went each day and what she wore, was the Royal Watcher blog. Thank you, Saad Salman. I'm also grateful for the writing and research of Michelle Morgan (*When Marilyn Met the Queen*, 2022), and Margaret Forster's biography of Daphne du Maurier (1993).

As always, I'm grateful to Emily, Sophie, Freddie and Tom. The boys have put up with my very late-night writing to deadlines for fourteen books now, so I owe you a lot. Thank goodness you can make pasta and pesto. And Alex, this is fundamentally a story about love, so you are at the heart of it.

Last but by no means least, I want to say a huge thank you to all my readers. Nothing gives me a thrill more than hearing from someone who has newly discovered the series. I'm especially grateful to the band of subscribers to my author newsletter, who have become part of my life. I'm honoured that these books have lifted so many of you up when you were down. I love hearing your own stories and memories of the Queen, knowing you enjoyed the short stories, and reading your entries to the competitions. Please keep them coming!

You can contact me via my website, at sjbennettbooks.com. It's always lovely to hear from you.

Hello!

Thank you for picking up *A Death in Diamonds*.

Four books into the series . . . I'm starting to feel that Queen Elizabeth II really *did* solve mysteries in her spare time. She'd have been so good at it.

This book started with my research into the year the Queen met Marilyn Monroe. I was going to set it in 1956, but the more I looked into the period, the more the following year reminded me of the times we're living in now. The UK was living through a period of austerity, was questioning its place in Europe, and was sending out the royals on bridge-building visits abroad. I realised it was the year the Queen visited Paris and New York – and the die was cast.

It may be book four, but *A Death in Diamonds* is part of the origin story of my fictional sleuth. It's not the first time Elizabeth has solved a crime, but it's the first time she's recruited an assistant private secretary to help her – the role I once interviewed for myself. I know many readers love this idea of a secret club of female sleuthing sidekicks, and this is where that club started: with Joan McGraw.

Joan is based in part on my grandmothers: Joan Price, formerly McGrath, née Cuthbert; and Jessie Pett, née Adamson. Joan grew up in Urmston, Manchester, left school at 16 and worked as a secretary before marrying and moving south. Jessie grew up in a mining village in Ayrshire, became nanny to the children of a wealthy Scottish family, and eventually married my Grandad, whom she met where he worked, at the Grosvenor House Hotel. Both were strong, multi-talented, capable women, whom I miss very much. Neither got to work at Bletchley Park, but each of them, I think, would have taken it in her stride.

Like previous books in the series, all the official events in this story are based on fact. The Queen really did travel to all those places, really was presented with the Mona Lisa in an impromptu display, and really did have a friendship with Daphne du Maurier. Only the murder bits are made up. Those, and the dastardly sabotage plot. To the best of my knowledge, nobody tried to put itching powder in the royal Elizabeth Arden face cream. With Bobo Macdonald looking after her, I pity any man who would try.

If you would like to know more about the background to the books and follow the series as it progresses, then you can sign up to my author newsletter via my website, at sjbennettbooks.com. It would be lovely to welcome you to the worldwide community of readers.

And if you would like to get involved in a wider conversation about this book, please review *A Death in Diamonds* on Amazon, on Goodreads, or wherever else you share your thoughts online, or talk about it in real life with friends, family or reader groups! If you've already done so, I send you a heartfelt thank you.

With warmest wishes, S. J. Bennett

www.sjbennettbooks.com